AZALEA AND I – ON THE ROAD TO SPAIN

By

RM HOWE

A GOLDEN STORYLINE BOOKS PUBLICATION

This paperback book was first published by Golden Storyline Books in the United States and internationally.

COPYRIGHT @2024 RM HOWE

COPYRIGHT STATEMENT

All rights reserved. No part of this publication may be reproduced, stored in a retrieval system or transmitted in any form or by any other means without prior permission in writing of the publisher, nor likewise be circulated in any form of binding of cover other than that in which it is published without a similar condition, including this condition, being imposed on the subsequent purchaser.

Dedication

To my dear friends Susan Hedworth and Hans Mittag. Sue for her invaluable support in writing the book and Hans for providing a lovely character with sparkling blue eyes.

CHAPTER ONE
Sun, Sand, Sangria – and Murder.

Murder always comes as a bit of a shock – even when encountering it for the third time.

As amateur sleuths, we had already had more than our fair share of drama. But when Lea opened the massive rubbish bin on this hot Spanish evening and we saw a twisted, grotesque body lying on the top, we were rooted to the spot.

'That's not a gruesome toy, is it?' My voice shook.

It took Hans a minute to answer: 'No, Barbara. That's Enrico.'

We were each as white as a sheet in contrast to the crimson, blood-soaked body dumped unceremoniously in the basura.

Lea was leaning against a wall – frozen, shocked, glazed eyes staring into space.

I gradually became aware of a mix of houses, shops and café bars all around the area, filled with the early evening activity in the second half of a typical Spanish day.

Two days before ...

As we descended the steps from the plane just landed in Malaga, very hot sun hit us instantly. The tarmac shimmered with the heat haze. It was an expected shock and we started acclimatizing immediately. Dressed for heat in shorts and trendy tops with our factor 50 sunscreen already on, we were prepared for almost anything.

It had been an uneventful flight, for which I was grateful. I am not a fan of defying gravity and Azalea's incessant babble had taken my mind off flying. The babble continued even though now I could do without it – almost. I did enjoy her 'off the wall' view of life.

'– bi-polar, narcissistic, sociopath windbag. Wouldn't you agree, Barbara?' Azalea was squinting at me with an intent look as we slowly wound our way to Customs, which was not far enough away to need a bus to the terminal. She had said it with feeling and paused now, waiting for a reply.

'So! You're not sure about him then?'

Silence – a confused look on Lea's face.

I had to smile. 'I mean, that's why you dropped him? I hazarded a guess. 'Apart from only knowing him a very few days, of course.'

'No, Babs, he was a car salesman. A girl can only take so much and he was determined to sell me that snazzy, gold model. I only admired it in passing.'

'Oh, but it was so 'you'! Anyway, we're here now and who knows what lies ahead. Last time an innocent start with simple tasks ended in art theft, smuggling, murder and mayhem – and two nice men. Two lovely men.' I smiled, reminiscing. I had been very happy with my brief, romantic encounter with romance. Ah, Gareth!

A representative was collecting the new arrivals, directing them – and us – to the coach waiting in the parking lot with the name 'Club La Roca Resort', our destination for the next couple of weeks at least.

Lea and I were on our second fact-finding mission for my Uncle Charles who owns and runs a coach travel company with a very hands-on philosophy. Madden's Magic Carpet Tours was his first love and where we had cut our teeth with amateur sleuthing on his behalf. He had recently acquired this holiday complex to expand his ventures and I had been made junior partner – on a steep learning curve in the practicalities of running such a company.

Club La Roca was situated between Malaga and Alicante. We had come incognito to give our opinion on how it ran, or didn't run, and try a little investigation as to what had happened to the disappearing under-manager, Gerhardt Schmidt. Uncle Charles had had an anonymous letter by snail mail telling him of certain concerns about this which he took seriously. Lea, my zany, starving artist friend, was the perfect foil to my more serious self. We made a good team.

The coach trip took a while, so the early evening sun was still hot but not unbearable when we arrived in this glamorous part of Andalusia. A refreshing breeze followed us to our room after we had left our names and passports at reception. Barbara Wells and Azalea Dunbar had arrived.

We quickly dumped our bags in a huge room with king-size twin beds and an even bigger balcony. It was in a vibrantly coloured, flower filled block of eight bedrooms. Five other similar blocks were nearby, all in sight of the hotel. We went straight out to explore and eat in the beautiful surroundings. Trees swayed, and the sound of the sea lapping on the shore could be heard from the pool and bar terrace, where we sat eyeing up the fully inclusive, seriously varied buffet behind floor-to-ceiling open glass doors.

I had a long wine and soda drink with lots of ice, and Lea had fresh orange to quench her thirst. We felt we deserved this bit of relaxation before the work began.

Azalea was impressed with the food from the buffet. Food seemed to loom large in our lives. 'I'm going to look at the chicken dish. We won't need breakfast at this rate. Shall I bring you something back?'

The buffet was a good idea but I couldn't decide if it was potentially wasteful. The table groaned under the weight of all the food trying to cater for many different tastes: English, Spanish, Italian, Indian, German, vegetarian and more.

I felt slightly overwhelmed. OK, hugely overwhelmed by the choices, so I was happy to leave it to Lea. She came back with as much as she could carry, followed by two waiters with more. Definitely wasteful.

'Perhaps a note to Uncle C to advise cutting down on the assortment available,' I pondered.

'I'm sure I saw an Indian restaurant on the road in. He could at least leave it to them instead, and save a bit of effort here.' Seems work had indeed already started so I duly wrote this thought down in my notebook.

Lea looked confused. 'The chicken doesn't have any legs. I do like a leg.'

'Well, if we find a supermarket, we'll buy some and ask the chef to stick some on in future.'

'Would he do that, do you think?' Lea was quite serious.

I managed to keep a straight face and my opinion to myself. I should have been used to being bewildered by Azalea but every so often she caught me unawares. I had no doubt that if she asked the chef to attach legs to the hapless chicken, he would try to do it with the greatest of pleasure, smitten with her unwitting charm. Her eating slowed to a stop.

'You're not struggling with the rest of that plateful, are you?' I was ready to gloat.

'No, I'm resting like an actress in between roles.'

We agreed to relax for the rest of the evening as Spanish evenings were long. Orientate ourselves to our surroundings and unpack, then look at the possible tours we could go on in the next week. Uncle C provided these local tours on coaches, adding another string to the bow in this new acquisition.

First though, we followed the white picket fence down the shallow steps to the beach and found a peaceful atmosphere under some palm trees. We settled on the loungers provided among the lovely, soft, clean sand, noticing the hotel's private jetty with several boats moored up, gently bobbing. People lounged on them relaxing with drinks. It was getting dark and pretty lights suddenly came on, inviting an evening crowd. Coolers stood near every lounger with water bottles which attentive waiters kept an eye on. Lea was ready for a snooze and arranged her large squashy bag to use as a pillow.

Silence for a while. Then, 'Babs, do you remember that elderly couple on the bus? You know, they were holding hands all the time.'

I thought a bit.' Oh yes – couldn't keep their eyes off each other. Didn't they tell us they'd just got married and they were in their eighties?'

'That's right! The woman kept giggling, and her husband was grinning from ear to ear. They were off on a honeymooning adventure in South America. I wonder what lies ahead for us, Babs? What shall we do when we get old?' She flopped backwards blissfully stretching out.

'I can't imagine we'll grow old gracefully – not you anyway. Mind you, we might not make it to old age! Do you remember when that cable car got stuck hundreds of feet above a ravine and you saw an absolutely massive toilet kitchen towel roll type thing stuffed in a corner, and asked if it was for nervous people to use in emergencies? No one laughed. Then the engineer wiped his oily hands on a piece of it after he'd managed to get the brakes unstuck. He'd had to climb on top of the car with only two railings for safety! Made my palms sweaty, I can tell you. Ugh!'

Only her soft breathing came in answer. She had gone out like a light. She always did have a tendency to fall asleep after food.

I left Lea there and slipped off to have a nosy around. I paused under a tree to get my bearings and a waiter approached, asking in English if I needed anything. A tall, slim great-looking specimen. I was happy to engage him in conversation.

'It's my first night here so perhaps you could tell me a bit about the place. Do you all speak English?'

'We must if we want to get the work. It is the international language for communication. My name is Alvaro and I will be pleased to help and make your stay one to remember.' He sounded rather formal and stiff.

'Thank you. That's good. Your companion up there doesn't seem too worried about making an effort to help the guests.' I nodded towards a guy who looked like a bulldog chewing a wasp as he leaned against a door post on the terrace going back into the buffet area.

Alvaro glanced up. 'Oh, him. Mmm. He is the new deputy under-manager. Very efficient – at what he does.'

Something in his tone made me more inquisitive but cautious. 'Sounds like there's a 'but' coming. Know what I mean?'

'Oh, yes. I learned English in England, with many of its idiosyncrasies. Not all, though. Too many.' He smiled as if some memory amused him. Then he spoke more seriously: 'It is not for me to say anything about anyone, especially a manager. But if you have a problem with any member of staff, I will get it sorted out.'

Then he brightened up immediately: 'My job is hosting, which I really enjoy. Being out and about all the time so the day flies. Or evening. And it pays well since we have a new owner. I hear he takes a personal interest in the running of things so this can only be good for guests. I hope he will come here one day. Now, can I do something for you? Show you around? Or I can get drinks for you?'

'Show me around, please. It's a larger complex than I realized.' I thought better of furthering the questioning. A potential source of information and help had been established. I would reveal my identity only when I had a firmer 'friendship', depending upon what Lea and I found. I could only think he had been referring to Uncle when he spoke of 'the new owner'. I also kept it to myself that I spoke Spanish.

We started the tour around the immediate La Roca hotel with its elegant, white porticoed entrance leading into the cool, high-ceilinged reception area and on to all the other facilities. These consisted of two restaurants – the informal buffet we had just experienced which doubled for breakfast, and a fine dining room. Two pools, one for children, and the adults' pool with loungers, bar and umbrellas giving shade on an otherwise sun-filled terrace. Alvaro drew my attention to the separate menu that cost extra in case the buffet got boring. Hard to believe with so much choice but, hey ho, you never know. More discussions to have with Uncle.

We came back out, moving deeper into the gardens which were full of various Mediterranean trees, palms and abundant colourful flowers, especially the bright flowing bougainvillea. Ad hoc seating allowed guests to rest, taking in sweeping views down to the sea. A golf course rambled upwards and disappeared over the top of the hill, I noticed. A series of tennis courts completed the area.

Uncle Charles had led me to believe it was a small resort so I was suitably impressed. Small?

Compared to what? 'Welcome to La Roca. Luxury hotel, Golf and Spa Resort' was written in English, Spanish and German both in the brochures and at the entrance to the resort. I was excited to be a part of it. That it mixed coach parties and private bookings was a source of slight irritation to me but so far it had worked in the few months Uncle Charles had owned it.

Alvaro told me there were other areas to explore but that it would be better to do it in daylight. Two other autonomous complexes had more restaurants, shops and offices, mixed with swanky time-share, privately-owned villas and apartments. Anyway, he had to get back to his other duties as a 'host waiter'. The night was young: much partying lay ahead for the tourists, and much work for him.

I knew the villas and apartment provided a lot of the trade for Uncle's Club complex so I asked, 'Are you free tomorrow to show us around by any chance? We could have a look at these other parts.'

'Us?'

'Sorry. I forgot to mention my friend, Azalea. We are here together, for a week or so.'

'Together?' Alvaro raised his eyebrows in involuntary enquiry.

'Ooh, not like that.' My cheeks began to go red. 'Just friends – girls enjoying a sunny break.'

'Sorry, I didn't mean anything by it. Really.' He seemed worried he had overstepped the mark, preparing for a hasty exit.

'Honestly, no offence taken. We would love to have a tour tomorrow if you can make it. Can you OK it with your boss? We can pay if he likes? I don't want to take you away from your duties.' I hoped I sounded conciliatory.

'Oh. Well then, it would be a pleasure. No need for payment. It's my day off and I would be delighted to take you and your friend around.' He was both visibly relieved and delighted.

'I don't want to spoil your day off. You need to relax!'

'I would be relaxing. I enjoy being a guide. I can show you the best bars and a good place for lunch.'

'In that case we will buy lunch. What time in reception? No rush.'

'About 11 am then. Hasta luego. Um, your name please?'

'Barbara. Babs.'

'Till then, Barbara.'

Just then Lea came in view. She sped over, all curiosity, with that smile on her face.

'Negative patient outcome, Babs.'

Some introduction. Alvaro and I stared at her quizzically.

'When I woke up and found you had gone, I went to our room to see if you were there. Thought I would wait a while and started reading your book – from the end backwards.'

Alvaro looked puzzled.

'I like a happy ending so I always read the ending first,' she explained. 'The patient died, so – negative outcome. Anyway, I'm Lea. Azal-e-a.' She articulated the syllables carefully. People were always assuming 'Lea' was 'Lee' and that would always make her bristle.

Then she beamed and held out her hand to Alvaro who responded in kind, but formally: 'Hello. I'm Alvaro. At your service.' He shook hands firmly.

'Alvaro has kindly agreed to show us around tomorrow on his day off. So, we are buying lunch. Well, Uncle is.' I hadn't meant to mention Uncle Charles so glossed over it rapidly: 'I'm buying it. We look forward to it, Alvaro. Excuse us. We have tourist chores to do. Someone has to. Come on, Lea. Time for a glass of something cold and alcoholic.'

We all smiled and went our separate ways. There was music coming from inside so we headed towards it, finding an elegant white and gold piano lounge. Normally, white and gold glitter sets my teeth on edge but this was very understated. Settling in low large comfy chairs big enough for a whole family, we looked around. The chairs were very pale green, complimenting the profusion of potted palms. They looked wonderfully elegant but were totally impractical. The notes were mounting up.

We were near the pianist who was noticeably short. In fact, I wondered how he managed to reach the pedals. I was about to fill Lea in on my findings so far, when she awkwardly pushed her way out of the chair. Good job the arms were stout and supportive. After a few wines I could imagine it would become a battle getting out of the monster chairs.

'Think I'll ask if he does requests.'

She went straight over to him. He was rifling through sheets of music, putting some away.

'Excuse me - are you finishing now?'

'Oh no. Just a break. I do four sessions, so three more to go. I finish about 1 am. Off to eat now. If you want a request I will be happy to do it later. You can look through the list of all the songs I do.' He handed her a four-page, double-sided epic. Lea's eyes widened as she glanced through.

'Is there anything you can't do?'

'Not much. I prefer classic rock n' roll but all the styles are there. Ballads, swing, top hits and stuff. No heavy metal, hip hop, reggae. That's for the late music club. Or old-fashioned disco.' He smiled pleasantly.

'Well – my friend Babs and I are here for two weeks so we'll work our way through. I'm Lea.'

'David. Pleased to meet you, ladies. My apologies. I should say 'señoritas'.' He inclined his head charmingly. 'See you later then. I'm off back home to eat. It's not far and I get to see my kid before he goes to bed.'

He was English. I thought I would cultivate him as well as Alvaro. Time was on our side.

'Now I'm up, Babs, I think I'll go to the bar for a drink. Joining me or shall I bring one over? All these mini palms are good to lurk behind and observe people. Do you want white wine or one of those posh fruit G and T's?''

'Joining you. Yes, the palms are just right for décor and lurking behind – and rhubarb gin with ordinary tonic, thank you.' All one sentence. Whew.

I got up before she could comment on any of that and stood at the bar with her. We sprawled over it, handbags taking up quite a bit of space. Lea's was the biggest and I swear she had brought it specially in case we found a stray dog needing rescue. We had found on our first trip for Uncle – and had indeed rescued it.

The array of gins was impressive. I remembered Uncle C telling me a lot of English people lived around here and frequented this resort. But maybe gin was an international fashion now. I told Lea about Alvaro and his hesitation on the subject of the wasp man.

'Hmm. Shades of the Hyena,' she said thoughtfully. 'Could we end up in another pickle? Probably reading too much into it, I think. Just an employee with a bad attitude – which is not good, of course,' she conceded.

We pondered for a while on our previous adventure with the terrifying man we had named the Hyena. We had had lots of scares on our previous trip, both perceived and real, so in the future I wanted to be focused between reality and getting carried away.

Three slow gins later, David returned accompanied by a tall, slim blonde who towered over him. They came to the bar and ordered drinks for themselves. David waved to us, then spoke to his friend, and they made their way along the long bar.

'This is my wife, Helen. Helen, these girls have just arrived and are finding their way around. Perhaps you can entertain them while I play a few numbers? Lea and Barbara, is that OK?'

We all smiled at each other. I took in Helen's height – at least five foot eleven to David's four foot ten – or so. Strange what attracts people to each other. David took his drink to the piano and we were left with the attractive Helen. Her long, wavy hair nearly gave Lea's a run for its money.

I hoped Helen didn't feel put upon so I dived in: 'I hear you have a child at home. Doesn't he mind having to look after himself?'

Then I hoped I hadn't sound accusatory. I had a bad habit of speaking before thinking.

'Oh no. He has a babysitter. He's only a year old. We have a sitter three nights a week so I can see more of David. He works late six nights a week so he sleeps a lot during the day. I work day time but we meet up afternoons in siesta time before I go back to work for the evening shift. Though the Spanish think of it as afternoon. It works well ¬David is around for Daniel in the mornings, even if he is asleep.'

'How very organized. I'm impressed.' Lea was always impressed by people and things that were organized. Uncle's sophistication had made me more blasé. 'What's your work?' she asked (Good, I thought. Always talk about the other person. They always find that interesting!)

'I work in an estate agency on one of the other complexes. It's a lovely job, swanning around showing the area to potential clients and seeing all those luxury villas. There's a timeshare office on another one but that's not my style.' Helen smiled the smile of someone who genuinely enjoyed her work. 'We came out here for David's job four years ago and are really lucky that part of his contract supplies free accommodation. We love it, and with me working, we hope to settle permanently by buying our own house one day.'

'So – you really know the area?'

'Yes. We've done our share of exploring. Have you seen the old mine shafts– or rather air vents –for the underground mining? Oh, you won't have. You've only just arrived.' She gave a 'silly me' smile.

'We're having a guided tour tomorrow with Alvaro – the host waiter.' Helen nodded obviously knowing Alvaro.

'I'll mention the mines,' I said. 'Alvaro's very accommodating. If all the staff are the same, it's a great asset to the place.'

'He is and they are. It's the expats that you need to watch. A lot of gossip and bitchiness can go on. Though I say it myself as an expat. I try not to get tarred with the same brush. Sometimes you can't help it. Nothing is malicious – unless it's deserved. Bit like small country villages back in the UK. I was born and brought up in a small place. Loved the anonymity of Manchester but I still had lots of friends.'

'I know what you mean. We live in London – that's got 'villages' too – and lots of gossip.'

'People probably gossip about your Uncle, Babs. Big fish, small pond.'

I wished Lea hadn't said that and glared. It was OK for me to make a blunder but not Lea, I thought.

'My uncle has a small travel company. He heard about this place and wondered if he might want to send clients here, so asked us to check it out on a holiday. But please don't say anything. It may never happen and I don't want people being nice simply to impress in order to get more business. It has to be genuinely good.' I congratulated myself on my quick thinking.

'No problem. I understand.'

I got the feeling I could trust Helen, warming to her quickly. I was usually right with such things.

'If I can be of any help, just ask,' she said. 'Come to my office tomorrow on your tour if you like – or whenever you can. I'll give you my business card. Alvaro knows where it is. The only fly in the ointment at the moment is that the under-manager disappeared suddenly. No reason given and can't be found. No communication from him – all very strange. The new under-manager is … is … how can I put this?'

She was obviously struggling to be diplomatic.

'He was head of housekeeping so it's not really his thing with all the extra responsibility front of house. I think he's not used to it so goes overboard to be nice to guests. Bit sickly. When the under-manager, Gerhardt, disappeared it was obvious this guy would get the job – unfortunately. The gap had to be filled quickly and no one else was available. But things can change.'

'What's his name?'

'Karim Badour. He's Moroccan. There are a lot of Moroccan gypsies around. There's one enclave in particular where you just drive through and hope you don't break down. You know you're in that area because it's so run-down. They wouldn't harm you but you might come away without your valuables. It would be an unpleasant experience. Maybe Karim is from these people but has made a better life for himself. I am supposing and gossiping, which isn't really fair of me. I don't know – but I suspect his character fits.'

'Why don't the police do something?' Lea asked.

Helen spoke thoughtfully. 'You can't convict on speculation. No one actually has broken down there, but people who live around have had things stolen even though everyone watches out for each other. Houses near the area were cheaper so it appealed to some cash-strapped expats as a bargain. The Policia Local keep an eye out and the Guardia drive through a lot.'

'Guardia Civil I've seen. What's the difference between them and the Policia Local?' Lea raised an eyebrow in enquiry.

'Guardia. Oh the Guardia are very serious. Live and breathe the job. Sometimes die for it. Used to be known as Franco's police as they were – are – very strict. Burglary, assault, smuggling, drug trafficking. They work hand in hand with the elite Trafico who have motor bikes, helicopters, boats and more to call on.'

'And the Local Police? Policia Local?'

'Responsible to the mayor basically. Police equivalent of 'First Responders' then they hand over to the Guardia. Not much in the way of resources. Traffic and parking offences, helping kids across the road. The Policia Nacional are a ferocious bunch. Smart black uniforms. Get all the big jobs. Wear scary gear – face masks and stuff on missions. Most police have handguns as a matter of course.'

Now we knew.

'We have all the equivalents in the UK but by other names don't we, Babs? Minus a lot of the guns.'

I was hoping we wouldn't ever need to find out which ones we needed while we were over here. Maybe a Policia Local would be very happy to see Lea across a road but I didn't think our lollipop people would go down well with Lea. Not as romantic as a foreign policeman giving a helping hand.

'Yes, it's interesting to see the way other countries operate. Travel broadens the mind especially in places like India with huge populations, poverty or superb wealth.'

I was getting carried away and was suitably cut off. 'Can we just concentrate on Spain, Babs? I have enough trouble figuring out why the Spanish have a siesta.'

'That's because … '

'I wasn't serious. I know it's because the shops close for the afternoon.'

Helen and I looked at each other. It was difficult stifling a laugh so we smiled broadly and changed the subject.

Helen volunteered, 'There's a mining museum nearby. Worth a look. You'll find the old mines interesting too. A lot were opencast so you can see what was being mined. Big holes in the ground with so many different colours – bright yellows, purples, blues. They really have a unique beauty. Shame it poisoned the earth. The area's taking years to clean up. It's still ongoing. The EU refused money for it, so in the end, private investment has had to get involved.' As an afterthought: 'If they wanted to develop the land, that is.'

Just then a short, stocky man with a bag clutched under his arm entered the room, walking or should I say mincing, rapidly across to the bar. He had a clipped sort of walk which, combined with the mincing action, drew attention. He spoke in a friendly, familiar way to one of the barmen. This took our attention – it didn't seem to fit the setting.

'That's Enrico. The one and only known, openly gay around here. He is tolerated because he's local but many of the Spanish are not so broad-minded. They're mostly country folk. Wouldn't matter in a big town. In fact there is gay pride march every year in San Cartana. Enrico is OK.' Helen shrugged, accepting of him.

'Well, I agree with the 'known' bit – but doubt he's 'alone', judging by the way he and the barman are smouldering at each other.' They seemed to be unaware of the way it appeared.

Helen looked sharply towards them. 'My goodness. I certainly didn't see that coming. That's Gonzales's son. His family's ultra conservative. I am surprised they've let him work in a bar.'

Near the flesh pots of the expats. I hope for his sake we're misreading the situation.'

Lea piped up. 'Live and let live, I say. Parents can surprise you anyway.'

'Not these.'

Dead flat statement. I believed Helen.

'Anyway, the mines sound fascinating.' Lea pressed on. 'What were they mining?'

'Oh – it wasn't so much the mining as the slag heaps that were created after smelting. So much was created that it pushed the sea back about a mile. You can see the old harbour and restaurant which are now on dry land. The restaurant is still open and has lots of character. Has a great reputation for food and is well patronized. I went a few nights ago with some girls. We had to drive but it's on a quiet road and one of us had only one wine. The police used to be very tolerant about drinking and driving – unless you maimed or killed someone. Then they threw the key away. Now, you really have to watch it all the time.'

She paused. Then – 'A friend of mine killed a child. Not his fault and he was sober but he'd had a drink – they smelled it on his breath. The family wanted to kill him. Dragged on for two years. Eventually he was found not guilty but then the family went after financial compensation. A deal was struck. Needless to say my friend went back to the UK very disillusioned and much poorer.'

'I'm beginning to think the Spanish laid-back attitude is not all it's cracked up to be.' I knew Spain from my gap year but Barcelona is unique, and a far cry from La Roca.

'I've just googled mining,' Lea piped up. 'What a history indeed! Goes back to the Romans - and before.'

Small silence so I filled the gap. 'Do tell,' I invited.

'Well, as Helen's told us, the modern mining has produced the most awful mess and pollution. Minerals, zinc, copper, nickel, arsenic, iron oxides, compounds for flotation. Sodium cyanide, aluminium, calcium … prrr,' She blew out her lips and vibrated them. 'Not sure I understand all this.'

'Me neither,' I replied. 'Are you sure you have everything in the right order? '

'Of course not.'

'Ah well, just so long as we know.'

'There's a tourist trail down in one of the mines. It has an orange lake. You have to book. Shall we go, Babs?'

'Absolutely. Wouldn't miss it. Let's do our tour with Alvaro tomorrow so we know a bit better where everything is. Do you think we should be heading for bed soon? I'm beginning to flag.'

'I suppose so. David hasn't done any requests for me yet and he has two more sessions to go.'

'How do you cope with it, Helen?'

'I'm used to late nights. Siestas make up for it - and I pace myself.'

'I suppose we have been knocking it back a bit. First night and all that.'

'Speak for yourself, Babs. I'm as fresh as a daisy.'

Dangerous words.

Helen waved from her stool to a tall, slim man who had just come in. He came over smiling, kissed Helen on both cheeks and waited for the introduction.

'This is Hans. Local entrepreneur. Has a finca down in the village Las Aqueas. Hans, this is Barbara and Lea.'

'Encantada. Wilkommen. Welcome. Are you on holidays or hoping to move here? '

'Holiday for now. Who knows later on. We live in hope,' I responded.

'I came here twenty-six years ago, coming and going for work then back to my family. My wife didn't like it so it became right to stay and not go back to Germany. This is home now – with no wife.'

He chuckled and we had to smile.

Hans had the typical look of a blonde, blue-eyed, straight-backed Teutonic specimen. His vivid blue eyes sparkled. He was somewhere in his fifties. I noticed Lea had a strange endearing smile on her face while she studied the newcomer. Oh yes – the more mature man. He returned her interest. No surprise there. Well, I didn't mind in the least as I preferred my men younger – like Alvaro. And Gareth. Hmm.

'Finca – what goes on there?' Lea's smile widened.

'I have a big building with land where I sell jacuzzis, whirlpools, small pre-formed pools and estufas – sorry, fires for the winter. It gets cold also in the south of Spain. Most of my clients are German and English. It's a problema as they are efficiently by nature and expect results rapido but my suppliers are Spanish who have big mañana life with severity. So laidback they are almost flat. You must come with pleasure. I live there too.' His English had a slight accent.

'We would love to, wouldn't we, Barbara? We have two invitations already. Aren't we lucky?'

'Everyone is so friendly.'

'Here's my card. Helen, can you bring them one day? I can do lunch for you all.'

'Of course. We'll try and arrange it asap. I do like a man who cooks.'

'No choice. I am alone. No one cooks for me – but I prefer me to myself. I go to the ventas to make life easy. I get tired of puree.' He pronounced it 'puray'.

'Puree?'

'Mashed potato from a packet. I keep many of them. Seven for any week. I will need an extra packet when you come.' Hans's smile was charming, his eyes twinkling.

'We'll sort it out after our trip with Alvaro. I hope that's OK with you, Helen?'

'Absolutely. Looking forward to it all. Nice change for me. Er, phone numbers, girls?'

'Oh, of course. Here.' I handed a card over. 'Now Lea, it might be early in Spain but our minds are still recovering from a busy few days so what say you to an early night and unpack.'

'Not until David plays a request for me. Just one,' she wheedled, and whipped off to the piano.

David nodded agreeably. Lea sent a drink over to him which a barman took over and put on a drinks mat on the top of the piano. He had three whiskey and waters in a row now.

'I'll put it on the room bill. Anyone else want a drink?' Lea offered generously. With Uncle's money backing it up. But to be fair, we were allowed expenses.

'One for the road,' I responded.

'Thank you! Tea and biscuits on me when you come to my office – providing I'm not busy,' volunteered Helen, 'and then we can firm up Hans's invitation. We can talk in the morning.'

'Sounds like a plan. Ah, my music's being played – 'Brown-Eyed Girl'. Then I've asked for something by the Rolling Stones: 'I'm an Old-Fashioned Girl'.'

'You didn't comment, Babs – so I added one. And, by the way, I meant me – I'm an old-fashioned girl!'

Big sigh from me. A sort of smirk from Helen who was already getting the measure of Lea and a smile from Hans.

'Right, that's the two songs now. Bed, Lea. We have a lot of exploring to do tomorrow. You can do what you want another night. In fact stay up all night if you want. Just not tonight.'

'Oh – OK!' Crestfallen and deflated, but a last fight emerged. 'I am tempted to be seditious with you, Babs.'

'I'm not an authority, a state, a monarchy or, or – ' I glared. 'You're doing it again. Not quite in context.'

'No, but I'm trying.'

'You certainly are that.'

'Ah well.' She shrugged, smiled and gave in. Even looked a bit sheepish.

'Night everyone. Lovely to meet you all. I just know we'll have a lovely time.' She waved cheerily to David and we both received the Spanish double-cheek air kisses from Hans and a thumbs-up from Helen, who chose not to move from her bar stool.

Back in the bedroom Lea hit the bed without brushing her teeth. Most unusual. Nothing to do with all the gins of course. Gentle zzzzzzzs ensued. I pondered on smothering her with a pillow but decided against it when I remembered I needed her input. I lay face down, head sideways so I could still breathe and put a pillow over my head instead.

'Good night, friend,' I said to myself. What nice people we had met tonight. So nice. My mind drifted, with warm, fuzzy thoughts of Angelique, the rescued dog, and Azalea with periods of lucidity. What would this trip bring? Adventure or just fun?

Lea, Le -ah. Hair covered her face, threatened to take over her whole being. Jealous, hair, hair, best friend, would give her life for me, me for her. Gareth not agreeing. My hero from Venice.

Yes, Gareth, who had saved my life in Venice. Would Alvaro be my hero? Alvaro future …

Gareth past. Nooo. Lovely Gareth. Sexy Alvaro, Gareth, Alvaro … merging, mingling. Warm fuzzy feeling more and more. Thoughts, coming, going. So clear. Reminiscing, drifting, Alvaro. Gareth – Food zzzzzzz . Delicious. Yummy. Food. Mountains of it. Table falling, so much weight. Always food around Lea and animals. Always animals. Compulsory animals. Drifting, swirling, warm room – and G and T's zzzzzzzzzzzzzzzzzzzzzzz. ☐

CHAPTER TWO
Adventure Begins Early

'How annoying.' I blinked at the sun pouring into the bedroom and half sat up.

'What is?'

'You are. All that drink and you're up, bright-eyed and bushy-tailed. Seven thirty am. Why? You're making so much noise. Too much teeth-brushing going on. Your electric brush sounds like a drill. My mouth feels like the bottom of a parrot's cage.'

'For someone with an apparent hangunder you aren't doing badly.'

'Hangunder?'

'Too small for a hangover. Besides – the sun is beckoning. My bed has rejected me. The day begins. I'll make tea for us. We have lots of tea and coffee stuff here. Very generous.'

I sat up and waited to be waited on. 'I should think so,' I muttered to myself.

'What?'

'I should imagine Uncle's instructions are to be generous.'

'Speaking of which, are we going to breakfast? Do you know, all animals are sentient beings?'

Lea was being her normal off-the-wall self, but this flawed me. I was more annoyed now – mainly with my stupefied self. Lashing out helps, though.

'Why did animals come into your thoughts and how can you think of food so early – and after so much last night?' I paused. 'And 'sentient' is a big word for you – I mean this early.' Smirking, I made a face somewhere between revulsion and amazement. I finally sighed and gave in. 'Yes to breakfast – but in view of lunch out, let's just have a light one.' I plumped up my pillows, taking the proffered tea. It was so good. It was gone in a couple of gulps. Best drink of the day. 'Can I have another one, Lea. Please!'

She looked askance and snatched the cup, ignoring my 'word' dig. 'What did your last servant die of? I trust you will return the compliment asap. Animals are always in my thoughts but I was watching some pretty birds on the balcony just now. I don't care about flies, though.'

No arguing with that.

'You should. They're food for many things. You like frogs, don't you? Don't want them to starve.'

She considered this as I lay back recovering. 'You look like a llama surprised in her bed.'

I was coming round gradually and responded, 'No, you should have said 'llama surprised in her bath'! What on earth made you quote Churchill about De Gaulle? Are you saying I look awful? No don't answer. I can't cope that well – just yet.' I relapsed.

In due course we wandered into the main dining room after unpacking, something that hadn't happened last night. We were confronted with another wonderfully appetizing but over-burdened buffet. I went for Greek yoghurt with honey and more tea. Lea ploughed in with mixed meats, some fish, boiled eggs, crispy bacon, a sausage, yoghurt with honey too, and two types of cheese with small tomatoes on the side. And an orange.

'I see you've gone for the healthy option – but haven't you forgotten toast?' I said sarcastically.

'Oh, yes.' Off she trotted to get some.

'You'll never eat all that, let alone lunch. What a waste – the buffet I mean. I'm going to tell Uncle, especially as he's still so personally involved. He's allowing too much food to be put out. I can't imagine what sort of budget he's given the chef – or catering manager.' For some reason I felt annoyed. That she could eat so much and stay so slim? That Uncle was potentially wasting money? I didn't know.

'I'm soaking up the gin. I'll be ravenous by two o'clock.'

'You'd better be – or else you'll be on rations.'

'If you've finished moaning and eating your yoghurt, why don't you go and get ready while I eat in peace.'

I gathered this was an order, not a request. So I did – as I had. Finished, that is.

I came back, all prepared for the day, to find Alvaro sitting at the table with Lea. They were talking animatedly, he with a coffee in front of him. There was an endless supply of beverages and juices. I joined them, feeling less bad-tempered as his smile was infectious and his manner so easy. I couldn't be seen to be grouchy. The hangunder was receding and I acquired more tea.

'Hadn't you better get ready now Lea? We don't want to waste Alvaro's time.'

'Oh, no problem. I was up early. Couldn't relax so thought I would wander over. Then I saw Lea here. I've been explaining where we are going.'

'Sounds great. I'll go and get ready anyway.'

'Can you move after all that food? You've eaten every last scrap?' I narrowed my eyes, scrutinizing her empty plate. I could have sworn she had licked it clean.

'Fit as a fiddle.' Off she sashayed, dodging nimbly between tables and the large potted plants, and ducking under the rather low hanging baskets everywhere. Health and safety note. Low flying hanging baskets after a few drinks was not a good idea.

It was nice to have Alvaro to myself, albeit briefly. 'What's the plan of action, then?' I asked him.

'First we go around the rest of this club complex. I have a golf buggy for us. You arrived fairly late last night so won't have seen much. Useful to know where all the facilities are. Do you want to hire a car, by the way? I have some good contacts in the town. Much cheaper than anything from here.'

'I think so. Yes please. Let's check.'

We chatted on and Lea returned looking sort of dreamy in a light, floating type of garment, cinched in at her waist and almost see-through but saved by a matching slip underneath. Beautiful pastel shades showing shapely legs. She had added a choker necklace and two knuckle duster rings. Bling!

I felt underdressed all of a sudden: plain, black, figure-hugging short dress, colourful sandals and bag. But I'd forgotten the jewellery. Bother.

'You seem to have packed some nice things, Lea. You won't need to borrow my clothes this time.'

'I'm so grateful to your Uncle Charles for treating us to some outfits. Money makes a difference. I always have to scrape by in markets.' She did a twirl to show off her dress and then plonked down.

'You look very sophisticated, Babs.'

I hadn't thought of it that way – but, yes, I suppose I did. 'Well, when we've finished with our mutual appreciation society, shall we get going? Alvaro has a golf buggy all fuelled up and ready to go.'

A confused look crossed Lea's face. 'I didn't think golf buggies used fuel.'

'They don't.' I didn't enlarge on it.

Brain visibly working, she didn't comment further.

'Joke.'

'Oh I see.' She clearly didn't.

Alvaro had a bemused look. 'This way to the buggy.'

We whizzed around the whole area, taking in the basics of last night – golf courses and tennis courts, pools that were shared by the private urbanizations for a fee, then set off around those autonomous areas. It was all green, landscaped and tree- lined. Street lighting for the evenings was a bonus. Uncle's hotel club complex had 24-hour security guards at a barrier – though apparently sometimes they weren't there. Due to lack of staff – some problems are the same the world over. Oddly, there was a back road that led straight in without barriers or checks. Alvaro shrugged. One of those Spanish anomalies.

We came across Helen's Inmobilaria in a big square which had two banks, various service shops, three independent café restaurants and wine bar, each oozing a different character but all covered with a myriad of colourful plants which I now realized were the norm. I thought it looked wonderful. Picture-postcard perfect. The Sergio Rodriguez Estate Agency was tucked in a corner. Somewhat hidden, but not forgotten by house hunters specifically wanting to be in this area.

Inside it was large, light and airy. Helen was the main salesperson. I imagined that, as a fluent Spanish speaker, she'd be useful to many of the expats, helping them through all the legalities and settling-in issues. She'd openly admitted her grammar was bad but this wouldn't be a problem.

As she was with clients we could only wave at her, but she scampered out to tell us she would arrange lunch with Hans another day – it had been an open invitation and I hadn't realized how seriously she'd taken it. She was meeting him with these clients later as they wanted to discuss swimming pool ideas. We could catch up later maybe. At least we knew where she was now. And where to find nearby watering holes. We could walk there and back – if we had to. Bit of a hike but the anticipation of some fun to come would buoy us up.

'It's all exceedingly pleasant so I can see why Uncle's invested in it. He has a captive clientele from the urbanizations plus the village – Las Aqueas isn't it - at the bottom of the hill. It's full of expats who work around the area.'

I had been whispering to Lea so Alvaro wouldn't hear me, but he volunteered, 'Neighbouring villages contribute to the business here. Not so many Spanish. Back to the club then, pick up my car to go further.' Alvaro was organized and his car was spacious, so the three of us managed to squeeze in the front.

I sat next to Alvaro, my leg gently against his – which I liked a lot. Oh, Gareth. Am I so fickle! Snippets of my thoughts and dreams last night wafted in and out of my mind.

It was a dream that brought a smile to my face. Two men – how lucky can a girl get?

We sped down the hill towards the village Las Aqueas, and past the Indian restaurant I had spotted the night before. Note to self to have a meal there and discuss the possibility of mutual marketing – if it wasn't being done already.

'Does that restaurant have a good reputation?' I pointed it out. The golf course came right up to the boundary fence. I wondered how many windows had been smashed and if there was a bit of resentment against the resort. Would I have to smooth ruffled feathers or was I pre-empting things too much. Another bad habit of mine – worrying about worrying.

'Yes, run by Prem. Does all her own cooking, with help, then she can socialize too. People go as much for her company as the food. She is very – er – have I got this right? Gregarious?'

'Mmm ... you did. Or you could say 'outgoing'. Anyway, we must go there, Lea.'

She was looking intently at the golf course.

'What about introducing foot golf to the Club? Getting popular you know. I saw a TV programme about it.'

Her enthusiasm took me by surprise. 'What on earth is foot golf?'

'Combination of football for the exercise and golf for the skill. Great exercise. People who find golf boring but football too energetic have this halfway game. Big holes in the ground for the football and the golf club is your foot.'

'Well, I'll have to think about it. Research it.' I was neutral but willing to investigate.

Just then we came into the village and spied a garden centre on the edge. There was a long, wide street with room for cars to easily pass each other, plus parking on the sides and pavement cafes, bars and shops. It reminded me of a French boulevard except that the shops and houses were all low-rise, boxy affairs. Modern, cheap Spanish building. The side streets were the same, so charm was not predominant.

However, we could see in the distance that the area was near the sea, with old buildings scattered around, more full of character. Alvaro told us that villages in the vicinity were older, and I could see that they had managed to keep some prettiness. I could understand the building frenzy that had gone on with the expansion of the mining industry. For some unfathomable reason I had had a strange feeling about the air vents we saw for the mines on our way down. They were all over. Round structures that stood about five feet off the ground. They had no safety cap on the top so if you fell down, that would be a hundred-foot drop, according to Alvaro.

In the meantime, we dived into the garden centre to see what kind of flowers they had to offer in southern Spain. The bright pinky purple bougainvillea were there in abundance. So stunning. I had always wanted one but bougainvillea didn't fit in with the London scene. So I had better buy a Spanish house then, I thought idly. Or Italian. Or ...? Dreaming is wonderful. I would suggest to Uncle that the Club should surround itself in a blaze of colour, more than it already had, which was a lot. But more would be better, I decided. The never-ending list! But making such a list was one of the reasons we were here, so I felt justified.

We wandered down the main road, peering in the cafes and bar restaurants that filled the pavements. It was hard not to find something that suited every taste. A variety of shops, both fashionable and cheap n' cheerful, appealing to tourists of all kinds, were squeezed in between the cafes. Obviously the locals, and probably the expats too, tended to shop in the equivalent of the pound shop for all household stuff and for things you didn't need, like jelly moulds and decorative, dust-collecting ceramic statues which would suddenly seem to become essential because they were so cheap.

A ferreteriá or iron monger's shop was doing a roaring trade We peeked in. The Spanish staff spoke English, which I thought was a shame, but we supposed that from the shop's point of view it would mean more sales because it would be easier for the non-Spanish speaking builders, painters, decorators et al. How lazy, I thought.

Another Spanish ferreteriá down the road that Alvaro pointed out was quiet in comparison. It was cheaper by far but in sticking to their principles and speaking only Spanish, it had limited its trade. Dilemma. Alvaro said he remembered as a boy that butchers had sold chickens with full heads and legs on all neatly tucked away out of sight but when the expats discovered this they had objected and when the EU laws were introduced, things began to change.

The sun was getting hot, and shade in the form of a potted tree-lined patio area in a tapas bar beckoned. Freshly-squeezed orange went down a treat all round. Twice. Satiated, we decided it was time to move on. Lunch, the main meal of the day, would come at about 2pm so we had time on our hands.

'Can we go into the hills please, Alvaro? You mentioned some opencast mining that looked a bit like a lunar landscape. Probably what Helen talked about.'

Off we set. The air conditioning didn't work in the car so we had all the windows open. Up, up, into the hills and back towards the Club. Generally flat, the area had undulating hills that every now and again gave glimpses of sparkling sea with lots of leisure craft racing around, some cruise ships gliding into or out of San Cartana, the big town and main port, and commercial ships heading in and out of the smaller commercial port, San Cartana Dos.

'Right. Here's an air vent.' Alvaro stopped the car. It was near a rough but well-used track so we popped out to have a look. I hate heights and Lea is pretty squeamish too so we approached the top of the air vent cautiously. I gripped the top hard just to make sure I couldn't fall down. Pathetic really. I have stupid desires to jump off cliffs or balconies just to see what it would be like to fly. The edges mesmerize me. I went in a tandem hang glider once and had to stop myself thinking it was a good idea to undo my straps and seat belt and jump out. Weird.

'Eew!' Lea screwed her face up and dropped a stone down the shaft. It took several seconds to land with a resounding thud.

'Think I've had enough of this, thank you,' she said heading back to the car at a gallop. 'I'll settle for the lunar landscape.'

It came as a surprise. It had the most unusual beauty. One of several areas developed, it was gouged out of the earth and hundreds of metres across. Vehicles would have taken minutes to drive around. Rusting diggers, dump trucks and things we didn't recognize lay abandoned amongst a myriad of dramatic colours – golds, purples, pinks, yellows, blues. Stunning but shameful. As Helen had told us, an environmental disaster that still waited to be cleaned up. As the mine owners should have done before leaving. Having ravaged the earth for profit, when it came to a costly clean-up they'd walked away – and literally got away with it. Lawsuits are costly and get you nowhere.

'That looks strange.' Lea was peering intently down the side of the mine face to our left. We were near the edge but not too near. I still had to quell the strange feeling of being mesmerised.

'It all looks strange.'

'No – I mean – it looks like someone is down there. Moving around.'

We all peered. A flash came and went – something caught in the sunlight.

'Perhaps a dog scavenging. There are lots of them. Harmless. They're left to live as best they can,' Alvaro observed.

'A dog on two legs that has something on it that shines in the sun?'

'Well, whatever it is, we can't do anything – and there is no reason to, Lea. It could be a person simply having a nosy. I imagine people do. We are. Shall we go to the restaurant – the venta by the old harbour – for lunch? I'm famished now.'

A slow drive downhill with stunning sea views brought us to the restaurant.

The Old Harbour Restaurant oozed character. 'El Restaurant del Puerto Viejo' – its name was displayed proudly. The outside space took up most of what used to be the quayside. Bright umbrellas perched above tables and chairs. We went inside to ask if we could have the 'menú del dia' – the three-course, all-inclusive meal which, apart from wine, would be cheaper than ordering individual dishes.

The inside was a treat for the eyes. Whole Spanish hams hung from the ceiling, covering every spare inch. There were little plastic covered paper cups attached underneath to catch any dripping fat. Old photos adorned the walls, showing how the venta used to look, with ships moored up at the quayside and weather-beaten fishermen mending nets. Lots of brass pieces from ships shone in corners and nets were thrown around on anything that dared to be exposed or have a vacant space. These had fishy ornaments caught up in the netting.

We chose to sit outside not far from the door to see all the comings and goings – people drifting in as it was still early, the food going out, the waiters scurrying around. It was a mecca for tourists and expats. Many from the club – I noticed some from the previous night. A few Spanish locals sat inside drinking cool beer and eating tapas. I wondered why they weren't having the full meal but thought maybe they were the farm or land workers who rise before dawn to work in the cool and finish early. They have a break about eight am with food and often brandy, a few more hours work then home, or refreshment, then home. Depended if there was a wife waiting with full lunch.

A waiter came over and warmly greeted Alvaro then us politely, in quick succession. Obviously working in a fairly small area, people were going to know each other. The waiter then told us, not unsurprisingly in English, what was on the menú del dia. Pronounced 'menoo'.

First course - a choice of fish soup, spaghetti bolognaise, or meat balls in tomato sauce. A huge mixed salad accompanied this, for us to share.

Second course – lamb cutlets, pork loin or grilled fish. All with chips and whole pepper, like them or not. The downside to menú del dia, the new waiter told us.

Third course – decide later.

'Oh, I do love eating.' Lea sighed in contentment. 'Fish soup and then grilled fish. Heaven. What is the fish, please?' I was always surprised Lea wasn't vegetarian with her compassion for animals. But as she said, she was born to eat meat and fish.

'Emperador.'

'It's always emperador. Like – um – cod. No, it's sword fish. Cod, that's bacalao I think.' Alvaro pulled a face in case he was wrong. 'I'll google it.'

'No need. It'll be fine. So long as it's still not flapping. I once saw a TV programme about a Japanese restaurant where the fish on a plate suddenly started doing that. I felt so sorry for it. I can't get it out of my mind.' She looked distressed.

'No flapping,' said the waiter smiling. We were impressed with his grasp of English. Lea gave a dazzling smile back. He melted. She was happy.

I ordered the same, as hot weather always made me want light food and I can't get enough fish in England.

Alvaro plumped for soup and lamb. Chuletas de cordero. It was too hot for wine so we settled for iced water. The ambiance of the place was marvellous. Busy as time went on but somehow calm. It was the efficiency that struck us. Everything operated smoothly.

The salad arrived first so we got stuck in and chatted happily. Our waiter came over and spoke in Spanish to Alvaro with a quick apology to us. A discussion ensued so Lea and I talked away but I can listen and talk so was intrigued to hear that the gay guy we had seen last night had disappeared. I think it is always good policy to have some words of a foreign language, no matter how rudimentary. Good will etc. But I was rather stuck as I had understood everything. I was thinking on my feet for the second time in two days.

'Did I hear someone had disappeared? Hazarding a guess. Key words, you know, are invaluable.' I did my best to look nonchalant.

'What?' Lea had suddenly realized I wasn't talking to her any-more and that my attention was elsewhere.

'Yes,' Alvaro answered straight away. 'There is someone in the village who is always around from early in the morning. Has a coffee, off to the bakery, stops and talks. Never ever misses. A busy, fussy person. He may be ill. It happens.' He shrugged.

'I wonder if that's that the man we saw last night chatting up one of the barmen. Very obvious. Helen mentioned it. I only ask as I heard you say 'maricón' – a friend of mine on holiday in Spain was once asking for fish soup but instead of saying 'sopa de mariscos', he asked for 'sopa de maricón'.'

'Speaking of which, I see the soup is coming.' Alvaro started chuckling away to himself. In fact, the merriment didn't stop. Kept coming in waves as he obviously had an image of a soup bowl full of gay men.

'I'm sorry. Such an easy mistake to make. I shouldn't have used the word 'maricón'. It's a bit uncomplimentary. The other mistake – if you don't mind me mentioning it – it will save you lots of embarrassment, is 'cajones' and 'cojones'. One is a drawer, the other is – er – men's balls.' He burst into laughter again. Using Spanish pronunciation the 'j' sounds like an 'h'.

The soup landed. It was swimming with chunky fish. We dug in. It was very filling so we asked for a break before the main course.

Just then a beautiful dog came along, winding in and out between the tables. It was an affable, long-coated, huge German Shepherd with striking markings. I expected it to be shooed away but many guests greeted it warmly. Alvaro told us it belonged to the restaurant's owners and was called Sam. The owners were a Spanish English couple. As Lea was watching the dog closely with a little smile on her face, it came over and sat by our table. It started licking its private bits with relish and great alacrity. Just as well we weren't eating just then.

'I wish I could do that.' Lea was impressed.

'Ask it nicely and it might let you.' I quipped.

'Babs!!' she squeaked. The main course arrived. We made a pathetic attempt to get Sam to leave, so he stayed, looking content. Alvaro's lamb bones were too tempting for him to move away.

'I don't think you should give Sam the bones. Lamb bones can be sharp.' As I said that a bone still with plenty of meat on it suddenly flew off Alvaro's plate as he stuck his knife in. It landed by Sam who moved so quickly he could have won a gold medal. It didn't even get chewed. It was gone.

'Well – I've made someone's day. But you're not having any more. Sam. Now go away.' A sudden shout took the dog's attention, and he flew inside to be seen a minute later carrying some juicy tidbits round a corner.

'Pampered dog. Lucky dog. Think I told you about the country dogs.'

Lea looked sad. She would have rescued every dog in the world if she could. Not to mention knitting warm coats for any wild animal she felt needed one. Sheep and cattle would live in warm, cosy stables and have clean, green fields in summer.

Postres – desserts – were chosen. We all had the caramel, a sort of blancmange that slipped down. A fitting end to a great meal.

Sam came back so we were spurred on to ask for the bill, paid for Alvaro, gave Sam a big fussing and went back to the car.

'Do you want to siesta now, Alvaro?'

'No, I'm fine but a slow drive back would suit me and then I have things to do. I hope you've both enjoyed it today?'

'Immensely!' we chorused. Smiles all round.

'Is there a way down into the open mine?' This from Lea. 'I'm curious. It has such an atmosphere. Can you drop us – or me – off please? Do you want to come, Babs?'

'Not really. It's very hot. Not much shade at the moment and I think it's quite a walk back. I should have brought my sun hat.'

'I can show you the road down that the trucks used to take. Then you can do it another day. It does take a while to walk from the Club. Or back. It's about four kilometres over rough ground.'

Will that do?'

'Oh, yes please. Perfect. Then we should relax by the pool, Babs. Or beach.'

'Sounds like a plan to me.'

Alvaro not only took us to the road down, he took us into the bottom of the mine, driving us around. It was even more awesome when you saw the whole layout and vastness at close quarters and looked upwards to see all the colours shimmering in the sun. There were various entrances to tunnels dotted around. It seemed that both open and closed mining ran side by side.

'Home, James, and don't spare the horses,' quipped Lea.

'Now that I don't understand. Please explain.'

'It's an old English saying when you want to get home quickly. Goes back to times when horses were the main transport. The pool is beckoning, Alvaro.'

We set off going a different route, on the back road without the security checks. It brought slightly different scenery, with rough roads and small pine forests. Here and there, houses appeared, quite desirable but older ones, not as posh as those around the club.

'Helen lives around here. It is good for expat workers, reasonable rents or cheaper to buy. '

Soon we came back to the Club. We all got out and exchanged air kisses on both cheeks with promises of meeting up again soon. Oh, good, I thought, and smiled deliciously to myself.

'Come on Babs. Race you to the pool. Last one buys the drinks tonight.' Off she sped. No point me rushing as it was Uncle paying anyway. I would email him later with news of today's events and my ideas. I looked forward to a swim and leisurely shower later before a pleasant evening in glamorous surroundings. This undercover work had its rewards. I could get used to this amateur sleuthing.

The pool area was too crowded for us so we headed to the beach following the white picket fence like someone from

'The Wizard of Oz'. It was a large cove with shallow water going a long way out, and with netting denoting the end of the safe area. On the rocks furthest out were signs saying 'Muy peligroso' – very dangerous. The waves looked choppy even though it was a calm day. No wind to speak of. I could see a sort of swirling ripple effect far out.

We settled ourselves on the towels we'd brought and made use of the large straw sunshades. Having got everything to our liking, Lea announced she was bored and off for to explore. I closed my eyes, preparing to drift off. Two minutes later she was back.

'Have you got a plastic bag I could have, Babs?'

'I think so. Why do you want it?' I rummaged in my beach bag, producing the plastic bag we had put fruit in.

'For the jelly fish.'

That was it. I sat for a minute considering my immediate future. A snooze was not going to work now that my curiosity was roused. Damn and blast that woman. I sauntered to where Lea was walking around in the shallow water, scooping up bags of water?

'What on earth are you actually doing, Lea?'

'Isn't it obvious? Rescuing jelly fish. You can help. That would be good.'

I studied the situation. 'They will only drift back. you know.'

'I don't care. I'll put them out as far as I can. Go over the rocks past the safety net to throw them into the open sea. The ones on the beach are most urgent, Babs. Go on! Get another bag. Beg, borrow, steal if you have to.'

I threw my arms up above my head in a gesture of resigned defeat, and went to scour the beach for bags. It didn't take long as many plastic bags had washed up, getting caught in calm tiny inlets around the rocks. Bit of a mess, I thought, making a mental note to organize a clear-up. I thought I had read the beach was cleaned daily but this had been missed. Anyway, for acquiring a plastic bag right now it was useful. I didn't want to have to ask someone.

'Well – here I am. What do I do?'

'Grab as best you can. Watch me.' She was on the beach digging out jellyfish with the bag then leaving it in there while she got another to put on top.

I wondered if the jellyfish minded or would sting each other. If they were alive - hard to tell.

Lea soon got four bags full, and with my four bags we were weighed down, and struggled across the rocks with the weight. But success buoyed us up and we continued till every last jellyfish was back in the water out to sea. I ignored the looks of amazement from other sunbathers, evaded attempts to engage me in conversation and solely focused on the task in hand. I felt as mad as Lea – but somehow it felt good to save a life. Finally we made to sit on a comfortably flat rock by the 'Dangerous' sign, catching our breath.

'Hope you have your factor 50 on, Babs. I have. We don't want to get wrinkly.'

'Of course.' The breeze out here was stronger. I laid back on the stone with a sigh and almost instantly had to sit up again. It was really hot. I wriggled around to no avail. Only my beach shoes saved my feet from burning. Just then a large wave came around the corner and slapped me full in the body. I wobbled, caught off balance, shocked by the very cold water and the force behind it. Lea saw just in time, grabbing me by the arm and pulling me back.

'Good job I had a hot bottom, Babs, and had to stand up, otherwise you could be in that boiling mass out there. At least you've cooled off.'

I was drenched. Salt water was in my eyes. The waves settled down again. Through rubbing my eyes I wondered if I was seeing things. Was someone out at sea waving?

'Lea – look out there.' I pointed.

She squinted, blinked and squealed, 'Someone's out there waving. Think I heard a shout too. OMG. What do we do? What is the emergency number here? Did you bring your phone? I didn't.'

The wind brought more cries from across the water. I spotted two lifebuoys attached to the rocks.

'No, Babs!' Lea had seen my look. 'You don't help if you end up needing rescuing yourself. No point two people drowning. Remember your scuba-diving training.' She was frantic.

I was frantic.

The wave came back and knocked Lea into the sea. She quickly came to the surface, spluttering. I grabbed the lifebuoy and threw as hard as I could.

She managed to grab it. It all happened so quickly. She got it round her and, with a shout, headed out to the person in trouble. I held on to the lifebuoy for dear life.

This was madness even though Lea was a strong swimmer, stronger than me. But, as she had pointed out when we learned to scuba dive, you just needed to have confidence in water – you didn't need to be a particularly good swimmer. Fins would take the hard work out of it.

I watched, unable to do anything except hang on and hope. My shouts fell on deaf ears. The line was long and Lea was doing well but I could see she was tiring.

My heart pounded. For precaution against another wave, I got the second buoy over me and tied it around the hook in the housing. I made a decision and jumped into the water to follow Lea. Stupid, but I felt if Lea could risk her life, then I should too.

I couldn't see much now but in what seemed an eternity I was suddenly thumped by something. It was Lea. The waves had thrown her into me and with the man too. The man was not responding, just floating around but secured to Lea with a bit of the rope from the buoy. As the undercurrent towed us out, the waves gradually threw us back against the rocks.

'FEET FIRST AGAINST ROCKS!'

Lea had her feet on the rock, hauling herself up with the man a dead weight. The water helped, throwing him upwards, and Lea managed to secure him on a bit of ledge.

I followed, hauling myself up. We all kept the lines on us. Our scuba training had done us proud.

Even though I'd hardly done anything, my knees were shaking and I only had the strength to sink onto the hot ground. I started to laugh – jellyfish had a lot to answer for.

Lea started to put the man in the recovery position. He was alive and conscious. I glanced behind us. A crowd of people were there and one took over the task from Lea. Others offered hands to help us back onto safer ground a little further away from potential rogue waves. The man was now breathing well. We saw a boat approaching.

'We've called the coastguard,' someone announced. 'Are you OK? You were both very brave. But very foolhardy!'

Comments flew around as we recovered, but one droning, pompous voice broke through. and made us listen:

' – the calm appearance of the sea around here can really fool unsuspecting bathers.'

'You mean they could drown?' Lea snapped.

The owner of the voice looked surprised and moved away.

'That's a bit like my 'nearly news': the waiter 'nearly' got sucked up into the eye of the hurricane in Guatemala, but didn't - we rescued a man who 'nearly' drowned, but didn't.'

Clearly, she was on a mission to counter the high she was on. I thought better of commenting.

'Not the time for telling them off,' someone else piped up. 'How's the man?'

'Going to be OK. Very lucky.' Amongst my shivering and trembling, I noticed they were all speaking English. My feet were beginning to burn as the rock dried out, waiting for the next wave. I was beginning to hop around so someone offered me flip flops. Mine had disappeared in the sea.

Lea had a small crowd of her own around her. She was smiling. People were patting her on the back. I vaguely wondered why she wasn't traumatized. The men on the inflatable were now on the rocks asking questions and seeing to the recovering man, organizing his evacuation into the boat.

In the general hubbub I was aware that we would be questioned later but that in the meantime we could go back to the hotel. I wondered if a follow-up would be necessary. We had plenty of witnesses to the whole event and they all spoke up vociferously on our behalf. We steadfastly refused to go in the boat to hospital as well. The man was looking in our direction. The three of us stared at each other and the boat departed.

Lea and I talked for some time with the beach people exchanging names and numbers just in case. Finally, Lea announced she would like to clean up and rest. We went back to our room. Lea showered and lay down for a rest. She slept for hours.

It was evening when she woke. 'Did I have a bad dream or were we in the water rescuing someone?'

'More of a nightmare. But real.'

'I thought so. It was all a bit asinine.'

'What? Where did you pick that word from?'

'I'm trying to improve myself, Babs. Means 'stupid', doesn't it? What a situation! Is the guy all right?'

'Yes, but – oh never mind. I felt so useless compared to you.'

She looked askance at me.

I continued: 'Yes, he's staying here. His wife heard what happened and went to the hospital. He is staying in for the night. A few people came back with us to the hotel and found her to explain. Small world round here.'

'Large resort. Small world. Time for a G and T, I think. By the way, you were superb' A second later she added, 'Great back up.' She smiled engagingly.

I almost got a compliment there, I thought. I sighed inwardly, resigned to having to play second fiddle, but allowing myself a smile as I thought of my work for Uncle with Club La Roca. It was such an attractive, addictive place.

Azalea stretched, yawned, leapt up, rummaged in the wardrobe and threw on some rather fetching little number in a deep blue. Quick make-up, bling on her neck and fingers and we were off.

CHAPTER THREE
The Double Barrellers

When we got downstairs, Reception was heaving. A coach party had arrived. Suitcases were everywhere. Porters hovered. People drifted to the bar while they waited to be checked in.

Lea and I thought wine would be nice for a change so we drifted as well. We sat at the pool bar. A couple from the coach stood nearby, sipping refreshing spritzers. Never one to stand on ceremony, Azalea got straight into introductions.

'Hello, I'm Azalea Dunbar and this is Barbara Wills. Our second night here.'

'Hello. Stella and James Prescott-Willoughby. You're old timers then?'

'We learn fast.'

A tall, stately-looking woman joined them. 'Queue's getting smaller. Time for a quick one though, I think. The sun has set somewhere in the world, hasn't it?'

We all agreed. More introductions.

'I'm Louisa Helena Josephine Augusta Spelier-Bielby. Louie for short.' She held out an elegant slim hand and smiled radiantly. She was stunning. The kind of person you looked at twice, no matter what age they were. She was fifty something. Her presence filled the room. Surprise in our eyes flickered only briefly when she announced her name. One such name was interesting, two was an amazing coincidence.

'Over here.' Louie waved to catch the attention of a smart, dapper-looking man sauntering around reception. 'This is Air Commodore Francis Culmé-Seymour.'

We barely concealed surprise this time. Lea all but squeaked and blinked a lot. 'Goodness – may I say what fabulous names you all have. Makes 'Azalea' seem quite tame. That's me. Lea for short. Le-ah. You all have fabulous names.' She addressed all four people, swiftly covering our amazement – and curiosity. They smiled and I could have sworn I saw them wink at each other.

'Well – not everyone can be called Smith. Some people drink like rugby players who hadn't been allowed near a bar for weeks.'

'Gosh, that was a coincidence. I wonder what the Spanish will make of their names? They drink fast,' she added as an afterthought.

'The Spanish?' I sometimes considered that 'thought' was not one of Lea's fortes. I was immediately sorry for that. She was a whirlwind of life, fun, compassion and loyalty.

'No – the Double Barrellers.'

'Same as we make of Spanish names – probably – possibly – maybe. Time for a G and T?'

'I prefer wine with my meals. It'll make matters much clearer!'

We giggled. No idea why. We felt young and invincible, I think. We chatted about the day's events. I told Lea off. She congratulated me on my heroism but said I was equally foolhardy. We batted events back and forth. I did concede she was the hero of the hour.

The evening was such fun. We went down into Las Aqueas by taxi, visiting several bars. The locals were interested in us, and we in them. We came across Helen who was having an early drink before going home to relieve the babysitter, who had a date. Hans came into view carrying swimming pool plans. Obviously they had just finished work with the clients Helen had been with. I was getting to like the community who welcomed strangers so openly.

The four of us headed for a Spanish bar recommended by Hans. Typically, it had two televisions on loudly playing different channels, another that was silent, and one which have been broken as it was turned off. People talked all through this noise, and children ran riot – the owners' children, home from the second round of the day's schooling. They'd obviously had a siesta, same as everyone else in the afternoon, and were ready to come alive again.

We all had a light white wine under Hans's direction. There was a quieter, large cavern affair at the back of the bar full of barrels and seats. Exposed brick gave it a country atmosphere, and copper-coloured trappings everywhere made it seem exclusive. Some expats were trying various tipples before filling large plastic containers with the desired drink. We moved in there and admired all the food on display too. Hams, sausages, cut meats, cheeses, salads and tins of exotic Spanish produce. It was in total contrast to the bar at the front. We sat on tall stools round a barrel which had been made into a table.

'This is the bodega run by the son of the family. His idea to make the business bigger, to be attracting the tourists and foreigners living here. It's doing good. His mujeres – wife – works here too. People come in to talk with them so between them they have a large crowd. The big – whole – area is changing. More money for locals. Some good money and some bad. Mainly it is the property developers who go hand by hand with the local council that us need to be watching. I am sure something will be done – sometime.' Hans was philosophical.

'Yes. It's almost public knowledge. So, why something hasn't happened already I don't know. Still, as I said about the gypsy enclave, you need to gather evidence for things. Hearsay is no good,' added Helen.

We should investigate more, I thought.

'Another round?'

'Round of what?' asked Hans.

'Drinks.' We all said in unison.

'Oh, I am a horse and you can lead me to water and make me drink.' He beamed, blue eyes sparkling – a look that was to become very familiar.

'I think it's a bit of a mixed metaphor but under the circumstances appropriate.'

'What is a mixed – thing?'

I sighed. 'Can I explain later when the horses have drunk a bit more? Same again, everyone?'

'Well, we can't have the same again as we've drunk it. But we can have similar.'

'Pedant Lea. Just because you're a heroine doesn't mean you can be annoying and get away with it as well!' I smiled to soften it.

'What's this, then? Heroine – or is it hero now. We don't have actresses any more do we. Just actors? Sorry, I digress.' Helen looked expectant.

We told her and Hans of the day's events. Suitably impressed, they bought the next two rounds plus some sticky rib tapas to keep us sober. There are some advantages in having been half-drowned, I thought.

We decided to move on to another watering hole. The warmth outside was luxury. The sun had set so the heat wasn't overwhelming. It was wonderful to walk around without coats or jackets of any kind knowing for sure they wouldn't be needed. Helen said she must go home but Hans was keen to continue and we liked his local knowledge of the most interesting places to go. Lea seemed happy in his company. She had gathered some tissues when we ate the tapas.

'I'm just going to pop these in the basura. See, I am learning the language.' We all moved off while she went across the street and I idly watched her open the lid of the huge rubbish container, big enough to house a family. I was wondering if she would struggle to open the heavy lid with her slim figure. But her strength was surprising as she had proved today. She put the tissues in and shut the lid, then opened it again as quickly. She seemed to stare at something.

She turned round dropping the lid and without speaking waved us over urgently. She just stood and pointed.

We went over – concerned but more puzzled. Hans and I lifted the lid together and peered in. We froze. We stared back at each other. Shock. Horror. Any advantage gained by Lea's mute warning was immediately lost.

'That's not a gruesome toy, is it?' my voice shook.

It took Hans a minute to answer. 'No. That's Enrico. The maricón. Um, the gay man.'

We were each as white as a sheet in contrast to the crimson, blood-soaked body dumped unceremoniously in the basura. Lea was leaning with her back against the nearby wall.

There were mixed houses, shops and café bars all around, I noticed, but the basura was set a little way down a narrow, poorly-lit alley. Strange how the mind works! Hans and I took another look before closing the lid. Just to make sure it was not some horrible but gruesome joke.

Enrico had had his throat cut. There was a gaping hole with flaps of skin hanging down as though a rough serrated knife had been used to hack away at the plump, wobbly skin under the chin, prolonging his agony. His stylish, colourful clothes and everything surrounding him was bloodied. The look on his face was of fear and pain. His eyes were wide open, staring. I felt I would always retain that image.

I went over to Lea, who had moved to another wall a little further away from the rubbish bin. We just stood there mute.

Hans finally got his mobile out and made some phone calls. One, I gathered, was to the guardia, the civil police. The other was to Helen. She hadn't yet reached home so re-appeared within minutes.

She was as shocked as we were but at least she hadn't seen the body. She automatically went to look but we stopped her.

'Are you OK, Barbara? Everyone?'

We all nodded automatically. It seemed undignified to find a human amongst all the rubbish, rubbish intended to be collected and to rot away. It would have been nearly as upsetting to find an animal there. The man who had caught our attention rather dramatically, mincing his way to the bar to talk to a friend or lover, had now had his life prematurely ended. Gone. Just like that.

'I will stay with you to translate if necessary,' said Helen gently. 'Are you coping? I'll explain to the babysitter and ring my husband.'

Coping? We were just there – dazed. As we stood around silently, our attention was caught by a man swaying his way over, as if in slow motion. He was carrying a plastic shopping bag and seemed focused on the basura, an object to head for in his alcoholic state.

He stopped by us and looked enquiringly. 'Ish something goin' on? Can I put thish – thish – ' he waved the bag — ' in' – he waved the bag again towards the basura – ' there?'

'No!' we all shouted together.

He looked startled. 'Wash – what? Why?'

He wobbled and I thought he was going to fall over so I grabbed an arm to steady him and pulled the bag from him. 'I'll put it in for you. No bother.'

'Oo – oh, I can do it. My wubbish. I musht be tidy.' His arm flailed around, trying to get the bag back but I easily evaded him. He wobbled so I took the opportunity to gently lead him further along the street. I threw the bag towards the others and Alvaro picked it up putting it near the bin.

'Look, there's a bar. Your rubbish has gone so you can have another drink.'

'Don't want another drink. Taxshi. Want a taxshi. Going back the reshort. Where's my rubbish? Need to put it in the bin.' He started back towards the basura.

This is all we need, I thought. A tidy drunk with a conscience. At least it occupied our minds.

'We'll take you to the bar and phone a taxi for you. How about that? Won't we, Lea?' I waved her over. They were all staring at me but Lea roused herself and came over. Her very presence took the drunk's interest and he focused on her.

'Your nishe. Fancy a drink?'

'Yesh – yes. But only a quick one as I have to go somewhere. I know a good bar round the corner. Follow me.

Thanks for this, Babs.' She glowered at me, took the man's arm to stop him falling over in his rush to follow, and steered him out of sight.

She was back in a few minutes breathless and alone. 'I raced him around a few corners and pushed him towards a bar, then legged it. Hope he stays away long enough for the police to arrive. If he finds his way back here, he's going to be cross.'

'Sorry, Lea, I didn't mean you to go to a bar. Just give me a hand. The guys would have seen him off if necessary.'

'Done now. Never mind.'

We stood waiting again, guarding the basura. Never more could we have done with a stiff drink. All of us. It seemed ages since Hans had made the phone call but suddenly we were surrounded by flashing lights and blaring sirens.

The guardia had arrived and the circus began.

Just then, the drunk came speeding back into view, obviously not happy. He had spotted us and was making a beeline in our direction, wagging his finger and saying uncomplimentary things from what I could manage to hear – sirens have an international quality.

Not realizing what was happening, the drunk continued to waver forward, bumping into a tall, uniformed officer. Staring into a stern, unsmiling, face, he finally got the message. Obviously he thought discretion was the best part of valour, and, muttering apologies, he slunk away wobbling – if it is possible to slink when wobbling. Many other rubberneckers had arrived and the first wave of police were busy putting up cordons around us and the basura.

The guardia cars had come in force. There were no screeching brakes but a definite 'I am here' feel ensued. Quite right too. Someone had to take charge. We were all beginning to recover our senses, in part thanks to the drunk who had got our attention, albeit for the wrong reasons. The numbness was wearing off and we felt secure in our innocence.

The main man introduced himself. There was no attempt at Spanish. He went straight into English, encompassing all of us. Obviously, we had that 'English' look. Or at least 'foreign'. Hans was German after all, but most of the Germans speak English.

'I am el capitan. Please show me the body.' We all pointed at the basura but made no move to go to it. He hesitated only a moment then strode over with some compatriots. They peered in and talked quickly amongst themselves. Spanish is a quick language anyway, at least I thought so. Maybe English is as bad if you don't know it. We got several looks in our direction which made us shuffle.

'Isn't it amazing how you know you're innocent but the police can still make you feel guilty,' Lea observed. 'They only have to be around to manage it. I feel the same going through Customs. I know I'm not smuggling anything and I've packed my own bag but I always feel guilty. I always wonder if I've taken my eyes off my bags even for a second and someone's put drugs in.'

She was recovering rapidly and was even beginning to – dare I say – relish the situation. Her artistic side was taking over and I could imagine she was visualizing dramatic paintings. I had stopped trembling and feeling sick at the sight of the body but the 'positive side' hadn't yet kicked in for me.

El Capitan came over to us. Not unsurprisingly, he had a serious look on his face. 'Who found the body?'

'I did.' Lea stared at him steadfastly. She had her arms folded in front of her and something in her stance made her look defiant. El Capitan stared back. Lea's chin jutted out. Temporary stand-off.

'How and when?'

'I went to put some rubbish in the bin – basura – and saw the body. Half an hour ago maybe. We had been to the bodega just over there.' She pointed across the road.

'Who is 'we'?'

'Me, Babs, Hans and Helen.' She introduced us all. 'Hans phoned you. Barbara and I are on holiday at the resort, only our second day, but Helen and Hans live and work here. We all met only recently but it feels like we have known each other a hundred years. Murder does that you know. We were all stunned. You don't find a body very often.'

'Oh, how often is not often for you – and how do you know it is murder?'

'What? It's just a saying. Anyhow, the way his throat was cut means he couldn't possible have done it himself, to himself – even if he was suicidal. I notice these things. I'm an artist you know.'

'All what things?' El Capitan had a slightly bemused look.

'I mean – in the English language – we say things that we don't mean but they can still be relevant to a situation. No, I didn't mean that. Whew. I was saying that there are things people say from history based on – hmm – history. Or to be clearer –'

'No! Thank you. That will do.' El Capitan's look had changed not only to confused but faintly amused. It was just a flicker across his face but I noticed. His hard face came back immediately.

'Oh, but I need to explain ...'

'No. you don't.' He was very firm. 'Now I want to know why, how, or if you all know this person. Names, addresses. Many questions to follow. My colleagues will take statements. Are you all alright? Do you need some time or help to recover? It must be a shock for you all. We can do more tomorrow if we need to.' He smiled curtly and without waiting for an answer departed, leaving others to carry on.

'Well!' snorted Lea.

'What do you expect? Same all over the world.'

'He offered help but I somehow felt it was insincere. Are we suspects, do you suppose?'

'Guilty till proven innocent.'

'I agree.' Hans piped up. 'Could be a long night.'

I realized Helen was going to be caught up in all this. I suddenly felt guilty. Such a short acquaintance.

'I am so sorry, Helen. This isn't your problem.'

She cut in immediately. 'No problem. I wouldn't leave anyone in these circumstances. I'll be a good witness. I can vouch for you only arriving the day before yesterday. The police know me – and Hans. I know it seems like a lifetime since you arrived, but the fact is – you're new here.'

The rank and file questioned us. Forensics arrived and lights flashed all over the place more intensely than before. The crowd of onlookers grew but police systematically dispersed them. Finally, el capitan came back from directing matters and told us we could go back to the hotel but that he would be in touch.

Lea promised with a serious look. 'We won't leave town. Scouts' honour.'

El Capitan scrutinized her face, searching for any sign of disrespect but, finding none, he left without another word. Even with the testimony of our friends, I wasn't sure if he believed in our innocence.

Now we headed to the nearest bar. News had travelled fast. Hans was inundated with questions from the inhabitants, all agog for news. We seemed to be celebrities in a strange way. In some ways I wanted to join in the conversations but instead settled for quietly talking over events with Helen and Lea. Would I ever sleep peacefully again? Would any of us?

By the time we had got back to La Roca itself – Hans dropping us off – the new under-manager, Karim, the bulldog with the wasp, sped towards us full of concern. He was indeed unctuous. However, we were grateful for the reassurance that all help necessary would be forthcoming. Could he phone anyone? Contact the UK? Get us food or drink? Room service? No, no, no and no – but thank you.

We were strangely grateful for Karim's oily attention. It was now early morning and bed beckoned. Our heads hit the pillows and soon I heard Lea breathing rhythmically. Her clothes were tossed on the floor, inviting all manner of wildlife to a cosy bed.

How could she turn off so quickly? It was surely the childhood loss of her parents in a motor accident that had made her into such a tough cookie!

I tossed and turned for what seemed hours but tiredness eventually overcame me and I felt myself drifting. ☐

CHAPTER FOUR
Anticlimax Turns Dramatic

Strong sunlight woke us both up as we had not thought to close the blinds.

I lay awake mulling over the night's events but Lea leaped up and made tea for us. My head felt as if an elephant had given birth in it.

Lea was quiet but active, going to shower with her tea in hand. She had told me she always slept well in fresh bedlinen or just after a night-time shower – generally speaking – so she was often refreshed when I wasn't. These things did nothing for me. Clean clothes were on in a trice then she turned her attention to the heap on the floor. It was moving. Her eyes widened and she approached with caution while I looked on, still stupefied. Finally, she snatched the clothes up and shook them, a small lizard dropping to the floor. It scuttled off to the balcony, disappearing over the balustrade and into a nearby tree.

'I hope I didn't hurt it. Are you going to be long, Babs? I'm famished. Breakfast is calling.' She looked thoughtful. 'So you remember when I was a squirrel racist? I didn't care about invasive grey squirrels, only reds. But they both have rights.'

I was totally nonplussed. Had I dreamt it all? Unfortunately not, but apparently life went on, certainly for Lea who was champing at the bit to get going. She went to see if the lizard was around and apologize to it. I obligingly, if slowly, got myself together, showered and we set off for breakfast, the heat already starting to make itself felt.

'Another hot day.' I commented conversationally.

'What do you expect in southern Spain this time of year. It's lovely in the evenings. Fab foreign weather.'

I was put in my place, deciding to stay there for the quiet life.

It was a nice walk across open ground among flowers and bushes from our block to the main hotel and dining area. We liked being slightly apart as it gave a sense of privacy. The gardeners were already busy watering plants.

'Did you know Babs that you should never water plants in the heat of the day as it gives them a shock? You do it early or late when it's cool.'

'Can't say I had thought about it – not this morning anyway. My mind's been a bit occupied. I must speak to Uncle if only out of courtesy.'

We arrived at the breakfast buffet. Here was normality. Food.

We sat in the restaurant looking at our breakfast in a rather stupefied way. Neither of us spoke. Had last night just been a particularly bad dream? Tiredness had tied our tongues after the initial early surge urged on by Lea. Shock had worn off completely but the process of the police enquiries along with the graphic memories of the body were still taking their toll.

Lea had a particularly odd look on her face, staring at the fried eggs on her plate as though they were aliens.

'Olive oil becomes carcinogenic when you cook with it,' I observed, breaking the silence.

'What?'

'Your eggs are cooked in olive oil. I read the menu. Properly. Lots of people cook with it but it's not necessarily good for you.'

'Well, I have to die of something so I think I'll chance it and hope I'll still be alive at the end of today.' With that she tucked in with gusto, piling lots of butter on her toast as well. Minutes later she was back at the breakfast bar surveying the usual mountain but with much more food this morning. I had not had time to tell Uncle Charles about the food issue and now I had a lot more to tell him. Lea came back with a little of everything. OK – a lot of everything. And another orange.

'I see you've gone for the healthy option.' My meagre bowl of cereal seemed lonely.

'Murder makes me hungry. Poor guy will never eat again. Think of all that food that's become available because he's not able to eat it!'

'So – you're eating his portion? Shouldn't you be generous and let someone else eat it who needs it more? The world has room for your generosity.' I wasn't sure where this bizarre conversation was going.

'Don't be silly, Babs. I can't take things out from the buffet.' She didn't blink and continued eating without a break.

I looked up when she waved and saw Hans approaching. He'd got coffee and toast, and sat down, smiling. Those twinkling, deep blue eyes were doing their thing again as he turned his attention to Lea.

'Buenas dias guapa, guapas. How are you today?'

'Good, surprisingly.' I had to answer as Lea had her mouth full. She smiled back at him waving a fork. She was very 'guapa'- attractive or beautiful – in spite of a strange night. Dressed this morning in the shabby chic way she achieved from her cheap clothes markets, it was a look that went well with her fecund imagination.

'Two shocks in one day, guapas. Nearly drowned heroes, then el homicidio – murder! I hope you don't think Spain is always like this. Aqui - here - it is usually quiet.' He reflected. 'Well, apart from local politics. Much stress.' I wanted to follow this up but just then Karim Badour, the under-manager from the previous night, started to slime his way over.

We all watched. It is hard to describe his movements but my thoughts were of a plump Uriah Heap. Slightly bent over, almost wringing his hands as he stopped at quite a few tables to enquire how the guests were. They responded in various ways. We were amused to see the different attitudes.

Some couples had a quick word and carried on with breakfast, others glanced at each other with a knowing look after the Bulldog Wasp had gone. Some older ladies appeared charmed, the young ones clearly found him repulsive. Finally, it was our turn. Neutrality was best. His opening gambit was obviously going to be the previous night's event.

'Good morning. How are you this morning? Anything I can do to help today?' All said on one breath. More hand wringing.

'We're fine, thank you. In daylight things always seem better. Not the usual problems your guests have, though you must have come across strange things in this job. How long have you worked here? Any stories to cheer us up this morning?'

'Er – I can't think of any.' Karim seemed embarrassed at this – perhaps not used to such attention yet. 'I have been here a while …' He trailed off.

'Forgive me for asking, but local gossip has told us about your predecessor disappearing. It must be a worry.' Karim looked a bit startled, so I repeated, 'People keep telling us about it.' I gave what I hoped was an engaging smile. Guests' questions should always be answered, I thought, just in case he was going to argue. I had no right to ask but I was going to take all opportunities to get any information, any time from anyone!

He struggled with my sentence. 'Predecessor – gossip - um, is what please? My English always needs to be extended.'

'I mean the person who had this job before you. Didn't he go missing – unexpectedly?' Momentary silence.

'Ah, I see. Thank you. I will add that to my vocabulary.' He seemed to overly evaluate the question. 'It is a mystery indeed. No one knows anything. The police have been informed and family have not heard from him. It is a worry. Please excuse me. I have my morning work to do.' With that he smiled in a crooked way and sped off, the unctuousness following him almost visibly. Even his hair was slicked back with oil.

'Did you get the impression he didn't want to talk about it?'

'Potentially tumbleweed. Anyway, perhaps he has a lot to live up to in a job that he was not really destined for in normal times.' Lea always saw the best side of everything.

Hans looked puzzled. 'Sorry – I didn't understand all that. Tumbleweed?'

'New word for maybe 'embarrassing' – your question, I mean. A silence followed. Tumbleweeds don't say a lot. Heard it on a quiz.' I changed the subject. Silent shake of my head.

'Do you know Karim, Hans?'

'Not well. I don't hear good things and I don't like what I see – but he is in new job. We must not be judging.' It suddenly struck me I hadn't met the general manager yet.

'Do you know Carl Wellington then – the top man?'

'Carl – yes. Friend of mine. English. We have some good drinks together. Now you are not in the EU, all jobs are in question but I think he is in safety. No reason why not. He has a long contract which I think must be kept – for honour? Right? We hope.'

'Yes, much change. Maybe other countries will follow us out. Merely speculation.' I shrugged.

'You must introduce us sometime. I only say this because my uncle has a tour company in the UK and he has heard of this resort and wondered if he could – or should – send people here on his coach tours. I did tell Helen and asked her not to mention it as we want an unbiased view of this place without special treatment. But, in the short time that we have been here, we can see the place is both beautiful and well-run.' (said as a conciliatory after thought in case I'd inadvertently been rude).

I went on: 'Just a little worrying because of the local politics. Can't be worse than going to an area where you might have religious problems, though,' I commented and was going to expand on Hans's earlier comment when Lea jumped in:

'You mean, Babs, you might be murdered by some fanatics?'

'Well, yes, the thought had crossed my mind. My uncle does like to go to unusual places. Not that this is unusual. Just reminds me of Midsomer.'

Hans was obviously lost by all this. 'Of course, I will introduce you. But I don't understand Mid – um - somer?'

'It's a small country place in a TV series where there is at least one murder every week. Here we have one murder and a missing person. I was just being silly. But it is a thought that murder, a missing person and local politics may be linked. I wouldn't want tourists to get involved in anything. I am sure I am being – '

'Paranoid?' supplied Lea. She had a funny look on her face like 'shut up - I want to talk to you later'. We glared at each other.

Hans didn't seem phased by any of the interchange. He studied us both, a slight smile on his face and just for a change his eyes sparkled with a cross between merriment and curiosity. And, dare I say, excitement.

'I like mysteries.' He was beaming. 'Do you think we have something that should be investigated? Oh – but you are on holiday. We hardly know each other.'

'It feels like we have known each other for years. We had a murder together last night. It brings people together.' Lea was passionate and bent forward to put her hand on Hans's, which was resting on the table. They locked looks in a mutual feeling of sudden companionship. "I feel I am positively hugged by the sincerity of the people around here. The love in this place is amazing!"

I felt a bit on the sideline. Where were Alvaro and Gareth when you needed to be 'hugged' by them?

As it happens, here. Alvaro walked over. Things had evened up. Hans and Lea continued to smoulder but took in Alvaro's arrival.

Alvaro looked full of concern, and questions.

'Pull up a seat, Alvaro. Are you working or off today?'

'Off for two days. What am I hearing? Murder? Are you involved? Are you OK?' He was genuinely worried and concerned.

Oh bless him, I thought. Nice man. Very, very nice man. 'We are OK and you hear right. Can you sit down or is it not allowed?'

He was hesitating. 'Not really allowed. We can go to some areas on days off. Like the main music club and we can pay for golf. The swimming pools are not allowed. We would be too under dressed! Might give everyone the wrong idea. I will hover around. It is easier when Karim is off duty.'

'Shame. How about we all move to our room, Babs? We have a lovely balcony. We are in one of the separate blocks but near the hotel. We can order drinks.'

We all moved as one and went to our room. We ordered coffee and croissants. Lea added butter and jam. We shuffled chairs around on the balcony, a very generous affair with sun loungers and big table. The views were of the sea towards the beach and part of the club so people watching was a definite pastime. We were just settling down when the food arrived. I went to see to it.

'Please put it on there.' I pointed to a coffee table. I tipped the waiter and called for help to move it all. Everyone came. Many hands and all that. There was a mountain of croissants.

'Lea, just how much did you order? Did you sneakily order more?'

'I said there were four very hungry people here. That's all. I'm hungry, at least. I can eat for us all – if no one wants anything.' She looked guilty. Subdued even in front of friends, but it didn't last long.

'Did you know there is a fabulous new drug out but the side effects can be headaches, nausea or death.'

I opened my mouth to comment but nothing happened. I sighed internally – character will out!

'Drug for what?' Alvaro asked, a familiar, bemused look forming.

'No idea,' she beamed. 'I missed the first part of the programme.'

'Well, we must be sure to avoid that one. I'm hungry,' Hans and Alvaro more or less chimed in together.

We all ate. Some of us again. My waist expanded a lot but Lea's flat tummy bulged only a tad and I was jealous again. I tried to find a reason to love her and forgive.

Just as I was about to get back to what we had been discussing in the restaurant, Alvaro jumped in with some news, addressing me formally as 'Barbara'. I was intrigued.

Of course, the murder was a very serious matter, he said, especially that of a long-term resident of the village, but as well as that there had been a big problem within the hotel and someone had had to be fired for very bad conduct. In case Uncle was to be a good source of potential clients, he wanted to assure me that things were dealt with quickly and efficiently.

Carl, the manager, had asked him to get all our bread from the village bakery early that morning. Alvaro lives in the village so it would be easy – except he had to use both bakeries as one of them hadn't been able to do the whole order without leaving the shop empty.

Given the general circumstances I couldn't begin to think what was coming but clearly Alvaro had something on his mind. More than murder. We sat agog, almost glad to have our minds taken off the serious event that had played out.

'I'm glad you had croissants, not bread. There was a problem with a chef who bakes the bread. Spanish bread is not always good, it doesn't last long, so Carl wants fresh bread cooked here. But the chef – I mean baker - was dismissed early this morning. Please – don't repeat what I am about to tell you.' He looked at us seriously.

Goodness – what was coming? We all nodded with our serious faces on too and murmured agreement.

'The chef was caught doing bad things with the bread.'

'You mean like putting too much salt in or something?' I queried.

'Not salt. He was playing in the bread. He put himself in the dough. Or a bit of himself.'

'What?' Comprehension was slow.

'Interfering – how can I say this?' He was beginning to look uncomfortable, not because of the English as his was pretty near perfect, but because of the subject.

It began to dawn on me, my eyes widening. 'You mean like interfere – as in sex?'

'Yes. Whew! That's it. He was playing with the dough and – er – himself. Instant dismissal.'

'Eww! Was it soft dough?' Lea enquired.

'What difference does that make?' My eyes were wide.

Hans looked a bit lost.

'Lots of difference – if it was soft and warm and then cooked later we could all have eaten some. Ugh! But if it was already cooked, he wouldn't have bothered with it as bread.'

'If it was cooked it wouldn't be dough!! I'm surprised you didn't ask if the rolls were plain or seeded – or those nice mustard-top ones, or something.'

'Oh, I don't think he would have used seeded or mustard!' Lea emphasized. Amazed and amused at the same time, we gave Hans a few explanations to sort out the look on his face.

'No wonder Karim Wasp-Face looked fed up with that to cope with. I might let him off this time. Maybe not all bad, eh?'

'Anyway, I think croissants are more suitable for breakfast in heat like this. A light meal. Too much hot food is so heavy in heat. Bit like having that cold soup – what is it – gazpacho – in the middle of the Arctic.'

After Lea's gargantuan feast I couldn't believe what I had just heard!

I was forming a ripe reposte but she carried on: 'This reminds me of the time two of my friends went to rescue a sheep and its lamb stuck in mud. They were accused of murder.'

I was a little stunned by this deviation, even for Lea. Unique and off the wall sometimes just didn't seem a good enough description for her. 'How does this relate – in any shape or form?'

There was silence as she considered this. 'Well ... it doesn't. But it's interesting – and after our night and this rather big blip in the kitchen department, it's a nice distraction. Some light relief! Oh, no pun intended! Call it what you will.'

She paused waiting for comment but none came. 'So ... my friends were out walking along the seashore and saw this sheep with a lamb stuck in the muddy sand. They graze sheep on salt marshes in some places – then you don't need to season them.'

It flitted through my mind she was possibly, even probably, serious and said so. Big mistake. Huge. 'You don't really believe that – do you?'

If looks could kill, I would have been the next victim.

Anyway, they managed to pull the sheep and the lamb out but had to carry them back onto dry land. Not easy with struggling, mud-caked, heavy sheep. Unknown to them, someone from shore had been watching, and completely misunderstood the event, thinking the sheep were bodies. Not much later the police arrived and swooped down on them. Amazement all round. Fortunately, the sheep were still there and everyone had a good laugh – in the end. I'm glad our murder was real so we didn't waste police time.'

'You mean you're glad someone got murdered just to keep the guardia happy - and that's quite a tale. If it's true.'

Miffed, she went into attack mode. 'Of course it is. Why would you doubt me? And I'm sorry someone is dead. Obviously. I just don't like wasting people's time. Do you remember when you told your mother that you loved her but you didn't like her?'

'Azalea! That's personal – and also irrelevant! I wasn't wasting my mother's time, I was trying to communicate. Failed, of course, but that's how it always was. Stop baiting me just for the sake of it and let's get going – somewhere. We have lovely company for the day. What do you suggest guys?

We girls have finished out little spat, haven't we, Lea? Sorry about that!'

Alvaro was the first to speak. He had moved to the balcony during this little exchange, sitting in a comfy but elegant white rattan chair, resting his elbows on the ledge with a leg doing the restless leg movements. My mind ran through all the causes of this but for now I stayed quiet as I didn't know him well enough to mention it. I looked forward to when I did know him better.

Hans was looking both bemused and amused with his eyes still twinkling and a smile playing around his mouth. He was sprawling in a chair, long legs straight out in front of him, bottom on the outer edge of the seat, his normal habit being super-relaxed. We provided good sport for him.

'I think someone is trying to attract your attention.' I moved to the balcony and saw some of the Double Barrellers waving and shouting up. How did they know which room we were in? I must ask later. They had lots of people around them.

'Are you alright?' came drifting up. Different bits. 'We heard about the body you found. Anything we can do to help? I told my son I knew you, so don't worry.'

How kind of them, was my first thought. My second, were they just being nosy? I gave them the benefit of the doubt. 'Thank you!' I shouted down. 'We have two able bodies – I mean friends, helping. Maybe see you in the Piano Bar later? We get there later rather than sooner, depending where we get to during the day.'

'Splendid idea. We have more friends to introduce you to. I think your friend Azalea – Lea – will be interested. 'Bye for now.' They waved and left.

Now – who were they? I mulled over the names. Hard to forget but I had so much going on. Lea joined us on the balcony, Hans standing up to join her. She peered over, called hello and waved. Obviously they waved back.

'Oh, that's Louisa Spelier-Bielberg and the Prescott-Willoughbys. What did they want? Such nice people! Strange – you can know someone for years and still have no lasting rapport but know some else for five minutes and they become lifelong good friends.'

I vaguely wondered if she would feel the murderer was a nice person who had some good reason to snuff out a life. I could imagine her listening intently to the murder's explanation. Her eyes would narrow in concentration staring at the person. Next, I was irritated because she had remembered their names. Silly really. Too late it suddenly clicked with me that someone – a female voice – had shouted about not worrying because she had told her son about us. It had been such a melee of people and words. I didn't bother to further it with Lea, being annoyed, mostly with myself.

'We'll meet them for a drink later in the Piano Bar, I'm sure. More friends of theirs to meet – you heard. Quite a crowd of them booking in last night.' She had organized our evening and why not?

This was a little annoying when I thought about it – she had made more of an impression on them than I had. I must work on this – me being – well, not invisible but slightly, slightly – what? What was I less of? My insecurities were coming to the fore again. No reason to, especially after I had done so well for Uncle Charles on our previous trip. I comforted myself. But it niggled me that so far Lea had rescued a drowning person and made an impression on – just about everyone. In spite of being such a scatter brain. Annoying – but I only had myself to blame.

No, I didn't. I must be positive. I would be.

I felt better. Lea and I were not in competition. We were so different, we couldn't be. Besides we were best friends. Yes. We were lucky to have each other. I kept telling myself this and meant it. Lea told me I had the Midas touch but that she had the minus touch. Regarding money she was right, but in other things she won hands down. Ah well – onwards and upwards. Now to Hans and Alvaro.

'I think you said you had some good contacts for hiring a car –'

Before I could finish the sentence both Hans and Alvaro jumped in. 'Yes, I do!' exclaimed in unison.

'Ooh, choices. How nice! What next then? Over to you, guys.'

'I have a contact down in the village.' From Hans. 'We can compare prices, Alvaro, with yours?'

Lea moved more into the sun across the balcony and her tight short shorts showed her bottom off beautifully. The small wiggle she had when walking reminded me of two ferrets fighting in a pillowcase. The men appreciated the view.

I smiled. I remembered a very stout solid Matron in a hospital I was in for a short time as a child strutting forth with her buttocks going 'boom, boom' one after the other, as she moved in her formidable way. She was an amusing person in spite of her ferocious appearance and kind towards children – if firm. She had some strange sayings for us but quite common now. Some of us kids let slip the odd noise or smell for fun and if she noticed she would either say 'Church or Chapel let it rattle' or sometimes 'Wherever you be let it run free' which made us all giggle like mad – so we did it more.

Strange what runs through minds in a few split seconds. It was Lea's bottom that set me off on this track. I came back to earth. I must have been 'gone' longer than I thought because all I heard was:

' … my friend went on holiday and put her cats in a cattery.'

'… Oh, I have never put my dogs, Bessie and Guapa in a doggery.'

'… massage parlour – just come and go.'

Smirking all round.

'… seriously though, I really am into dowsing, ley lines, alternative therapy and all that. Physical energy. I like to be healthy – you can't cure death. I do like and admire older men who stay fit – but fossils aren't my thing. I can't fuc – er – oops. I mean I have my limits.'

'What?' I enquired with raised eyebrows. I noticed the men perked up with the physical energy reference but the fossils went over their heads. Thankfully.

'I doubt even with Alvaro's good English he will understand ley lines – and how did you get onto dogging and massage parlours from car hire?'

'You went into your own little world, Babs, and it was catteries and kennels. I was going into more detail about the murder with Alvaro, and then Hans was telling us about the joke down in the village. A gift shop has closed and some wit has put posters on the empty windows advertising a massage parlour saying 'just come and go'. I'm not explaining that bit! Anyway, the locals took it seriously and have been up in arms, even though it was only a joke. Everyone knows there are lots of legal 'clubs' or brothels, for that sort of thing.'

This was said in a worldly sort of way, not quite Lea's style, so I had another smile, not at her expense, but because of her being her. I was sure it was me who had told her about the fully legal clubs for men only, dotted here and there. In fact, I knew I had, because she had snorted with indignation that there was nothing legal for women (bit of an equality buff, our Azalea).

I explained that anywhere in the world if you pay, you can get pretty much anything, plus there were lots of private clubs for couples who could do as they wished when inside the premises. Not the same, she had declared. Pouted even.

I had asked if she would frequent these legal clubs for women if they existed and got an interesting reply: 'Yes. I would just to see what it was like and then say I didn't like it with conviction because I had tried it. You can't say you don't like something if you haven't tried it.'

'Does that go for heroin or cocaine too?'

'Babs! I'm not getting drawn into a full-scale discussion of everything you should or shouldn't try. Now you're baiting *me*! I thought you wanted to go out?' She couldn't resist one last quick dig, though. 'Drugs are a separate issue. Potentially harmful. Brothels aren't in that category – though an aggrieved wife might disagree. Mind you, if her husband did it regularly and these places didn't exist, it could be worse. He might have endless affairs instead! You've got me going, so I'm going to stop.'

I smiled to myself.

The men looked amused. Again.

'Please – what is dogging?' from Hans.

'Argh - can you explain, Alvaro?' He nodded amiably, doing so instantly, which caused Hans's shoulders to start a life of their own with amusement and much chuckling. Alvaro scattered words around – cars, rocking, peeping, steamy windows.

'This is a special English thing? Or international?' Hans enquired gleefully. 'I must look out for this to see where the Spanish or Germans do it. It is good for international relations, yes? I look on the internet to be educated.' More chuckling erupted into guffawing. It was infectious.

Lea was staring hard at her legs. 'I didn't realize my legs were so hairy after the winter,' she mused. ' I tend to ignore them when I'm in jeans. Wonder if the gardener here would lend me his lawn mower? Ooh – my toenails! Terrible. Awful. Horrid. I'd better borrow the garden shears too.' She squealed. 'I'm not going anywhere till I've sorted myself out. I hate feeling like a whale with a golf club. You lot go ahead and hire a car.'

'Whale? I thought you wanted to be a driver? You'll need to be there with paperwork.'

'Oh – yes.' Her shoulders slumped and a big sigh followed. 'I feel out of place if I'm not neat and tidy in myself – like the whale – out of place. I'll come then. Can we go now, then I can get back to this asap? Boring task so I like to get it out of the way.'

Typical Lea. Similar attitude to clothes so I wasn't surprised. We gathered ourselves and 'got going'. It was already hot so I filled the 'cool bottles' we'd purchased from the hotel shop, which was an Aladdin's cave, an upmarket version of the 'Todo Uno Euro' (Everything One Euro) shop in the village which we'd discovered briefly with Alvaro. You could buy practically anything there – pots, pans, knives, forks, toys, ornaments, gifts, bedding, linen et al – including an elephant. Well, that's how it felt.

I had chatted with the assistant in the hotel shop who informed me it was rented from the hotel as a private enterprise. I was impressed with the set-up and made a note for Uncle Charles to maybe expand into more rentals of this kind. A wine, beer, cheese, posh food shop for picnics or guests to eat on their balconies. We knew of the Bodega Bar shop in the village which was patronized by the autonomous villa owners and renters but the village was growing, literally, with more housing being built for all comers, so competition should be healthy. More clothes shops, independent bars and restaurants, thereby taking the rent without the hassle of running venues like Prem's.

'Can we go to the open mine? I want to take some photos.' This from Lea who now had an enormous shoulder bag bulging with 'things' just in case.

'Are you taking the kitchen sink?' I enquired sweetly.

'Everything's necessary. Swimming costume. Change of sandals in case my feet hurt. Camera. Purse. Money, notebook and pen –'

'Yes! I get the picture.' I swept up my ever-ready bag and we went out to Alvaro's car. Hans had his car too so we went one in each. Alvaro, Lea and I with Hans. We felt pleased.

We went to Hans's contact on the outskirts of the village as he came first geographically. If you hadn't known the office was there you would never have found it. Small, dark, cool and very appealing on a hot day. The only thing of note was a tall palm tree in front of it. Hans did all the talking to the Spaniard, who smiled a lot at Lea. She in turn smiled back, not understanding a word but enraptured in the flow of the language.

It wasn't worth going to see Alvaro's friend. Paperwork was done quickly and we were shown to the car around the back of the office in a surprisingly big back yard full of stock. A four-door, medium-size car, bigger than we expected. It was perfect – large enough for Lea's oversized bags, plus guests should we have any. Lea liked the colour, a bronze, shimmery affair, similar to the one she'd rejected from the car salesman seemingly ages ago. Both were a bit flashy for me but as we had been given an upgrade for such a good price I wasn't going to say anything. Once we had taken the hire stickers off, we could even be taken for locals.

'Thank you, Hans. That was a very good deal. We'll drive you around somewhere so you can relax. And Alvaro, you too. Do say sorry to your contact.'

'No problema, Barbara.'

'Shall we go back to the hotel and get sorted out, Lea, or are you staying out now with your suitcase? You wanted to de-fuzz and stuff.'

'I'll de-fuzz.' Considered answer as she looked with revulsion to her legs and feet.

'Do you want to do anything, Barbara, or are you going with Lea?'

'Please call me Babs, Alvaro. Barbara is such a mouthful. I'm happy to see somewhere, if you don't mind. How about we call on Helen and you come too, Hans? I wouldn't mind going down the mine again and walking around. It's not far from Helen, is it? We can pick Lea up later – or better you take the car, Lea.'

'Yes, I'd better – in case I don't want to come later.'

'Hmm?'

'Well, if you want to pick me up, I'm committed but if I have the car I can please myself. I can text you, Babs.'

'Fine.'

'So ? What do you think, guys?'

'Let's get going. Are you OK with the car, Lea? Both of you? Shall we go over all the controls first?' Hans volunteered.

'Yes please. Seeing as it's the wrong way round, probably best.'

We took notice of all Hans showed us. Easy really. I'd done it before but Lea was not used to it so I felt a bit of trepidation on her behalf. She was a good driver, though, and the roads were quiet around this area. We left Lea getting used to the car and got ready to set off to Helen's. I was going with Alvaro and Hans in his car.

'I'll be fine.' She waved us off. Hans's friend came to join her and point things out all over again with some hesitant English. Everyone needed some English. I felt a little ashamed but it was good for business as Alvaro had pointed out. Besides Hans's friend was enjoying himself.

Helen was alone for once and very pleased to see us. Relieved even. She sped out from behind her desk and air-kissed us all.

'Oh, tell me everything. Are you OK? How's it going? What's happening next?'

'Well, um, the police were very good with us, probably because we knew you and Hans. I don't know if we will be questioned again – can't remember if they said, actually. Ah, I remember! El Capitan said we would be. Bit of a blur. Anyway, we've just hired a car, courtesy of a friend of Hans's, so we can get around under our own steam now. We're getting organized. We will have it all sussed by the time we leave. All the watering holes, anyway. Always the way.'

Hans and Alvaro had sat down in front of empty desks as the other staff were out doing viewings.

'What is 'sussed' – and 'watering holes'? Should I be another horse?' Hans piped up.

'Allow me.' Alvaro looked pleased with himself. ''Sussed' means 'found out' or 'just found', maybe. As in 'found' all the watering holes, bars or cafes to you, Hans.'

'So, I can be a horse again.' His infectious good humour made his eyes twinkle again.

We all smiled. We chatted on for quite a while but declined the offer of drinks, still overfull from breakfast.

'Can we go on to the mines now?' I asked. 'I want to get some photos with my phone. I have an idea for the place. As the mines are such a feature here, maybe they could become more of a tourist attraction? I know there are some mines already open to the public – as mines – but I wondered about getting some shops, bars, cafes down in the basin we were in. Mega bucks, I'm sure, but worth a thought.'

'Oh, big idea! Do you have big money and many years to spare? Some cleaning must be done before it is safe for lots of people to visit constantly. A lot has been done on the beaches but it has taken years.' Hans's local knowledge was useful.

'I know. Just dreaming, but I love a challenge and investigating things. Maybe after so many years the pollution is receding, simply through time. After all, the resort exists now. My uncle might want to send people to the resort on his coach tours I told you about. Well, I think I told you! So having as much for them to see as possible can only be good.'

'Then, vámanos!' He jumped up without questioning my statement. We said our goodbyes to Helen, hoping to see each other later in the hotel bar maybe along with the Double Barrellers.

The drive down to the open mine was still spectacular the second time around. I texted Lea before she texted me, to join us if she was 'all done'. She was and would set off immediately.

We got out of the cars into a very hot environment. Not a breath of air. It was sheltered by the surrounding high walls of the mine that had been dug out over years. It was probably 30 to 40 meters deep.

The heat could be a problem, I speculated, for any businesses. Problems are there to be solved. I would have trouble persuading Uncle C to invest money into such a big project. A project I would like to be mine – no pun intended. Would it be allowed? I speculated that local authorities would jump at the chance for investment and a clean-up plan. This would also give me the chance to see where maybe the bribery and corruption came in.

We were walking around, having parked more or less in the middle but to one side, where you could see partially into some of the dark tunnels. I wandered into the entrance to one. It went into oblivion and blackness.

It was cooler inside. The guys joined me and we wandered further in. As our eyes got used to the dark it was not so bad. I was taking photos all round. Such amazing colours! My imagination ran riot. What a wonderful restaurant this would make, with lots of bars in other tunnels. Crazy ideas. I was fired up. Then disappointed with myself for being so stupid. Millionaires lived in this area and had not done anything about such a project so there must be a reason.

We didn't hear Lea approach. We all jumped in unison. 'Who's your friend out there? Glared at me from another tunnel and disappeared in an instant. Don't think he thought he had been seen but my peripheral vision is exceptional – though I say it myself.' She smiled at us all blinking a little, questioning.

'We didn't see anyone. No idea. Why would anyone be down here? I know we are, but that's different.'

We all nodded. We went further into the tunnel and then turned back to the cars. What we found was not good. In fact, the more we all thought it was potentially seriously worrying.

Two of the cars had flat tyres and scrapes along the sides. Fortunately not the hire car.

'Well, we know we didn't scrape anything or run over a rock coming down here so it must be deliberate. That person you saw, Lea -' I ground to a halt. 'If someone wants to put us off coming down here, it'll have the opposite effect!' My stubborn streak was showing.

'I have my thinking – doubts about this place. I don't know what – but I think there are bad things here. I mean it. Only rumours but ...' Hans tailed off. 'Anyway, we must exchange the tyres and – vámanos – I think. It is not nice work in this heat. Babs and Lea, you can go in your car. Alvaro and I will sort this.'

'Oh no! I got you down here and I want to see we all get out OK together. I have water in a cool bag. I always carry it. Sun lotion as well - anyone? Factor 50. Even men should use it.' I waved it around. Surprisingly they did, and had some water before setting forth to tackle the tyres.

Lea and I waited in the relative cool of the tunnel.

'It's so wide you could get a car in here. Maybe even a truck,' I commented.

Finally, the repairs were done and we set off to a bar for a long, cold, much-deserved drink. Cold beers all round except for Lea who wanted an iced coffee. The café con leche was fine but with ice – con hielo – caused some explaining. A bigger cup, mug, receptacle to take the ice and cold milk, not hot. Lea did most of the explaining with Spanglish and demonstrations. She even went behind the bar area pointing. She got what she wanted, making quite an impression in the process.

'Apart from freshly squeezed lemonade or orange or white wine and soda – or very cold sparkling wine – or tea, hot or cold, iced water – this is my favourite thirst-quenching drink. Bit like you, Babs, when you have a hangover – you ask for a hair of the dog and a cup of tea in case you can't make your mind up.' She saw Hans starting to ask about 'hair of the dog.'

'In answer to the question that you haven't asked yet – a hair of the dog is having a drink of something alcoholic from the night before to even up what's in your body the following day. Drinking doesn't give you a hangover, it's stopping that does. Withdrawal symptoms.'

Amen to that.

So far, a near drowning, a murder and slashed tyres had invaded our few days at Club La Roca. What would happen next. I shuddered to think. Was I really up for this I reflected. Or Lea? □

CHAPTER FIVE
The Finca

We were sat in a café bar which was more modern than the Bodega Bar of the previous night.

The tables, which were spread over the pavement, had a windbreak affair surrounding them and umbrellas against the sun as there was no other shade. We all plumped for copious amounts of freshly-squeezed orange. It was quiet as time had flown and it was now Spanish lunch time with everyone in restaurants, so we were a little surprised when the waiter didn't seem pleased to see us. Having our custom was apparently a great inconvenience to him.

'I think he's had a whole bottle of vinegar to drink,' observed Lea.

We mulled over the tyre event. Nefarious activities! But how serious were they really? Hans was worried for us all. It certainly had not been an accident. This was even more worrying and I had no intention of leaving it alone.

As Lea had said earlier, 'shades of the Hyena' – a most unpleasant encounter with a murderous maniac on our first adventure. Either this was perhaps a harbinger of death or her imagination was working overtime – or was it? I kept this thought to myself, although I could tell Lea, quiet for once, was possibly thinking something similar. We would have to talk later.

Voices from the past echoed in my brain – evil intent towards anyone that interfered with illegal trade, and 'anyone' had included Lea and me. I didn't know how much I should involve her or how much she wanted to be involved. Also, I must tell Uncle Charles. I felt we had good friends in Alvaro and Hans, and I would tell them of anything I planned, without actually involving them. Just so we could be traced if necessary.

Traced if necessary! What was I thinking. I frightened myself. A cold shudder went down my spine.

Hans suddenly piped up, 'I think you guapas are playing it close to your breasts. You are quiet. To cheer you up, how would you all like to come to my finca and I will make pork chop, sausages and puree. I have enough. It would be my pleasure.'

I looked at Lea for consent. She was beaming so I gathered it was indeed fine.

'Yes please. Lea's starving. And by the way, it's 'playing it close to your chest'.'

'Yes, this is what I said.'

I gave up.

Lea brightened. 'I'm very hungry. It's been a long time since breakfast. Oh, look at that couple coming in. Fugly. I am sure they are wonderful people so it is irrelevant that she looks like the back end of a cow. Takes all sorts to attract. The waiter won't be pleased – and they're like a couple of boxing hares.'

'Miaow, big time! What do you mean the waiter won't be pleased that she looks like a cow and they are boxing like hares? Not descriptions I would attribute to a couple normally.'

I vaguely wondered if she was jealous of people who had steady relationships. Hers always seemed fraught with danger, and expired as quickly as they started. At least she was never bored.

'They're interested in each other but sparring and she's making sure he keeps in his place. That's what hares do when they are going to mate – the female boxes with him until she is ready. And I meant the waiter won't want the trade.'

I rolled my eyes. 'Vamos!'

'Let's go.' Lea echoed. 'See, I'm learning. I learned quite a bit from Hans while he helped me take the hire stickers off the car.'

'I'm sure you did,' I muttered.

'What?'

'I'm sure we should get going. Time's getting on and we've people to meet in the hotel bar tonight. I hope you'll both come?' I threw a glance over to Hans and Alvaro.

'We wouldn't miss it. Would we, Alvaro!' said Hans.

'Certainly not.' They winked conspiratorially and seemed comfortable in each other's company. Not best buddies but cruising along very nicely. We all were.

Hans led the way to his finca. It was a large plot of land on the outskirts of Las Aqueas with a boring, square, single-storey building in the middle, all grey concrete. It was behind enormous gates that had a befittingly big padlock which he had to get out of his car to open while we waited in the pull-in before the gates just off the main road. We drove in after him and parked where there was room for about ten cars and trucks.

The showroom had floor-to-ceiling windows going across the whole of the front, which displayed several types of whirlpools, jacuzzis, and fires (for winter) a little further back in the room. Some tall, impressive figurines stood around, almost full height. Hans assured us they graced many a pool he had installed. Out of nowhere came two dogs as soon as he had opened the front glass doors. Going to a fridge through a side door, he fetched food bowls to put down for them. 'Semi-campo' dogs.

'Meet Bessie and Guapa. Guapa is called Guapa because she is ugly. Muy feo.' But the dog wasn't ugly and Hans was smiling indulgently. She was a scruffy, mid-brown mutt with character. Bessie was a short-haired German Shepherd cross. Nothing to do with Hans being German, he assured us.

'Fugly she is not.' Lea piped up. Why, I asked myself, did she have to say all these things that needed explanation!

' 'Fugly'? I don't know this one.' Alvaro was curious.

'Oh dear. You explain, Babs.'

'No! You said it. You explain. Teach you a lesson.'

She visibly squirmed. 'Phew – er – well ....Alvaro, if someone says in English 'it's an effing shame' do you know what the 'effing' is short for?'

He considered this and then, luckily for Lea, the penny, peseta or euro dropped.

'Ah, it's short for 'fuc - '

'You got it. Fugly. Explain to Hans now. Por favor.'

Hans got it, and was delighted to add it to his English repertoire. I wondered how often he would engineer using it as he obviously really liked the word and kept rolling it round, repeating it with glee. Lea got people unwittingly into bad habits.

Bessie and Guapa swooped down on the two full bowls. A horrible smell started to envelope us.

'Is there a mine round here emitting some gas? Or is it the food? Smells like something crawled up Bessie's or Guapa's bum and died.' Lea was graphic. I was glad it wasn't time for us to eat.

We were ignored until they had eaten, then got the full, once-over, being sniffed nearly from head to foot. Hans had shown us to a table and chairs right at the back of the showroom which was full of paperwork so we settled there and waited to be accepted by the dogs. Eventually they wagged, graciously accepted being stroked, and left through the open gates.

Hans went to close the gates. I must have looked concerned because an explanation followed:

'The dogs will stay now out till I leave again and then come in for the night. In the day they go in the campo - the countryside around. Chase a rabbit maybe. Then they come back and sleep under the palm trees. They have small houses if they need them but in summer it's too hot.'

'Can I take them to the Harbour Restaurant near La Roca to meet Karim's dog? He goes there.' Lea was enthusiastic. 'I'm sure the German Shepherds would get along.'

Oh brother! Talk about making work for yourself, I thought.

'If you are wanting to, but they are not so used to a car. I know they will like the other dog as they are brother and sister. I think we should come with us for this going out.'

Lea was happy.

I changed the subject: 'What do people do when your gates are shut? I know you have Spanish hours but you've been out strange hours lately.'

'People know that when my gates are closed I am out working and to come back later or phone me. I was out on an appointment before I came to you so I locked up for the day. I'll re-open tomorrow as I see you all in the bar tonight.'

'Quite right too. Murder doesn't happen to us every day,' Lea chipped in, 'or having car tyres slashed by phantoms.'

'I will go and prepare the food. Would you like a drink?' He laughed. 'I have only water. Or coffee – but no cold milk with ice.'

'My favourite drink.' Lea stood up. 'Besides my head felt so fuzzy earlier. No idea why. Can I help? Anyone for water?'

We all nodded.

As she went to follow Hans, I had a great view of her back and surprisingly long – for her – shorts. They bordered on smart, elegant casual. Her newly de-fuzzed legs shone with her aftercare cream.

'Can we all come and have a look at the kitchen?' I enquired and didn't wait for an answer. Alvaro followed me.

Hans's personal space was basic. A small kitchen with a two-ring electric cooker and no oven. Open shelves with many tins and packets. Fresh food he bought every day. There was a fridge which, when opened, revealed many bottles of water and various salad items. Lea took out a large bottle of water and poured us all a glass. Wine was also bought daily, we were informed.

'Where are your servicios, Hans? All that orange juice followed by water and iced coffee makes a girl want to make room for more!'

'Ah, Lea, I think you mean you want the throne room? Right?'

'Yes please. The loo.'

'So many ways to say the same thing. Is this another special English thing?'

'I don't think so,' I piped up. 'Trying to learn Spanish, I've come across similar ways to say the same basic thing.'

'You have un exiample, um, example please?' Hans's smile was mischievous. A challenge had been thrown down.

'I'll think about it and let you know. In the meantime I need the toilet, bathroom, washroom, to spend a penny, have a pee, a wee …'

'This way girls – guapas.' We followed Hans out of his kitchen, down a corridor with three large storerooms on one side containing all manner of equipment, in and out of packaging, leaning against walls, stacked up, thrown in corners. Jacuzzis, whirlpools, posh power showers, small plunge pools – the big ones were in situ in the finca grounds – woodburners and pellet fires for the winter along with their fuel. The walls were rough concrete blocks. On the opposite side were Hans's own quarters.

The walls had been plastered and floors tiled to give some measure of comfort. Some rugs were scattered around, relieving only a little the Spartan atmosphere. In the bedroom the bed was large. It dominated, looming over two small chests of drawers and a pole stretching the whole length of one wall secured at either end in rings fixed into the walls. It was full of smart shirts, trousers, jackets. Shoes lay in neat rows underneath, raised just off the floor on what seemed to be a series of pallets.

It occurred to me the pallets were a good idea. On my first trip to Spain I had pushed a foot into a proper walking shoe to feel a crunch. A quick retreat revealed a squashed cockroach. I won't tell you what I said. I had felt obliged to wash and re-wash both my foot and shoe, the horror ensuring I never did it again and Lea had learnt an early lesson over the lizard in her clothes.

The bathroom came as a massive surprise. It was fully tiled, finished to a high standard with power shower, a handbasin and a jacuzzi big enough for a family or even a whole party, all surrounded with matching units. The toilet could well be described as a 'throne' and there was a bidet as well. Floor-to-ceiling cupboards in a pearl-ish creamy colour were stacked with linen, and bulging towels bulged out of slightly open doors. Heated towel rail and panel heaters for winter promised long happy sessions in here. We were impressed. This luxury certainly eluded the rest of the interior.

'Think I'll move in. It's magnificent,' said Lea appreciatively. 'I'm going first. I thought of it first. Have you noticed how some people say 'bath' – bAth, barth, bath?' she declaimed, with a different pronunciation for each version.

'Hmmm.' I continued to have a nosy around while trying not to move too much. I didn't want to be caught actually snooping. Hans had left us to it. My turn came for a taste of luxury.

When I got back to the kitchen, Lea was grilling Hans.

'Why is the bathroom so luxurious but the rest is – well – not finished? The basic bricks and mortar are sound. Have you ever noticed how some people say 'mor –a', instead?'

'Lea! Honestly! 'Mor – a'! It's an accent. 'Sarf' London as it happens. How is Hans to understand all this?' I gave a verbal dig. 'You'll be telling us all about your dowsing rod next.'

'Well, I am into physical energy.'

I know you are, I thought almost snickering as I remembered certain men of hers.

'Hm?' Confused look with raised eyebrows. 'I must ask another time, guapas. I haven't had time to do more yet. The bathroom was una ganga – a bargain – I found. Working on my own many of the times es no rapido. Es lento, slow. I don't have much time for me but I do like comfort in the 'throne room'. I have help but when I move here it was mas grande, bigger building with muchos costs so I had to fire – you say fire - my assistant to go. Big shame for me – and him. The English and German, my most clients, want immediate quick work but it is slow when me is on my own. So I have a difficult situation.'

We all stayed in what can only be described as a rustic kitchen, watching Hans. He was well practised at using his limited equipment. He produced smart matching knives, forks, spoons and table mats, instructing us to clear the desk in the showroom and set it up. Paperwork was to go on a nearby shelf. We organized the chairs and waited, chatting. A large salad appeared with oil and vinegar for dressing. Next the chops, puree and, magically, peas. All done on only two rings.

'You've worked miracles, Hans.' We all nodded in agreement. The food looked good and was well presented. Hans was a no slouch when it came to cooking.

'Hans, you are the eponymous owner of a fab restaurant. Hans's Bistro.'

What's got into Lea, I wondered.

'Please start.' He sat down with us, either ignoring the comment or not wanting to hear it.

We all tucked in. We had two chops each. Conversation lapsed for a while until a big hole had been made in the food. So simple, so unexpectedly delicious.

'I'll come to your restaurant anytime, Hans.' Lea was beaming. She was in food heaven, crunching on al dente vegetables. 'You can hear it tastes good. Where did the vegetables come from?'

'The top shelf in my kitchen. I'm sorry I haven't postres. I only bother with dessert if I am having menú del dia.'

'I meant which shop? Or did you grow them here on the finca?'

'Oh, I buy in the big super.'

We assumed 'supermarket'.

'Well, how very pragmatic! That's your philosophy, is it? Existing, feeling, acting upon circumstances? Hey ho – why grow your own food if you don't need to?'

I blinked at this interpretation but was not moved to comment, elaborate or question. Hans only smiled. The food had put us all in a soporific mood. I was all soporiffed out.

Lea leaned back, putting her chair on its back legs, stretched, yawned widely and we watched lazily as a huge fly went straight into her mouth. Instant coughing and spluttering, followed by an undignified rush to the bathroom, all in contrast to her previous superior attitude. We all smiled, smirked and burst out laughing.

'I'm too full anyway. This was wonderful, Hans. Now I need a long siesta.' Alvaro chipped in after a lengthy silence as we waited for Lea to return, which she did, somewhat subdued.

'We all second that. After all the drama yesterday and today and all this food I need to sleep by the pool. What about you, Babs?' She was grimacing obviously still revolted by the fly.

Then another look appeared on her face and I wondered what was coming so I jumped in: 'Oh yes. I agree to that. Room or pool – whatever. Now – we'll wash up Hans. Least we can do.'

'Then let's sort out meeting up tonight. We have the Double Barrellers to meet as well.'

I gathered all the plates together and took them back to the kitchen area, putting everything on the only bit of free space. Pots and pans were all around. Lea and Alvaro followed with the water and glasses. Hans brought up the rear.

'Please leave it all. I have to boil water for washing up. Only the bathroom is connected to hot water. I will boil some pans.'

'What's wrong with a kettle?'

'Kettle?'

'Hmm, yes. Kettle. You know?' I began to realize he didn't understand kettle. 'Specially for boiling water. Nothing else. Very fast.'

'Oh, but I can use a pan for many things.'

'But a kettle means you don't need to wash your pan just to boil water. I will – we will – buy you one. Won't we Lea? For all the help you have given us and this wonderful meal.'

'I happened to be there. Nothing special and the food I am happy to give.'

'Well, we'll see. We will certainly treat you to lunch one day. Or maybe dinner at Prem's. Yes, how about that? I'll ask

Helen. And Alvaro, you've been so helpful. You must come too. Do you only have tonight free?'

'Tomorrow I work through the day but have the evening off. It changes from evening to day work so we all have a chance to work reasonable hours.'

'Let's make it tomorrow then? You OK with that, Hans? I know you have your main meal in the afternoon but perhaps you can eat less or have Indian tapas – if Prem does them?'

'Fine. I will see us there because I don't close the showroom till 8pm. There is a nice area outside at Prem's where you can wait with a drink. She doesn't take bookings. It's a good idea from her – of her – so when people wait they spend more money drinking. Very clever. You will like her and please to mention me, then you will get good attention.' His whole face lit up with pleasure.

'I will lock you out now for my siesta.' He went on. 'My bat nap. If you come down to the village later, you will find me somewhere near my van or car. It is how to find me always but if you want to be quiet this afternoon – your English evening – we'll see us tomorrow.'

'Indeed we will 'see us tomorrow'. I must tell you it is a cat nap. Not bat nap – unless you want to hang from those beams in your showroom. You know 'bat' – the small furry animal often associated with Dracula?'

'Oh yes. I understand now. Dracula. I will remember.'

He did a little bow and walked us to our cars, smiling all the time, while we discussed with Alvaro what to do next, then he closed the huge gate after us, waving madly. Lea was driving so I turned round and waved back. Hans had a very fond look on his face as though he had found long lost relatives – or new, dear friends. I looked sideways at Lea, wondering where her liking for mature men would go: Uncle C and now Hans!

We had all decided to go our separate ways, with loose promises of meeting up in the hotel bar as we had the Double Barrellers to meet – sort of. If no one was around about 8 to 9 pm we would go our own ways. The five of us – Hans,

Alvaro, Helen, Lea and I – all had each other's mobile numbers if all else failed.

Alvaro went to siesta too and that was what I was going to do but for some reason Lea followed through with the funny look she had had on her face a few minutes ago. She decided she wanted to go back to the quarry.

Bother. Big time. I felt uneasy with that.

'Why on earth … ?'

She cut in immediately. 'Because I have a feeling something bad is going on there and my curiosity is peaked. No not curiosity – serious concern. My mother was a psychic and I get 'feelings' too.'

Silence. I didn't comment.

'Go on – laugh if you want to.'

I was compelled to answer. 'I'm not laughing. If you feel that strongly we'll go. Besides, if I didn't come, I know you would only go on your own and that really would worry me. So vámanos.'

I smiled graciously and, I hoped, with friendly resignation. Although the beach was calling me strongly, I felt obliged to go with her, albeit begrudgingly.

We were finding our way around well and came to the mine without a wrong turn but with a small side trip through the gypsy area. It was very run down. Basic, small, square, white block houses were all in a row along the road. Chickens, dogs and dirty children in colourful but raggedy clothes ran all over. They stopped and stared at us while we drove slowly through, avoiding accidents. We didn't want any excuse to have to stop. The road was dry and dusty, with potholes clearly not anyone's priority to mend. The clean and sparkling car got covered in the dust.

About a mile and a half further on, the road improved and so did the housing. Not wonderful, as we had been told by Helen, but not at all bad. The houses had gardens with high walls, some with barbed wire fencing on the top or broken bottles cemented in. Gates were quite elaborate affairs of wrought iron with scrolling and swirling so no one could ease through a gap, and with huge padlocks and intercoms. What you could see behind the gates suggested this area had been quite upmarket in its day.

'They have some communal gardens too.' Lea observed. 'Have you ever noticed how some people say commun -u - al? They stick another 'u' in the word.'

'I will give it some consideration.' And immediately forgot it.

The mine was as deserted as it usually seemed but the drive down into it began to fill me with trepidation. We had not told anyone of our change of plans and now they would be having a siesta. Suddenly I thought I would phone Uncle Charles, bring him up to date and give him our new friends' phone numbers for emergencies, without worrying him.

'Lea, I think it's wise to let someone know where we're going so, rather than disturb Hans or Alvaro, I'm going to phone Uncle. Shall we go into the entrance to one of the tunnels to keep cool? This is a new one where we've parked. Even bigger than the first one. Amazing size.'

We got out and I dialled. Surprisingly the signal was good and Uncle answered immediately.

I took a deep breath and plunged in. I kept my voice light. 'Hello, Uncle! You have a fabulous resort. We are impressed – Lea especially – with the food. '

'Barbara, good to hear from you. Glad you like everything. Say hello to Lea for me. Any thoughts ¬ or is too early to form any opinions on anything?'

'Well, we think the food is wonderful as I said but I honestly think there is too much and a lot is wasted – or it goes to the staff – which isn't a waste but usually the staff menu is more limited. I mean cheaper to produce.'

'Ah – that. You know me. I do like happy staff. It engenders loyalty and continuity which is lacking in most hotel type work. That's why catering staff move around so much. They just use the system. A broken system if it ever worked. Anyway, that's my philosophy – so I gave the chef permission to feed the staff well and in fact they can have whatever is left over. I had long talks with all the heads of department and some of the staff when I was there signing the deal.'

'Did you meet the under-manager?'

'Yes, that's why I am concerned about him just disappearing. The manager let me know but didn't want to bother me and then I got this anonymous letter about it. Time to take notice. Any leads?'

'Not specifically. But we have made contacts and got some ideas with – um - feelings. Intuition, I suppose you could say. Persistent feelings. Hard to explain. One to watch is Karim Badour, the new under-manager. He has an unfortunate attitude, over friendly going towards slimy. Doesn't make him a criminal of course. It's just one of those feelings. However, he's Moroccan and there's a Moroccan gypsy enclave that it's thought he may have come from. Local poor boy made good. Anyway, I have to tell you about an unrelated incident. Nothing to do with us but we just happened to find the body.'

'Body – oh don't tell me you're in danger already!' Instant concern bordering on panic.

'Now what did I just say? No danger. A gay man we saw in the hotel bar on the first night got murdered and Lea happened to be the one to find the body. Some friends we have made were there too and helped with the police and stuff. Probably a jealous lover type thing – so no panicking.'

He didn't answer.

'OK?' I said again.

'All right. I trust you on this.'

'What does concern me – us – a bit, is the huge opencast mine. But it has lots of tunnels off it. Did you ever see it?'

'No. I heard about it but didn't have the time.'

'Well, another feeling. All four of us came down here – '

'Who's four, and do you mean you're there now?' Uncle was sharp on the uptake.

'Hans a local, but German, Alvaro who works in the resort and is a diamond. Lea and me. We've become like old friends in just two days. You know how curious Lea is? So we all came to have a look and it really is magnificent in a strange way. That brings me to another subject. Oh - but more of that later. While we were in a tunnel someone slashed a couple of tyres on two of the cars and scraped down the sides. Luckily not our hire car. Hans got us a great deal on that by the way. On another occasion we also thought, or Lea did, that someone was down here We were peering over the edge at the time. I mean this place is deserted.'

'So are you there now? If so, why? Sounds as if there could be trouble with a capital T.'

'Yes, but we won't stay long and I am about to give you Hans and Alvaro's numbers for the future. They are the good guys. Believe me. I would have told them we were coming here now but it is siesta time and I didn't want to disturb them – specially on Alvaro's day off. Plus I had to phone you anyway.'

'Right – I've got a pen. Fire away.'

I gave him the contact numbers and told him it was for emergencies only. Hans and Alvaro didn't know about my full relationship with Uncle and his company. I would keep it that way unless there was a reason to change it.

'What is this other thing you mentioned for later? Do I need to worry about that too?'

'Oh no. Not unless you think I'm mad. These tunnels - well, they would make stupendous bars and café and restaurants and shops and – ' I had got carried away.

'Whoa!!! I think I'll worry. The question is, why aren't they already up and running in such a well-developed area?' Uncle sighed. 'Tell you what, I'll do some asking and research. It is always nice to be first with something innovative. I'm not promising anything and I do know that a lot of money was spent cleaning the whole place up a few years ago.'

We chatted a bit more and rang off.

I turned to speak to Lea but she wasn't there. Immediate shock. My stomach did flips. She was nowhere in sight – or sound. Total silence.

I shouted and shouted and started to panic, going further into the tunnel.

Suddenly she appeared from around a corner.

'Oh, my goodness, don't ever do that to me again! My heart's going nineteen to the dozen.' I was all but shaking, and I actually had to steady my hands. A few minutes had seemed like hours.

'So! I didn't mean to be so long and I thought you would be ages talking to Charles. Uncle Charles. I can't call him 'Uncle' to his face can I so I'm going to call him 'Charles' from now on.' She was lightening the mood but acknowledged that I was genuinely upset. 'Really, I'm sorry.' She looked at the floor, suitably downcast.

'Oh – whatever. I'm so pleased to see you. Did you find anything interesting – or anything at all for that matter?' I was recovering fast and didn't want to make her suffer any more.

'As a matter of fact, yes. It doesn't get darker as you get further in and there is a strange sort of humming. Far away but definitely there. Thought I ought to give up for now and maybe we can come back in force if the guys are up for it. What do you think?'

'Very sensible. We can leave someone to watch the vehicles too. In the meantime the pool beckons. Let's go. No argument.'

'You're not getting one. Vamos!'

On our way back we saw some hot air balloons floating majestically overhead. Various patterns and colours. The baskets seemed to hold about ten people, maybe more. Hard to tell from the ground, but they were large.

'I want to have a go in one. Always have. Can we, Babs? Let's find out where you get them from. We could order a big one and we could all go together – pay extra if we have to.'

'Why would we have to? Really – you're the kind of person who would offer £170,000 for a house that was for sale for £150,000 either just to secure it or because you felt sorry for the sellers. Anyway, I'd love to. We'll ask in reception. Sun sand and sea first, though.'

Lea had her book with her and she was muttering 'Book, booke, buck, beewck – argh! You can say the same words in so many weird ways. I can hear your eyes glazing over, Babs, so stop it. I don't need to look before you comment on my comment.'

We finally settled under some waving palms on the beach as the pool was crowded. Lunch took effect and we dozed blissfully drifting in the warmth with a cooling breeze wafting over us. Heaven. Sheer heaven. ☐

CHAPTER SIX
Evening Fun and Discoveries

Oh, to be young and carefree. It was glorious being a tourist!

We came back from serious relaxation on the beach. We had scanned the long curve of the golden sands, people-watching like a U boat looking for victims. The only things missing were binoculars.

We deserved to relax. The thought of the evening ahead was pleasant and we were dressing for the occasion. Girly discussions on outfits ensued amid a feeling of some trepidation. Our first adventure had been a learning curve of how people can be deceitful and downright dangerous. I shuddered at the memories of me in a dark room with a murderous maniac. Someone I had trusted – a chilling revelation I must keep in mind. I had been able to feel his breath on me, he had been so close.

Once again, I asked myself if I could face this – again? And could I ask Lea to share this again? I certainly didn't want to face things alone. Already we had encountered unpleasant incidents albeit that the murder had nothing to do with the resort and therefore us. I shook myself out of my reverie and got back to the banter.

'I want to see what you brought.' I was firm.

'No problem. Look in my suitcase – and the wardrobe. Then I'll look in yours.'

Our cases still had clothes in that we hadn't hung up in spite of an unpacking session. How much did we bring? Too much. But then – when you have clothes, you just much show them off, and you need the bling to go with them. The bling weighed more than anything else and we had only narrowly escaped paying excess baggage.

'I love this little number, Babs. Sleek. You do go for black a bit too much but this has colour that lifts it – and such style. You always wear such sophisticated clothes and you always look a million dollars.' Big sigh from her. 'I'm always in cheap stuff.'

'But what you wear looks fabulous. No one would know it's cheap because you're so fashionable. And you don't get things from the high street. Getting clothes from markets and those posh second-hand shops and – oh what do you call them –dress agencies, means you have individual creative fashion. Award-winning. Ugh, I sound like an advert, don't I? I mean I don't have the patience to look but I would like to come on one of your shopping sprees one day. I mean that. I could learn a lot.'

'Oh!' She was contemplative. 'You would be very welcome. We'll make a day of it.'

'Well – I go to small individual shops. On the back streets. They've got fashions you won't find anywhere else. So we've really got a lot in common, just in a different way. We get similar results by different methods. Let's just swap methods for a change.'

Our mutual admiration session came to an end.

'Time to get ready, shower and straight to reception to ask about the hot air balloons,' mused Lea, still very taken with the idea.

'I'm still a bit groggy so don't rush me.'

'Do you know where that saying came from?'

'No. But I'm sure you are going to tell me whether I want to know or not!'

'There are variations of how the phrase came about. It's from the time when the Navy issued alcohol – to keep the crew happy or if not, at least it was a reward. Basically, as a drink it's rum, one bitter, one sweet, two strong, one weak – not sure of what, mind you – but also in the West Indies in the 1800s the British Vice Admiral Edward Vernon wore a coat of grogran cloth and got the nickname Old Grog.'

'Well, I'm glad we cleared that up. Even if you're not anywhere near one hundred percent correct about any of it, that's as much as I want to know. Anyway, I'm ready now.'

There were tourist leaflets by the bucket load, in a big display unit in the reception area. We took a ballooning one to read at the pool bar because we saw the Prescott-Willoughby's and Louisa Spelier-Bielby there. They were with some other people so we sat nearby, not wanting to interfere. As was our habit, we people-watched for a while without the intensity of the U boat. Lea was keenly observing a good-looking man – or specimen as she called them – walking round the pool.

'You're staring. It's rude.'

'Not as rude as what he's wearing. Or not wearing. Comfortable roomy trousers, that is. There's no need to guess which side he dresses on with that bulge.' She sniffed indignantly. Not sure why, as she was no prude with her tight, short shorts. Which were a bit too tight at the front lower down - if you get my drift. Ahem. I considered mentioning that – for her own good. But maybe not right now. I chickened out.

'Oh please – we have to eat yet.' I got back to eavesdropping on the DBs.

Oddly enough, or luckily enough, they were talking about a balloon trip one of them had taken, so listening in was useful.

Apparently, the start was from a very large flat area to accommodate all the vehicles involved in the whole exercise. Vehicles taking the balloon or balloons, and all their paraphernalia to inflate, baskets for the customers to stand in, some larger than others depending on how many groups were going, ropes, weights, back-up vehicles to follow the balloon to pick everyone up from where it landed (it was not an exact science apparently) and, last but not least, to collect people from hotels in the first place and return them.

Louisa suddenly saw us and waved an elegant hand. Just then an aloof, sleek cat strolled into view. She spotted it and put her hand down to stroke it. It came over to her, arching its back, and responded by gliding under her hand, beginning to purr. I thought they made a good pair.

So did Lea who squealed, 'Ooh, I could paint that – or sketch it.' She got up and shot over to Louisa and the cat, fumbling in her cavernous bag as she went.

'Hello!' Louisa greeted her. 'Lovely to see you both. Come join us.' She began pulling a couple of chairs over from the next table. People shuffled around making space. Lea gave a hand, smiling engagingly, all the while assessing the rest of the party. She settled next to Louisa while I made my way round the table and chairs to sit, feeling a little overwhelmed for some strange reason. Perhaps the party being so large unsettled me.

Not so Lea. She already had her sketching pad out. Headfirst into everything! Occasionally with some regret, but not often. The memory of our departure from the UK on our first adventure flitted through my mind. She had arrived late at the small airport accompanied (or should I say besieged) by two men who were clearly besotted. As we flew out from the small airport we could see them waving madly. She had sighed and told me she was 'only being kind talking to them – they had mistaken it for flirting.'

The cat was now focused on both Lea and Louisa. The purring sounded like an approaching train.

'Would it be convenient to draw you, Louisa, while the cat's here? You make such a lovely pair. So suited.' She glanced around at everyone else. 'I'm Lea by the way. Pronounced 'Le-ah' with an 'h'.' She practically blew them away, forcibly emphasising the 'h'. A hurricane would have caused less impact. 'Babs and I found the body, you know.'

Everyone nodded, knowingly and sympathetically. No one asked questions. I assumed this was out of polite restraint. Difficult subject.

Louisa started to make introductions. Everyone knew who we were. I couldn't decide if this was good or not, but I soon became caught up in the names, which started to flow from left to right. Louisa was waving her hand from one person or couple to another. The cat remained transfixed on Lea but decided a stable lap was better than a moving pair of legs (Lea was half standing, shaking hands where she could reach, or acknowledging where she couldn't) so it jumped onto Louisa's lap. She accepted it willingly.

'Esme Arundel-Crackenthorpe-Gore, first time with us since her husband passed away last year. Susanna Campbell-Casson-Parker, also on her own aren't, you dear but not for long, I'm sure! Mr and Mrs Todd-Bailey-Pullen, our happy couple. Mr George Farnworth–Seager, an old hand now, helping to make travel arrangements for us all. Air Commodore Francis Culmé-Seymour, retired – though you wish you weren't, we all know this! His good friend and companion, Augusta Harrington–Smythe, and in turn, her good friend and travel companion – the latter have been all over the world between them you know – Theophila Frances Brown-Lowe.' Louisa paused, briefly.

'Then we have our engaged couple so we wait with bated breath to see how the names work out, Sebastian Halton-Bamforth-Scott with his lovely Juliana Haymer-Howarth. Neither wants to give up their full name. Goodness knows how they'll resolve that! Not present are Clive Stanford-Barclay, a tad curmudgeonly but only a tad, and his lovely wife, Fiona, who won't come out of the room until she's immaculate. I don't say that maliciously, purely factually. And last but not least, Rosalind and Alexander Gore–Marsden, who are always late for no reason. All part of the fun and we get on famously don't we everyone? Well, nearly all! And so long as it's only once or twice a year. We don't expect you to remember all these names, of course.'

Everyone nodded amiably.

I was so entranced by all the names and mini-information packs that my eyes sparkled in amazement. Lea's positively danced. 'I'm astounded and – well – fascinated by all the names. It must be a riot checking into places if you all arrive together.'

'We try to. Mayhem is fun!' Louisa winked at me.

'I do like a good sense of humour. Now, before the cat gets bored, can I get my sketch done? Free of course. It's what I enjoy. '

'Of course. How do you want me?'

'Just as you are. Waist up.' Lea began to sketch, concentrating in a relaxed way, totally absorbed in her subject. 'We heard you all talking about a balloon flight. Was it good? Was it worth the money?'

A waiter came over to take drink orders. A bit too leisurely for my liking but I saw the pool bar was busy so gave him the benefit of the doubt, deciding to say nothing in my notes for Uncle. There was no point making minor waves. I thought I would blame the magpie I saw earlier, then wondered if they had magpies in Spain. I quickly googled it to make sure I could blame it. I found Spain does have them and they are called Iberian magpies. I didn't want Lea – with an 'h' – to look it up to tell me all about it at length if I mentioned I wanted to know. I was thankful there were no crows in sight as I would have mentioned they were called 'a murder of crows' and with murder already seeping into our lives it could have caused a meltdown in communications.

'Two spritzers please. Plenty of ice.' I ordered for Lea who didn't like to drink too much too early in the day. Later was another matter.

'Fabulous.' As far as I could remember, this came from Esme. 'We all went in two balloons. Plenty of room. Champagne to start with and some snacks. What you get depends on the time of day. Not too much alcohol as you can't have people being silly all that way up. The same company also has a leisure boat or two. I saw them in the sports harbour. One was called Teabag! I asked why and was told it was because it was full of holes. I assume they were joking. It was that reception manager from here, on the boat. Think he's Moroccan.'

My eyes widened in surprise. 'Is he part of the company?'

'I believe so. He was chatty – if you can get past the smarmy side to him. Helps run it anyway. Don't think he owns it but I don't really know.'

Mental note to investigate further. How would he have time to do this extracurricular work? If he had stakes in the company, how did he afford it? Just who was in charge? Another Double Barreller piped up. It was Air Commodore Francis Culmé-Seymour.

'It was good value. Spectacular views. Bit surprising to land near that big hole in the ground though. The old mine. There was a balloon that actually landed in it. We didn't know the people. Another party. The company is very busy. I have seen lots of balloons going up. Anyway, I suppose you can't choose where you land – or not so much. I'd go again. As a friend of mine would say, ''Twas banging, mate'.'

I raised my eyebrows. That was not a phrase I would have associated with this bunch – even through someone else. First and last night of the Proms more like. Typical Brit stuff. Bit of Wagner, but I thought that was maybe too heavy for them. More of the Offenbach or Strauss with the drinking song, and bobbing up and down to the hornpipe music after they'd sat through all the obligatory concerts to get tickets for the last night. I had tried to get last-night tickets once but hadn't had the patience for what went before. I was more rock n' roll with light classic mixed in and around.

Francis must have seen my expression as he smiled and added, 'I have all sorts of friends, Barbara. A sheltered life has not been mine! I have a friend that I go walking with a lot. He's from Liverpool and proud of it. The right side of Liverpool, mind you. He has a lodge in the Lake District and one sunny day we went across Morecambe Bay on a guided tour. It's guided so you don't get caught in the quick sands. They've claimed many a life. Don't mind a little story, do you?'

'Not at all. Carry on.'

'Well, he took water for the dog but for some reason the dog wouldn't drink it. Drank sea water all the time. Couldn't stop it. After a while, strange rumblings started to come from its stomach. It was windy so we didn't always hear it, but, oh boy! We found out what happens when dogs drink sea water! There was a sort of explosion from its rear end. With the wind, anyone nearby got covered with the diarrhoea. Went everywhere. We had a lot of explaining to do. Why we'd not given the dog proper water etc. Took several rounds in the pub to get back on the right side of everyone caught in the mess. So, you see, we're not that posh. Well, some of us are but I mention no names.' He beamed.

'Well, I can,' sniffed Esme. 'Seeing as they're not here yet! Ros and Alex, the Gore-Marsdens, are right up their own arses. They think they're posh.'

I blinked – did I hear that from this sweet, stylish, well-spoken woman?

'They seem to care too much for the finer things in life. Because they're not used to them and really have to acquire things and then talk about them endlessly. 'Look what I've got now' and so on. So annoying to those of us who already have these things. Often, our things are family heirlooms and we take them for granted, rightly or wrongly. Feel free to disagree. It's just not done to talk about it, not in the way they do, I mean. Boasting. Oh yes, the Gore-Marsdens have had a lot of foreign trips to buy antiques and, oh boy, don't they make sure we all know about it!'

'A little uncharitable, Esme. We can't all be born with a silver spoon. They have money and like to spend it. The difference between old and new money as they used to say but it's levelling out now.' Francis was a charming man.

Esme countered: 'Bah, humbug. Lottery winners – not literally – still want to go to work to make a point but can't stop spending. He works for a maritime insurance company so he travels a lot anyway. Specialises in ships. He told me so.'

A few of the others started pitching in with opinions. For and against, but carefully tolerant. They were a nice crowd.

It emerged the group had started because Louisa had met Theophila with some friends – 'ladies who lunch' – and for fun had put an advert on the internet for people with such names to start meeting up once in a while. It had taken off very well and been established for five years now. The Gore-Marsdens were a newish addition and been keen on the travel side of the club. In between travel, dinners were arranged over weekend breaks. A club for the moneyed.

I kind of envied it all. What a shame my name wouldn't fit in!

Our drinks arrived in huge glasses. 'Lea, drinks are here.'

She looked up and sat back in her chair, seemingly satisfied with her work. She smiled and passed the sketch over to Louisa who studied it only for a second before addressing Lea. 'It's absolutely marvellous. Almost like a photo, yet only in pencil. Several kinds by the look of it. Soft and hard. I love the black and white contrast and smudged edges. I definitely want to commission some more work.'

She turned it round for all to see and it was received with amazement. Oohs and ahs followed. I peeked round the corner of it and was truly in awe – it was indeed like looking at Louisa in the flesh. It hadn't taken long. Lea had a true talent. Shame about her cooking, which was with a can opener and microwave! But you can't do everything.

'I want to commission a painting too before we all leave. If you can't do it here I want to get in touch when we are all back home. Of course, I'll pay what you want.' This from Juliana, part of the engaged couple. 'In fact, here's my card. Can I have yours? I will pay you too. I insist.' She was firm.

'I'm a Pisces so I am either at the bottom of the pond or on the top. Sink or swim. No inbetweens for us, so maybe with some good commissions I will rise to the surface – again. I would like to stay on top.' She smiled so sweetly and innocently it galvanized everyone into action.

All of a sudden, they were getting out business cards and handing them over, asking for a time for a portrait while at La Roca or to arrange one later. Lea was overwhelmed, and grateful noises ensued. The cat apparently was overwhelmed too and took an aloof attitude, jumping off Louisa's lap with disdain for all the noise. It cruised away to a quieter area and started to lick itself, sticking its back legs in the air while licking noisily around some interesting parts.

'I wish I could do that.' Lea was impressed with the dexterity of the cat.

'You said that about the dog, remember!'

'What? Oh yes!' Slight dejection tinged with minor annoyance.

Before we went any further, I changed the subject back to art – and contact. 'Well, we all agree Lea has done a wonderful sketch with minimal tools and I often say you can't make a Chippendale with a hacksaw, but she has. We don't have any cards, either of us, but I can give you my uncle's card and I'll put Lea's number on it.'

Murmurs of assent followed all round so I got Uncle's cards out and started writing. Lea muttered thanks.

'I must explain, my uncle has a travel company and he sent us here to see if it might be suitable to send some clients over. We are incognito so we don't get special treatment. It means we can see the real picture. So, please don't tell on us!'

As I distributed the cards, comments were rife, all understanding, sympathetic, and eager to be in touch. Lea made a joke about Chippendale men which thankfully I couldn't really hear but produced some merriment all round.

'Maybe in future we can use your uncle's company for our travel? No special treatment.'

'Oh, I'm sure there can be discount for bulk travel. I'll put a word in. I'm going to be junior partner.' A wave of pride came over me when I said that. The praise that Lea had had heaped on her was now matched by appreciation of my situation and offer. We were equal. I was aware two people were coming our way.

'Hello, everyone! Sorry we're late.'

Smiles all round. Did I imagine it or were the smiles a bit thin? Obviously the Gore-Marsdens.

'What's all this?'

I left someone else to explain.

Francis did the honours. 'Ros and Alex, this is Barbara and Azalea, or Babs and Lea. In a nutshell, Lea has done the most wonderful and impressive sketch of Louisa and we are all swapping numbers. Babs has an uncle who has a travel agency so we think it's a good idea to keep it in mind for the future.'

Louisa waved the sketch towards Ros and Alex. They were indeed impressed. 'Wow. What works have you done? Where do you exhibit?'

'Exhibit? I am a starving artist. I don't display anywhere – yet. I live in hope.' Lea gave one of her winning looks which didn't cut the ice. As soon as she had said she didn't have anywhere to display the Gore-Marsdens seemed to lose interest – or at least Ros did.

Louisa spoke up: 'She is going to be a star, you know. We are all going to have paintings done, aren't we guys?'

All nodded as one.

'Well, in that case …' the sentence was left open by Alex.

Lea had a strange look on her face. A cross between distaste and annoyance. I knew her so well and could see she didn't like this couple. But she smiled sweetly in their direction with a look that only I could know was insincere.

More drinks were ordered and Louisa bought us a round. It was time to relax for the evening. We began to slide down into the large comfy chairs used even around the pool area, put legs out in front of us and slouched. We were all of the same mind except for Ros and Alex who didn't bother to bring chairs and join in. For some reason they seemed edgy, and my and Lea's company obviously irritated them. In a few minutes they said they were going off to 'do their own thing' and left.

As Lea would have said if we'd been alone, the couple were well suited with their good looks and style. In their case they were well-suited in their shallowness. We had discussed such attributes before and Lea was adamant that attraction takes many forms, including physical but that it should be a mix of mutual interest and complementary personalities – in fact, whatever form it takes for two to tango. I had once accused her of being fixated on good looks only.

'Absolutely not!' she had snapped.

We all chatted more and then Lea announced she was 'starving.'

'You're always starving. You've got to have hollow feet. Where and what do you want to eat?'

'How about one of the tapas bars in the village? We can look around. Have a drink here and there. We could leave the car there and taxi back then I'll walk down in the morning to get it. I'm always up before you.'

'Sounds like a plan. So, everyone – it's been a real pleasure to meet you and, as Lea's agent I'll arrange some sketching or painting sessions. Here and back home. I'm the organized one. Lea's a scatty artist – aren't you, dear!'

Lea smiled a quiet smile. 'If you say so – dear! I really do look forward to painting you all. Or some of you. My stomach needs attention so we must go or I'll get ratty.'

'Oh, I think I can speak for everyone. We all want to be painted. Have a great evening! I can recommend a bar called Milos. Local atmosphere with basic homemade type food according to Milo. Lots of Spaniards in it and Milo is very friendly. Talked to him while waiting for the girls to come out of a shop – shops. Girls will be girls.' Francis winked at his two lady friends. Esme looked agreeable.

'Thank you, Francis,' I said. 'We'll take a look and report back. Vamos, Lea. Adios amigos. Hasta luego.' We waved a general encompassing wave and went to pick the car up.

'You still have the chariot keys, so shall I wait here? No use both of us going back to the parking lot?'

I made myself comfy, leaning against a palm tree, enjoying the balmy air. My eye was attracted towards the comings and goings of all and sundry. I saw the Gore-Marsdens and wondered what 'doing their own thing' consisted of this evening.

Soon a partial and interesting answer came. The bulldog, Karim, came to speak to them and I can only say they huddled together looking furtive. How do you look furtive, I wondered idly. They certainly kept glancing around to see who else was around. Curious. Suddenly Karim went to a nearby car, opened the doors and they all got in. They went in the direction of the village, Las Aqueas.

Just then Lea pulled up.

'Follow that car!' I ordered and jumped in. 'It's Karim and the Gore thingies. It all looked a bit suspicious. I mean, it's only a short time they can have known each other. That we know of.'

'Great. I've always wanted to do this. I won't get too near.'

The car windows were wide open, the air-conditioning as always ignored because closed windows gave Lea feelings of claustrophobia. Her rapidly growing hair – cut it short on our previous trip - had reached the shoulder-length 'messy sexy' stage.

I could kill for hair like that, I thought. But not when driving with open windows. 'How on earth can you see through all that hair?' I couldn't help myself.

The response was a dismissive wave. But she did put the windows up – a bit. And that gave me some smug satisfaction.

We followed Karim and the Gore-Marsdens right into the village – and out again. Lea drove wonderfully, staying when possible two cars behind, all the way to the commercial harbour. We parked up and watched them go through the gates into the actual harbour where we couldn't follow.

'I can just about see them. They're heading for that second ship along. Look! Someone's greeting them. Good job it's very well-lit inside there. What're all those metal structures with walkways and chimneys doing? They're all lit up like Christmas trees! Gas tanks? It's a whole industrial village!' She pointed to some grain stores in the distance.

We had certainly come to the working port, and an area most tourists would never see. It was vast! Fascinating to see how another country dealt with industrial sites.

We waited another fifteen minutes.

'Can we go now?' This from Lea. 'We can't ask them what they were doing when they come out anyway and my stomach thinks my throat has been cut. Oh – I shouldn't have said that.'

Both our minds had gone back to the murdered body. 'Let's go straight to that bar Francis recommended,' she added. 'I know where it is. I saw it when I took the drunk round that corner.'

'OK. Lead me to water as Hans would say.'

The bar was on a back street but still had outside space with tables. It was a cut-through so people-watching was easy. We sat outside and studied the menus propped up between the oil and vinegar bottles.

Milo came out. We knew it was Milo because his T-shirt said so. He had the image of a very amiable person, Father Christmas plumpish with a big greying bushy beard. And indeed he turned out to be amiable. Stopping him talking was the problem. He enthused about every dish on the menu and some that weren't.

'What do you recommend?' Lea looked up directly into his face and two sets of kindly eyes met hers with a twinkle. I thought of Hans. It must be catching.

'How about you leave it to me and if you don't like it, you don't need to pay for it?'

'Now that's an offer that can't be refused.' We both said more or less the same thing together.

'But whatever it is, we're paying for the wine. So please may we have una botella de casa? Vino blanco – secco.'

I stared at Lea in surprise. 'Where on earth are you getting these phrases?'

She dived into her bag – the big one reserved for sketch pads, pencils and stray dogs. A dictionary and phrase book appeared.

'I bought them in the hotel shop and I've been studying any spare moment.'

'I'm impressed. Not just a pretty face. Talented artist – and linguist now. Don't forget I'm your agent.' I told myself one fit of jealousy was enough in a day. Besides she was jealous of me – so I felt vindicated and relaxed.

The wine arrived so we got stuck in and Lea toasted to 'Partnership – whatever that is!'

Food started arriving in small dishes. Meatballs in a rich tomato sauce, potatoes with lots of garlic mayonnaise, fried squid, fresh grilled sardines, succulent serrano ham, some strong cheeses. Copious amounts of crusty sliced bread.

Lea was tucking in while I was still surveying the spread. My mind was still full of Karim and the Gore-Marsdens. I put a few things on my plate and pushed them around.

'I want to eat my food not dissect it.' snorted Lea. It was a worthwhile observation so I made more of an effort.

Milo came to see how we approved. 'Let me know when you are ready for the main course.' He never stopped smiling. How lovely to be so content, I thought.

'Main course? Oh my goodness. I thought this was it! Phew.' Shock without the horror. I patted my tummy.

'Ah, not so. You have my version of goulash next. House speciality.' With that he left us to finish the first course. Lea had the good grace to look at the remaining food in a quiet, speculative way.

'Perhaps I'd better not have any more of this. Well – maybe just one more sardine. And a piece of serrano ham. That's all.'

'I'm going to the servicios. I assume you know this word by now?'

'Of course – the loo. Bathroom, Washroom. Lavatory. Anymore? Gazunder – gazunder the bed!'

'Ha! Bet you didn't think of that. But I wouldn't, if I were you. Think, that is. That man over there,' she pointed, 'went in twenty minutes ago and has only just come out of the servicios. Either he was enjoying himself or he has problems and you need to wait for the smell to go. Either way, I'd give it a wide berth for a while. I don't like following people into toilets after you know what, any more than I like standing at a bar full of gabby old men.' She shuddered for emphasis. I wasn't sure whether which upset her the most, the toilets or the old men.

'I'm glad we're not eating at this precise moment. I could be put off. Do you time me too?' I demanded.

'Never.' Another sardine disappeared.

Milo came out of the kitchen area, peering our way. I waved him over. 'Wonderful, Milo. Looks like we'll be paying. The food has been positively dancing across – er - on my tongue - and my heart is singing too with this positively amazing banquet. Por favor, another bottle of wine. Have I said this before somewhere?' I hiccuped.

'What – another bottle of wine? Or tongue and heart? Excuse my friend. She has had a hard day – week – month. I'll translate if you want.' Lea patted her language books.

He beamed, shaking his head and started collecting the dishes.

'No need. I understand the sentiment. I am happy as you are happy.'

Through his arms I caught sight of Karim and the Gore-Ms heading our way. Next moment they were inside. Milo saw them too and greeted them like long-lost friends. Of course, he had a table – inside or out? Suddenly they caught sight of us. A quick polite recognition came our way and they opted for inside.

'Well! The plot thickens, Lea, and don't think I didn't see you sneak that last piece of ham from the plate.' A new waitress came with the wine, leaving it in a bucket of ice this time. We filled up.

'I think I can queak a snick wine in before the next course.'

'Er, I think you mean 'sneak a quick'!'

Lea giggled. 'Oops. I need more food.' More food arrived.

I took a chance on the new waitress and asked if she knew Karim. 'He's from our hotel – La Roca, you know. I was wondering if the staff often got out from the Club. They seem to work very hard.' I hoped I didn't sound nosey, so I deliberately stumbled over some Spanish. I didn't know how much English she spoke, and I wanted to take her mind off why I was being inquisitive.

'Yes. He and his friends have often been in here. They are English. Mr Gore told us he has to check ships out before they can sail. What's the name of his job – insurance. Er …'

'Insurance investigator?'

'Yes. They all go sport sailing together and sometimes as Karim helps in the balloon company they get rides in the balloons. But mainly the English hire a boat from Karim through his boat company. Or maybe he just works there. Very nice. I would ask if I could go for a reduced rate but – ' she pulled a face, 'how can I say this? I hear Karim is good in his job at the Club but I don't like his style. Only my personal thinking. I am sure he is very good to you so please don't say I said this. You asked me.'

'Don't worry! Thank you! I was only curious because hotel work doesn't pay well but Karim seems to do well. I am glad for him, of course. I suppose because he has two jobs. I was surprised to see him here and with some of our fellow guests. But – I'll tell you a secret – my friend and I have been out with Alvaro who works in the Club. Just sightseeing. Do you know him?'

'I don't know. Maybe. I am happy if my customers are happy. Are you happy? With the food and service? Milo is a very happy person and wants everyone to be happy. Very important to him. He is a very good boss.' She glanced into the dining room.' I must go. Karim wants to order.' We all smiled and she went on her way with assurances that we were 'happy'.

'The food's getting cold. What do you make of Karim being friends with the Gores? Boats, balloons. We only need trains and planes now and we'll have the full set.'

'I think we go back to the Club and mull it over in the Piano Bar. Then tomorrow we'll run it all past Hans, Alvaro and Helen. That's what I think. I must tell Hans he has a splendid finca and I love all the fields around it. You know we are a small country, Babs, but we have large fields too and huge equipment to deal with it. It impresses me. I am interested in how things run – like the commercial harbour. Fascinating.'

'I agree, Lea. Let's drink to snooping and your coat of a thousand budgies.' I raised my glass.

'I'll drink to anything.' She raised hers. 'What made you mention my coat?'

'Why not? Hans's finca reminded you of England and that woman over there in the corner with her family has a multi-coloured jacket similar to yours. Fluffy too. Hard to believe two of you have millions of budgies between you. Did you hear what that kid over there said to his dad when his mum went to the loo?'

'No. Panting with anticipation.'

'The kid asked his dad a question and Dad didn't know the answer – so the kid said, 'But Mummy says you know everything. You're a know-it-all'. I loved the look on Dad's face. Classic.'

Just then Mum came back. She had her T-shirt on show and she did a twizzle. 'How do you like my T-shirt? Got it in the market today. Cheap, you'll be pleased to hear.'

Dad glared for a few seconds then: 'Is that with or without the rolls of fat under it? Mind you, a clever dick like me can't have any valid opinions.' Mum was open-mouthed. Kid looked confused, aware something was not right. We chose to close ears to whatever was to follow, picking up our wine glasses and clinking.

'Cheers and oops!' Lea whispered. 'Oh dear. Out of the mouths of babes. Lucky the coats are man-made then. You know how I feel about animals – even if I do eat them. I must become a veggie. I think we need a taxi soon before squiffy becomes legless. How can you be tipsy with so much food in you? Hans would like this – squiffy, legless and tipsy. Ha! Have you thought of any words for him for the challenge he set?'

'Not yet. Working on it. Taxi soon then. To mulling in the Piano Bar. You pay and order the takshi and I'll get some fresh air. See you by the dor - er.' Hic.

'Door, doo – er, dor, dore, daw – how many ways can you say 'door'. Don't answer that. Hang on to something –

like the door post. If we stay any longer you'll be using double negatives.'

'I mean, like, I don't not want a taxi. Remember that woman who said 'We can't not do nuffink'? I hope there's a taxi quickly. They are never around when you want one. Did you know Heathrow flights land every forty-five seconds?' Having been subjected to a bad grammar and speech lesson my brain was turning to jelly.

'I'm not going to Heathrow to catch a plane back to the club no matter how frequent. I bet taxis are like rocking horse shit at this time.' Hic.

'Why couldn't you say like hen's teeth? Much more polite?'

'I was guuna – guna – gunner – gonna - goin, going to do that - but er, um, hmm, erm ...'

The taxi came swiftly and we were ensconced in the Piano Bar rapido. I would worry about my hangunder tomorrow.

CHAPTER SEVEN
Bats

'Spooky old bat,' Lea snorted as she brought tea over to my bed. She was fully dressed, bright- eyed, bushy-tailed and raring to go. The sun beckoned. Her bed had rejected her. Situation normal. She stared hard at me. Her deep eye-sockets suddenly seemed out of proportion and grotesque in my stupor.

'Robinson Crusoe. He's leaving Friday,' I countered. She was too much in my mornings. Loud. 'Why do you do this to me every morning.?' I pulled the sheet over my head and slithered down in the bed. 'I'm too hot with the sheet and this top and shorts on.' I hadn't undressed the night before – just fallen into bed. I was grumpy again. At least the patio doors were open with a gentle breeze wafting in, thanks to Lea's claustrophobia. Sod the insects flying in – or lizards creeping into clothes and shoes.

Was I dreaming or did she say the weather was rather inclement? Unbelievable. 'What? Inclement? It's sunny. As usual. End of. I can't be doing with inclement in my state.'

'Well, under all my clothes I'm naked so I should be cool. I only wear Chanel no 5 in bed, like a certain film star. What are you talking about, Babs?' She was sniffing her arm.

'What are you talking about? Spooky old bat. I don't remember anyone like that in the bar last night. And why are you sniffing your arm?' I slowly crept up out of my sheets and peeked over the top, still somewhat stupefied. Hangunder.

We only had sheets. It was far too hot for anything more substantial.

'That's because you had gone to the servicios. I bought some lovely shower gel in the hotel shop yesterday and it makes me smell gorgeous.'

'So, why didn't you tell me last night? '

'I didn't think shower gel was important. Oh, I see. Because she was still there and then you got talking to one of the Double Barrellers and then I went to bed – early. Well, it was early morning. By the way, what's your definition of a gentleman?'

Still half-dazed: 'Bring me more tea and I'll tell you. Or at least I'll think of something.'

A nano second later: 'Well – here's your tea. I'm waiting. And I think I'm going to rename the late bar 'Amnesia'. At least you might remember that.' She threw herself into a chair, crumpling like a rag doll, all legs and angles.

'Er, oh, erm – a gentleman is a man who uses a butter knife – straight on the packet of butter.'

'Ha! I can beat that. A gentleman is a man who has corns on his elbows.'

'Old joke. Am I to assume – because I can't quite remember, I was too busy solving our mystery – that we were telling jokes last night? And did you know – last night you had white hair, white teeth and a white dress. A white shark needed rescuing but you told me it was a dragon and because you put its fire out to save it, it was annoyed, so you had to find a lighter to give it its fire back.'

'I think the white was because of the lighting in the disco dance bar. Remember? Obviously not. The rest – nice dream? And no, it was definitions. Bit similar. Those Double Barrellers are a hoot. Very game. I would like them on my side anytime. Francis has had quite a lot of adventures and since he took early retirement he's bored. He's only in his fifties. Louisa hinted she used to have a secret job. She said even spies have to get paid. They do need human resources and accounts offices. Then she roared with laughter. Nod and wink. I'm never sure if she's joking or not.'

'Explain 'spooky old bat'.'

'Prrr! Well, she was dressed to the nines. Too much make up, like a vampire - smart clothes, flashy jewellery, but she still looked like the girl next door. Woman next door. I don't know how she managed it. She floated in when you were in the loo – and out again. She was looking for Karim. I think she was Moroccan too. Sort of dark, sallow complexion. She had claws for fingernails and she grabbed my hands. Asked where he might be. I asked her what made her think I would know. She said she was asking anyone. Everyone. As it happens, I did tell her I had seen him in Milo's. With friends. She went berserk and left. Old enough to be his mother. Maybe she was.'

'There's something not quite right going on but I can't think what. Either that or I have an overactive imagination. I think I'm joining the world, but a third cup of tea would help. Please.'

'I'm getting used to this pattern. I need to go and fetch the car. Remember?' Two seconds later the rag doll had been drawn up like a puppet on a string, straight and energetic, and the third cup of tea was plonked on my bedside table.

'Can't you throw it a bit more quietly?'

'I'm escaping before you make demands I can't cope with. If I was with that Double Barreller Esme, no doubt she would have me cutting grass. She said that grass always seemed to grow a lot in summer. I may have missed something but it always has in my experience. I can only think that while she loves her garden she leaves the technical side to her gardener. She's the old money you know.'

'I would never have guessed.'

'For some reason I feel rather intrepid. Like some of those early, much under-rated women adventurers. There was Nellie Bly who went around the world in 72 days in the 1890s and was a journalist. Imagine that. She was only twenty-five. I have – we have – a lot to live up to. Still, if you never expect anything, then you're never disappointed.'

With that she swept up her bag and left. The room suddenly felt quiet. I couldn't decide if that was good or bad.

Irritating though Lea was in a morning, the silence was deafening so I got up and made some noise, clattering onto the balcony with my phone, my teacup and with loose sandals flopping around.

I wanted to see what was happening in the world. Our balcony was already warming up even though it had the shade of the tree that the gecko had run into for safety. The hotel also provided table umbrellas which was as well as we got the sun all day in our room. I leaned over the balustrade, people-watching. Even thought it was only 9.30 am the heat was getting up.

I saw Lea with her one-piece top and shorts on, showing up those fighting ferrets. I really was going to have to mention them to her! The sun hat overshadowed everything and the sunglasses made a statement. I shouted, 'Factor 50!' She replied with a wave, not looking back, and then a diver's OK sign.

Three cups of tea were taking effect so I headed to the bathroom. Time to join the world. My tongue was furry white. Must have dandruff on it. Quick shower, all the lotions a person could subject their bodies to, let them soak in so they didn't spoil your clothes, make sure bags had all necessary items for the day, like phone, sun lotions, water, cool box for the car, maps, extra shoes in case some unexpected walking had to be done, money, credit cards (or should these be left in the hotel safe?), comb, lipstick, swimming costume, some kind of weapon – what? A terrifying thought! I settled back to mundanities. Kitchen sink. Dog biscuits just in case Lea found a new stray dog. Shower and thinking over. What was I going to wear? Decisions, decisions.

What were Lea and I doing today? Dinner tonight (looking forward to that at Prem's) but, engage brain, check out tunnels, ask around about Karim, maybe get an introduction to the manager Carl Wellington, at some point – but on what basis? Ask Alvaro about Carl Wellington's work hours and general movements and just watch out for him. Then what? Thinking was hurting my brain. So I decided to go back on the terrace and relax. Coffee this time and a hotel biscuit as we would miss breakfast by the time Lea was back.

Back to people-watching. It flitted through my mind that even my short shorts and combined top – a short onesie – was more robust than Lea's. Better made – but not as pretty. The difference between us. One of many - but so what! As Gareth would say, I had class. Not that Lea didn't – it was just different. We both had style in bucketloads, just in different ways.

I texted Uncle with the idea as I wanted to be seen to be working in a businesslike way. Also he might give it due attention. To my complete surprise he texted back immediately with a 'Good idea – work on it for discussion.'

I was elated so I added to the text, pressing my ideas about networking with other restaurants, bars, cafes or even shops to join up to promote each other within a certain area. A special website to link everyone together for a fee or commission. The answer came back: I should work with Carl Wellington on this when the time was right. More Brownie points for me. Not bad with a hangunder.

Comings and goings began to amuse me. The staff were doing a shuttle between the four blocks of rooms, carrying all the linen in big carts that trundled around. Our block faced the hotel reception area so we always had loads to watch. All blocks consisted of eight bedrooms, four on the lower floor and four on the top. Some had a bit of a hike to the hotel but we were lucky. We could see all the comings and goings. Good mornings shouted, guests waving to newly-made friends from the evening before. Holiday friends were instant and close – but only till the time of departure.

Lea suddenly erupted into the room. She saw me on the balcony and headed straight out. Her arms were full of large-brimmed, straw sunhats. And a bucket and dog water bowl and large plastic container. They all landed in a heap on the floor. I stared at them, waiting for an explanation.

'I need a cold drink. Have you had breakfast? I'm starving. If not, can we go for a snack by the pool and I'll explain.'

'That would be nice. I'm ready, ready for both,' I got up expecting her to follow but she was busy collecting all her purchases together.

'Can you give me a hand, please? I should have left them in the car. I need to buy some scissors for the hats. Before you ask – dog, donkey and horse.' She looked enigmatic so I did as requested without further comment. We headed for the car and put them in.

'Right. I'll see you by the pool. I'm going via the farmacia for some more scissors. Hans got me some from the ferreteriá but I think they're too small. Get a menu, will you?'

'Any more instructions? Shall I order and eat for you too?'

'You'll understand in a minute, I promise. It's all in a good cause. I just hope I don't make a pig's ear out of it all 'cos I want to make a silver lining for a sweet duo.' It was too enigmatic for me.

I settled myself by the pool under a tall, shady tree then spotted Alvaro. He was on duty so I waved. He came over instantly with menus. They nearly filled the table. Two-sided laminated affairs in case people dripped pool water on them.

'How are you both today? I'm looking forward to dinner tonight so I'll only snack.'

'Me too. We missed breakfast this morning as Lea went to pick the car up. She's found a mission to carry out so I'm dying to hear what's happened. She'll be here in a minute.'

'I saw Hans giving her a lift down to the village.'

Lea arrived on cue with an enormous pair of scissors, noisily scraping the vacant chair out across the patio slabs. Non-slip, I noted.

'Do you do anything quietly?' I handed her a menu while she ignored me.

'Good morning, Alvaro. How are you? '

'Working unfortunately, but fine. Looking forward to this evening as I was saying to Babs.'

'Oh yes. And Hans. He gave me a lift into the village. Even so early the sea was shimmering, all blue and sparkling, and I'm sure there was a heat haze on the road. Like a mirage.

I thought I saw the village below.' She sighed with contentment. 'Anyway, he'd been out early to see some clients about installing a pellet burner for winter. I told him it was conflagrational combustibles. Firewood. He didn't ask me to clarify. Spoilsport. He's reported the slashed tyres to the police by the way. Said you both had.'

'You're using some big words this morning.' I had to comment. 'And aren't 'shimmering' and 'sparkling' the same?' By way of a change I was ignored. I was too full of my ideas to care.

Alvaro said: 'It will be easier to claim on insurance now that we have reported the tyres. Also, it was very strange to have it done in that place. They may go and have a look. Or not. They're busy with the murder. Not a great deal happens around here so I'm sure they will make the most of it. I mentioned to Karim about our tyres. I'm not sure why I did.' He shrugged 'Anyway, Babs said you had a mission today. Can I ask what? It sounds mysterious. I like mysteries.'

'Well then! On our way down to the village Hans was driving slowly so I had time to look around. He said the road being so straight and downhill had proved lethal on quite a few occasions so everyone drives slowly now. Biggest shock was when a local family was walking up the road and a toddler with his mum ran away from her, and a car going too fast ran into him. Killed outright.'

We looked suitably sympathetic.

'Anyway,' Lea continued, 'I saw a donkey and a horse in a field. Tethered without any shade or water. That's what the hats are for. I must get my pigs' ears and silver linings right. I'm going to cut holes for their ears and leave a bucket of water and top-up container. I'll see how the owner reacts to it all while we're here. I may even try and find the owner. Hans thinks I'm mad but I can't leave the donkeys in that state. I'd never sleep. Then when Hans dropped me near the car I looked down a side road. There is a bit of a factory building or metal barn and a dog was tied up outside in full sun. No shade or water again. I just don't understand how people can do this to animals.' She was a mix of angry and distressed.

'So – what's the plan? I was wondering how we were going to spend the day.'

'I go into the field and hope the horse and donkey are friendly then offer them water and see how it goes. Keep as far away from flying hooves as I can. If they like attention, I'll try to get the hats on them. It's the best I can manage for a risk assessment. See what happens. I did notice the gate isn't far away if they break free and chase me.'

'What if the owner comes by and gets angry?'

'Cross that bridge when I come to it. I don't speak Spanish so leave it to me. Actions speak louder than words. Anyway, right now I need to eat – and drink.' She flew through the menu.

'Fresh-made real lemonade first, please. Then – hmmm – the fried mixed fish with special salad.'

'The luxury bacon baguette – and I'll share the special salad. Don't mind do you, Lea?' She nodded consent. 'Is the lemonade sweet?' I asked Alvaro.

'It's with fresh-squeezed lemons and some sugar but you get extra sugar separately in case you want more. Is that OK?'

'I guess so – I don't like anything too sweet, so fingers crossed. Thank you, Alvaro.'

He went off to deal with our order. We sat back and relaxed in the shade, feeling the warmth around us. People drifted in and out so we commented unashamedly on their appearances. For one, the man with the huge belly and shirt that wouldn't do up, both flowing over the top if his long shorts. We tried guessing his nationality.

'German.' My guess.

'English.' Lea's.

Then a family came in and settled a few tables away. No sooner had they sat down than two noisy fidgety children got up again and started running around tables. I hoped the parents would stop them but nothing was said.

Our lemonade arrived so we poured and drank deeply then took a big breath and re-filled from the pitcher. I stirred it first and the ice clinked. It was delicious in its freshness without being too sweet.

We sat back again just in time for the kids, a girl and boy, to come racing round bumping into our table as they lost grip on the tiles. The lemonade from the glasses spilled over the table. We started to use all our serviettes to mop up, leaving a soggy heap.

'Hey, look what you're doing.' I shouted crossly and automatically, loud enough for the parents to hear. Accidentally on purpose. They did look up and whilst not really apologetic they ordered the children back to the table. I glowered. The children at least looked subdued. Peace reigned. I made a note for Uncle to have a word with the manager to put some signs up about well-behaved, accompanied children only allowed around the pool and pool bar.

Then I changed my mind and texted him immediately with details and why it would be best for all concerned. This club didn't strike me as being particularly adapted for children. Coach tours were in the main filled with adults. Then you had the 'upper end' where more adults came to play sport and relax in a luxury environment. La Roca did not have a 'water theme park, play area' atmosphere such as you get on the edges of towns. I told him Azalea was off to rescue some animals and that all was well.

Two women came in next, all glammed up. Not a hair out of place and with immaculate, expensive clothes and accessories. Make up was so perfect it almost looked like a mask but it covered lined faces and brightened tired eyes. They were probably fifty-ish but hoping to achieve thirty, all girly, giggling, smiling at waiters in particular – smouldering even. This got our attention.

'They're only having fun.' Lea was sympathetic. 'They're on holiday so why not.'

'I suppose so.' I said grudgingly. 'I hope I never act like that when I get older.'

'Oh, stop being such a spoil sport. They're less of a pest than those children. They've started running around again, by the way. At least it's not near us. Ha! I'm going over to say hello to the women and see what's what.'

Off she went. In a minute she was sitting with them, all smiling and chatting, arms waving, pointing, more smiling, listening, sympathizing and finally parting like old friends. I saw our food coming so it and Lea, arrived at the same time.

We admired the veritable feast. The varied fish was in a lovely, light crisp batter, not overcooked, so Lea got stuck in before anything went soggy. The salad had everything in it you could think of, including boiled eggs and canned tuna. A meal in itself. My baguette was bulging with bacon and topped with melted cheese. All this and a meal tonight. Phew.

'So – what's what with the women?'

'They're both widows. Known each other since school and this is the anniversary of both their husbands' deaths just one month apart. They're well off and want to enjoy the rest of their lives before it's too late. Their husbands were only in their mid-fifties. They're both fifty today, hence all the fancy clothes. They're off on a balloon flight, then a tour around the area and dinner tonight in a club with cabaret. All inclusive package. I say good for them. They're very friendly, down-to-earth but well-spoken. They've both got good jobs in management. Don't judge a book by its cover, Babs. After all, people could see you as a priggish, posh, spoiled slapper – if that's not a contradiction in terms - and they could see me as a brainless airhead, only focused on fashion.'

'Brainless airhead, eh?' I had to smile. 'Don't forget you're focused on animals – and art.'

'Well, you're a linguist and game for an adventure, even out of your comfort zone. You do your Uncle proud.'

We smiled at each other. Alvaro came over to see how the food was and to stop for a natter. We agreed to all meet at Prem's at 8 pm for drinks.

'Luckily today with my breaks I have to eat early so eating at 8 is fine.' We were stuffed so he took the plates away.

'Let's rest by the pool for a while and snooze this off before we gallivant around horses. It will be Spanish lunchtime in a while so less likely to bump into angry owners.'

I acquiesced and we set off for the pool with the remains of our lemonade, settling under an umbrella on loungers. From around a bush Karim came into view making his way over to us. 'Ladies, I have heard two of your friends had an incident with their car tyres being cut. Alvaro told me. I am most sorry to hear this. If you go into some areas you should be aware of who is around. There is a gypsy area near the quarry. It is probably safe but best to stay in your car anywhere near them. If you have any concerns about anything, do let someone in the hotel know. I am here to help and of course the manager, Carl Wellington. Oh, excuse me. He's here.'

Karim waved Carl over. I was absolutely dying to talk business with Carl but there was no way at this stage. As it happens we hadn't said a word but Karim didn't seem to notice and we had wanted to make his acquaintance. Now we stood up feeling slightly at a disadvantage lying down and in skimpy clothes next to two fully-dressed people. Karim made the introductions. Carl was tall, slim, brown-haired, good looking, English and as charming as you would expect a manager to be. Not slimy like Karim, though Karim's concern was welcome and he even passed for normal now that he'd left the slime behind. I noted he had made no objection to our friendship with Alvaro. I must ask Alvaro later.

'This is Carl Wellington, and this is Miss Barbara Wills and her friend Miss Azalea Dunbar. They have unfortunately had two bad incidents in the short time they have been here. Witness to a murder and while they were out with friends, their friends' car tyres were cut. I was saying we are here to help.'

Carl took over. 'I heard of the murder. All over the village and in town too now. It's in the papers. I am so sorry you are mixed up in these things. Is there anything we can do?'

'We didn't actually see the murder. We found the victim. Not nice at all but I suppose someone had to find the body. The police were very good with us. We seem to have found friends here already. Lea collects them, you know.' Carl looked puzzled at this, and the remark went over Karim's head.

'She makes friends easily. She's a people person. An animal person as well. We're about to go and rescue some donkeys when lunch has settled.'

'Well – what can I say? I – er. Can I – um – do anything for these animals?'

'Oh, no thank you. I don't want anyone to get into trouble on my behalf.' Lea smiled sweetly. 'I'm only going to give them some drinking water. I don't think the Spanish are always thoughtful towards their animals. But then, the English can be cruel too. Any individual can. It's very good of you to offer.'

'Our pleasure. Karim and I are always around between us though he has another job in a boat- hire company. If you want to hire a boat or just go for a trip, I'm sure he will look after you. He has made good deals for our customers. '

'Yes, of course. I will get you a leaflet from reception,' said Karim. 'I will be very pleased to help but I am very busy since I was promoted to under-manager here at the Club. It was unexpected and of course a great privilege.' His English was very precise. Textbook learnt, I guessed.

Carl smiled. 'Karim does well to cope. One day we will sort something out for him a little less strenuous. Unfortunately, our other manager disappeared without warning. We are worried but nothing can be found out about him. The police haven't turned anything up. All very strange. I trust none of this has or will, stop the smooth running of the Club complex for you but as we have a new owner, please do really let us know if anything's not right or if we can help in any way at all. We want good reports to pass on.' He sounded absolutely genuine.

'Of course we will. And thank you.'

They both left but Karim sent a waiter back with his leaflet on boating just as we were settling down again. Lea put it in her bag and we drifted into a lovely soporific state.

'Right. Time for action.' I was suddenly brought back to reality. Lea was packing bits and pieces in her bag.

Sunglasses, wet wipes she had dug out when the lemonade spilled over and made us sticky, a towel she had put on the sun lounger. I hadn't done anything, except lie down. So, I got up.

'Ready. Let's go. Vamos!'

We went to the car and removed all the temporary sun sheets from inside the windows. They helped but not enormously. Parking in the shade had helped too. The hotel provided undercover parking with lots of green vines trained over metal poles. It both looked nice and was quite effective.

'Who's driving?' asked Lea.

'You are. Then I can do what I have to, and you can get us a quick getaway if I need one.'

'That's encouraging!' We set off down the hill towards the village.

'Relax. You won't get the blame for anything.'

'No – but I might have to rescue you and use my 'non-existent' Spanish. From the owner not the donkey.'

'I told you. Leave it to me. Not your problem. Don't you think Karim was fairly decent today? I suppose if he's run off his feet he could be stressed and come across as smarmy?'

'You see the good in everyone. You would promise that a circumcision could be reversed if they had kept the foreskin just to make someone happy. What if he is just smarmy?'

'Yuck. What an analogy. Then so be it. If he's smarmy, he's smarmy. Hitler had some good in him you know. He loved his dog. A beautiful German shepherd.'

'How do you know this?'

'I saw it on some historical footage about him. He was on a big terrace with lots of others – I can't remember who. Eva Braun was there, I think, and this dog was running around looking really happy. I wonder what happened to it. Poor dog. Not his fault his human was Adolf Hitler.'

'No, indeed not. But all the same! There seem to be lots of German shepherds in our life at the moment: the restaurant dog, Hans's, for instance.'

'Stop by that gate on the right.'

'Thanks for the warning.'

I slammed the brakes on, still managing to park neatly in the gates recess. Lea jumped out, collected two sun hats, a large water bowl and the plastic container full of water. Heavy. Gallons of water.

'Don't you want help with that.?'

'Help me to the gate and pass it through. I checked earlier and the gate has a rope loop over a post.'

We dumped the things by the gate and I watched Lea approach the horse and donkey. They watched intently. She was making cooing, friendly noises and I could see their ears twitching and the horses' eyes rolling. They were both tethered for some reason, close together but not so as to get tangled. Lea got right up to the horse and stroked its neck then moved over to the donkey. Both were interested in her and friendly, the donkey more so. She came back for the water and bowl. I automatically took half the strain of the water carrier and went with her a certain way towards the animals.

She did the rest herself. She settled the big bowl near the horse, put some water in and held it up to him. He looked, put his head near it as though assessing the situation and then drank a bit. Lea put the bowl down and he drank some more. She repeated the process with the donkey who did the same. Then she left the bowl in the middle so both animals could reach the water, and came back for the sun hats and scissors.

The animals continued to watch with interest. Lea threw the hats down and petted each animal, weighing up the distance of the incisions needed for the ears. The hats were soft but not floppy so raw edges wouldn't be a problem, according to Lea. The donkey seemed most co-operative and had taken a shine to Lea so she started by rubbing its head a lot, letting it see and get used to the hat. Then with a deft movement she slipped it over its ears, continuing to rub its neck and talk to it. This seemed to work as there was no adverse reaction.

The horse was a little more spirited and I was glad it wasn't me attempting the manoeuvre. I had had a few riding lessons but the horses I had been on always seemed to have minds of their own. I had been glad to give the whole thing a miss in the end. I watched the horse move away each time the hat appeared, with a toss of its head and some blowing of nostrils. Lea relaxed and let the hat drop and she stood around patiently till things calmed down. Then after a few minutes that seemed like an hour, she started her 'cooing' again.

'What are you waiting for?' I snapped. Every time a car or truck passed I wondered uneasily if it was going to be an irate owner. All vehicles had to slow down here as it was near the end of the road before it took you onto the roundabout either into the village Las Aqueas or the town, San Cartana. It was a busy junction with most of the...

'To gain the animal's trust.'

'Well, wait faster. My nerves won't stand much more of this.' I deliberately drifted away.

Uncle certainly had invested in a fascinating project and I was excited to be a part of it – with my own ideas. I drifted off into visions of converting the tunnels in the mine. I looked over to Lea and found the horse had its hat on. I'd missed the moment. Bother. Lea was coming back to me smiling. The water container had to stay in the sun but it would cool down in the evening and overnight. Perhaps animals didn't mind drinking warmish water.

'Success. I'm surprised they didn't drink more. I wonder why? I must ask about that. Now – to the dog please. Go to the bar called 'Celestino's' and then round that funny bend. We were next to it, having a drink and food when –'

'Yes, I know the one. There's a road down and round a tight, narrow corner and the building's down there. Right?'

'Lead on, Macduff.'

The drive wasn't long and there was plenty of parking. Only trouble was, there was a large popular venta, or bar restaurant across the way, full of workers. Fortunately, they were busy eating and there were few people outside. Thank goodness lunch hour lasted ages before siestas were taken or people had to return to offices to rest or, if lucky enough, to go home. It had been quite an issue in Spain for some time as it was very awkward for those workers who had nowhere convenient to go till things opened up again for the evening session.

'If I park longways across this bit,' I indicated the area where the dog was, 'you won't be very visible when someone comes out of the restaurant. They'll be heading for their cars just in front of the venta.'

'OK.' She picked up the other dog bowl and water container, walking slowly towards the tethered dog. It sat up and watched. Then it stood up. A few feet away from it, Lea started her 'nice doggy' routine. It barked and wagged at the same time, straining against the rope, coming towards Lea. So she stopped moving but kept talking, then squatted down at the dog's level. It continued to wag and bark so she put some water in the bowl and pushed it forward just shy of the mouth full of teeth. I shouted that there was a stick nearby to push the water closer for the dog so she retreated to pick it up and then pushed the water within reach of the dog. Going round the dog towards its stake, she pointed.

'It's got a hole in the door it can get through. That's good. I'm going to leave the container by the door. It's too interested in me to drink so maybe we should go. I'll look back to see if it drinks. I might try the hat another day. Let's go.'

'No need to ask me twice. Where to? What next?'

'Let's have a look at the harbour in San Cartana. We've only seen it in the distance.'

The harbour was by a tree-lined wide boulevard with parking on both sides and walkways leading to various bars and restaurants. We parked, paid in a machine and started walking from one end to another. There were three parts to the harbour. Small fishing boats where we were, clearly used a lot. Fishermen were sitting around mending nets. Next there was a mini dry dock with one yacht in it then we stopped by a large working ship which was being loaded with fish from the quay.

'Why aren't they taking fish off?' Lea queried.

'I'm going to ask. I'm curious too. Can you see anyone we could ask?'

'How about the man doing the loading behind the fence? You can shout.'

'Ah. I didn't see him. Senor!' I got his attention.

We moved right up to the fence and I asked what was going on. I think he was amused to have two pretty girls talking to him through his fence. It turned out the fish being loaded were food for the tuna farm out to sea, way beyond the harbour walls.

We spotted a huge ship moored out there too. I enquired again what that was, realizing as I said it, it must be a warship as I started seeing men and women in uniform strolling around. 'Americans!' Lea and the worker both came up with the same answer simultaneously. There seemed to be about two thousand sailors enjoying a few days' shore leave, coming and going in waves so there were always crew on the ship and not enough on shore leave to overwhelm the town. Seems we had hit an interesting time in this corner of Spain. I thanked the guy behind the fence with Lea beaming at him and adding her unique goodbyes in Spanglish.

We walked on and came to the sports harbour, jam-packed with small to medium power boats. American accents were everywhere, in all the bars. We supposed that like us, the Americans were sightseeing or more likely just drinking. We gave them the benefit of the doubt: some sightseeing with a wobbly walk. Spanish don't like open drunkenness but the money must be good from a ship that size, so tolerance was the order of the day, along with a large police presence. We couldn't imagine very bad behaviour being tolerated by the commanders on the ship. We enjoyed the buzzing atmosphere and being two pretty girls on our own got compliments by the bucket load.

We made it into the centre which was elegant and grand, with tall, stately buildings on either side of a fairly wide pedestrian street. We noticed bullet holes in walls probably left over from the Civil War. Any Roman buildings were carefully guarded under glass or behind bars. History abounded.

Bars nudged each other up and down the street, all overflowing with the Americans. Finally we found one with some space and relative quiet, thankfully sinking into chairs. Service was slow so we people-watched for over twenty minutes before a waiter came to us. Plain old agua was fine as it was hot and stuffy in the crowded street. We saw adverts for a big Gay Pride event and remembered Helen had said they were tolerant in San Cartana of such things even though individuals like the old-fashioned parents of the gay barman in our hotel might not be. Barcelona or Benidorm this was not, but many people, especially the younger ones, obviously moved with the times.

The tall buildings kept the sun out but the narrow streets felt hot and clammy with the crowds milling all around. We fended off several attempts at being picked up as apparently we 'owed it to the people defending the world' to provide girly entertainment. We smiled – after all, the Brits do their own share of defending. It was all good-humoured. No offence was taken on either side, there were just polite refusals and general banter. The more senior officers weren't drunk and generally kept an eye on the masses, so we had one sensible conversation with two truly appreciative officers who found our 'Englishness' charming. We found being addressed with 'Yes, ma'm' quite amusing.

One officer pointed out more bullet holes in the building opposite which we all concurred did indeed come from the time of the Civil War. He was sober and charming and had done some research on the town. He told us many guns were left over from these times, families keeping them as souvenirs or protection – or for the hell of it. Someone might need a gun sometime and you could hire them out. Or favours could be returned. Well, well, well, how interesting. I thought. Perhaps a bit scary but – hmmm – useful. Was I scaring myself? Who would I approach if I needed to? This was a town with history worth further exploration.

'I really think we should go, Babs. We have dinner to get ready for and we've been out for hours. We set off late.'

We paid up, ended our chat and made our way back to the car. All in all, a successful and fun day with a lovely evening to come. Bliss.

'Do'

'Why would we so soon? Don't you trust me – as a woman driver? Sexist!' I was miffed.

'Course I do – but you've been musing so I'm being practical. I have used the car quite a bit. I must check on the horse and donkey – you only need to slow down so I can grab a quick look.'

I slowed down. Lea could see over the wall and both animals still had sun hats on. So far, so good. ☐

CHAPTER EIGHT
Dinner at Prem's and Some Ideas

I had coped well with my hangunder in the morning and was now ready for tonight's action. Lea was full steam ahead too.

'I think we should have a pre-dinner drink in the Piano Bar before Prem's.'

'We're having one at the restaurant.'

'Then a pre-drink, before the pre-dinner drink.' Lea twirled in her white, figure-hugging, off-the-shoulder little number. Her suntan was glowing with some body shimmer she had put on. I complimented the outfit and took my twirl. Mine was a luscious red with capped sleeves but a slightly open, downward V front. Not too much. Lea's hair was growing fast and she'd swept it up with some loose ringlets at the sides. Mine was glossy and wavy as usual.

I gathered up my courage while we were still messing around in the bedroom to mention her short, tight shorts.

'Lea?' I fell silent so she looked at me enquiringly.

'Is this something I'm not going to like?'

'Well – you know you always look gorgeous –'

'Why are you buttering me up? Spit it out.' She looked at me suspiciously and I squirmed inwardly.

'You know you were miffed – for some reason – when that guy by the pool had very tight trousers on. Well – '

'Don't tell me you fancy him!'

'No! Course not!' Deep breath. 'But it's just that you wear very tight shorts that show a lot of – things! And I don't think it is quite right for you. I like you to look fabulous all the time, not like a, a, a – '

'Tart.' She finished for me. 'Hmm. As it happens, I've been thinking about it myself. I caught sight of myself in the bedroom mirror and now if you notice I only wear the very tight ones round the pool. I never go out in them. I've put weight on so they probably are too tight now. So – I agree. I'll give them away – and thank you for caring.'

She blew me a kiss across the room and continued: 'Off we go then. Piano Bar. Helen may be there and we can ask how she is. Or if not, we should phone. Seeing as she was so good to us. Ask her to join us for dinner maybe.'

'I agree. Vamos!' What a relief. Whew! I got away with that.

We settled by the piano and not long later David came in. No Helen.

'Hi, David. Is Helen OK? Can we buy you a drink? Least we can do for letting us borrow your wife to help with a murder. We were wondering if she would join us at Prem's for dinner too? Our treat for everyone as you all helped in some way. We insist.'

'I'm fine for drinks, thank you. I will have loads lined up later but I'll ring Helen and see if she wants to go to Prem's. What time are you going?'

'Making our way slowly and meeting with Alvaro and Hans. We just wait till everyone gets there. I did ring and ask if we had to have a specific time but as long as we don't mind waiting it can be anytime.'

David rang Helen. 'Helen, Lea and Babs want to know if you'll join them, and Hans and Alvaro at Prem's. No rush, just when you get there. Their treat and they are all dressed up. Take note.' He listened and nodded. 'Ok, I'll tell them. Night, sweetie. See you later.'

He turned back to us. 'She'd love to. About an hour. Has to finish at the office with a client so will come in uniform, which is smart anyway. You've seen it.'

'Perfect. Time for another here then.' Lea beamed.
'Lush.'
'Yep. When on holiday –'
'Unusual holiday you've had so far. Murder is unknown here, though not in San Cartana. Drink or drug-related mostly, though we did hear of one revenge killing of an English woman running a small hotel in Cartana. She had a gay chef and the chef wanted his boyfriend to come and work in the hotel but she said no to it. She had enough staff and didn't want to attract only gay staff. There were two already, including the chef. Anyway, her son went into her private quarters the next morning and found her hanging from a beam in her bathroom, covered in cigarette burns and cuts. No chef to be found. The police caught up with the chef and his boyfriend trying to get back to the UK. They had done it between them so they are still in prison here. It was a shock for the whole area.'

'It would be anywhere.' We chatted on ... the murder, slashed tyres, donkeys, dogs, the Spanish, the English, the Germans and a smattering of other nationalities.

'Time to make a move, Babs. I'll drive like before and we can taxi back. I'll walk to get the car tomorrow and I can check on my donkey and horse at the same time.'

'Twist my arm, why don't you. We may see you later, David.'

'Hope so. I need to work my way through your song sheet. Night for now.'

Lea parked in the forecourt of Prem's restaurant. There was room for eight cars and four were already there. More than eight would have to park on the road but we had heard people preferred not to in case they got scratched by careless drivers. This was a notorious road, even after the tragedy.

No Hans or Alvaro yet. We went in to be greeted by Prem herself. An attractive, elegant, slim woman in her early fifties, beautifully dressed in a sari of turquoise and silver but somehow adapted to be practical for running around in a restaurant.

'You are Lea and Barbara. I can tell. Hans has told me a lot about you both. All good. Please sit by the bookcase on the comfy sofa. Best place. Everyone wants it.'

The sofa was enormous, in muted reds and golds near a curtain of the same material dividing the drinking area from the dining area. Other chairs in the waiting area were of the white rattan style that reminded me of the Indian Raj. Matching low rattan tables with glass tops continued into the dining area where the tables gained height. It all flowed and sparkled but without garishness. It was elegant, like its owner.

'When did Hans come in, then?'

'He often drops in on his way into or out of the Club when he has clients to visit. We have coffee and a chat. I don't open for lunch but I come in to prepare with my chef. It's a nice lazy time through the day. Sociable. What would you like to drink?'

'Fine. House dry? There's another person joining us by the way. It's Helen.'

'No problem. I'll get your wine and menus.'

With that Prem disappeared into a room behind the bar. The kitchen was off to one side of the bar. Doors swung open and shut. The people from the parked cars were already seated in the dining room. Lea was looking at the books behind our sofa. I followed her gaze.

'Look at these. Some funny titles here. 'It's Hot in the Kitchen' by Mrs Cook, 'Mawn Lowing' by G R N Grasse, 'Memories of Stairs' by Lord Bannister, 'The Death of Mrs Lamb' by Wolfe.'

I continued 'Ha, yes. Good, eh? 'Memoirs of Loch Ness' by T H E Monsta, 'Revenge' by B A D Losa. Clever. Wonder why? Pick one.'

Just then the wine and menus arrived, brought by a dark, pretty girl. I wondered if it was Prem's daughter.

'Thank you. Tell me – why the funny titles.' I pointed.

'It was Mum's idea. When we were refurbishing. They aren't real. If you press the right side of the furthest book, it pops open. It hides some electric switches. You can't see any switches anywhere. They are all hidden by something. In the dining room you'll see some wood panelling and they hide other switches. '

'I bet you're tired of being asked that question. So, you're Prem's daughter?'

'Yes. Shelley.' She had a lovely smile that lit up her face. 'The regulars know about the books. I help out now and again since I've left school so it's not so bad. I'm learning the business too but I'm considering a course at uni. I can't make my mind up yet. Keeping options open. Do you want to taste the wine?'

'No, it'll be fine. If it's corked we'll let you know. I'm beginning to dehydrate.'

'No surprise there, Lea.' Just then Hans walked in. We waved and I signed to ask him what he wanted to drink. I asked Shelley for a bottle of house red and she too disappeared into the room behind the bar.

'Good afternoon, ladies. Still not evening in Spain. How was your day?' His whole face conveyed humour and happiness. He sat next to Lea.

'We rescued that donkey and horse – and a dog. Well, gave them water and made hats for them. Babs was lookout.' Lea went into detail and Hans was suitably rapt and amused, those eyes again twinkling merrily.

I spotted Alvaro and Helen coming in together. Good. Someone for me to talk to. Two low rattan chairs were pulled up by Helen and Alvaro. Wine was accepted so I asked by sign language again for two more glasses as Shelley was on her way over.

'Well – how nice to be all together in such pleasant circumstances. Cheers, everyone.'

We all clinked the glasses that I had filled and then settled back into the comfort of our seats, definitely not designed to get rid of customers quickly. We all started talking quietly as nothing seemed loud in this establishment. There was a background murmur and some unobtrusive background music of no particular kind. It just merged. I couldn't put a name to any of it. Soporific. Then I heard:

'– discombobulating.'

'You certainly are,' I addressed Lea.

'Hmm?'

'Confusing. Discombobulating. You keep doing this. I've noticed long, complicated words have been creeping in for a while now. So what are you talking about? I have to ask so I can translate for Hans. Unless his English runs to 'discombobulating'?' He shook his head, amused as ever with our antics.

'Since I looked in my English–Spanish dictionary. We were talking about the balloons. I saw ten drifting around today. Seems a lot, though I'm happy they're busy. Also, I noticed one came down in the quarry – again. One of the Double Barrellers said one did.'

'Maybe it's a convention or competition.' We all speculated and conversation turned to the funny books which we had to explain.

'Now I can tell my German friends. Prem has book exchanging, so people drop in and leave or take books for reading on the beach. Or – ' Hans emphasized, 'there is a grande big second-hand shop passing the English speaking ferreteriáo on the main road. Has all kinds of things in it. Many books but no swapping. That's why a lot are to be coming here. The shop has clothes, sheets, duvets' – he pronounced it as it was spelled – 'household stuff, re-conditioning fridges, freezers. The expats buy a lot of those for their own selves in rented accommodation or for property they are renting to others. It is – you say – Aladdin's Cave? I bought my knives and forks and plates there. Some pans too. No kettle.'

'Sounds just like my kind of place. I'll look when I pick the car up tomorrow morning. You can sleep in, Babs – as usual. I'll take my shorts there.' She shot me a look. 'How are you guys getting home tonight? We can all share a taxi. Ideal for us and Helen, and you two,' nodding to Hans and Alvaro, 'don't have far to walk back here for your cars.'

'I won't drink too much as I need my car for an early start at work tomorrow. I can take you back, Hans, if you want to walk back for your car in the morning?' So it was settled. It was so nice that the 'guys' automatically spoke English for us though it made me feel guilty. My thoughts must have transferred to Lea because she fished out her Spanish phrase book and dictionary from her matching white bag – but still large enough for a stray dog if she found one. Some things never change.

'I am determined to learn, but I'll have to carry on back home.' She waved the books around, which met with approval.

'The mistake most people make is relying on others to speak Spanish for them, or using only English-speaking shops. Of course, pointing helps and gestures, but even a few words is appreciated by the Spanish. Try every time with Spanish first.'

'Good advice,' I said, and Hans agreed.

Shelley came over. 'Are you ready to order?'

'Sorry. Lo siento. Not even looked yet. Can we have two more menus, please. Dos mas – er – menús, cartes, por favor?' Lea looked both pleased and half-embarrassed with her attempt. Shelley smiled and Hans beamed.

'Well done. Bien. Dos guapas este noche.' Twinkle.

'You said we are pretty this evening.' Lea was happy. We studied the menus.

'Order whatever you want. We have an expense account from my uncle for things like this and there is so much to choose from. It needs to be tried. Unusual versions of some classic dishes.'

Helen gave some opinions from tried and tested dishes so between us we ordered seven starters, seven main courses, plus side dishes. Way over the top but we wanted to sample as much as possible. Last but not least, more wine and water.

In due course an absolute feast arrived – and that was just the starters. Prem accompanied it to explain her spin on things. We got stuck in – a bit of this and a bit of that. It was warm feeling, as though we had known each other for years. It was an easy friendship and we all looked forward to seeing each other. I wasn't sure about romance though. How would that fit in? Would it spoil things? Or would the disappointment of no romance spoil things equally? Dilemma. Anyway, food first.

'Doggie bags later? '

'Well, you never know when there will be a dog to rescue, though I doubt they would like all the garlic. Imagine dog breath with garlic.'

'You just don't know, do you, Babs? And if they were hungry, garlic is a small price to pay. I doubt their friends would mind.'

Hans interrupted. 'My dogs eat anything. They are catching things from the campo and try to catch trains passing. But they couldn't eat a whole one!' He guffawed.

'I gather they chase things?' Lea smiled. 'In the meantime, can anyone tell me a bit more about Spain's relationship with Morocco? Only I watched a TV programme about it a while back, never realizing I would ever be here.'

Helen piped up. We enjoyed her knowledge but just before she went on, a terrible noise erupted. We all glanced up questioning.

'Sounds like a donkey on heat.'

'And what does a donkey on heat sound like. Lea?'

'Like that. It's coming from the field where my horse and donkey are.' She shot out of the restaurant. We could see she went to the end of the terrace and peered down the field which was next door. I was about to join her when she started to come back. We all waited for an explanation and be ready to help rescue a distressed animal.

'It's okay. My donkey was letting off a bit of steam. I had forgotten how awful they sound. It was being hedonistic.' She resumed her seat without batting an eyelid. I purposefully ignored the big word and we all encouraged Helen to resume her information package.

'I do know the Spanish are hypocrites over Gibraltar. Sorry Alvaro –it's true.' He nodded acceptingly. 'They have a Ceuta and Melilla on the North African coast which no more belongs to them than Gib to the UK. They are referred to as enclaves and Morocco is constantly asking for them back. The legality of it has never been recognized. Spain doesn't treat the people there well. The Africans that is, legal or illegal. I know some Africans who came from as far as the Gambia in search of a better life. They got to Spain but I don't know if their life was better. Different kind of poverty, working incredibly hard for a pittance. Ceuta's not like Gib which has a good standard of living and where everyone is free, has education, work and good homes. Most in Ceuta are very poor. It is a jumping-off point for all Africans to try and get to Spain and the rest of Europe.'

'I've been to Morocco and Ceuta,' Alvaro chipped in. 'Ceuta has a wire fence around it. Massive, with barbed wire on top. It is to stop smuggling and migrants from entering Europe. Morocco objected as it doesn't recognize Spanish sovereignty. There are watch posts, spotlights, noise and movement sensors, videos, Guardia and police patrols and boat patrols. The whole enchilada – or is it shebang? You can correct me?' None of us bothered to say anything.

'I saw the hopelessness of many there. I suddenly really valued my passport. The Straits of Gibraltar to Morocco is only nine miles or a half-hour journey but for many it's a million miles away. We take freedom for granted. I saw women of all ages there struggling with huge heavy loads of goods coming and going from Morocco because it's allowed to cross the border with cheap good – and for a lot of women it's the only work they can get. They don't have much status there.'

We all pondered this while starters were cleared.

'I know some finca owners here who exploit Moroccans. The illegals have no say in anything. They can get permits to work in the vast plastic greenhouses or polytunnels, which is hot, sweaty work for sure. It's worse in Almeria where there is so much of this type of work. I know a boss who charges his workers per month to share a room with sixteen other people and awful facilities. One bathroom and toilet and a kitchen with one cooker for sixteen that has dangerous wiring. Complaining only means the authorities side with the owners, not the migrants. When an area is earning one billion euros a year you don't disturb it.' Helen looked disturbed, with a 'what can you do about it?' look.

'What happens to all the plastic?' Lea was as ever concerned about nature but with reason, I conceded.

'It gets abandoned. Blown away – literally. Torn down and left. Most washes into the sea. Gets covered over to make layers of sand and soil and plastic, over and over like a cake. I am told twenty-seven million tons of plastic gets into the sea from Spain every year. I don't know. I should check it out.'

'I'll do that Helen. Then maybe start a campaign. I'll have to think about it. It's awful. I did see in the |TV programme that some fishermen are now paid to fish for plastic to help the situation. Someone is seeing the eco side of things.'

'Well, I wish they would in Benidorm. It looks like the Manhattan of Spain but somehow misses the romance, in spite of the TV series set there. Which was quite fun, actually. Again, I've been told they have five million tourists a year. At least the Straits of Gibraltar has some good news – apart from the bad news of massive drug smuggling around and into Gib, thence into Europe. One hundred thousand ships per year pass through it, which hasn't helped the dolphin and whale population – that's down fifty percent since the 1960s. But it's changing for the better. That and the plastic. Not fast enough, but changing, like those fishermen.'

'Wasn't Almeria where they made spaghetti westerns in the old days? 'The Good, The Bad and the Ugly' stuff? The only desert in Europe.'

'You have some winning phrases, Lea. Old days! It's not two hundred years ago.'

'What's grown in the greenhouses?'

'Oh – so much. Aubergines, melons, courgettes, tomatoes.'

Hans interrupted. 'Opposite my finca there are fields. A few weeks I was watching lights. I'd seen it before but not for a while. The whole field was lit like a beacon with trucks and people everywhere. Some of the people came over to me and asked for water. Moroccans. I am giving them water but when they ask for food, I am saying no. After 8.30 night time my gates are closing. I am not to trust the Moroccan workers. Sorry.'

Silence then he continued: 'I am understanding their situation and sorry. I think they would steal. Why not when they are so poor? They were picking crops. Next morning the field was emptying – empty – but trucks are coming in and starting ploughing, fertilizing and watering. Entonces – then – it was left for a week and planting is going starting again. Big cycle. Many years ago I remember all fields were planted and crops were left to die in the ground. Farmers paid to plant and leave the crop without harvest. Crazy. At least we have moved in front ahead from that. Now we have new problems. Pollution. Over fish farming. Extinction of species for many reason. Greed usually.' He stopped again. 'Sorry! I am speaking too much. You say 'going on'? I feel strong for this situation.'

Most of the time Hans's English was good if mixed up – which made it amusing though we would never say so. If he got really excited, it went downhill. Not that it mattered. We understood.

The main course arrived again with Prem attending. Wow! We all muttered appreciatively together.

'Prem – this is amazing. The presentation is exceptional. I have to assume the taste follows.'

'It will.' Helen looked at us all with pleasure and confidence.

Again we got stuck in, sharing this and that. Wine flowed. More bottles were ordered and Alvaro's resolve melted 'I can resist everything except temptation. Can I accept your offer of a taxi and I will worry about tomorrow when it comes to tomorrow?'

'Course you can.' Lea raised her glass and we all cheered. We were happy. Desserts were declined, apart from Lea, who wanted ice cream to settle her stomach. We all had liqueur coffees and then it was time to pay the bill. The comfy seats by the bar beckoned but the Piano Bar did too and it was Helen's husband who would like to see her. A child minder was there anyway so we were all set. Hans and Alvaro couldn't say no to coming along. The taxi was quick and rebooked for later.

When we got back to La Roca we sat by the piano with smiles all around. Lea started looking through the songs and I resigned myself to another late night. Drinks were ordered and Hans and Alvaro sorted the bill. We observed many of our new acquaintances coming in – the Double Barrellers. Lea flew over to speak to them so I chatted with Helen and David who was on a break. Alvaro hovered. I suppose I flirted with him. Hans spoke with several people we didn't know which was hardly surprising. He knew loads of people.

Finally Lea came over and announced she was going to bed. She looked a bit mysterious but I couldn't be bothered to respond. She had to pick up the car tomorrow. Er – no –this morning, actually, I pointed out. Best reason to go to bed, she said. Must speak to me tomorrow or even today. The taxi was back for Hans and Alvaro so air kisses went all round, and some genuine hugs with our good friends. It took a while for us all to depart in dribs and drabs.

An elderly couple who had been watching us in general came to speak to us. They said it had been such a delight to watch our fun, which reminded them of their youth. They were celebrating their golden wedding anniversary, paid for by their family. A whole week in La Roca on a coach tour. Hans was charm personified with them. They looked at him fondly and asked if they could ask a question. We all held our breath. They noticed we were ordering taxis on mobile phones and one had phoned back. How did they know at the other end which number to contact us on? They were all for learning about technology and another present from the family was 'one of these moving phones' – but they couldn't work out how to use it. Hans spent some time explaining and Lea promised to give further lessons another day. Grab her when they saw her anytime. We were all enchanted. Helen went with the guys on a round trip as David was still on duty for another hour.

They were all so grateful for the dinner and, as they said, genuinely good company. When I looked around Lea had gone without asking for any music. She had said she had some very interesting gossip for me. I ordered another drink and sat at the piano. I would sleep in – definitely.

I had a laugh when I overheard two ladies bantering – a bit the worse for wear.

'I don't know – all that money you spend on face creams. You would expect them to work better.'

'I take it you don't use any at all?'

I smiled to myself. Time for bed!

CHAPTER NINE
Things to Speculate On

When I woke up, I was alone. It gradually dawned on me through the silence and my fog that Lea would have gone for the car. Oh – tea was all down to me. I eyed the kettle up – across the room. It seemed very far off. Too far. Phooey.

So I sat up and pondered. Last night had been fun and we felt we had repaid our dues to everyone for all the help and kindness we had received in such a short time. The balcony doors were open, letting a cooling breeze waft into the room. I stretched and got up lazily, going via the kettle to turn it on, then onto the balcony. I wondered who would be about so I hung over the balcony paxrapet, resting my elbows on the wide top, peering over the edge. I didn't recognize anyone and was just about to organize my tea when Esme came out of her block across the way with Louisa. They spotted me.

'Morning, Babs. We're off to see my son,' Louisa called up, shading her eyes against the already bright, hot sun. Sunglasses sat redundant on her head. I was very surprised and curious.

'You never mentioned before that you had a son here.'

'No, I keep it quiet so people don't feel they have to watch what they say around me.' A sly look crossed her face. 'Police make people nervous – for no reason.'

I cut in suitably curious: 'Police?'

'Yes, for my sins I was living in Spain when I had my child and he grew up here. You've met him.' She looked directly at me smiling cheekily with amusement, obviously waiting for a reaction.

I obliged. Tea could wait. 'Oh, do tell me! I can't imagine who.'

'El Capitan Edouardo Spelier-Bielby.'

I must have looked blank. She continued: 'The policeman who was in charge when you found the body.'

'Oh, my goodness! I thought he spoke wonderful English. No wonder. I never did catch his name. So he has Spanish nationality then?' I was indeed surprised. Taken aback in fact.

'Yes, and I have permanent residency – but I commute between here and England. I have a house there as well as here but I like to stay with my friends when we come on one of our jaunts to Spain. The Club is one of my favourite places to stay. Such wonderful breakfasts. Speaking of which we should go before they finish. We're behind this morning. Slept in.'

'Me too. Lea's gone to pick up our car. We left it at Prem's last night and got a lift back. See you then.'

We all waved. Tea beckoned so I went in to make it after a short trip to the bathroom to splash cold water over my face to properly wake up. I thought, not for the first time, how lucky Lea was to drink as though she had hollow legs and still be up, bright-eyed and bushy-tailed. I took my tea onto the balcony and settled down. I watched some large birds soaring around on the thermals and, whilst I was sure they were birds of prey, I giggled when a thought struck me that if it had been Lea spotting them they would have been vultures. Her type of bird that was so ugly it became cute.

It was late morning now and no doubt Lea would be wanting lunch on her return. I phoned her but it went to answer. It was another hour and a half before she returned and I was getting worried. A shower and getting dressed distracted me then suddenly the door burst open.

Lea looked flushed and excited, and she was rather breathless. 'You'll never guess what happened to me.' She flung herself on the edge of her bed and sat unlady-like, knees wide apart, feet resting ha feet resting haphazardly on the cool tiled floor. Her top half flopped forward, rag-doll style.

'You're right. I wouldn't.'

She drew a deep breath and blew it out. 'To start with, I went to check on my horse and donkey. They're fine but I met the owner. I was getting some water for the container at Prem's –'

'Hold on, you went to see the animals first or filled another container from Prem?'

'When I got to Prem's I told her all about my rescue mission and begged water for the container after I'd gone to check things out. I was going to empty the container and fill up at Prem's. She was very sympathetic. Knew the horse and donkey as she passes them every day to and from work and agrees they should like the hats and water. Knows the owner too. Often pops in for a coffee. Anyway, when I got back with the container the owner was there. Wow. What a break. When she introduced me I thought I was going to be told off because he's Spanish. But he was OK about it. Amused even. He'd called on Prem to see if she could throw any light on who had done that for his animals. What a coincidence. What luck.'

She took another big breath and dived for the mini fridge and a bottle of water, drinking till I thought she'd burst. She gulped air and wiped off the water that had dribbled down her chin.

'We spoke Spanglish. He told me he does give water to his animals but at night. Never thought of hats – he said it was very English. I made him promise to keep the hats on and top up the water for daytime. I had to twist his arm but in the end he agreed. I gave him a big hug and I said I would do it till we left. We'll meet up at some point.' As an afterthought she added, 'The dog was OK too. Still barking a lot so I just topped the water up.'

'I'm sure he agreed because he liked you. What age was he?'

'Oh, old. About seventy. Bit battered-looking. All this sun, you know, and farmers don't bother with sunscreen.

That's not all though. Prem told me she'd had trouble with theft from her restaurant. Someone broke in and took food and wine. She doesn't leave cash overnight. She reported it and when the police came up, do you know what they said?' Pause.

'Oddly enough, no. Can't think why.'

'They said that if she ever caught someone and killed them, she'd drop them down one of those airshafts. The body would never be found.' Dramatic pause now.

'Very handy. Wish we had a few of those back home. I'd start a list of who to throw down. Now, I have news for you.'

She waited all agog, straight-backed on her bed but legs still akimbo.

'Louisa's son is Spanish and he's the one who was in charge when we found the body. El Capitan Edouardo Spelier-Bielby.'

'OMG! What a small world! I wonder how his comrades get on with his name? Perhaps they just say 'Sir'. Well, he may come in useful. Or at least having an intro to him might.'

'Any particular reason?'

'You never know. We do seem to run into problems on our trips.'

'What, all one and a half of them? Trips, I mean.' I added when she looked blank.

'Actually – I haven't told you everything.'

I raised my eyebrows questioningly.

'I went past the quarry. Not on purpose – it was on my route. I find it fascinating you know – '

'Me too. I want Uncle to take a look and see if it's feasible to turn some of the caverns into wine bars and shops.'

'I thought you mentioned it in passing after you phoned your Uncle. I didn't think you were serious.'

'Well – I am.'

Lea blew out her lips in a way that meant she thought it was indeed a big project, with more ifs and buts than I was prepared for. Possibly. She went on: 'Well, anyway. I stopped and looked down into the mine. Guess what I saw?'

'Lea!' I was exasperated by now. 'Get on with it!'

'A small boy running around, and there was an adult chasing him. The boy looked dark-skinned. Didn't really notice the man except he was medium-height and ordinary in everything. Hair, skin, clothes. Nondescript. It didn't look friendly. I could have been mistaken but I really don't think so. I am getting really worried now, Babs. Aren't you?'

'Yes, I am. But, mistaken in what? That you saw it or because it didn't look friendly?'

'Oh. Don't make hard work of it. Didn't look friendly, of course! The kid was caught and just sort of gave up. They headed into a tunnel. Not the one we were in, but nearby. I waited for a quarter of an hour and they didn't come back out. That's worth worrying about.'

'They could have come out somewhere else. I think it's a rabbit warren down there. Was there a car around?'

'No but a balloon was drifting overhead. One was on the ground too – on that flat bit where they set off on the top, towards the cliffs. For heaven's sake! Take it and me seriously, will you? And there was something else I saw –' She put a hand up to stop any sarcastic comment from me. 'I'll tell you. Some huge, beautiful birds floating around on the thermals.'

'Ah ha! Oddly enough I saw some too from our balcony and thought of you. Only thing was my thought that in your case they would be vultures.'

I couldn't stop myself giggling which brought an indignant, pointed stare in my direction.

'As it happens, I really like vultures, especially the babies. So cute. Just as well I like you too because I know you meant it as an insult. Let's be serious again, please!'

'Insult? Who me? Never. Hmm. Anyway, OK. Seriously, I really don't know what to think. We still have the disappearance of the under-manager to look into. Don't know how we start on that. Maybe he didn't like his job and quit without giving notice. Something and nothing. It happens. Can you remember if we were told if he left any personal possessions behind?'

'No. Can't remember. Who can we ask without it sounding odd?' The grey cells were positively noisy while the cogs and wheels went around.

'Maybe this is where we confide in Louisa and see what she recommends. See if it's worth mentioning to her son. The Double Barrellers seem a game lot, especially the Air Commodore. Louisa hinted she used to do a secret sort of job. One confidence deserves another,' I speculated.

'Yes, let's do it, and if we've read the situation completely wrongly, we can always ask that it's all forgotten. Swept under the carpet … I don't think we should make a big thing of it,' she went on, frowning. 'Spur of the moment sort of thing. Whenever. I also think we should go and look at the tunnels again, what with me seeing this kid and the nearby balloons. But this time we should go with Hans and Alvaro, like we said. If they're still up for it. I am sure Hans will, for me.' Lea smiled quietly to herself, I noticed.

I followed up with, 'I agree. We need to see Alvaro and find out when it's his next day off, or morning, or just when he can. If we wait for his next day off it will be a week and we will be into the next week here having achieved nothing except obtaining suspicions by the ton. Shall we go and find Alvaro and get lunch too? We seem to keep missing breakfast.'

'I'm up early enough for breakfast. It's you that's not. Not that it matters. We're on holiday – sort of. But, yes I'm ready to go now. Dressed for any eventuality and with spare things in my bag. Sensible shoes, sunscreen, some long thin trousers in case we need to be more respectably dressed, swimming cozzy. Artist sketch pad, pencils. We need the cold box though.'

She went to pack it with water bottles. Thank goodness she remembered the water or the list might have got longer. I glanced at her non-sensible glamorous, sparkling, colourful sandals. High-class label bought cheaply at one of her second-hand and dress agencies. She had long shorts on for going out today. Lesson learned, so I felt in tune for once. My shorts were better cut but somehow hers looked more stylish as usual. I was always telling myself that and comforted with the fact that I had a serious secure future. And good clothes. Her future was indecisive but somehow I knew she would be just fine. I must pack a day bag too – or should I just fudge through? My shoes were sturdy sandals.

'I'm ready too.' I wasn't but, hey ho, I could always come back to the room when we decided what we were doing next. We headed for the pool bar. No Alvaro. We were handed a menu by a smiley waitress so I asked where Alvaro was. Apparently in the buffet restaurant setting up lunch.

'I'll go and look,' I volunteered a bit too quickly.

'So – Gareth is out of the picture already? You are a fickle creature. Good job you're my friend or I could dislike your lack of loyalty.'

'Don't jump to conclusions, Lea. We're only having fun here. Besides, you're smouldering at Hans and you smoulder at my uncle when he's around. I might feel awkward with that – my uncle, I mean!'

'Babs, I 'smoulder', as you put it, at everyone but it's only because I'm an artist. I like to get a close look at their expressions and faces. I could 'smoulder' at Esme or Louisa but it doesn't make me lesbian.'

'Ok, Ok. Point taken. I'm still going to find Alvaro, so could you order me the mixed meat and fish pizza with anchovies extra?'

'Yuck!'

'Not to me.'

'Will do.' She waved a dismissive hand.

I found Alvaro bringing more dishes into the buffet bar. His face lit up the instant he saw me. I walked over to talk to him, also smiling – almost childishly. Was I being coy?

'Barbara, it was a lovely evening. Thank you again.'

'No problem. We all enjoyed it. Actually, I have another favour to ask. Lea and I want to go back into the mine and search some of the tunnels. We'd feel safer if we had company so, to suit you, could you come with us? Lea is going to ask Hans too. Someone should stay as lookout by the

143

cars after what happened.' I told him of Lea's sighting of the kid down there too.

'Very odd. Mostly the mine is deserted but some people are curious, so, yes! Of course I can come. With the under-manager disappearing, there are some strange things I can't quite understand I'm working a split shift today and can be free by 3pm till 7pm, or tomorrow I am off till the afternoon. Which would be best? I'll fit in with Hans. Let me know his free days and I'll work round it.'

'Brill. I'll let you know later. Thanks.'

'Brill? I know most words but 'brill'? Sounds like a type of fish!'

'Short for 'brilliant.' Wonderful. Indicates gratefulness.'

'Ah. Are you not eating here at the buffet?'

'No, we've just ordered at the pool bar. So nice under the palm trees. See you then.'

We gave each other a little wave. Back at the table Lea had ordered the fresh lemonade for us both.

'He's up for it. This afternoon or tomorrow morning. What about Hans?'

'I phoned him. He says any time. He doesn't have any specific appointments so he'll close the finca gates.'

'Well,' I considered. 'This afternoon, when it's siesta time. Tell him to meet us down in the mine just after 3pm. He can have his lunch then, and I'll run back and let Alvaro know. We can take him down there.'

While I'd been away, the food had arrived. Lea was eating her mixed fish salad. It looked appealing. I eyed up my overstuffed pizza and knew I was going to struggle.

'Shall we relax and swim after lunch?' With barely a pause she continued, 'I had a strange dream last night – or this morning. I found this cute, sticky, dripping monster, looking sorry for itself. I rescued it and washed it, but it was cross with me and went off in a huff, getting sticky again. Not all animals want my help.' She looked sad.

I ignored all this. 'Swim, relax. I think that's a good idea. Ready for any eventuality later.'

'I saw Karim skitting about. He always seems busy but I suppose, as they're a person down, he must be. You know, he can't be all bad. He has a dog.'

'What, here?'

'Not that I saw. But I noticed when he got out of his car this morning just as I was leaving – there were smears on the inside of the windows. Nose marks.'

'Humph.'

'So then, as I said, he isn't all bad.'

'Most people wouldn't agree but I think we'll leave this conversation alone. There are limits to your generosity of spirit.'

'Just saying. If Karim turns out to be mixed up in something bad – and apart from him being a bit smarmy we have no particular reason to think he is – I will have to try and find his dog now I know he has one.'

'Ask him about it. They do have rescue centres here, you know. You can't take another dog home, especially when it belongs to someone. You're presupposing Karim is guilty and that he'll go to prison.'

'I'll make sure the dog is found, that's all, and taken care of – if necessary.' She was adamant and I could see a determined look on her face, like the one she had had before when she'd rescued the lost puppy, Angelique, on our first trip. I knew when I was beaten. I dropped the subject.

'Can you eat some pizza? Too big for me.'

'One piece – maybe we can leave the rest for the cats that come and go. Or I can take it for the dog in the village. I'll get a doggie bag.'

So she did, signed for the food and we moved off to the pool. It was perfect after a big lunch. Quiet with a soft breeze, and gentle swimming helped us digest the food. Time flew. It was my turn to drive so I took the opportunity to grab a few things from our room and fling them in a bag. I rounded Alvaro up, who had a sandwich in his hand as he would miss staff lunch, and met Lea by Reception.

By the time we got to the mine we saw Hans's van parked up. We slid in next to him.

'All this space and you have to park right next to me. Mujeres!' He looked amused.

'Well, this 'woman' wants to go into the tunnel first. I told Hans about me seeing the kid here,' Lea addressed us, 'so I'm keen to follow it up. Now that I have a full tummy. Hans, shall we? I feel much more secure now there's male company around – and we're being sensible by doing this in twos. Two in, two out.'

He agreed without demur and off they set. Alvaro and I knew our place. I was happy with that and we fell into conversation.

'Do you have any particular ambitions?' I was curious.

'I want to own my own place one day. Then a chain of hotels. Why not aim high and see what happens. I'm in a good place to learn.'

He was matter-of-fact but it was said with, not amusement, but a certain lightness. He seemed serious, but my impression was of a person who would one day be successful – at something. I admired his determination. It seemed to have come without the stress that so often accompanies ambition. He obviously had plenty of ambition, however. I had to avoid saying too much about Uncle so we got onto speculations about the disappearance of the under-manager.

'What was – is – his name?' I couldn't remember if we had been told.

'Gerhardt Schmidt. German. We are very international in this place.'

'Indeed. It's a good thing, I think. Did he leave anything behind? Passport, driving license, clothes?' A perfect opportunity to ask questions without it seeming odd.

'When it became clear he was not around, I think Carl Wellington, our manager, found a few clothes – but no documentation. We don't know when exactly he, disappeared. He'd been off for a couple of days and then just didn't come back. We kept thinking he would phone in or turn up with an excuse. But he didn't, and this went on for a few days. Carl mentioned it to el capitan but hotel staff are known for flitting so really nothing serious has been done. He was a Spanish resident, so nothing much is known about any family in Germany. I think on his job application there is a next of kin but Carl didn't want to alarm anyone for no reason. He did phone former employers but came up with nothing.'

'I hope he's Ok. We can try and follow it up if you want. Or Carl wants? I suppose we should ask him first. What time did Lea and Hans go? Seems ages ago.'

'It is. About 45 minutes. Should we go in?'

'I'll see if I have a signal first.' I didn't. 'Well, if they come out a different way we could miss each other, then they won't know what to do. I think staying put for now is best. Lea and I were on a scuba dive in a quarry back in England and we had gone in some tunnels leaving another diver at the entrance who didn't want to go in. We were going to come back to the entrance wherever we came out but when we did, she wasn't there – so we came up. She wasn't on the surface either – or on land. It was an altitude dive so we couldn't go back down. We were worried sick. Do you know about diving?'

'Yes, I took some PADI lessons. What happened?'

'She had got lost in the tunnels and ran out of air. No idea why she would go in on her own. Awful. I wouldn't go in tunnels ever again.'

'We only did it the once for the experience. The route was marked but somehow the girl didn't see it. It was an eerie place. A hundred feet down to the water, down a sheer cliff, then a hundred feet of water to dive in. Again – dramatic sheer walls. She could see tunnels left over from the quarrying days, now filled with water, and a number of cars that had been shoved over the edge assuming no one would find them. The entrance was another tunnel that you walked through to the edge of the water. Spectacular dive but only in the sense of the logistics of getting in and out, and the awesome setting. If you looked over the top of the quarry, down about forty meters to the water, it was a grim sight. Made your stomach churn. No fencing, though eventually huge stones were put round the perimeter so cars couldn't be pushed over. '

'Here they are! You've been ages!'

Lea and Hans came out from a different tunnel. Their expressions were concerned.

Lea explained. 'We got a bit lost. So many twists and turns, though basically the tunnels are in straight lines. Just that one leads off another. I really think we need to tell Louisa's capitan about this and get him to look. Or at least ask Louisa. I told Hans about Louisa's son.'

Alvaro looked for clarification. Lea filled him in. 'One of the guests at the Club has Spanish residency as she lives here a lot of the time and used to be a full-time resident so brought her son up in Spain. He is now the local capitan. As it happens, Hans knows him but still it would maybe be best to go through Louisa first.'

'What do all you think? It's fairly easy to see in the tunnels. There are a lot of the air shafts so just as it gets a bit dark, another shaft appears. I don't know if the tunnels have wind or some natural sounds in them, but we thought we heard some sort of moaning, talking, humming – a combination. I even thought I heard a door open and shut. But I couldn't be sure. We tried to follow the sounds but they came from different directions. Or seemed to change directions. I thought I heard speaking or whispering.'

Lea paused for thought, then went on: 'Pretty certain anyway. There was creaking too, like things being opened. But maybe the tunnels have sounds from the rocks, air circulating. Heat makes things creak. I don't know but I – we – felt there were people in there. We didn't want to get any more lost than we were. It was more luck than judgment that we came out over there. We followed the best source of light to an entrance – or exit. I think we should all go and have a drink to cool off and discuss the next move. No need for you two to go in, unless you want to, but if you get lost too, remember Alvaro needs to get back for work. Our treat again,' Lea volunteered as an afterthought.

'Up to you, Alvaro. I'm happy to leave it for now and come another time. Until we can find our way around the tunnels or mark them out, it seems a bit pointless. So I vote for going to cool off.' I was firm.

'I agree. And I will buy the drinks. Hans has given us a meal, you and Lea bought another meal so it's my turn. How about the bodega with the barrels for tables at the back. That's nice and cool.'

Alvaro's offer was accepted very quickly.

We got in our cars and set off to plan our strategy in the bodega. I felt we could now add Gerhardt Schmidt to the list of things to investigate without raising suspicion as to why we should want to. I still had to keep Uncle out of it – for now. But I felt the time was coming to get him involved. I must phone him with an update.

We settled in the welcome cool of the bar amongst the coppers and brasses. Cold beers all round. We all downed them in one and set up another round. I went to phone Uncle with this update while the others decided upon follow-up action. When I got back they had moved on to other subjects so I thought I would surprise them with my news.

As usual Hans was sprawling his bottom on the front edge of his chair, legs stretched out in front, shoulders just touching the back. Relaxed to a fault, so I took heart: 'Hans, Alvaro. I haven't been quite truthful with you. Lea and I are here both on holiday and assessing the Club for the suitability of my uncle sending coach tours here, though they already come here. What I didn't tell you, only so we would get an unbiased view of things without people being specially nice to us, is that it's my uncle, Charles Madden, who owns the Club. He wanted us to stay secret but now he agrees we should come out in the open – only the information is for you two and Carl Wellington. No one else. I hope you will respect that?' I emphasised the last words and waited for the reaction.

The looks of amazement and smiles immediately made me feel good that the secret would be kept.

'Of course. My pleasure.' Hans was positively chuckling. His eyes were doing their sparkly thing. 'So your Uncle is the boss? The hefe? Will we meet him?'

'That brings me to the next bit. He is going to join us in a few days. He'll let me know asap. He was concerned about the disappearance of Gerhardt anyway. Someone sent him an anonymous letter. So now with all this other stuff he wants to be out here.'

Lea looked startled. No doubt her mind was buzzing. Hans versus Uncle Charles. Would they get on? Interesting. I had to smile to myself. She would be 'discussing' this with me later.

Alvaro was looking pleased but a bit nervous. 'I too have a confession to make. It was me that sent him the anonymous letter.'

'Alvaro! Wow. How cool!' squeaked Lea.

'Yes, well done!' I chipped in. 'We are truly in this together now. That's great! I mean it.' Alvaro looked relieved and happy. 'How did you find Uncle's address?'

'I didn't. I read that he is very hands-on and goes into the office a lot in London. The office address is not secret. So I took a chance and put addressed it 'personal'.'

'Well, I'm glad you did. Now, what plans have we?'

'We agree – if you do – that you and I, Babs, speak to Louisa on the QT asap.'

'QT asap? What is this?' Hans had a quizzical look.

'We will have a discreet – that's QT – talk with our fellow guest, Louisa, as soon as possible – that's asap– and ask her about involving her son, el capitan. Now, one more beer for the road and we should take you back, Alvaro. What are you going to do, Hans?'

'I must work this afternoon but we see us tomorrow maybe?'

'Yes. Let's do that. We may have news from Louisa by then. We'll phone you. Alvaro is free tomorrow morning so that's good.' We said our goodbyes and went back to the Club to try and find Louisa.

Lea was already thinking loudly about Hans and Uncle Charles.

I could hear the cogs turning.

CHAPTER TEN
Introductions and Progress

'The first thing I want to know is what you did with the pizza doggie bag?' We were back in our room on the balcony, which was still bathed in sunshine, so we were sat under the tree. Alvaro was back at work. I hoped Lea would forget to mention Uncle Charles coming over and meeting Hans.

'I left it for anything that may need feeding around here. When you brought the car around, I thought I saw a cat lurking so I threw it in the bushes. Satisfied?'

'Well at least it isn't going mouldy in your bag like the one I found on our last trip. It was disgusting. Nearly liquid.' The memory made me feel queasy. 'Don't you think throwing it in the bushes might encourage vermin?'

'No, because any starving animal will eat it too fast."

'No, don't bother. If I want to know, I can do it.'

I got up to have a nosy over the balcony. As luck would have it, Louisa was walking towards her block so I shouted down to her. She looked up and waved.

'Louisa – could you spare a few minutes please? We want to ask you something. Private.'

'Sure. Sounds intriguing. Shall I come up or will you come down?'

'We'll come down, Meet you in Reception. Find a quiet seat, will you?' She nodded and set off.

'Come on, Lea,' I said. 'Don't bother grabbing anything.'

Louisa was seated on a large, cream-coloured sofa surrounded by potted palms, It looked like a cosy, private space. What an impractical colour, I thought. I must point it out to Uncle Charles. Mental note to add it to the list which I was adding to regularly. We sat on two of the matching, fully-stuffed chairs opposite. The look was one of cool serenity with the cream and the green of the plants. Almost a shame to spoil it.

'Thank you, Louisa. Would you like a drink of any kind?'

'No thanks. I'm fine, but you go ahead.'

'Lea – do you want one?'

'No thanks.'

I breathed out in a big sigh. 'Where do we start?'

'How about saying we have some suspicions that some odd things are going on around here, potentially serious, and with your son being el capitan, we want your advice as to whether we should mention it to him.' Lea looked directly into Louisa's eyes.

'OK. What things?' She had taken this onslaught well, without blinking or shrinking. Head on, in fact. I admired her attitude. What was her background?

'Over to you Babs.'

'Thanks, Lea. You can help out if you want.'

'I just did. I introduced the subject.'

So I dived in. 'When we arrived, we thought we saw a man and dog in the big open mine which is nothing in itself. But now there've been developments. Out of pure curiosity, Lea and I, Alvaro the waiter here, and a guy called Hans from the village, went down there again. More than once.'

'I know Hans. Not well but I have seen him and of course my son knows him as they both live around here. I live about forty-five minutes away.'

'Oh, that's good. That you know Hans. Well, when we went down into the mine again, we went into one of the tunnels, and when we came out, a couple of tyres on Hans's and Alvaro's cars had been slashed. It was a shock.'

'I bet it was. I heard about that. Did you see anyone?' Louisa was concerned.

'No. It had been deserted. But Lea saw a man down there the other day and she thought he was chasing a little kid. Not in fun either.'

'Yes,' Lea chimed in. 'I got the impression the kid wasn't happy – but that far away, it was just that. An impression. Then the under-manager here, Gerhardt somebody, disappeared a few weeks ago without trace. All this just amounts to feelings, images, suspicions. But all four of us went back to the tunnels this morning. Hans and I went in again and definitely got the feeling that there are people in there. Noises, possible voices, doors opening or closing. Could just be tunnel noises, of course. That's why we want your advice. Don't want to waste anyone's time. But I can't emphasise enough how deadly serious we are at the same time. We are not time wasters.'

'Hmm. Can I think about it and get back to you? I don't doubt your concern. I have a nose for the truth.'

'Of course, but to lend it a bit more weight, I think I should tell you that it is my uncle who owns this club complex and he got an anonymous letter in the UK informing him about Gerhardt's disappearance. I have gone out of my way to keep all this quiet. I must bore people asking them to keep secrets. It's one reason why Lea and I are here – to investigate the disappearance. As it happens, Uncle is coming out soon and you should meet up. I would ask that whatever you decide – here I go again! – you don't tell anyone. By the way, it was Alvaro who sent the anonymous letter to my uncle. I'm playing things down.'

'Rest assured, I won't say anything. I can keep secrets. I have had practice.' She winked at us. 'Maybe I'll tell you another time.'

'Then there's Karim and the Gore-Marsdens, your fellow members of the Double Barrellers. They seemed very cosy with Karim on one occasion, and we do wonder about him too. Nothing specific. '

'I'll have a word with Edward – Edouardo – and let you know. It might be we need to delve into this more before he can get involved. I know he was informed about Gerhardt's disappearance but hotel staff – well – even ones with good jobs – have a tendency to up and leave.' She unfolded her elegant legs and stood to leave.

'What do you mean 'we' will have to delve into it more?' I asked.

She smiled enigmatically. 'We'll put our heads together when your uncle gets here. I want to ask permission to tell the Air Commodore about all this. It will go no further, I promise. Or let me know later.'

I thought quickly. It seemed like a good suggestion so I gave my permission.

Off she went.

'Phew – that went well,' exclaimed Lea. 'I'm off for a shower and then I want to study a bit.'

'Fine'

Alvaro was very accepting of our strategy and pleased to be included.

Lea went off. I rang Hans and told him too. We would wait for Uncle Charles. In the meantime – holiday mode.

'Oof. Well done then. I look forward to meeting your uncle – and do we see us tonight?' Hans asked.

'Fine by me. I think Alvaro is working so how about we meet in the village and wind up back at the Club? Maybe sit round the piano and talk to David?'

'Good. Ring me when you get back here. So – we will see us then.'

'Hasta luego, Hans.'

When I got back to the room Lea was under the tree on the balcony, all washed and shiny, in a silver floaty number, keeping cool. She had her high-heeled sandals on so she looked more tall and willowy in the gown, which draped itself around her, clinging here and there. It was partly diaphanous – with an underslip. I thought I would match it. We had a reputation for being constantly glamorous so we needed to keep it up. Didn't want to disappoint. We sat for a while and I told her about Hans. She was delighted about meeting up but a little quiet about him meeting Uncle Charles. In fact there was no comment at all.

'The only trouble with this tree are the insects that drop off it. I've had to shake my hair out twice in the last ten minutes. Think I might get my hat. I prefer the bougainvillea at the other end of the balcony."

'Yes, but it's more work for the housekeepers sweeping it. I'll get your hat. I'm off for my shower.' As I moved, I saw what she was studying and writing out. 'What on earth are you doing?'

'Spanish. What do you think? I've told you.'

'Yes – but don't you think you should start with some basics? Like, 'can I have', 'I want to buy', 'how much,' 'what size blah, blah'? I really don't think 'eviscerate', 'disseminate', 'nebulous', 'lugubrious', 'moribund' are going to be useful any time soon. Do you?'

'Well, 'moribund' might be. We might be confronted by death like we were on our last trip. And Karim, the bulldog often looks lugubrious – well, dismal anyway. And then we're eviscerated – short of essential things – like facts. Don't forget we need to disseminate our ideas about what might be going on to certain people, and anyway they are certainly nebulous so far – don't you think? Bit hazy, fuzzy, ill-defined ideas?'

I was stunned into silence.

'Well – I'm waiting.'

'I'm speechless. Can you say all that in Spanish and if you can, can you say 'I want' in Spanish too and form a sensible, everyday sentence?'

'Yes!' Triumphant look. 'And by the way I think Louisa is very perspicacious.'

'I agree she is very insightful and understanding but – I ask again – can you say 'I want' in Spanish and form a sensible sentence? Swallowing a dictionary can wait for your advanced Spanish. Besides, maybe you should – and this is only an idea – increase your English vocabulary.'

Well, that did it. She had a look of determination and stubbornness. I knew the look. She was not to be sidetracked from her mission. Once more I remembered the dog rescue on our first adventure.

'Right – just because I did Art at uni it doesn't mean I'm a dumbo at other things' Her chin jutted up and out. A demonstration of her Spanish followed: 'Por favor, me gustaria tres gramos de jamon Serrano y un kilo de naranjas. Gracias? Tienes un banco aqui? Que tan lejos caminar? En que direccion y en que calle? Quanto cuesta el jamon y las naranjas? Ta da! See! May not be perfect but I can do basic questions.'

'I'm impressed. Really. I mean it. Keep it up. Whatever you are doing is working. I'll get your hat then I'm off for my shower. Are you staying like that for the evening?'

'Yes. This outfit's easy to wear, and I can eat and breathe in it. My stomach can expand. Are we tapasing with Hans?'

'Whatever we want to do.'

She seemed to be thinking, then came out with 'I think dilemmas have a habit of solving themselves. Example – Hans meeting Uncle Charles.'

'It's not really a dilemma. It's just going to happen. They have no reason to dislike each other.'

'They are both lovely people, and, let's face it, neither of them is your boyfriend. Yet. Maybe never – so don't worry about it. We're young enough to find Mr Right.'

I left her musing on this point. Cool if not cold showers were always in order. Such a refreshing feeling after the heat of the day. I found a floaty outfit of my own and together we floated downstairs and across to the Pool Bar. We spotted Alvaro and asked if he could join us later.

'Only in the nightclub. The Piano Bar is out of bounds for staff.'

'That's OK. We'll find you in the nightclub later. About midnight or just after. Anyway, wait and we'll be there.'

We had our pre-drink drinks and settled by the pool. Louisa found us and sat down at our table.

'The balloon flights were wonderful. You must go. Now, girls, Listen. Since you mentioned balloons, I noticed something odd. I would never have thought about it twice but for all the odd things you described. One balloon had a family in it – at least I assume it was a family – of what looked like –

how can I put this – immigrants. About twenty. The baskets are all different sizes. They didn't seem excited like the rest of us. They were quiet, didn't take photos. Not acting like tourists somehow. Nothing conclusive. Same type of feelings that you describe. I don't remember them taking off with us either and they landed somewhere else. Could be that take-off and landing is from different parts depending how busy the flights are. I couldn't swear to it but in retrospect, I thought they came from the seaward direction. Whereas we went out over the sea. May all be to do with wind and being blown here and there. Or, an overactive imagination! What if – if there is some illegal immigration going on, and they are coming in from different directions to avoid a routine that can be followed. Maybe from the sea one day, and land another?'

I ruminated.

Lea spoke thoughtfully: 'They have to come from the seaward side at some point – unless they take a long journey entirely overland, which is more risky, even without borders now. As the EU changes, so will borders. The UK's left – who knows which country may leave next? I know some of the tunnels run right out to sea – or up to the sea. Maybe, there's a mix of boat landings and then some balloon flights to get them to other places, be it here or further afield.'

Louisa continued: 'I'll ask around about the owners of the boat-hire business. Edward might have some background knowledge, so I'll tell him all about you – if that's OK now?'

We concurred.

'And the Air Commodore is really very interested. Can't wait for some action. I told him he could live to regret it. At least I hope he lives to regret it. People smuggling is a ruthless business. Could be that the kid you saw, Lea, was being kept in the tunnels and tried to make a run for it.'

Now this was being discussed in the open it seemed to become more tangible – and worrying. A ruthless business indeed. We were all a little quiet, cogitating.

'Karim is involved in the boat hire. We know he works in it as well as here, which is why he seems harassed sometimes. I don't know if he is an owner or in the top management or just works on commission, passing people on from here. I'll ask Edward.' Louisa smiled and jumped up. 'Must go. Get changed, eat, drink, sleep. Don't do anything till I get back to you. Maybe your uncle will be here by then. In the meantime, enjoy your evening – and holiday. Adios amigas.'

'We also noticed Karim was – either uptight, busy, stressed – whatever.' We smiled our thanks.

'This is escalating into something, isn't it?' A sombre Lea stared after Louisa. I felt equally sombre. In a minute she snapped out of the mood. 'Come on. Let's meet Hans. I need food and more drink. Wine next. Spritzers. I'll drive then I can walk back as usual and check on my animals tomorrow.' She sprang up and I gulped the last of my G and T.

'Your legs are hollow when it comes to food and drink.'

'We know this. Handy, isn't it?'

'Expensive.'

'I'll do some more drawings to pay my way. Fear not, your uncle won't have to lash out too much for me but as I remember, I'm on the payroll now. Sort of. For a while.'

'You certainly are. And earning every euro. Vamos!'

'I'll drink to that.'

'What's that in Spanish?'

'Bebere pore eso. Yippee, we are on holiday now for a few days. Estamos de vacaciones por uno dias ahora – before it gets serious and it becomes dangerous.'

'Hmm. Yes, let's enjoy it. How are you speaking so well? I can't believe it's just from coming here.'

'Ah – it isn't. But you didn't ask, and I did need to buy a phrase book from the hotel shop. And a dictionary, so I wasn't lying. I've been studying for a while. Just fancied it as I always wanted to come to Spain. I'll never be fluent like you, but simple communication does me fine.'

'I'm going to have to watch you. I can't say something without you knowing what it is now – or at least guessing. No talking behind your back.'

'I should hope not. If you do I'll learn Polish – or Chinese.' We went for the car and set off to meet Hans for another fun evening.

I was just settling down in relaxing anticipation of our fun evening when Lea sniffed loudly and pointed. 'They really do have lots of crems over here. Look! That one's cooking today.'

I was jerked out my reverie. 'Did I just understand what you said? Do you have to be so totally revolting?'

"And did you know that when human flesh burns, it smells like pork cooking?'

Well, that did it. I poked her hard in her side and the car wobbled dangerously.

'Ok! Ok! I'll behave. But it's factual.' She was smirking.

Irritating woman – I really would have to learn not to react.

Oh, happy days!

CHAPTER ELEVEN
Uncle Charles Arrives – Plans are Afoot.

Uncle C. was coming. Yippee! I felt altogether relieved and happy.

We sat lounging on our balcony in the morning sun. Best time of the day. Still cool but sunny, so very pleasant. Lea stretched out, still holding her cup of tea. Bit precarious, I thought. I was remembering our trip to the tourist caves. A few days had slipped by waiting for Uncle. We had toned down the investigations and gone exploring in general.

In particular, we'd been on one of the official mines tours. We had been surrounded by spectacular colours and a series of mini lakes that were bright orange. Lots of space so it wasn't as claustrophobic as we had feared. Some tunnels narrowed, but then opened up again. An artist would have wondered how to portray it all without it looking false, so Lea hadn't done anything about it. We contented ourselves with taking photos instead to see how she could handle it later. We had been around the mining museum first, which was full of old photos and implements, with full mockups and information. A well-spent two hours even though we weren't aficionados of mining.

There had been about twenty-five people on the tour and by chance we met Simon, the man we'd rescued from drowning. He was with his wife this time. Lea and I glanced at each other but said nothing. We try not to judge but sometimes can't help it. Simon was fortyish, very fit-looking, slim and handsome. His wife had a pretty face, but she could only be described as obese. She didn't walk – she half-waddled, half-shuffled. They were totally incongruous. Her bosom – it could only be described as such as it was amply impressive – was encased in a bra that made her breasts stick out in an amazing way. Madonna, eat your heart out!

We observed the couple, hoping we weren't staring. Suddenly they saw us and came over, all smiles. We greeted them, warmly chatting while we waited to go in the mine – the dinner he had treated us to – his wife hadn't been well on the night – Spain, tours, what to see etc. We all went forward, slowly getting separated.

'I'm going to follow the gun turrets,' Lea announced. I wondered why and supposed I would find out in due course. I was too hot to bother or argue. Towards the end of the tour, she engineered getting close to them again and we ended up outside together. A café was near the entrance, so Lea suggested us all going for a drink as it had been thirsty work. We settled in a shady place, agreeing to pay separately. Idle chat followed. With hindsight I saw how Lea subtly steered the conversation round to relationships. In retrospect I am full of admiration.

'Can I ask you guys a question? It's not rude. Being an artist, I like to study things. Many things, not just art.'

Curiosity flitted across their faces with immediate consent.

'So – after facing death, Simon, how do you and Liz approach life now?'

'Full of crystals.' Not the answer we expected. He smiled. 'I was pumped full of drugs and was seeing all manner of colourful crystals. So pretty. Liz asked me how my ankle was – it seems I'd cracked it. Apparently I said 'Crystals don't have ankles.' I'd thought I was making perfect sense.'

Liz laughed. 'You know I've seen so many TV reality programmes where people say that life-threatening events have changed their perspective on life and just thought, yeah, yeah. But …' Liz paused. 'Simon's accident made me think. Now I've decided you have to do all you can to grab life, enjoy it, make the most of everything, do your best in every situation – and think of others too. She paused again and looked down, 'For instance, I know Simon thinks I'm very overweight.'

Simon's surprise was obvious, and he started to speak. Liz cut him off. 'You've never said but I know you don't fancy me anymore. Yes, I know you still love me! Oh goodness – we can discuss this later - just that for ages I've been wondering how to bring this up so – thank you, Lea for giving me the chance! I won't embarrass you all, don't worry, but I want to say I'm going to do something about my weight for the sake of my health, and for you and the kids. After I had them, I took everything for granted. I had my husband and family. I stopped being an individual. I've booked into a clinic for when we get back. I'm paying for it from my own money. This is important. Now you can say something!'

Simon was silent for a moment. He seemed stunned. 'I'm not sure what to say, Liz. I'm full of admiration. Yes, I do love you. Always have. And you've such a lovely face. You'll blossom again., I know it. I'm so proud of what you've just said. So proud of you for what you're going to do. So out of the blue.'

He leaned across the gap and put his hand on her arm looking into her eyes, his own full of love. 'I must drown more often!' He smiled broadly. 'You've surprised me in a wonderful way. Girls – you've unwittingly performed a miracle. I have to be honest, I've been wondering all holiday how to broach the subject of Liz losing weight. Our son came back from school one day. He was very quiet. Long story short – kids had been teasing him that we were both fat, Liz more so. Sorry, Liz. I made the effort and lost weight, but you didn't – for many good reasons, I know. Being a busy mum is hard and I was away at work a lot. My fault. I suppose I was pleased to get away. So, I've got my faults too – need to work on them. Need to realise it's wonderful to have a home and family to come back to.' He ground to a halt.

Liz looked all teary and said she must go to the servicios to mop her eyes.

When she was out of earshot, Simon confided: 'I think we've got to know each other a bit over the dinner. I really meant it when I said this is a miracle for me. To be blunt, while I love Liz, I've been looking for fun elsewhere. It's been a dilemma of monumental proportions as I'm not a person who takes such things lightly – unlike like many – men and women both.'

'I suppose it's like having steak at home,' Lea said earnestly, 'but every once in a while a person wants a burger. But if you don't want to stray and like having scrambled egg for breakfast every day you need to vary it – and it is possible – without being unfaithful, and if you both consent, you can add to scrambled eggs. Just a thought. You know – try different things. Poached, for example. Am I teaching my grandmother to suck eggs?'

'You would have to use a food analogy, wouldn't you, Lea! I apologise on her behalf, Simon. She's food-obsessed.'

Simon was half laughing. 'I agree. Since you mention it – and please don't repeat this – we went to a sex swap club to try to liven things up. It was full of black-leather-clad men, and women with whips sitting around looking bored to death. When we came in basically normal and Liz with floaty lingerie on to hide her figure, they fell over themselves to engage with us. We stayed a couple of hours drinking and talking, and left with a little more knowledge of what goes on than when we had arrived. We put it down to experience. Anyway, she's on her way back.' He winked conspiratorially.

We chatted on in general and parted good friends in a strange way. I asked Lea if she'd steered the conversation deliberately.

'Well, I sensed something amiss between them. You know I'm a bit psychic. I really do want to help people if I can. I could see Liz used to be so attractive and then that she'd let herself go. I hope I really did help.'

I concurred and we left it at that.

Lea ran to the loo again, I noticed. She had taken to going at every opportunity.

'Have you got a bladder-leak problem? Ought you buy some of those extra thin, protective invisible pads they advertise on TV? Turns it to gel.'

'Babs!' Indignant squeak. 'I'm not old yet and I haven't had a baby. I just like to be sure I'm not miles away from safety if we get caught in a tunnel, cave or in a broken-down lift with murderers, muggers, rapists et al.'

'You mean if the lift didn't have murderers or muggers in it, it would be all right?'

'Now who's being a pedant. You know perfectly well what I meant. Humph! Tell you what – if you get a tummy bug and have to run to the loo a lot, I recommend you buy some extra absorbent nappies. You're not getting any sympathy from me. And you can make your own tea in future!'

Our next jaunt had been the balloon flight. It was fun being involved in helping to set up the equipment. There was so much to do what with securing the basket with all the ropes and weights, and watching the balloon fill, bit by bit. We were in a party of ten and there still seemed plenty of room.

The views were spectacular, the sea sparkled and though we were high above the ground, it was near enough to see people and ground activity. Everyone waved a lot. The sound of the balloon being periodically inflated with air made people look upwards. We knew from having watched from the ground ourselves what a grand sight it must have been, with several balloons floating around in the sky together, all with different colours and forming so many different patterns. Our forebodings seemed to vanish, although I did wonder if this was just the calm before the storm.

The balloon floated, drifted and swayed. We all ooed and aahed at the scenery, enjoying drinks and snacks. The descent and landing came about a little more rapidly than we had bargained for. It was a little like being in a plane when the pilot announces the approach to the airport and warns that the descent could be a bit bumpy due to the prevailing, following, side winds – or whatever the excuse happens to be. Here, we were told to strap in and hold on for dear life, expect a bumpy landing, and pray. Well, it wasn't that bad but the landing was indeed bumpy, and the balloon half tipped over before righting itself, jolting us back and forth.

We suddenly became best friends with all the others as we squealed, laughed, and put on a brave face – stiff-upper-lip Brits all together. Relief and smiles all round. Congratulations to the pilot!

The ground team with the following vehicles were there snapping into action. Holiday fun? Yes, of course. Lea sneaked in a comment about a huge commercial roll of tissue or toilet paper sat in the basket being for the people who needed to clean up after the landing. Fresh underpants not included. We found it was for general purpose use for oily bits and spilled drinks n' stuff. What oily bits?

Now here we were, sitting on the balcony, happily reminiscing.

'The last few days have gone so fast. A blur of sun, sea, sand and sangria. Well, G and T's and wine. And that was a fabulous, thank-you dinner meal Simon bought for us. Nice to have caught up with Liz as well when we were in the mine. And sorted their lives out – by accident. Made a change from Hans and Alvaro – much though I love their company. Do you know, we've been here eight days now. Or nine or is it ten? Never mind. Oh – and that hoary old guy was a laugh.'

'Tautology.'

'Um?'

'Hoary and old. I see you've been at the dictionary again. 'Hoary' means – '

'Yes, yes. I know and I have. Well, I'm egressing out of here.'

I fell about laughing. 'You can't just slap words like that any old where. Sounds odd. Besides, where are you egressing to? Without me, may I ask? '

'Hang on – am I wrong in what I'm saying?' She was beginning to look a bit aggrieved.

'No and yes. It's not how people would speak in an everyday situation.' I was still chuckling to myself but keeping it under control now. Almost. Shoulders still shaking a tad. Silent laughing.

'So if I said I thought someone was perfidious would you say it was wrong?'

'No. But – well the sentence has to flow for the right reasons. You have to have big or posh words in the right context. Not much good saying 'I'm egressing down the takeaway for a greasy kebab or burger.' See what I mean? Anyway, who do you think is perfidious?'

'Karim – but I could be mistaken. The more I speak to him the more I think he has another agenda apart from this complex.'

'He does. The boat-hire business. We know that. And where are you going?'

'To the dress shop here in the hotel and to clean the car. They had some new outfits in yesterday. Are you coming?'

'Yes, I'll have a look. You don't buy from places like that. You aren't becoming posh, are you?'

'Rhetorical. See you down there. I need to change. It's OK for you – you get up early.'

I was down in record time and found her huddled in a corner of the shop listening intently to Louisa.

'Anything afoot.' I enquired.

Louisa looked around and smiled encouragingly, getting me into the huddle.

'I've talked to my son, Edouardo – Edward – and he's taking it seriously. He thinks something is going on as he's heard rumours himself - on the QT. We mustn't talk carelessly. Also – I have asked some unofficial favours from ex-colleagues. 'Now –' she blew her cheeks out, 'I'm ex Interpol. If one can ever be 'ex' from that institution. We dealt with a lot of smuggling of all sorts. People and art and stuff. Different departments, but not surprisingly they often crossed over. My fellow holiday pals don't know and mustn't – apart from the Air Commodore. We go back a very long way.' She smiled, almost to herself.

'Of course. Whatever you say. How do you know we're trustworthy. We are, of course.'

'I know you are.' This time the smile was sweet, and she looked at us directly, almost piercingly. Lea and I looked at each other. We got the feeling we 'd been checked out. Telepathy is a wonderful thing. Not for us to complain if we were to get help. My concern was having the mission taken away from us, leaving it all to the professionals. I still had things to prove, both to Uncle and myself.

'Well – this all a bit serendipitous'

'You're doing it again.'

'This is a happy, beneficial development for us, don't you think, Babs?'

'Yes, but just think. We may end up in a titular position with all these proper experts around. What we started might not be ours in the end.' Lea had a rather blank expression. I could see 'titular' whirling around. She said nothing, then suddenly came out with 'You mean some esoteric people might take over?' She looked first at me, then Louisa enquiringly.

Louisa wore a puzzled expression.

'Er, yes. Sort of,' I tried to keep a straight face but my shoulders were at it again. 'Some people with specialist knowledge might just have the edge on us.'

'Well,' Lea said, 'I was reading about drug trafficking amongst other things, and found that a lot of cocaine entered the EU through Spain after Gib. Helen mentioned that too. There's the so-called Galician Mafia and there were 364 murders in 2012. Iran smuggles things into Serbia, then to France, and then from France to the UK. I wonder if we could extrapolate?'

Extrapolate? Louisa and I were rather bemused!

'I really don't know what to say, Lea,' commented Louisa. 'We'll all do our best, I know that, and we'll all stay in touch. You girls must be careful. I understand how curious and enthusiastic you are, but if all this really is going on, it's dangerous and you're, dare I say it, civilians. Please don't do anything from now on without telling me – or leaving a message to pass on. This is my very private mobile number.

Give it to Hans and Alvaro. Oh, and your uncle too. He arrives today, doesn't he?'

'Yes, we're meeting Uncle this afternoon at the airport. After that I don't see how we can keep it secret that we're related, or at least good friends. Or something.'

'Up to you. I don't suppose it'll matter. You've a good idea of how things run here. I'm looking forward to meeting him. Let me know when it's convenient.' She got up. 'I must get on now. I'm off with the rest of the Double Barrellers to terrorize some of the natives over a lunch. It's a long drive to a fabulous restaurant I know, so we're setting off early to enjoy the scenery. I must get them going. It's like trying to round up a herd of cats. Enjoy your day. 'Bye 'Thanks for everything. See you, Louisa. Tell us about the restaurant later.'

I relaxed. 'Now, to serious matters. Retail therapy. Which outfits have you got your eyes on?'

'Hmm. Lots. I still love my street market and second-hand shops. I won't be deserting them, but this is foreign fashion and there are labels I've never seen or heard of. It's exciting! Let's do some browsing.'

We spent the next half hour happily trying on various dresses. Several purchases later we tripped in for breakfast, bulging with parcels. Oh, the joy! After the leisurely feast there wasn't much time before we had to get ready to pick up Uncle Charles.

There seemed to be a lot of sand both in and on the car as we started to declutter it.

One of the beaches we had been going to had parking under some palm-thatched roofs but the track to it was all sand. I smiled at a memory from a few days earlier. The beach had been divided into sections. There was one section for everyone, one for topless and the final furthest bit for nudists. We had compromised and gone for the middle section. The fact that you could see each section from the other one was apparently irrelevant.

We had just settled on our beach towels, having found the perfect spot with sun and shade not too far from the sea when a man had come jogging along from the nudist section. He had a fine, suntanned body. All over. What did take our attention was the bouncing action of his nether region. Eye-watering – at least for us but it didn't seem to bother him. We admired the view for some minutes as it took a while to arrive and pass by. Deep joy. We had smiled for quite a while and were blessed with a return passing.

Lea must have remembered this incident as well, because all of a sudden, out of the blue, she said, 'I do love 'The Last Night of the Proms'.'

'What brought that on?' I sighed. This was Lea after all.

'I suddenly thought how bucolic it was that day on the beach. Just popped into my head. That and the – er – jogging guy.'

'Well, it can just pop out again. Please will you stop using these words out of context. It means relating to pleasant aspects of country and life, not to men's bits bouncing up and down.'

'Oh – OK.' She sounded so disappointed. 'I thought I was doing well. I am relating all this to Spanish you know.'

'It's advanced stuff. You're doing well with basics. Stick to that. Honestly. Do yourself a favour.'

She breathed deeply. In and out – a big, long sigh. I wondered what was coming but all she said was, 'Shall we go now? Nothing else to do. We can have a drink at the airport and plane- watch.'

'Suits me. Vamos, mi amiga!' I felt a bit sorry to deflate her happiness.

I suddenly felt a rush of pleasure, knowing Uncle Charles was coming. It felt homely. My family – my beloved uncle – was coming to help me. I'd had so many issues to deal with when I was growing up. It was thanks to Uncle that there was stability in my life now. Feeling warm inside, I looked at Lea, wondering exactly how differently she viewed him.

The airport was crowded and the plane was late. It was the height of the tourist season with myriads of people all milling around. There was nothing to do except watch and wait. Two coffees later we suddenly spotted Karim and the Gore-Marsdens together. They too seemed to be waiting.

We made ourselves scarce, hiding behind one of the obligatory small palms that seemed to be all over southern Spain. As we waited, we saw who they were meeting. It was a dark-skinned man wearing typical flowing Arab garb. They shook hands though we noticed Karim didn't seem to be included in this. A curt nod was all he got. We watched them leave the building then noticed the UK flight was due to land. About time.

Finally, we saw Uncle Charles approaching the gate. Immediate eye lock and smiles. Lea hung back a bit while Uncle dropped his bag and we had a big hug. Disentangling, he moved on to Lea and she got the same bear hug. She was so genuinely delighted I couldn't for one moment resent it. We were all happy to be together.

'The car's this way.' We moved off, Uncle pulling his own bag amongst protests.

'How is Angelique?' Lea enquired after the dog she had rescued.

'Happy and well taken care of. I have a friend who has taken her for however long we need her to. She's grown. I can't believe the size she is now. Amazing. She's good at 'Sit, stay, come here, stop, no!' We say 'no' a lot.'

'That's puppies for you.'

'She's a big puppy now and she's developed a habit of getting up on the garden balcony wall and putting her paws up on the top of the railings to peer over. Gives me the shudders to think she might decide to jump over out of curiosity, so I've had the railing raised. Plunging eight storeys isn't an option. '

'Bet that cost a bit. Should I be contributing?'

'Lea, it's a pleasure. You did me a great favour letting me keep her. I've always wanted a pet but never seemed to have the time. Barbara seemed to take up a lot of my time. Can't think why.' He winked at me fondly. 'Now she's flown the nest I have my new girl installed.'

We arrived at the car.

'We have a lot of catching up to do, Uncle. Lea will drive while I talk. You sit in the front.' 'RHIP.' Lea replied.

'What?'

'Rank has its privileges, Babs.'

We pulled out into the traffic, heading south, following the busy coast road. All manner of resorts were strung along the route. Towns, villages, urbanizations, shopping malls – one seemed to merge into another. Sprawling urbanity. Not particularly pretty but if you turned off into the various towns it was often much nicer. There would be a traditional old part and as this was being a coastal route, there would be an attractive harbour of some sort, big or small. We had pulled up in a few of these on our holiday, spending pleasant lunch times in small restaurants, all with magnificent choices of fresh-caught fish. Sometimes modern, square, concrete blocks had grown up around these delightful old buildings. It was called progress.

'I'll give you the few facts we have, then our thoughts and suppositions. Or should I do it the other way around?'

'Summarize it, Babs!' snapped Lea.

'Right. Here goes. We haven't got anywhere with the under-manager's disappearance, Gerhardt Schmidt. Our friend Hans knew him a bit but nothing of his family. We should have asked Carl Wellington, your manager, but at first we weren't in a position to ask questions like that, what with being incognito. It'll be easier now if we can come out into the open. We wonder if our latest contact, Louisa, whose son Edward is el capitan in this area, could follow that up. Maybe he has already. We need to check up on that. I've filled you in on most of these things already but some oddments may have been left out. Stop me if I'm repeating myself.'

'No! Carry on, Barbara! It's good to be reminded anyway.'

'The mine then. We've seen and heard strange things in it. A man and an unhappy kid – slashed tyres. We've been in the tunnels – or Lea has. She thought she heard voices, doors opening and closing. I have yet to get in them properly. I only got into the beginning of one. The one I thought would make a great bar restaurant.' I was pleased to get that idea in.

'Hmm. We'll have to see about that. You can take me down there, girls. I've made a few preliminary enquiries and get a feeling lots of money needs to change hands to get such projects off the ground. As in bribery. I spoke with the local mayor after you mentioned it all, Barbara. His English is good even if his manner is – hmm. Not committing myself on this.'

'I think we should spread it around that we are going to have a look around with a view to this possible project and see if there is any reaction. We should let Karin hear about it, and the Gore-Marsdens, and then just generally spread it around.'

'Sounds like a plan, Lea.' You need to point these people out to me. I didn't meet Karim when I came over to check out La Roca.' Uncle winked at Lea and immediately I wished I'd thought of that idea.

'Of course, and Louisa and her son Edward. We'll arrange a meeting for the Big Guns.' I smiled.

'Don't forget the balloons, the people trafficking, sex slaves, slaves of any kind. You know the usual kind of thing.' Big prompt from Lea.

'Whoa. You seem to have moved on. When did all these suppositions make an appearance. You didn't mention these, Barbara!'

'Agh! No, I didn't, Uncle. It's been quite a process. We thought maybe this was all in our imaginations. We've only just talked about it all with Louisa, who was going to run it past her son. They're keen to meet you. Hans and Alvaro too. Did I mention it was Alvaro who sent the anonymous letter about Gerhardt?'

Before Uncle answered there was a sort of shriek from Lea. 'Look!' She was pointing and looking to her left on the roadside. 'It's the kid with that man again. The ones I saw in the mine. The kid still doesn't look happy.'

She was slowing down and came to a halt some way off from them. They were in front of us, getting out of a car slightly to the side of a building. I hastily wrote the registration number down in my phone notebook. 'They can't be heading there – can they?'

'It's the only place round here. Where else can they be going?' It was a club, one of the many legal brothels. The man had a quick look round and then ducked through a door with the boy.

'OMG. I don't believe it. Well, I do. I've just seen it.' We were all silent. The first 'proof' we had come across.

We sat there, then Lea continued with a thoughtful look on her face. 'I think I've an idea. I'll think about it and tell you when we get back. I need to look some things up first.'

The rest of the journey went by without incident and we chatted in general.

Uncle Charles had become serious. 'I told Carl you were picking me up and who you are. Obviously when I said I was coming over he wanted to meet me – or send a car. We discussed the missing under-manager, Gerhardt. We'll follow it up at some point. So, to answer an earlier question, Barbara, yes, you are out in the open now. I don't know if it'll work for or against us all. But we couldn't have kept meeting in secret, so – onwards and upwards!'

We arrived at the Club, and unloaded Uncle and his luggage before Lea went to park. Uncle made himself known at Reception. Hurriedly Carl was sought out and while we waited for him, Karim came over, presumably having arrived back before us. He introduced himself with good grace and not too much unctuousness for once. Carl had informed him of the visit, which was only reasonable.

My phone rang and it was Lea. 'Babs, I'm going for a drive while you all get acquainted. Thought I would clear my head and pop up onto the mountain road. Won't be too long.'

'Fine. See you then.' I was a little surprised but I wasn't her keeper. Carl appeared with greetings all round. We adjourned to his office.

'Mr Madden – your room will be ready in about half an hour. Some minor repairs had to be done on the plumbing so it is being cleaned up. Would you both like some refreshments or to go to the restaurant for something? I thought Miss Dunbar was going to be with you?'

'She phoned me to say she was going for a drive into the mountains to clear her mind. It's not far so she'll join us in a bit.'

Both men nodded. Not much else they could do. 'She might come across some rain up there today. Even hail. It happens sometimes. You can see the clouds gathering. In the same way as Gibraltar is often wrapped in mist or fog though it's not high – only about four hundred and twenty and a bit meters. I'm not quite sure why it has a microclimate. Partly its position in the isthmus and the Levant wind that blows. Sometimes it creates a cloud.'

We peered through the office window to see brilliant sun down by us and a cloud bank high up.

'Well, she'll find out. We had lots of coffee while we were waiting for you, Uncle, but you go ahead with whatever you want.'

'Water would be good. Thank you.' Carl had a water cooler installed so poured two plastic cups for himself and Uncle.

'I told you some things over the phone, Carl, but according to my niece here, things have moved on a bit. As yet, unfortunately, nothing on Gerhardt but it's possible there's another serious problem. Unconnected as far as we know. People trafficking. Would you like to fill in the details, Barbara?'

I did. Carl listened silently, a look of muted, dawning horror.

'This is awful. You expect this sort of thing in the cities but not in a quiet area like this.'

'Perhaps that's exactly why this area has been chosen, to see how well it works round here. How well it can be hidden. The mines are a mysterious rabbit warren with both land and sea approaches,' I pointed out.

'This is something that should be reported to the police.' Carl was firm. 'It's not something we can deal with.'

'I agree.' From Uncle. I went into defence mode, explaining why we – at least Lea, me, Hans and Alvaro – should get involved. We were unknown, could pry without attracting attention and pass on relevant information to the police when we had it. Amateur sleuthing was alive and well. It was falling on deaf ears. I was losing the argument in the face of the possible dangers in a very nasty, violent business. And it was a business. A seriously lucrative one.

We agreed to disagree and Uncle was taken to his suite. One of the best inside the hotel. I vaguely pointed out our block when we passed Reception. Plus all the potted palms. Uncle's suite was on the second floor with a large lounge area, huge balcony bigger than ours, and 'his and hers' basins in the bathroom. The bathroom itself was decorated with gold leaf (which I found rather ostentatious) and there was enough space in it to house a double bed. The whole effect was bordering on vulgar. According to me. Uncle had a funny look on his face too.

'Barbara, remind me to get some decorating done will you. About time there was a bit of a makeover in some of the rooms.'

Just then Lea rang me. She wanted to know if we could all meet up as she had Hans and Louisa in tow. Hans's finca was closed for the afternoon and Louisa was back from lunch. I hadn't realized it was so late. We agreed to meet by the palm trees near one corner of the pool as they gave both shade and privacy.

'Third palm on the left' I joked. 'By the way, I hear you got caught in some rain in the mountains. Where were you?'

'In the car.'

'Where in the car?'

'In the driver's seat.'

My smile over the phone got a little thinner. 'Where was the car when you got caught in the rain?'

'Oh, I thought it was odd you wanted to know where I was sitting.' Big sigh from me. 'I was parked in the village at the top of the mountain,' she went on unperturbed. 'Er –

what's it called? Anyway, I got a good signal there and I've formulated a plan. I think. I did some googling.'

'Formulated – hmm – I'll let that one pass. It's a normal word. Just not usually associated with you. Or planning either.'

'I take umbrage at that.'

'Take what you like but we have some opposition to us being involved. Especially Carl who thinks it should go straight to the police.'

'Just as well I've got Louisa on our side then. See you in a mo – or several.'

We arrived in dribs and drabs by the third palm on the left. Uncle and I got there first, then Louisa, who was charmed with Uncle and charming herself, then Hans and Lea. Uncle and Hans's eyes met head on. They stood and shook hands in a positive, friendly way, smiling. No reason why it should be otherwise, of course. I had arranged chairs, wondering if Carl was invited as I had forgotten to ask Lea about his inclusion. I mentioned it now.

'I think leave it for now. He has a responsibility to all his guests. Alvaro is joining us though. I hope you don't mind, Charles? He's off duty at the moment.'

Lea was sat between Uncle and Hans and she wriggled around in her chair, tugging down her dress that had ridden up when she sat. I saw Uncle and Hans notice this and look at each other with a mutual pleasure and appreciation of their 'find'. They smiled knowingly at each other. It reminded me of the two guys who had dropped Lea off at the airport on our first trip who both clearly adored her and seemed to think they had invented her.

Alvaro arrived and took the last chair. I introduced Uncle and explained that he now knew it was Alvaro who had sent the anonymous letter about Gerhardt.

Alvaro looked a little uneasy but Uncle jumped in. 'I am so glad to meet you, Alvaro. It's been a mystery that I am pleased to have solved. It's good to hear you – and Hans for that matter – have been so helpful to my favourite girls. I do worry about them sometimes. Though it is partly my fault for sending them on missions.'

'My pleasure, Senor Madden. They are good company. The best.'

'Please call me Charles!' Pause. 'Well Lea, I hear you have a plan, so over to you. I am concerned about safety for everyone but let's see what you have to say.'

She gulped, suddenly being the centre of attention. We all stared at her waiting.

'Ok, bull by the horns. I'll tell you why afterwards. Louisa agrees with me and I can now say with her permission that she is ex-Interpol. As you also know, her son is el capitan in this area. If you didn't know, then you do now. This is all between us. Not even Carl knows just yet. A need-to-know basis.' She looked round but no-one said anything, whatever they may have been thinking. Not even a raised eyebrow. Stiff-upper-British-Spanish-German lip.'

'Right. I think Charles and Hans should go into the brothel where we saw the kid and the man this morning, posing as clients. It will need several visits to gain the confidence of the owner or manager to be able to ask for an underage boy – and maybe also for an underage girl. In a nutshell.'

She stopped and waited for a reaction.

Hans obviously knew some of her plan but he uttered an 'Oof!'

It came as a big surprise to Uncle, who looked stunned. He didn't respond right away.

Louisa jumped in. 'It's a huge thing to ask of anyone. Lea did some research which she'll tell you about in a minute, and she's done some soul-searching before she put this plan together. Hence the mountain trip. She talked to me about it. I've been personally involved in similar undercover work so I do know the dangers fully. But I also know the advantages of having two people like you, Charles and Hans, doing some research. Invaluable even, because of who you are. That is what it is – research – and when it gets to the point of contact I will be involving my son. I don't want to tell him at first because he would have to stop us, or try. So, I will decide when to tell him. Of course, he may be angry, but I have the trump card. I'm his mother.' Big chuckle. 'Plus, even he doesn't know for sure if I'm still working.' She had a sly look and winked, not for the first time I noted.' Over to you, Lea.'

Uncle interrupted before Lea could carry on. 'I must say I have been a bit dumbstruck. But – I can see where this is coming from. Hans, what do you say? I take it you knew Lea's plan?'

'Only partly, since she just phoned me this afternoon, but I am in agreement. I will do it. What about you?'

There's positive for you, I thought. He must be besotted.

'Let's hear the rest.'

'Babs, sorry – I literally didn't have time to let you know anything. I was so busy getting Hans and Louisa and Alvaro together. And getting back here. I did think you would approve though.' Ingratiating smile.

'I did wonder, but never mind. And I do approve so you'd better give it your best shot to convince Uncle.' I gave her a 'balls back in your court' smile.

'First, Charles, you will be known by some and easily verifiable to others. They may be suspicious about you owning this club. They would wonder why you would put yourself out on a limb in your circumstances unless you really wanted some discreet and unlawful sex. It could give them ideas of blackmail but I think when Louisa has sorted things out with Edward, that suspicion will evaporate. Same goes for Hans. He's known locally. Of course, you'll have to play naive, only hinting who you are, or better still letting someone else drop you in it. That's where you come in, Alvaro. You can legitimately go into the club, see them going in or out, or whatever, and over a few drinks let it be known who they are. You only need to ask for normal sex, which here in Spain is so accepted it would never in a million years be blackmailable.'

'Except I don't like sex clubs and don't want to ask for sex. Thank you. Any kind.'

'I know my explanation was a bit hurried but I did say you don't have to do anything except drink and talk. Just a 'do you know who that client of yours is? type thing. Not overdone.'

'Yes. You did say that. And if that's the case, count me in.'

Phew. Lea's idea was winning ground here.

'I still want to hear anything else you have to say, Lea,' said Uncle Charles, 'but in view of Hans and Alvaro putting their hands up for it, I will too. My goodness, what I do for my girls. Go to brothels, put high railings up costing well – quite a lot.'

'What is putting hands up with railings?' Hans enquired. 'I am learning such a lot more English these days since your girls came here.'

' 'Putting your hands up' is an expression. Like in school, you put your hands up to answer a question, but if you are asked to volunteer, you also put your hand up, or you admit to something you hadn't expected to. And as for railings – Uncle has a new dog that is very inquisitive and she is in a penthouse with a big garden and likes to jump up to see over the edge looking several storeys down. So he put high fencing around to stop her falling or jumping over.'

Another 'Oof' came.

'Now people, can I go on?' Lea looked to her phone. 'I made some notes from my research. You can probably see I'm passionate about helping underdogs. It was a shock to see the little kid today. I'm sure he's being trafficked. So – anyone wants a drink before I start?'

I was impressed by her sincerity which was expanding to encompass humans as well as animals. I was also formulating an idea of my own. We ordered drinks and chatted while I got busy thinking.

Hans asked what an underdog was as opposed to an overdog, or just a dog. Did underdog mean it was under another dog for some reason or over, as in mating? Lea explained in some detail about an underdog – a poor dog, most likely human, who didn't have the privileges of others, so he – or it – was 'under' rather than – er – um– 'over', followed by more flailing around for words, leaving Hans more befuddled than before. □

CHAPTER TWELVE
Action and Adventure

The drinks arrived and Lea went on, 'Are we sitting comfortably? Then I'll begin.' She launched into her research with sweeping enthusiasm. We were fascinated.

'The sex industry is huge. At least it's now under review. That way the sinister aspects of it can be controlled to some extent. In the Netherlands it's strictly regulated, but it's not here. It used to be, then it got too big and the whole situation got out of hand.'

'Most people assume that those working in the sex industry want to be in it for their own personal reasons. Such as supporting a family, getting on financially or – not such a good motive – supporting a drug habit. Unfortunately this isn't true. It's a billion-dollar industry that's attracted all sorts of illegal activities. This makes it very dangerous, and innocent people get unwittingly trapped. In Spain, in spite of the legal brothels, it's a leisure activity at crisis point with all kinds of underground illegal activities being fed by the trafficking.'

Deep breath, quick pause, then she careered on.

'Child pornography, grooming, pimping, street prostitution, ad hoc renting rooms to girls is illegal. But the actual trafficking creates debts for the sex workers. They're trapped until the debt is paid – they believe they're going to a better life. Commonly, 20,000 euros is the sum they have to pay back. Threats of violence against them or reprisals against their families back home keep them under control.'

She paused for breath again.

'Occasionally, the foreign worker has formed an emotional attachment to a man in her own country who then sets her to work in Spain either by persuading her it is a lucrative way forward or because she was duped by being promised a job as hotel staff, waitress, babysitter, work in a sweatshop, cleaner – whatever. Papers are forged for these illegal immigrants. The boyfriend pays and then the girl starts to be in debt immediately. There's a lot of psychological manipulation. Following me so far?'

We all shifted in our seats and murmured amongst ourselves. She carried on:

'Romania is one of the worst offenders, being so close by. Only an ID card is needed to enter Spain so it's easy to be here legally. The women from there have their families threatened and because so many police are corrupt in Romania, they turn a blind eye to such things. Then Africa's a short hop over the water, so many West Africans pop over to add to the chaos. Last but not least, with a strong connection of language and history, South America is fodder. Spain is both a holding country and a transit country for passage to anywhere else in Europe, some even for plain, domestic slavery. It's inhumane.'

Lea stopped to let it all sink in. Indeed, it was a huge and serious subject. She gulped some water and ploughed on:

'The demographics of who wants sex has changed. It used to be family men getting away for fun in fairly normal conditions – brothels have been licensed since 1956. Now they're loosely disguised as clubs – and a large proportion of Spanish consider prostitution inevitable. No grounds for divorce unless taken to extremes. Now it is mainly young men of around eighteen who think it is their right to do anything once they have paid a woman.'

Alvaro shook his head and looked uncomfortable. 'Not my thing at all. I did in all honesty try it, just once. It put me off. So mechanical. No true feeling. Cold, sordid – but obviously I am in a minority. I like a woman to feel pleasure too. That is part of it. Mutual fun.'

We all looked at him and he blushed. 'Sorry, did I speak out of turn?'

'No! Glad to hear it, Alvaro. And so say all of us men – don't we Hans?' Uncle winked. Hans smiled and nodded vigorously. Why did I not quite believe this?

'We girls will remember this. Some men are gentlemen – eh, Lea?'

'Quite. Glad to hear it too. Must put it to the test with someone, sometime. After all this is over. So, back to the matter in hand.'

So businesslike. Amazing. Proud of my Lea.

'I'll explain later, Hans. Carry on, Lea. You're doing a great job,' I encouraged.

'It affects all parts of society. Even taxi drivers are paid to transport people around. Immigration and customs officials are bribed, as well as general transporters ¬ trucks, boats, ships and so on. Money talks. There's a lot of collaboration. Maybe even balloons now? We shall see.'

She reflected briefly. 'There is some good news. Things are being ratified – don't say anything, Babs, my dictionary was on google – 'We got a funny look but no-one commented 'A new organization called 'Ayundarme' is going strong. One already exists so this runs alongside it now. Both aim to help 'saved' or 'reformed' women, and also pro-actively go out looking for other women, knocking on doors, talking on street corners to see if they want help to escape. Protection, reintegration and general assistance is offered. They have different uniforms, so you can tell who's who, and they each go about things in slightly different ways. Of course it's a dangerous occupation because of the money involved. Now, wait for it – '

I guess she hoped we would all be astounded by the next bit.

'Drum roll please! Something in the region of twenty-six billion euros is sloshing around in this industry so naturally people want to keep it going. Spain is behind only Thailand

and Puerto Rica in this, so it's looked upon by the rest of Europe as a problem country. Or a country with serious problems.'

She shifted position, making herself more comfortable, crossing and uncrossing her legs.

'Hiring sex workers funds so many other dangerous and sleazy activities. There are landlords who rent rooms unofficially to the girls. Loopholes are being tightened up – but slowly. Advertising in the 'leisure and relaxation' section of newspapers and magazines has stalled, but new moves to prosecute the clients is afoot, like tracking down DVDs which show all kinds of sex abuse. It's an industry with victims – and not just in cities either. I believe it's out here in our very midst and we should help in any way we can.'

She breathed out a big a sigh of relief. Job done. What next? She had certainly done her research.

'Well – I am impressed, Lea. Well done.' Uncle started to clap. We all followed suit. 'You have convinced me – more than I was already. We need a plan of action.'

I jumped in. 'I've an idea, Uncle – and, yes! Well done, that girl!'

Lea had gone all coy and girly. Not used to praise from me. But credit, where credit is due.

I went on. 'Boats. I think you might want some input into this, Louisa, and maybe involve the Air Commodore? Oh by the way, everyone, Louisa has a friend who is very game to get involved. He's called Francis Culmé-Seymour.'

'Oof – some name. The English have some big names.'

It occurred to me that 'oof' was one of Hans's favourite words.

'I'll tell you some more interesting names before the end of the evening, Hans. Your eyes will water! Yes, I am sure I can speak for the Air Commodore in saying he will, but I'll call him now and ask him to join us, if you can wait a minute, Babs?' This from Louisa.

'Sure. Shall we get another drink? More fruit juices all round? Speaking of which, if expenses are to be involved, who is paying?'

Silence ensued. Louisa got on her phone to Francis while waiting for an answer to this.

'Perhaps we can all chip in?' We all began to confer and caught the attention of a waiter for another round. Thirsty work – undercover operations!

While we waited for Francis, Louisa turned to Hans saying, 'Shall I tell you the names of my friends? You will find it interesting.' He beamed acceptance.

'Well, first my best friend after Francis is Esme Arundel-Crackenthorpe-Gore.'

Hans's eyes widened considerably and he emitted an 'Oof'.

'Then we have my name – Louisa Helena Josephine Augusta Spelier–Bielby – so my poor son Eduardo is saddled with this in his very Spanish job. I think sometimes his comrades make fun of him for it.'

'I think I can understand this. I know him but never knew his name – not this name. You have a magnificent name. Louisa Augusta.' He was duly impressed. 'Louisa Augusta – hmm – Spelier-Bielby.' He was rolling it around his tongue with great seriousness. 'This is a – what you say – posh name?'

'Maybe – but we just happened to have these names by luck – so I thought of getting a club together for fun to meet up with people with such names and have meals out that turned into days out, which turned into holidays together. We are stuck with these ridiculous names so we have fun with them.' She smiled wickedly. 'Some of us are more 'posh' than others, as you put it. Hmm – I shouldn't mention names but you might meet them, so if you do come across a Rosalind and Alexander Gore-Marsden, escape quickly. Noses in the air type!'

She saw Hans raising eyebrows, and added, 'We try to leave them behind, especially as they're always late for everything, but it doesn't work as much as we'd all like. They're the boring posh type you mentioned. Bit like a commoner – ordinary person – marrying into the English royal family, only realizing too late that there's a tremendous amount of corresponding work and duty. You realize that opening toilet blocks is not really for you. You thought the servants would do it. Yes, the Gore-Marsdens are definitely the fly in the ointment.'

Hans just looked. 'Fly in ointment – please?'

'They spoil things. Then we have the good, all-round nice people. Stella and James Prescott-Willoughby, Theophila Frances Brown-Lowe, Augusta Harrington–Smythe, Juliana Windsor- Scott, Campbell Casson-Parker, George Farnworth-Seager, the Bailey-Pullens – shall I go on? My own eyes are beginning to glaze over and there are a few more, but I could tell you another time. Or did I get everyone? Hmm. There are a lot more back in the UK who didn't come with us this time.' Louisa almost smirked with secret thoughts of the motley crowd of Double Barrellers.

'Thank you! Another time. Please, another time. I think I have the idea. I am impressed.' Hans looked a little dazed, even fearful of information overload.

Just then Francis arrived and pulled up another chair. The motley crew was growing. Louisa – we all forgot to call her Louie but she didn't seem to bother – asked if she could tell Esme later and maybe involve her too – depending. We said we would leave it to her and let us know. Francis had got a drink so I put my plan before them.

'I have a feeling that not only balloons are involved in the transport of people but the obvious means of boats too. Rightly or wrongly, Louie, I've noticed the Gore-Marsdens going out on boats more than once, and Lea and I followed them to a large ship in the commercial port one day. They hire the boats through Karim. Not that that in itself is suspicious. It's the addition of so many small things.'

Louie said nothing and her face was a mask so I carried on.

'I think some of us should hire boats and do some following and watching. If we can't follow and moor up in strategic places, I think you Louie, would be able to find out if and when the Gore-Marsden's are going boating again? This might be a nice job for Esme, you, me, Lea? Anyone.'

I considered my next statement. 'And some of us need to explore the tunnels –but at night and dressed in black, leaving cars well out of the way. Walk down into the mine or perhaps see where the entrances are from the seaward side. Explore from both ends. Horses for courses.' I held up a hand to Hans. 'I'll explain that later. We leave details of every trip with those that aren't going, and phones on at all times with speed dial, although we might not always get a signal in the tunnels. We all need to make sure we have each other's phone numbers. More than we have already. Maybe even hire a hotel safety box with all this written up. Can't be too careful.' We all started discussing matters.

'When should these things begin? And what about boat-hire costs? I don't mind pitching in financially.'

'Uncle, that's great.'

'We are all well-heeled here – I mean no disrespect – except Alvaro. The fact that he will help is enough, I think. And Hans, I don't want to pry into your finances but can you contribute some money? If not, don't worry. I'm only asking. The same applies to you as to Alvaro.'

'I am not so good. I moved my business not long ago to my big finca with many costs – but something I can help with. I will see how much money I have.'

'Me too,' said Alvaro. 'A bit, in a good cause.'

'May I suggest for now I bank roll everything and we sort it out later. I will be bookkeeper. Simpler. As to when, Barbara, we can start tomorrow as far as I am concerned. Hans and I will go the club and start the ball rolling. To suit you, Hans.'

'Tomorrow evening is fine for me, Charles. About 21.30 is good. Do we go together or separately? Do we know us each other for this purpose?'

'I think you know each other. To have two people who don't know each other wanting unusual things is unlikely – in my opinion,' I said.

'I agree. So, shall we meet about 9.45 pm, Hans, and finalise things? I can pick you up and we'll drive together. Then the next night maybe we swap so one of can be seen to drink too much and say things we shouldn't. Hint anyway. Then maybe give it a miss for a night?'

'Play it by ear. That's all any of us can do.' We conferred again.

'I'll find out about the boat trips,' Louisa said. 'Then maybe book something. We should talk tomorrow. How about we meet for breakfast? Those that can. Hans and Charles are sorted so it's up to you if you want to meet for breakfast. You are very welcome – and I know Alvaro has to work.'

Alvaro made a face. 'I can lurk around.'

We all smiled.

'You do that Alvaro. Nothing like a bit of lurking.'

'Please now can we all do the swapping of numbers? Some we have, some we need? This is a strong situation for me and I want much back up. Like in the cop movies I want to call for back up.' Hans grinned. As an afterthought 'What is lurking?'

'"Course. Let's get to it. It's a 'strong' situation for all of us and lurking – well, it's hanging around to see what's happening.'

'What is 'hanging'?'

'Don't go there. Another time. Later. With the horses.'

'I'm not going anywhere with horses.' Puzzled ...

'Not even to the bar? My niece tells me they lead you to water? I'm buying. We can sort the numbers out in the Piano Bar.' Uncle beamed and swept us all out and in.

Numbers were duly swapped, drinks ordered – mostly café con leche as it wasn't that late – and Francis cornered me. He was eager to know what part he could play. I called Louie over to confer. As Francis was her best friend, I thought it only right.

'What do you think of Francis coming into the tunnels with us?'

'Who is 'us'?' she asked.

'Well, I haven't been in properly yet so I want to go. I think Lea will want to again. In fact, I know she will. I think two men would be good. How about Alvaro? Shall we ask?'

189

We called him over as he looked as if he was leaving. 'Alvaro – are you off back to work?'

'Yes, a few more hours to go. I thanked your uncle for not minding me taking some time out – but I was due a break anyway. Bit of a long one though.'

'Would you mind coming into the tunnels with me, Lea and Francis here? We mentioned it way back but this is different. At night-time as I said?'

'I would be pleased to accompany you. An honour.'

'Steady on. It's possibly dangerous. So it's not exactly a privilege, you know.'

'I am happy to do it then. I have the next two nights off, so up to you.'

'Tomorrow then. Ok with you, Francis?'

'Fine. I was only going to eat and drink anyway. Boring really. Alvaro, nice to meet you not as a waiter but a fellow conspirator.'

Francis proffered a hand which Alvaro was keen to shake. He obviously felt part of 'the team' and loved it. Bless him – I just hoped he wouldn't come to any harm on behalf of any of us that were setting this up. I would never forgive myself if any harm came to anyone, in fact. My ideas had taken off into somewhat more than I had anticipated. It worried me. Lea on the other hand seemed to be in her element as I watched her talking with Uncle and Hans. They were very attentive so perhaps she was animated because of them.

Alvaro excused himself. Louisa saw the Gore-Marsdens and went to chat them up about boats without letting them get suspicious.

Francis and I chatted. I found him absolutely charming and what I would describe as a true gent with a magnificent 'gung-ho' attitude. I thought we would feel very safe with him around. I was pleased he was coming into the tunnels with us.

Louisa came back strolling casually. Then she smiled conspiratorially. 'They are going out tomorrow after lunch. An afternoon bobbing around. Taking a picnic. Starting from the Sport Harbour. They have a boast hired for the rest of the week. Karim did them a good deal. I think you should see him tonight and ask for a deal too for a few days. He will be pleased about- the business. I know he works hard here and there but I think he wants really to go to the boat business full-time. Would have done until Gerhardt disappeared and he had to take more responsibility here.'

'How do you know that?'

'I asked him one day when he was looking particularly harassed. Two staff were off sick and he had to do the lunch buffet shift. He was so pre-occupied he even forgot to be unctuous.'

'You don't think he's a suspect then?' I was almost disappointed.

'I'm not ruling anyone out.'

'I'll go and find him now and book a boat. Are they all self-drive? I'm not sure I'm good with boats.'

'There is some tuition. They don't let you out without any knowledge. Or you can get a skipper, but that costs a lot and it would restrict you. I may come with you. I've done boat handling, and for a biggish boat they want to see a certificate for their insurance. I thought you scuba dived? Did you never do a boat-handling course?'

'Ah, of course. We did. Lea was good, and we brought our diving certificates. I think Lea brought her boat-handling certificate too. I could never get the boat lined up on a trailer to either launch it or retrieve it but Lea was fine. She drives well too and could park a trailer up no problem. She could always do that banana shape you need when you're backing up. I remember once when I was at the wheel of a dive boat I was ploughing through big waves but I didn't see a particularly big one. You're supposed to go into them but not like I did. The others were shouting at me and pointing but I didn't hear them. Too engrossed in staying afloat. The wave hit us full on and swamped the boat. We all fell over any loose equipment that was floating around. Lots of bruises and my bruised ego. We had to do a lot of baling out. It was all OK in the end but I've never been keen since.'

Louie smiled. 'Can happen to anyone. Anyway, I'll leave you to it. Ask for a boat big enough to take at least six people. You never know when it may be needed. Now, I'm off to change so I'll see you at breakfast if I don't see you somewhere tonight. Adios! Or maybe hasta luego – the night is yet young.' She shouted and waved over the general buzz of conversation.

The rest of us began to break up and go our separate ways. I went to Reception to ask for Karim to reserve a boat. By the time he came, Lea had joined me, and Uncle had gone to his room to rest and meet us later, along with Hans who would join us for a drink later too. Maybe Alvaro after work. It would be nice to for everyone to mix and get to know each other more. I hoped Alvaro wouldn't arouse any jealousy if he was seen hobnobbing with Uncle – and us. Maybe I would tackle this issue at some point, asking Uncle what he thought.

Lea did have to produce her boat-handling certificate for speed boats. She had one from our diving course but had taken further instruction separately to include basic sailing. Karim did us a good deal. The boat would be ready from 11am the next day. We arranged to get our tuition done at 11.30 am. I would put my mind to it – just in case I needed to. I hoped I wouldn't. Once a Girl Scout, I should be prepared for all eventualities.□

CHAPTER THIRTEEN
Boats, Tunnels and Brothels

'The salient points are –' Lea announced at breakfast.

Long word far too early. 'There aren't any,' I snapped. I didn't do mornings. 9 am! I ask you. I was grumpy. It might as well have been 5 am. My brain was having trouble focusing on anything apart from tea. Uncle Charles looked in, rested and calm. Annoying!

'Yes, there are,' Lea retorted. 'We saw the kid with the man going into the brothel.'

'We did. Yes, I grant you that. But we have no further evidence of anything else at all.' I sat cogitating, legs splayed out under the table, low in my seat. I was annoyed. I could summon up the energy to be annoyed because Lea had already been down to the village to check on her horse, donkey and dog. Topped up their water, met the equine owner again who had fallen in love with her, and made enquiries as to the owner of the chained-up dog. She had been bubbly all morning.

Uncle chipped in. 'Now, now girls. Too early to be fighting. Besides we are all agreed that there is something bad going on, which is why we are all here. You agree, don't you, Esme?' Esme had joined us for breakfast and Francis was happily munching his way through the buffet.

'Sorry, Louie. I'll be human by 11 am. The boat will blow the cobwebs away.' We were to be at the boat for 11.30

am to get all our instructions. 'Can I get you something from the buffet, Uncle?'

Uncle went to peruse the groaning table. He inspected it and from the look on his face he was impressed. Not quite what I had hoped from a financial point of view. 'Do you want more tea, Barbara? Perk you up a bit!' Uncle shouted over.

I gave a thumbs-up sign. And that gave me an idea. 'When we're in the tunnels we'll need to be quiet, so dive signals would be good. We must get some powerful torches and – maybe some spray paint to mark our way in. Just blobs, and to indicate left or right turns taken. We don't want to go round in circles. I wonder if a compass would work under all those minerals and tons of rock? Only one way to find out, so I'll buy one. The ironmongers in the village should have everything.'

That cheered me up a bit.

'Good idea,' Uncle said and put my tea before me, rather a way off so I had to sit up a little straighter. I saw Lea smirk. Oh boy, was she annoying.

To annoy me even more she piped up, 'You're in a state of lassitude this morning – again. Not that I noticed, of course.' Another smirk. She winked at Uncle too and they exchanged a conspiratorial smile. Well, that just did it.

'You and your flaming dictionary can keep yourselves to yourselves. I hope it strangles you.' My outburst caused guffaws all round. I was piqued. I was not amused. More guffawing.

'Barbara, you always were a nightmare to get off to school. You haven't grown out of it, have you? No wonder poor Lea ribs you. The girl has to have some fun in a morning. She needs it when she has to share a room with you.'

'I must say, Babs,' Lea chimed in, 'your uncle is both a very avuncular and erudite person. Sagacious even. I am grateful to him.'

I was utterly amazed. My mouth dropped open. I was about to remonstrate then she burst out laughing and Uncle was smiling madly. So was everyone.

'Did you two arrange this?' I asked accusingly.

'Oh yes! We had such fun thinking up how best to do it. I told Charles about my dictionary purchase. Sorry, folks. Babs is so easy to wind up, it had to be done!' I sighed ruefully. I really ought to learn.

'I suppose I deserved it. No need for anyone else to do it, though. Thank you all the same. Well, it's certainly woken me up.' I managed a gracious smile around the table.

I had been looking forward to Hans and Alvaro joining us that evening but both cried off, citing an early start at work. How sensible.

I made an effort now. 'Uncle, do you think having Alvaro involved and being seen in our company will cause jealousy with his work colleagues. Will Carl resent it?'

'I've already had a word with Carl and he'll cut him some slack. Alvaro is highly valued for his work ethic so he's appreciated. And he's a big boy so I am sure he can handle it. See what happens. I did tell Carl that I need, my 'personal assistant or butler' to cover any petty issues arising from his association with us at various times. He understands the bigger picture. No one can argue against the owner demanding outrageous things.'

'Clever thinking. Shall we finalise our plans? Do you want to start, Louie?'

'No, you go ahead, Babs.'

Everybody looked at me expectantly, so I got on with it. 'This afternoon Lea and I will go out in the boast, basically shadowing the Gore-Marsdens as far as possible. Also, I want to see from the seaward side any potential entrances and landing points into the tunnels. Are you and Esme joining us, Louie?'

'Yes, we will. Just to get a feel for things. I think the G-Ms are setting off at 2 pm. Does that suit? It will have to, won't it? Esme and I will make out own way to the harbour. What's the name of the boat you've hired?' Louisa enquired.

'Sunflower.' Firm confident answer from Lea with a big smile. I bet she had picked it just for the name.

'See you there then.'

'Uncle, you're picking Hans up at his place at 9.45 pm. Still the same arrangement? I did tell you, didn't I, that Alvaro will follow you tomorrow, not tonight. Makes it seem less of a coincidence. He's coming into the tunnels tonight instead.'

'Yes and yes. Sort of. Alvaro told me this morning.'

'Oops. Sorry. Well, we'll stay in touch. Every hour, even if there's nothing to report. All you and Hans are doing tonight is drinking and talking. Not too much. Build up for tomorrow. And then if you're asked why you don't want a woman tonight …'

'Barbara, I expect I can think of my own excuses. Leave it to us, eh?'

'Oh. Yes, of course.' I coloured up. Uncle was a man of the world but I tended to forget. After all, he was my jolly uncle. My rock.

'Now, this evening I'm going into the tunnels with Francis, Alvaro and Lea. All in black and I think our faces too. Does anyone mind? I've asked Alvaro.' No dissent came. 'Then I'll get some water-based paint. There's no particular plan once in there, except keep together, and keep silent unless there's an emergency. We'll go through some dive signals later. If for any reason we have to separate, make your way out and wait as near as possible to where we came in. If the hound from hell is on your heels, obviously run. Let's hope it never comes to that. I suggest you come to our room, Francis, and we'll black you up. I'll tell Alvaro. About 8.30. OK?' I raised my eyebrows enquiringly, feeling more confident by the minute.

Francis agreed.

'Louie, does your son know about this tunnel expedition?' I asked.

'Not as such. I've told him bits, just in case we need rescuing or he needs to believe our version of events. Suppose we came across a body – we don't want to be the suspects.' We were a little sombre at the thought.

'Edward is against it, of course. Another reason to keep details from him. He hasn't got the manpower to start surveillance on us, on a whim.'

'It's very good of you to help, Louisa. It's fully appreciated. Everyone's help, in fact.'

'No problem,' she sounded enthusiastic. 'We've been looking for some adventure and this is all in a good cause. Bit like being back at work. Excitement with trepidation. If you don't have nerves, you lose the edge. Mind you, some cold-blooded killers don't have nerves. Enough of that. Another time, maybe. I'm writing my memoirs – slowly, of course. A lot of is still secret. Now, I'm full of breakfast, and off to recover by the pool under a palm. I usually sunbathe early. Later I'll spend my time keeping out of the sun. My home has garden seats all round it for sun and shade whenever I need it. I sit my way around. See you later.'

'Sounds idyllic.' I was keen to ask all sorts of questions but didn't dare. I know I wondered about her past and could only assume others did, though maybe Francis and Esme knew more. I couldn't ask so I busied myself getting some food.

'What do you think of the buffet, Uncle?'

He contemplated for a moment. 'Excellent. But I think as you do – too much. I'll have a word with the chef at some point. It has to be a compromise as I don't want standards to go down, or our reputation for value and superb food.'

'Well, death is nature's way of telling us to slow down. So we could all eat ourselves to death here – in the nicest possible way.'

'I think you mean that as a compliment, Lea. At any rate I'll give it the benefit of the doubt.' Uncle smiled. He would never see any malice in Lea. No one would.

I hadn't seen Alvaro this morning in spite of him saying he would hover around. In the same instant Gareth popped into my mind. I wondered what he was up to and what he would think of us on this new adventure. I suddenly felt guilty, and the desire to look for Alvaro evaporated. Lea was always loyal with true friends. Did this make me shallow? I would have to think about this in some depth.

I looked over at Lea talking with the others, and picking at this and that from the buffet. I could have sworn she had lost weight. If that was possible. After all, she had just put weight on at the start of our trip, with all the eating that had been going on.

'Lea, is it my imagination or are you getting skinnier?' She glanced up.

'I hoped no one would notice. It's all the water I'm drinking – and the heat. I just burn everything off. My clothes are beginning to hang off me. I must eat more. Excuse me, does anyone want anything from the buffet? I must fill up. Hard day ahead.'

Esme, Francis and Uncle went with her to forage, and to compliment Uncle on the food. He looked pleased but now had his own dilemma. To decrease the food portions or not?

Sometime later we were all sated. We went our separate ways to meet up later and I felt I must find Alvaro just to make sure he was OK. I found him in Reception with Karim. They looked up when they saw me approaching.

'Is something wrong?' I felt a sudden concern at the looks.

'I hope it is all fixed now, Senora.' I would take issue with 'Senora' as opposed to 'Senorita' later.

'What?'

'Housekeeping went to do your room as you were out early today, and on the balcony there were hundreds of spiders. From the tree over the balcony, falling down.'

'The tree or the spiders?' I hate spiders.

Lea joined me. 'Spiders? I hope you didn't kill any?' She wasn't keen on spiders herself but wouldn't kill one, especially as they ate flies, which neither of us liked.

Alvaro took over. 'I wasn't around this morning because Karim and I have been dealing with the spiders. These ones don't live in trees but in dry scrubland. That is the Black Widow. But ¬' he paused, looking a bit concerned ,'there were different types which you wouldn't expect to see so close together, all falling off the tree. I saw a Brown Recluse and a Mediterranean Funnel Web. Separately, a Tiger Centipede. I studied arachnids for a while as a school project. There is no way they got there on their own and in such quantity. Fortunately, they are not killers but they can deliver a nasty, irritating bite. Of course, en masse – if you were allergic – you could die.' His words faded away.

Lea and I just looked at each other. He had spoken quickly so Karim didn't catch it all.

'Senoras, I am having another room made ready for you,' he said. 'We have got rid of most of the spiders. I am sorry but some had to die – many apologies for this – but we need to make sure with time that more appear. I mean don't appear! Really we need to have the room fumigated. I don't know what could have happened to cause this. I will inform your uncle with many, many apologies. The manager is out this morning so I must take responsibility. Please can you carefully check all your clothes, even drawers, shoes – everything – and I will get the housekeeping team to pack for you and move your bags. I am putting you in a suite next to your uncle, Mr Madden.'

'Thank you so much, Karim. We will do that now, but we will pack our bags and leave them to be brought across to here. We are going out at 11 anyway. Please don't worry. It is not your fault, and we will tell my Uncle so. I'll ring him from the room.'

Karim looked awful. Despondent. I felt sorry for him for once – or was it a second time? I must stop doing that or I would regret it when the slime came slithering along.

'Really, don't worry!' I even patted his arm and he looked slightly less despondent. We moved off and signalled to Alvaro. I hoped Karim hadn't noticed. Alvaro joined us outside.

'You know what this means don't you?' I looked at Lea and him. 'Our hints are taking effect. Someone wants to discourage us. We have hit a nerve. I think the exciting bit is being taken over by severe trepidation.'

'I agree but that's what we wanted, isn't it?' Lea was positive.

'I'm still up for everything.' Alvaro was positive.

'Yes. Indeed.' I was positive too! 'Right! 8.30 pm in our room to get blacked up. With Hans and Uncle tomorrow night.'

He nodded. 'I must get back to work. Karim and I spent a lot of time clearing up the spiders. Horrible job.' We all shuddered.

Lea and I went to our room, which we entered with caution, and peered around. Only the odd spider was still sat there or walking about. Nothing that would have made your flesh crawl. I phoned Uncle first and gave him the full story.

'Barbara, you're getting closer. I do admire your determination but you really must back off at the first sight of any danger. These tunnels worry me a great deal and I'm wondering about handing the whole thing over to Louisa's son. I think there's enough for him to take action on now.'

'No! There isn't. Please, Uncle. It's all set up now. You have a major part to play tonight and that, with tomorrow's visit, should produce something positive. That's when we can think of handing over to Edward. We've got a sensible plan. Tonight we're not doing much more than you. Finding our way around. IF we see anyone, we'll back off, I promise that. Promise! Cross my heart and not hope to die!'

'Barbara, don't joke like that. But – against my better judgement, go ahead as planned. It will be nice to have you as my neighbour. I can keep an eye on you both.'

'Great! Thanks. See you then.'

I told Lea what he'd said and she sniffed.' Keep an eye on us! No men in the room then. Hmph.'

'Not unless Uncle is one of them.'

'Oh, I see. That could be interesting.'

'Not that way, Lea. Down, girl. It's my uncle you're thinking naughty thoughts about.'

She had a wily look. 'Certainly not. You're misinterpreting everything I say.'

Still - I must steer her back to Hans. Or was she just winding me up? I wouldn't stoop to ask.

We started packing and I phoned Louie. She was both concerned and excited. 'Babs, are you OK with this? You can back out now if you want and I'll turn it over to Edward.'

'Oh, don't you start please. I've had all this from Uncle a few minutes ago. I – we – are going ahead. We're all agreed.'

'Fine. Just checking. See you at the boat then.'

We finished up packing and set off for the boat. Time was getting on. Lea phoned Hans to let him know of developments in case he wanted to renege on his part. He didn't.

At the sleek, sparkling, white boat a good-looking specimen greeted us. Tall, dark and handsome – and Spanish. I had the feeling he had his way with many a female tourist. I wasn't going to be one of them. Nor was Lea. When he took us the boat to explain things, he used every opportunity to get close and touch – by accident. When he was explaining about boat handling Lea demonstrated her skills by telling him how it was done, citing several examples of how she had coped. He got bored, went off abruptly and left us to it.

We would have the boat for the rest of the week and hoped to get some relaxation out of it. It was nice and breezy so we sat around. A small cabin forward provided shade or shelter and a roof where we could sit and sunbathe, as well as the plush seats outside on three sides. It would take six people easily, more if you didn't mind being crowded.

The harbour had various cafes where we could sit and people-watch. So we did. I put my sun cream on. As usual Lea had hers on already. She'd brought her copious bag full of seasick pills, bandages, headache pills, a change of shoes, clothes, one size fits all, in case anyone got wet or perhaps covered in blood, towels to sit on – the list was endless.

I was delving for my sunglasses in my more modest bag when I spotted the G-Ms with the Arab guy. They were strolling, and finally settled in a café a few away from us. Shame we couldn't have listened in.

'Should we get some takeaway food? Could be a long afternoon.' Lea and food went together like ham and eggs.

'Trust you to think of food. As it happens it is a good idea. They do takeaway here.' When a waiter came our way again we asked for a variety of things, together with water. There was a cool box on the boat loaded up with ice.

'Is that the time?' Lea looked at her phone as Louisa and Esme approached. She wouldn't wear a watch in case it spoiled her tan lines. It was kept in her bag. We noticed the G-Ms moving off to their boat a few up from ours. Theirs was a bit smaller. They hadn't noticed us, not that it mattered. We picked up our picnic.

'Hello, ladies. This way to our chariot. We have sustenance. Hope you can face food after breakfast. If not. Lea will eat it all.' We settled ourselves in the boat. Louie and Lea started the engine and cast off between them. We motored slowly out of the harbour, following the G-Ms. We had to as there was no other way to go. Once out at sea, they turned towards the commercial harbour and when there, they seemed to be looking at the cargo ship that we had previously seen them go to from the land side. They didn't go into the harbour, and after some minutes left for a leisurely putter around the bay.

Conveniently this brought us towards the mining area. Several leisure craft were bobbing around so we didn't feel conspicuous. We decided to hug the coastline to get a better view of any landing places near the mines. It was all rather craggy. After some time we came upon a small inlet that provided some shelter for mooring so we slowed down, found a rock to throw a rope around and disembarked. Rather a grand term for such a relatively small craft. Anyway, we got off.

There was a natural platform, smoothed by the sea and the passage of time. A good place to sunbathe and eat. It was quite late in the afternoon now, so we set about our picnic. A bit of a rest followed but boredom got to me so I announced I was going further along the rocks. Louie joined me, leaving the others on guard duty.

We considered it wise to not to leave the boat unattended. About fifteen minutes of scrambling brought us to a bit of cliff that had various levels going up it – almost steps – or a cross between steps and platforms. We looked up and saw the dark shadow of what appeared to be an entrance – or exit – from one of the tunnels. Not something you would see easily from the sea as it was fairly low down, with a rocky outcrop in front. We felt pleased to have found this, whether or not it was relevant.

We set off back to the boat, going back faster than we had come, being more familiar with the terrain. Esme and Lea had packed the picnic away and were back in the boat. Lea got out again to deal with the rope while Louie started the engine. She jumped nimbly back into the boat and we set off for the harbour. It was getting late. I described what we had come across and on our way back we made a point of remembering certain landmarks, and timed the journey.

We were all keeping an eye out for anything at all. No sight of the G-Ms and the Arab but we did see the gay barman from the Piano Bar in a boat heading out more or less the way we had come. He had two passengers with him who seemed to be teenagers. They had fishing rods in the boat.

He saw us and waved while his 'mates' looked at us with a sombre expression. No reason why it should be otherwise as we didn't know each other.

'I don't know if I should ask Louie, but has that barman been questioned by the police? He was the boyfriend of the murdered man Lea found.'

'Yes, I know and yes, he has. Edward told me a bit. Seemed he had an alibi. Thanks for the food by the way. Very welcome.'

'Add me to that.' Esme chipped in.

'Thank Lea. She bought it.'

Lea gracefully accepted the thanks. 'Do you see that?' She pointed. We could still just about see the barman's boat as a speck, and it was heading into the little bay we had left. 'I don't know much about fishing, but it seems an odd place to fish. Though I suppose you can fish anywhere there's water. And it's going to be getting dark in a while. Maybe night fishing?' We all mulled this over but not knowing much, if anything, about fishing, we didn't get anywhere.

Back in harbour, we saw the G-Ms' boat was back and Louie and Esme set off for La Roca Club.

Lea and I went in search of shoe polish and a compass. The shops were open again for the afternoon session and as we wondered around San Cartana, we came across a fancy-dress shop. I dived in and asked for face paint. It was m lucky day. Face paint and spray paints. I suggested getting white spray paint as I thought it would show up better than any other colour. It also glowed in the dark. This may be good for us but bad in that it would be obvious someone was snooping. One of those dilemmas. It solved itself when Lea suggested getting ordinary white spray paint as well as the luminous one.

The compass eluded us but a ferreteriá provided us with really powerful torches, and I added four small ones for less of a show should we need to fade into the background.

'Right, we'd best get on back. We need to meet up with Alvaro and Francis and get set to go. It'll be dark soon. No point waiting. Hopefully we'll be back at La Roca before Uncle, and when he gets back from the brothel, we'll hear all about what happened there.'

Back at the Club we headed for our room – then it occurred to us we had been moved and needed our new key. We inspected our accommodation with glee. Like Uncle's it had its own large lounge area. It was posh, no doubt about it. We'd investigate properly in the morning. I gave Uncle a quick call to say we were off soon and just getting changed.

We found all our black outfits. T shirts, black jeans would do. Francis and Alvaro were on time, suitably dressed. I have to say they both looked very smart in black. Sexy even. Francis was no mean-looking guy for his age. Any age. We went through the dive signals: Stop, OK, Finish it – which was a cutting motion across the throat. I had packed the face paints in a small bag to put on when we parked the car. No point frightening the natives here at the Club.

Alvaro was nominated to drive as he knew the area and the best place to park out of sight but not too far away from the mine. We got there not long after 8.30 pm. I distributed the torches in four small bags and a paint each, then Lea and I did the honours with the face paint.

'Hands,' Lea said.

'Oh. I suppose it's a good idea. Well spotted.'

'Ready then?' I looked round. We all gave an 'OK' dive sign and off we set, keeping to any cover we found.

A moon made it reasonably bright. As soon as we got into the mine there wasn't any cover so we moulded ourselves to the sides in a line. No one lurked in the shadows of other tunnel entrances.

My heart had started to pound. My stomach was doing flips. The others looked serious, determined and focused, and I wondered if they didn't have the nerves that I had. We were heading down the gentle slope which must have been a busy road in and out at one time. Wide enough for two big trucks to pass.

We could whisper if we had to, but hoped we wouldn't need to. Large torches for now after getting part way inside. We only put two on. It got black dark quickly but lightened up again when we got near one of the air chimneys. Shafts for light as well. As we progressed, several of these came and went. I was marking the way. We ignored any turn offs, following the main wide tunnel which ran straight.

We had been going for about fifteen minutes – I was timing it – when we heard – something. I made the cutting sign and we stopped dead, listening. It was distant but rhythmic. A cross between clattering and swooshing. Machinery of some sort and then a bang. A door slamming. Lea had heard it before. My heart was now through my mouth, but I signaled for us to go on.

Another ten minutes at our slow, steady pace and the noise had increased considerably, but then we came across a wall in front of us. We looked for a way around but couldn't find one. No side tunnels. I signalled for two more torches to be put on and I flashed mine around the top, bottom, sides and middle of the wall. Under close scrutiny we could see the tiniest of gaps in the middle of the wall in a rectangular door shape. Our eyes met.

Suddenly, though muffled, we clearly heard talking. Various tones. Adults and a lighter tone of children. Shouting from the adults then thudding sounds. Shrieks lasting some minutes then silence. Total silence. We were transfixed. What next? Retreat.

I risked a whisper. As we hadn't been able to hear them properly, they wouldn't hear us. 'We should go. We have no idea what we might be facing or how many people. Or what state of mind they would be in. Probably hostile. '

The others all nodded and we set off back, Alvaro leading this time. The exit was a welcome sight. We were outside in record time as we'd practically run! A fast trot up the slope and back to the car. We all stood around, not sure what to say. Finally breaking the spell, Lea got her bag out of the car and produced wet wipes for us all to get our face paint off. We started talking.

'Do we report this now and hand it all over?' Francis asked. 'Shame if we have to.' He had a glimmer of a smile on his face.

'It would.' Both Alvaro and Lea said in unison. I was taken aback.

'I thought you would all want to want to give up now. Getting dangerous. I don't know about you lot, but my heart was pounding and my hands on the shaky side.'

'Mine too – but it got the adrenaline going, didn't it? I would go back maybe with more back-up, and perhaps from the seaward side. Just to look and see what there is to be seen without going in that entrance we saw this morning.'

'What happens if someone comes out?'

'Hence the back up. But there were plenty of rocks to hide behind. Enough for two to do a reccy at the entrance anyway before deciding what next.'

'I agree.' From Francis.

'And me.' From Alvaro.

I took a deep breath. My pulse was nearly back to normal. 'Then we should organize it. Let's get back, have a drink and unwind. I'll phone Uncle and tell him to phone Louisa that we're OK and we'll meet them in the Pool Bar when he and Hans get back from the brothel. I doubt their news will be as dramatic as ours.'

We piled in Alvaro's car and set off. Uncle was on his way from the hotel to pick up Hans so the conversation was short. He was relieved we were back safely. How much to tell him?

The breeze over the Pool Bar was heaven. We sat beside the third palm from the left, which had become a joke. We knocked our first drinks back in swift style. Thirsty work in the tunnel. The men had beer, or what passes for beer in Spain –basically lager. Lea and I stuck to long G and T's. I ordered the next round and decided I should add some colour to my outfit. We looked as though we had been to a funeral or were escaped baddies from a James Bond film.

'I'm going to put another top on so we don't look so odd all in black. Won't be a mo.'

'Good idea. Can you bring me some bling down. Any. I'll throw it on so don't spend ages thinking. Your drink will get warm, so hurry!'

Instructions from Lea made me hurry and I was back in no time to hear discussions about what should be said to others so we wouldn't be stopped in our tracks. I put some large pieces of bling on the table for Lea – a chunky necklace and matching bracelet with two knuckle dusters of rings.

It certainly brightened her up. I swept my drink up and joined in.

'So – what do you think we should or shouldn't say?' Francis started. 'Should I tell Louisa the truth? I know her and she won't stop us. She'll quietly have back up at the ready, just in case. She's in her element with this. Me too, I have to say. As for your uncle and Hans, I would suggest – or at least for your uncle, Babs – that we say we got further in and confirmed the noises that Lea heard before. She didn't imagine it. More investigation needed. No problems. Keep it simple.'

'I'll second that!' Lea grinned. 'You know I was watching a war film a few weeks ago about bomber pilots in WW2. How they managed with their nerves, waiting around for hours, day after day, before going up in the air – probably to be killed – I'll never know. Some did crack up and you can't blame them. How could they eat, knowing what was coming? I would never have made a bomber pilot. Spy probably.'

'I can see that,' I said. 'The enemy would have told you all their secrets just to shut you up and stop having to feed you before you ate them out of house and home.'

'I say!' Mock indignation.

We all smiled. Just then Hans and Uncle approached cheerily. Not very late.

'Good evening, I gather!' I said.

We all waited with bated breath as they drew up chairs. The huge comfy ones.

'Aren't you going to get the heroes a drink? Yes, we did, thank you.'

I waved a waiter over who took more orders. I had involved everyone in this so it was the least I could do. Plus, to my surprise, they were all up for supporting me. Francis texted Louisa at length so I guessed he was properly updating her. She joined us in time to hear Uncle describing the evening:

'We played it very slowly, mostly talking to each other. We called a couple of girls over and bought them drinks. More general chat. It's a nice place you know. Good décor. Long bar to the right then the girls sit or lounge about on sofas to the left. Lots of waiting. They were pretty disappointed when we left. We left a tip behind the bar saying we would be back tomorrow. We didn't hint at wanting anything unusual. I think the money got their attention. I did wonder if, when Alvaro comes in tomorrow, he should be the one to say he has heard rumours that we like 'special' things. He can then say he doesn't want to say what, and go all shy – then hint he would spill the beans if he had a drink, or several, offered. Then he has an excuse to leave without a girl because he's had too much. If it didn't work, he can drink too much anyway – throw it in a pot plant, there are a lot of those – and get too chatty. Can you act, Alvaro? Seem pleased with yourself for dropping us in it? Looking for a freebie in return for information. You know us from working in the Club. Think you mentioned that, Barbara?'

'Yes. Good idea – if Alvaro is OK with it. Are you? Can you act?'

'I act all the time with clients. Present company excepted, of course.' He beamed.

'Should you have another evening before this happens though, Uncle? Is it all a bit quick? You could say tomorrow you are looking around at other places for some special fun without specifying. They won't want to lose your custom. Then play hard to get and Alvaro can nail it the day after.'

'I'll go along with that. What about you, Hans?'

'Oh yes. Please can you tell me what is spilled beans. Is this difficult to do? Do I need to learn?'

'Old English saying. Ignore it. Nothing for you to do or worry about,' I volunteered. Then I filled Uncle in on our tunnel adventure, minus the bits about the eerie and scaring noises. Francis and Lea backed me up with nonentities. Shrugs of 'not much to report'.

We decided we would all leave things for a day and regroup the day after next, apart from Uncle and Hans going to the brothel again the following evening. Then we all went to the late bar.

After a while Lea suggested we have a drink in our room so we could relax more. She had bought some wine from the bodega. When did she have time to do that? I wondered.

We trooped up and settled in. Lea did the honours with the wine, handing pretty glasses all round. Again I wondered when she had acquired these. I must grill her later, I thought. She opened a red for Uncle and let it sit there – seemingly forever.

'Why is the wine just sitting there – instead of going down my throat?' He reached over and poured himself a glass.

'To let it breathe.'

'Ooh – where did you get this? It seems to be taking its last gasp!'

Lea looked dismayed. 'From the bodega Bar. It smelled good – and it was cheap. Um, I mean reasonably priced. I wanted to treat you all.'

'Admirable!' Uncle smiled encouragingly. 'And it is growing on me. After the first mouthful it mellows. Cheers everyone. Here's to success and safe adventure.'

CHAPTER FOURTEEN
Children, Children, Everywhere

'Well, I'm feeling incandescent this morning,' announced Lea at breakfast.

I peered at her over my sunglasses. Nothing surprised me anymore – well not her dictionary anyway. Why? I asked myself. Why now does she want to get to grips with words – words she has managed without thus far?

'So, are you emitting light as a result of being heated up or are you feeling strong, passionate and have a particular love of life this particular morning?'

'The latter.' She had a pained expression on her face now.

'May I ask why?' I stretched out for my orange juice. We were going to have a leisurely day and as it was late-ish, I wasn't grumpy. I was pleased that there was nothing potentially dangerous to do today. It had taken quite a while for my hands to stop shaking after the tunnel incident. Lea didn't seem fazed by the previous evening's events but she did usually tend to keep that sort of thing to herself.

'I feel strongly that we're doing the right thing in helping to catch these criminals. It's good to feel that we're rescuing people.'

'I agree, but it certainly is stressful – like you said with the WW2 fighter pilots.'

'Oh yes. Awful. I can feel their fear and stress, and I can only admire what they did. I only hope I can carry through with whatever we get up to. I wouldn't want to let anyone down by running away from something. Or not doing it in the first place. I did feel wobbly in the tunnel.'

'Only wobbly? My stomach was churning. Hasn't your dictionary got a word for it?'

She picked up her bag from the floor and fished out the dictionary. 'As a matter of fact –'

'No, no! Don't tell me. I couldn't stand another big word today, even though I don't feel particularly grumpy. Anyway, I'm sure people would forgive us for feeling a bit wobbly – after all, we're not professionals. Still, I do think I'd feel I'd let myself down.' An idea began to form.

'Absolutely.'

'What? That I had let myself down?' I felt a tad miffed.

'No! I meant I would feel the same. That I would have let myself down, that is. I've got just the glimmer of an idea. Might relieve some of the stress.'

'I've an idea too. Do you want to go first?'

'Ok.'

Damn, I thought. I should have kept my mouth shut.

'Instead of sneaking around at night I think we should storm in during the day.'

'Yes, but we need an excuse. I was thinking we should wander around in full sight, like nosy tourists exploring.'

Lea was thinking. I could tell. Mulling. 'How about we – just you and me – go in the boat to the seaward entrance all guns blazing, with a picnic. Pretend we're just looking for somewhere to sunbathe and eat. Nothing wrong with that. We explore up to the tunnel entrance carrying the picnic, and see where that gets us.'

'I see. And if someone, or some people are there, we apologize, offer to share the picnic, act stupid and very friendly, like we expect other people to have a picnic there too. Could work. Why just us?'

'Because two women on their own don't look suspicious, or aren't much of a threat anyway. I would – or we could – moor up and swim off the boat. Be noisy, make our presence felt, then go ashore and explore.' We both sat, mulling it over.

'When?' I asked.

'Why not today? Get it over with. Let Charles, Hans and Alvaro have the glory tomorrow evening asking for – you know.'

As soon as she said 'today', my heart did a flip. Less stress but not stress-free. That was because we knew something bad was going on. If we hadn't known it and had found that tunnel by accident, we wouldn't have given it a second thought. Picnic is as picnic does.

'I'll run it past Uncle. If he's fine with it, we'll ask for a picnic from the chef here. Have you seen Uncle by the way? He wasn't in is room when I knocked this morning.'

'Yes. He said he was off early to see some Spanish travel agents about bringing business here. He'd hired a car early and was setting off just as I was on my way to see to my animals – well, to say hello to them. They have plenty of water. They look out for me now.' She had a warm smile when she talked about them.

I phoned Uncle but had to leave a message. I was grateful for that – it meant he didn't have a chance to argue. As backup, I phoned Louisa. Fortunately, she was all for it. Did we want her to come too? I said not. But thank you. We'd keep in touch. Next, we ordered the picnic which would be in Reception in half an hour, so went back to our room – well, this one was more like a suite – and changed into 'boating' gear.

I told myself we were just going for an ordinary trip out. Nerves not required. Alvaro was nowhere to be seen so we duly left for the harbour. I drove, as Lea would be handling the boat. It was a calm day with minimum breeze. The boat sat there gleaming and looked so inviting I was almost – almost – enjoying myself. We loaded the food, a large heavy hamper, and set off.

Puttering along, it took over half an hour to get to the inlet. To our surprise and dismay, there was another boat moored. It looked familiar. We nudged in beside it and threw the mooring rope over the same rock.

'Isn't that the boat we saw the barman in with the fishing gear and the teenagers?'

'So it is. At least we know we have company from the start.' Positive reaction from Lea. She foraged in her bag and came out with binoculars.

'Why haven't I seen those before?'

'Because I only bought them this morning while I was out and you were still sleeping beauty. Charles said it was a good idea – so there!' She did a hundred degree sweep and went back to a point out at sea. 'That's the G-Ms with the Arab, but he's not in flowing clothes ¬ he's in shorts and T shirt. They all are. They seem to be heading our way. Oh.' Silence.

'Oh what.'

'They're looking at me looking at them.'

'With binoculars?'

'No! Just that they've amazing eyesight after being beamed up to an extra-terrestrial space ship.'

'Funny!'

She stopped looking their way and put the binoculars down.

'Let's swim.' Lea jumped over the side. She did it so fast I was left standing. How had she get her shorts off without me noticing? I followed more sedately with my hair tied back. The water was cool but with warm patches. It was so calm it was a pleasure to float. The sound of the water lapping around the boat and against the rocks was soporific. It was tempting to nod off, but even with that calm sea I could feel we were tending to drift out of the inlet.

'I think we should get on shore.' I was not apprehensive any more now that we had familiar people around, even though these were the Gore-Ms. For some illogical reason, our murder didn't occur to me.

'Rock,' said Lea. 'It's a rock platform. I wonder if it was carved specially for the mining days? Looks man-made.'

We got onto the rock, hauling the picnic basket out of the boat.

'I'll take another look for the G-Ms.' After a minute of surveying the horizon, she pointed. 'They're heading parallel to the shore – not coming in here but not exactly going away either.'

'Let's go to the tunnel entrance and get that over with. Think I'll take some water. Want some?'

'Yes please.' We scrambled up the way we had gone before and came to the entrance. Our swimming costumes had dried in the heat. The entrance was neither big nor small. It was high enough to stand with space above, then it opened out into a cavern which was dark towards the back but with shafts of light here and there from some small openings in the roof where the ground had given way after being excavated. Fallen rock and debris lay strewn around. It had the myriad colours of the minerals that had been mined, though we guessed this was a big area to be used just as an exit. In the dimness I thought I could see other small passageways, and as my eyes got used to the change in light I saw a wall right at the back that I would not have recognized except we had seen it – or something similar – the night before. It merged beautifully.

We were turning to leave when we heard noises. Chattering.

We edged toward the outside area and Lea whispered, 'Sit down and take a swig of water. Make it look normal.'

We sat and swigged. A few minutes later the chattering came much closer and didn't stop. Came right towards us and out. About ten children, ages ranging from about eight years old to about twelve, swarmed around, not too surprised to see us. Not surprised at all really. They were curious, friendly but somewhat reserved. All swarthy complexions. Girls and boys but mostly boys.

'Hello!' Lea broke the ice. 'Would you like a drink?' She proffered the water bottle but they didn't respond. 'Nice in here, isn't it? We're getting away from the heat. Do you speak English? We are from the big resort, having a picnic.' She was smiling a lot so I did.

One of the older boys made a move towards her. I wondered what was coming next but he only said, 'Yes, we speak a bit English. A picnic – what is that?'

'Food. The hotel made us lots of food to bring with us. Would you like some? It's by the boat.'

He looked interested.

Lea pressed her advantage. 'What are you all doing here? Exploring?'

Clever, I thought, give them an excuse so they don't panic.

'Yes.' The boy grabbed onto that. 'We come here often – to explore. The food?'

'Of course! Are you coming down?'

'No, we can bring it here.' He spoke rather sharply, but then more mildly, 'It's nice and cool in here. Nice views.' He waved a hand towards the horizon.

'Ok. Can you help bring it up? It's heavy for us.'

The kid said something in another language and two of the boys sped down towards the boat.

Lea was going to go with them but the main kid put a hand up. 'They will do it.'

Lea and I stole a glance at each other. We definitely weren't in charge here.

'My name is Barbara and this is my friend, Lea. As in the film. Princess Leah – you know the film?'

'Yes, I know. I see in Morocco when I used to live there. Very nice.'

'Your name?'

'Yusuf.'

'How do you get into this tunnel – by the boat?' I indicated the boat next to ours.

'Yes, the boat.' He seized on that too and I didn't let on that I thought the boat was far too small to carry ten children. I knew I had to pretend to be stupid. The hamper arrived with some puffing and was plonked in front of us. We opened it and started distributing the food. The other children crowded around. Table manners were not at a premium. Some grabbing went on but we turned a blind eye.

'We have a had a lovely swim by the boat. Do you swim?'

'Sometimes at night. Nice.' Yusuf always took the lead. The others talked in their own language.

'Are you all from Morocco?' Lea ventured.

'Most. We are friends. Nice here.'

'Don't your parents mind you being out here?' I wondered if Lea was pushing it a bit. There was a gap in the conversation, sporadic as it was.

'No,' was the only answer.

'What time do you have to go home?'

'When we want.' The food had all but disappeared and the kids had stopped waiting to be offered things and simply took.

'Can you play in the tunnel? Does it have light all over?'

'We play. Nice. Much light. Several tunnels. Some small. We hide. Look for each other. Some we make bed to sleep.' Sudden silence as though he had said too much.

'Does the boat next to ours belong to you?'

Whoa, Lea!

'Friend.' As an afterthought, 'He take us fishing. Nice.'

'Where is your friend now?'

Steady on girl, you'll get us into trouble.

'Is he playing in the tunnel? Maybe he will be sad to miss the food?'

'Yes, he in tunnel. No miss the food.'

'Yusuf, do you think you could take the basket back to the boat for us? Not so heavy now but not easy over the rocks. We have chocolate in the fridge on the boat. You can have it. We want to swim now and then go back. It has been lovely to meet you.' Lea smiled so sweetly that it would have been impossible to ignore.

'OK. No problem.' Yusuf gave an order. Two boys picked up the hamper and I hurriedly swept the unused cutlery back into it. We set off down the rocks. Yusuf followed. At the boat we got the chocolate and handed it over.

'I think we won't swim after all,' Lea said taking the rope from the rock. 'Need to go back to the hotel. Meeting people.' She started the engine and, waving, we slowly set off.

'Nice,' said Yusuf. He didn't wave or smile. No-one had smiled. Chattered, looked a bit worried. Obviously we'd been talked about.

After they'd grabbed food, someone had made a decision to let us go. Someone that we didn't see.□

CHAPTER FIFTEEN
Oof

Just as we had got out of the inlet and were back into the big blue sea, Uncle rang. Surprisingly good signal. We had waved till we were out of sight of the children and were about to discuss events, massively relieved that this episode was over. We had achieved what we set out to do.

'Barbara. Where on earth are you? I've only just got your message. No, don't do it!'

'Bit late. We're on our way back in the boat. All done and dusted. Very interesting. I'll explain in full when we're back. Don't forget you're going to the brothel.' Strange conversation to have with your uncle.

'How could I. You won't let me. See you later. I'll be a few hours yet. Tell Lea I said you are both obdurate,' he chuckled.

'Uncle has a message for you. You're obdurate. My turn to say 'So there!'.'

She beamed. Was she crowing? 'I know – so are you. Stubborn, obstinate, often inflexible, but otherwise lovely. And what do we make of all that with the kids?'

'Well – I think Enrico's friend is in it up to his neck. Bet they saw us and he sent the kids out to see what was going on. Who would suspect kids of anything?'

'I agree. No one was surprised to see us. Glad we went swimming – you know, all natural. Who's Enrico?'

'Takes you a bit to register some things,' I sighed. But really, I didn't care. I was happy with our adventure. 'The gay guy that was murdered. We must ask what his friend is called if he comes in tonight.' I paused. 'Actually, has he been in recently? I can't remember seeing him.'

'Me neither.'

By the time we got back to the harbour, the G-Ms boat was already moored up. We hot-footed it back to the Club. It was late afternoon now and we were relieved to relax. As we hadn't had any of the picnic we headed to the Pool Bar for a snack and found Alvaro there. Lea remembered to ask the barman's name: it was Miguel Martin. Apparently he had asked for time off after his friend had been found dead.

I texted Louisa to meet us later and catch up, and to bring Francis and Esme to join in planning any next moves. The more heads the better. I texted Hans too. Alvaro was working tonight so he was free the next evening. For some reason I felt elated and the fear had gone. I had faced my fears and come through. There would be more fear to face but this time I had found courage. And success breeds success. Surely our plans would go well. Suddenly, irrationally, I doubted my confidence. This is when things can go wrong, I thought. I shook myself. Only time would tell.

We brought Alvaro up to date and ate heartily when the snacks arrived. No need for a meal tonight. Just tapas. Or, as the Spanish say – 'tapa'. Bit like 'sheep' and 'sheep'. Who says 'sheeps'? A sudden image of sheep popped into my mind from some of our wonderful weekends away from London or uni. Welsh sheep, Lake District sheep, Scottish sheep. Sheep. Woolly backs. I giggled. How silly! But I deserved this little bit of self-congratulation.

'What next?' Lea brought me back from my reverie.

'Swim in the pool. Shower. Change. Wait for the others. You can swat up on your dictionary to surprise us all later.'

Feeling thoroughly rested, we made our way downstairs. Uncle was back and ensconced in one of the huge chairs in a quiet corner of Reception. He'd pulled enough around him to seat us all. He looked relaxed and pleased. He got up to kiss us, Spanish-style.

'How was your day, Uncle?'

'Very successful. I have a contract being drawn up with a big travel company in Madrid to send people here. We'll have a four-page feature all to ourselves in their brochure, plus TV advertising. They want me in the ad. I said only if you can be too. Do you mind? Means coming back here at some point – for the sun, swimming, glamour.'

'That'll will be great! Make a change from tunnels, human trafficking and stuff, not to mention fear and trepidation. But hey, all part of the travel business learning curve. Will posh people from Madrid want to rub up against coach tours?'

'Not all are posh, and besides the TV advertising will be national. The coach tours form part of the deal, with discounts on future tours with me. Us.'

'Why didn't you mention all this to me before?'

'Because, my dear Barbara, it was obvious to me at least, your mind was on other things, even when you rang me at home. I was setting it up then and was going to tell you but thought I would see how the land lay when I got here. You were even more pre-occupied when I did arrive. And rightly so. I am not criticizing you in the least. When things have been sorted, we'll be going to Madrid together. With your Spanish, it will be good to speak in their tongue – they had to speak to me in English.'

I was mollified. The others started drifting in. We all chatted about our respective days. When it came to the time for the nitty gritty of Lea's and my day, they listened intently.

'So – any opinions, folks? Suggestions for next move?' I finished up.

Esme spoke up. 'I think the adults – and this Miguel character – have something on the children. Threats and more as you told us, Lea. I would think they have a temporary base in the tunnels. How long that will last if they think they're rumbled is another matter! Children and adults alike.'

'Anyway, if they're well established there, they won't want to rush out to have to start afresh somewhere else. I think we have some time – but not too long. I did wonder if the spots you put in the main tunnel might be noticed and cause alarm. Let's hope they mainly use the sea entrance. Less obvious than landing a balloon in the mine. You can only do that so often before it attracts attention. Either that or it happens so frequently that people stop bothering.'

She continued, 'If they're genuinely expanding the balloon business they have an excuse to land there quite often by design. It is an intriguing place to finish the trip. Only – balloons do attract attention so it would be a bit hard to offload twenty suspicious-looking adults and children. Perhaps we should have a talk with the balloon company – though I'm not sure what we could ask without raising suspicion. From the sound of things in general, someone really is getting suspicious. A talk needs to be engineered.'

'I agree on both counts,' Louisa joined in. 'I had a glimpse into Karim's office this morning and saw a dog in there. And Karim, so I went in to say hello. Gorgeous dog, hard to resist. Like the one at the restaurant by the old dry harbour. Turns out the dogs are brother and sister. Karim is obviously very fond of dogs –'

'Told you he can't be all bad,' Lea interrupted.

'No. That was Hitler.' Everyone looked at me enquiringly. 'Don't ask. Carry on, Louisa. By the way – just curious. Can I ask – when 'Louie' is nearly as long as 'Louisa', why have it as a nick name?'

'Actually, my nickname is – or was – 'Georgie'. No reason. Someone called me that and it stuck, then someone else couldn't remember my proper name and made a stab at Louie. Then that stuck. The rest is history.'

I nodded my thanks. Francis winked at Louie with some private memory. I would have to ask about that – when I had more courage and opportunity.

'Where was I? Karim. Yes, he had to have the dog in the office today as the person who looks after it when he is at work had to do something else. He can shut it in his house but he hates doing that with his current long shifts and work at the boat-hire company too. He said on his way to the boat offices he often used to stop off in the mine and let the dog run free. It has a habit of not always coming back, and if he's short of time, the mine seems to keep it in one area. But recently, he was busy on his phone and didn't notice the dog had disappeared. He called and called and only after about half an hour it came back very subdued. It was injured – a cut. Quite deep. He thought it must be a cut from a rock and the dog had got stuck but when he took it to the vet, the vet said it was more likely a knife wound. Now the dog won't go near the mine.'

'Poor dog. I wonder if it was Karim I saw when we first looked down into the mine?' Lea pondered.

'Quite likely. But it does mean that anyone visiting is being discouraged. Though it can work the opposite way, like it did with us. Perhaps they thought better of killing the dog and set it free to save further investigation. We know for a fact now that the mine is the centre of our attention. Have I said that before?'

'I might be able to provide a way to question the balloon company,' Uncle said thoughtfully. All eyes turned to him. 'I'll mull over with them the possibility of specifically including them in my brochure, almost as though they are my company. It won't happen, of course, but it'll give me the opportunity to research the viability of the company, how it's run, by whom etc. I don't mean the public info, like who is registered on the books – well actually, that as well – but who on a daily basis runs it. How many? As in operating costs? How many bookings they have, where they go, how far they go, and so on. Even if they aren't interested before they can dismiss me, I will have been able to ask quite a lot. I think that would work! Can I leave it with you to set it all up, girls?'

'Wait, Charles,' said Lea 'how about it if you leave talking to the balloon company until after the last time you've been into the brothel. You can pretend to be disappointed that they've only got call girls – but only very mildly disappointed.

When Alvaro goes in later – drunk – he'll drop you in it. He can blurt out that his employer actually wants underage boys. That way the brothel owners might reveal more on the basis of hoping to tie you in, either as a strong partner or purely as a blackmail victim!'

Lea had hit on a good idea. We all agreed.

'So, Uncle, that's decided. You're going to the brothel tonight with Hans. Then we'll set up a meeting with the balloon company for a few days after tomorrow night, giving time for things to percolate.'

'I wonder – how about you and I take Charles and Hans to the brothel tonight, Babs.' Lea looked impish.

There was a general air of interest and amusement.

'On what basis? I know you're dying to tell us,' I asked. 'And we're all dying to hear, judging from everyone's expression.'

'Oof!' said Hans.

'Obviously two girls turning up at the front door of the brothel is going to be very unusual so it'll generate a lot of interest. You two men go in. You'll point to us girls parked up in the car, and say we're going to pick you up later. We can drive off for a drink, literally, and come back after half an hour. We'll wait, pretend to get fed up, knock on the door and ask for you. You still won't come out straight away so we'll sit around being conspicuous. If any gossip has got around after our boat trip this morning then people will know we went to the tunnel. Nothing wrong with that. They'll begin to think we're either very open-minded or half-crazy. The icing on the cake will be Alvaro tomorrow night. We won't say who we are tonight. Just guests at the Club.'

There was a general consensus.

'It will be very different,' said Hans cheerfully.' I am sure I can convince them to open the door to you later. We are the clients and leaving big tips. Sorry, Charles. You are leaving big tips. Me, I am leaving only merry with wine. But tonight you can leave merry. No driving.'

'Then so it is,' Uncle sealed it. 'In for a penny – '

'Do you want to change into something more svelte?' Lea put her head on one side, looking coquettish.

'Wondered when your dictionary would make an appearance!' I grumbled.

'It's a perfectly normal word. It's a fashion word – and you know I'm into fashion.'

'Yeah, OK. Whatever. Yes, let's. One should always dress up when visiting brothels. All you need is more bling. I'm going for black velvet. For the nightclub after. Aren't we, Uncle?'

He gave a mock sigh. 'If we must, child.' He looked at Hans and gave an 'I'm giving in' shrug. 'My pleasure, girls!'

'Ok, see you in a mo. Time to be off soon anyway. Anyone around later?' Various probablys and maybes ensued.

We were back in quick time, Lea all blinged up and me svelting for England. We all strolled to the car.

'Gentlemen in the back, please. You drive, Lea. They'll see you coming a mile off with all that sparkle on. You'll be glowing in the dark!'

'Thank you!' She beamed, happy at the compliment.

We drew up just outside the brothel door. The two doormen had a most quizzical look on their faces. Hans got out first and started talking and pointing to us. We pouted outrageously and giggled a lot. Blew a few kisses. Uncle followed, handing a handsome tip to each doorman. They smiled their acceptance.

Lea backed the car and we drove off to the nearest bar. Just our luck – it was very much a down-to-earth locals bar.

'Oh dear. Ah well, here goes nothing.' Lea jumped out so quickly I didn't have time to suggest finding something more upmarket. She was through the door and gone. I had no choice but to follow. By the time I got in there she had the barman smiling and the locals – all men – shouting out and clapping.

'How did you do that – and so quick?' Two white wines appeared.

'You were slow. I saw you trying to hide under the dashboard.' She stopped for a slurp of wine and said

'Cheers!' to the room, receiving a unanimous reception back. The admiring stares – not even surreptitious glances – didn't waver. I used English first so they knew I was a nutty foreigner, then used my best Spanish with many apologies, saying we were waiting for friends. Would they mind? Was it possible to have a drink, because it was such a treat to be in a proper local bar, not one of these posh places. I was going to one of those later but would rather stay here. I loved to meet the older locals with all the traditional values.

'You said all that in one minute? Plus with your Spanish accent they would know you were a nutty foreigner.' I had my sceptical face on.

She sniffed. 'You were three or four minutes. You weren't going to get out until I disappeared. But, yes, I said all that. The barman helped. He speaks some English. He told the locals. Not that it mattered but I said I didn't want to spoil their evening and could he ask them. Actually, he told them and they all were OK with it. Something to talk about.' With that she picked up her glass and went to say personal hellos to them. Table by table. They were enchanted.

I was left with the barman, who seemed happy with that. We started chatting. Half an hour sped by. In fact we were enjoying ourselves so much it slid into forty-five minutes. I glanced at my watch and waved over, pointing at the time. Lea slowly disengaged herself from the whole room. Goodbye here, goodbye there. Kisses all round. Waving. Come back soon. Please! Come back soon! They waved to me with – almost – the same enthusiasm. Lea was so happy.

'What a lovely bunch of people. So welcoming.' She couldn't stop smiling. We were back at the brothel in a few minutes. Parked near the door this time.

'Shall we both get out?'

'Why not?' We did, and rang the bell. The doorman looked through the peephole and opened up as soon as he saw us. We saw Uncle and Hans at the bar, with the girls sitting around the room. It was as pleasant as Uncle had described. We were surprised. It was a huge, comfy lounge. The wide stairs to the bedrooms were in the middle. Hans and Uncle were talking to a man at the bar.

'Please tell them we're here. Por favor, mi amigos.' Lea waved at Uncle but it wasn't necessary as the doorman knew what we wanted. He just said 'Si' and shut the door.

We went back to the car. Lea climbed on to the roof and sat there, legs splayed over the windscreen. I joined her. I felt devilish for some reason. I was minus the splayed legs. I had mine neatly, side by side. More me. If legs on a car roof didn't attract attention, nothing would.

We were there several minutes before the door opened again and one of the doormen walked over to us. He was eyeing up the sight in some amazement but obviously enjoying it too.

'Good evening. Buenas noches.'

Lea was 'incandescent'. Her reception at the previous bar seemed to have turned up the light she emitted by several notches. 'Will our friends be long? They didn't seem to find what they wanted here? Shame! It looks nice.'

'I am surprised they want anything else with two chicas like you.'

'Ah, when you have steak at home, sometimes you want a burger. Do you understand the English?'

'I understand. And what is it that they want? There are plenty of burgers inside.'

'Hmm. Not for me to say. We just have fun. Sometimes many of us. All ages. Not much choice here, they tell me. Never mind. Another day, another place. They will find something. Maybe. We leave soon for England. Would be nice to find some fun before we go.'

I gave her a very obvious dig. She said 'Ouch' and looked pained.

I cut in both for effect and to stop any more hints being dropped. 'We need to go. We are meeting some people, so could you get our friends for us, please. We will be late.'

My tone was final and the doorman moved reluctantly away. As he was walking back, Uncle and Hans came out. They said goodnight without any preamble. We didn't want things moving too fast. Lea's chatter could have been dangerous.

We got down from the roof.

'Where to? You taxi is at your disposal?'

'Do you want to find a nightclub then? What about driving?'

'Lea's driving so I'm OK.'

'Oh, thanks. One drink, then back to the Club. How did you both do in there, then? We saw you talking to a man at the bar.'

'It was just talk. Nothing of relevance. We left a gentle hint of having money enough for anything. Got a bit awkward when we were asked to specify but I wriggled out of it. Group fun, kept it vague, said we might be back tomorrow. Then we can leave it to Alvaro.'

'Lea did a good job with hints.'

'We had a great double act going. Babs poked me in the ribs to stop me saying anything more. It hurt. Genuinely. Still, one has to suffer for one's art.'

'So, let's enjoy tonight. More planning manána. Breakfast meeting? Late breakfast? Or brunch?' We left in good spirits.

Morning followed evening.

Alvaro off duty joined us for brunch. I had texted him. Hans had come up as specified by us last night. Apparently his clients at the finca could wait. I wondered if anyone ever got fed up with finding him closed.

No one else was around as it was up to us today to 'do' our final push. So Uncle, Alvaro, Lea, Hans and I were in confab. Not that there was much that hadn't already been discussed. It was mainly down to timing – and good acting. Should we girls go to the brothel again? I voiced my question. What could be gained this time round?

'I really don't think you coming along would contribute further.' Silence after Uncle's decree.

'Unless, unless ¬'Lea looked thoughtful.

'Unless what, Lea? Spit it out.'

'I'm thinking on my feet – '

'Oh, don't tempt me with such invitations.'

She had a suitably pained look. 'If we could borrow a child from someone – '

'What!' There was a collective yelp.

'You asked me to spit it out. If Babs and I come along in the car again, drop you off but with a kid in tow, it reinforces what you want when push comes to shove. Makes us seem more credible.'

'Oh, there must be simply loads of kids hanging around just dying to come to a brothel with us!' I snorted. Everyone else looked bemused.

'Well – I know one. While you were still in bed this morning, Babs – no change there, then – I was out and about and got chatting to a feisty little guy on my travels. Cheeky devil. Nearly pinched my bag. I came back from seeing my animals through the gypsy area. I stopped because some children were playing in the road and didn't move. Suppose it was designed to stop me and then they could pinch something. I made the mistake of opening my window to ask them to move.'

We wagged fingers at her.

'I know! Stupid! Anyway,' she continued, 'my doors were locked but I heard one of them fiddling with a back door so I whipped round and caught this kid. Turns out he was called Elijah. He ran off laughing but I called him back. Got chatting – as I do. Told them all that if they hadn't done that I might have given them some money, but I wouldn't now. They kicked the dirt around and looked sullen.'

'Were you speaking Spanish?'

'Spanglish. Anyway, I was forming this idea – the one I have now.'

'You were planning this?' I was amazed. We all were.

'Sort of. Are you going to let me finish?

We shut up.

'I told Elijah he could earn some money for his gang and I might be back later. I wanted to OK it with his family so I would know where he lives. My proposal is that we tell him it's a joke to play against the brothel and all he has to do is sit in the car looking sullen. Which shouldn't be much of a problem. We pay half up front and half on completion. Whatever we decide he is worthy of. Drive him back to his house.'

'You sound like a hardened professional criminal. Half upfront!' Uncle was amused. 'But – I do think it's worth considering. What say all of you?'

'I'm for it. Show of hands?' I turned to them all.

'What?' Hans thought he had been addressed.

'No – hands up in favour of Lea's idea.'

'Oh – sorry. Yes, me. Hands up.'

It was unanimous.

'Well, I'll go and look for Elijah and arrange it. So – how much do you think? Maybe less than half to start in case he just takes the money and doesn't play fair.'

'I think fifteen euros is enough. Five to start with. I'm the banker remember.'

'Fine by me, Charles.' Lea looked satisfied. We all agreed. Uncle pulled five euros out of his pocket and handed it over.

'Shall we come with you?' Alvaro asked. 'Safety.'

'No. Just me and Babs. You two hang around if you want.' Lea indicated Hans and Alvaro. 'See you in the pool later. Don't you have to open your finca, Hans?'

'Yes. I should. So we see us later. I will come for a swim after my lunch.' He left slowly, reluctantly. Obviously work wasn't figuring highly today.

'I wonder how he does with his business?' Uncle speculated. 'Such a big place. I've only seen it from the outside but it seems to have unexplored potential. My guess is it is underperforming. I might dwell on it – as well as your tunnel wine bars and shops, Barbara, of course. I'm off to relax before my final performance tonight. See you later, girls. Be careful. Alvaro – do you want to come up with me for a – er – hmm – coffee?'

I was immediately suspicious. What was Uncle up to? Alvaro looked a bit surprised but got up with alacrity as Uncle departed. I looked across at Lea.

230

'You're the leader. I'm just the passenger. Tell me what you want me to do and let's get going. On the way I'm going to tell Louisa about all this. We don't want to be accused of kidnapping. Now – vámanos. You have your bag, so no excuses.'

Off we set.

CHAPTER SIXTEEN
Revelations

I had cleared things with Louisa, and now Lea and I were approaching the gypsy enclave. It was quiet. A few adults were leaning against walls and doors, trying to keep in the shade. It was a scruffy area and whilst I had a feeling I should feel sorry for this poverty, I also felt uneasy.

Lea didn't show the concern I felt. She was slowing down and when we got to the centre, she stopped – and waited. We were being watched. I could feel eyes everywhere. She got out and stood leaning on the car door. It seemed ages before any movement came into focus. A kid came out of the shadows of a house.

'Elijah!' Lea beamed and moved straight towards him. He wasn't sure of himself but he had a half-smile on his face. Part curiosity, part nervousness. He stopped as she approached. She cocked her head to one side, looking completely disarming. She emanated friendliness. She put her hand out and said something in Spanglish approaching, 'I would kiss you on both cheeks Spanish style but your friends might laugh.' She ruffled his hair instead. He was taken aback but broke into a broad beaming smile. The ice had been broken.

'Elijah, I should meet your mother and father. I want you to do something for me and my friend tonight and it will be late for you to be out. Mi amiga tranduces para mi.' She waved me over.

I got out smiling in what I hoped was a friendly manner. Some of my smiles can look frightening. I duly translated but he already had the gist. He beckoned us into the house nearest. I hadn't locked the car and panicked. I had a feeling my smile had just frozen. I had my bag with me but Lea had left hers in the car. I stage-whispered to her. She ignored me.

We went into a large room, dark against the sun. It was basic but very clean. Kitchen facilities were adequate – table and chairs for four, an old, faded, worn sofa and three matching chairs.

Various small tables were strewn about with all manner of detritus everywhere. It wasn't untidy as such, but more a statement of children being around. Old shoes, T shirts, broken toys, books – yes, books. Also a dog was curled up in a corner. Lea saw it and asked immediately if she could pet it. It was passive, and accepted her fondling without demure.

Two adults emerged from a corner where a curtain separated this room from another. Lea straightened up and went to say hello. They didn't proffer hands or look much like they did air kisses so she settled for a small smile and a genuine look. How did she pull that out of the bag? She began to speak.

The father smiled back and came out with, 'Senorita, I speak English. No problema. I work for long time with English builders. Now no work but –' His words drifted off and he looked downcast. This rather stopped us in our tracks.

Lea was the first to pull herself together. 'Well then, we hope this will help you a little. We would like to borrow Elijah tonight for about two hours, including travelling. It means he will be home late, about 11 o'clock ¬ and we will pay you. Fifty euros. For all the children to share.' My eyes widened.

The man smiled and spoke rapidly with his wife in a language I didn't understand. 'Eleven is not late in Spain. But our concern is why you want him? We don't know you – and even if you pay for him, why?'

Lea and I looked at each other briefly.

I began to speak in Spanish but he held his hand up to stop me. 'Please, we all speak English. Elijah not so well but enough. My wife has good English. She worked in hotels for a long time.'

This took some thinking about. Why didn't they now and why would their son be a petty thief?

'We have a joke to play on someone. My uncle and a friend. It is complicated and so difficult to explain. Does it matter? We will pick him up at about 9 pm tonight and return about 11pm. I will give you our names and where we are staying so you can check. He will be safe.' I waited.

'Who is your uncle?'

'Charles Madden. He owns the La Roca Club. I am his niece, and this is my friend Lea.'

'Senora,' I immediately bristled internally,' what is this joke that you need our son? What will he have to do?'

'Sit in our car with us. Nothing else. We are taking my uncle and a friend to a club. You know, club?'

'Yes, all Spanish men - and women – know about clubs. But what kind of joke is this – and to involve Elijah? I don't think I am happy.'

'This is a private joke you wouldn't understand. English humour! Elijah is to sit in the car. Nothing to say. Just be there. Nothing more. Do you have a car? If so, follow us but you would need to stay out of sight. We drop my uncle off at the club, we go to a bar and buy Elijah a coke or something, maybe a tapa, return to pick up my uncle and friend and bring Elijah back. Or you can take him after we have picked my uncle up if you want to come with us. One hundred euros. I can't offer more.'

Lea's turn to widen her eyes? A family discussion followed, including Elijah who appeared very keen, obviously batting aside all objections.

'Senora, we agree. But, please – I want to meet your uncle to make sure of things. I come back with you to La Roca – yes?'

'Yes. No. Well, yes – but you can't mention the money or it will spoil it. We are meeting by the pool so you can have a drink with us there.' He nodded. ' Er – sorry, I don't mean to be rude, but perhaps you could change out of your work clothes into jeans, T shirt or something? Please don't be offended. I will give you half now and the other tonight.' He accepted without hesitation – the money and the suggestion.

'I understand. I did some work on La Roca. I know it is full of people with good clothes. I will come by my own car so see you by the pool soon. My name is Mansour if you need to give permission. Originally I – we – are from Morocco. Now we live here.' He waved his arm around desultorily, indicating the dusty, run-down collection of houses. Apathy seemed to pervade the atmosphere, with people just standing around and children of all ages playing in the dust.

'Just walk in, Mansour. You can say you're visiting Barbara and Lea.' We set off. Lea's bag was still on the back seat intact. She gave me a 'told you so' superior look.

'How do we play this, Babs? What do we say to your uncle?'

'First we tell him I'm a senorita not a senora. I'll think about the rest.' I was thoroughly miffed.

'Oh. Well, if it makes you happy it probably means Mansour thinks of me as childish and unworldly. Whereas you are mature and stately.'

'You make me sound like a stately home. Old! You're not helping.'

'Vintage quality then. Like a good claret. Gets better with age.'

'Do you want to live?' I flashed one of my grotesque smiles. She went quiet.

'There's nothing to tell Uncle apart from the kid's father wanting to know it's all safe. I'll pay the money. End of story.'

We parked up in shade and headed to the pool. Uncle and Alvaro were relaxing and chatting. So nice to see them getting on. It reminded me to ask what they had been talking about.

'We have sorted out Lea's willing kid – but the father is coming to check us out in a few minutes. We said it was all for a silly English joke. Don't think he was convinced but fifteen euros helped sway things. They are very poor though the father and mother used to work.'

'Money always talks.' Uncle smiled. I felt guilty.

'If he comes while we are upstairs, he's called Mansour. Swarthy-looking chap. Hard to miss.' We threw bags on two loungers and went to change into swimming gear. Hurrying back, we saw Mansour approaching the pool so we waved him over. He had scrubbed up well.

'Mansour, this is my Uncle Charles. Charles Madden.' Uncle stood up and shook hands.

'I hear you think we English have a strange sense of humour? Blame the girls. It's a challenge to invade to some extent the man's world of going to a club. That's the only way I can explain. Shall we sit at the table? Would you like a drink?' We all moved to the nearby table.

'Orange juice is good. Thank you.'

Uncle called for drinks all round. We had our fresh lemonade.

'I am told you are the boss here, Mr Madden? How long have you been here?'

'I'm not the boss – as in working here. I own La Roca. And a travel company – Madden's Magic Carpet Tours. There are brochures in reception you can take.'

'Thank you. I will look. I did some labour work here a few years ago. One of the new blocks for bedrooms over there.' He pointed to where Lea and I had had our room. 'A good English builder but he went back to the UK. Now work is no more. I try everywhere.'

'I am having some upgrading done on some of the rooms and suites – some taking down some walls and decorating. If you are interested?'

'Of course. But you must see my work first. I can do something small. Can you test me please?'

'I will think about this. We have some other urgent things to do, all of us, but before we leave, we will talk and organize something.'

'Good of you to keep me up to speed, Uncle.'

'Sorry, Barbara. I was meaning to tell you but you have been out a lot – doing things.' He looked at me pointedly.

'Suppose. Anyway – Mansour has a wife who used to work in hotels and she speaks English. Would there be anything for her – or not? Does your wife want any work, Mansour?'

'Very much. She came up here a few weeks ago but there was nothing. She wanted to be a room maid.'

'Things have changed. Someone left unexpectedly and we had to move staff around so now housekeeping is short-staffed. I will tell my manager, Carl, to give her an interview. Can you phone him to arrange something? I will introduce you before you go.'

'Thank you very much. It is very, very good of you. We work well. You will see. Some people don't like to give work to anyone from the gypsy village. They are worried we will steal things but my family is not gypsy. We are Moroccans and work well and cheaply. We have to live in that village because we can't afford more. It is worrying because Elijah has bad influence from the gypsy children. He say not, but I know it. I see him stopping people who drive through the village and the trick is for one to talk and another looks to steal anything from the cars. If they are caught or seen they run off laughing. We worry all the time for Elijah. He goes to school but not always.'

'The children tried that on me, Mansour – which is how we met. And then I came back with my idea for a joke. For once it worked well. Maybe, if you have work, his attitude will change. He could help you a bit? Give him a purpose – and pride.'

'Perhaps. I hope so. I will try. He is twelve and has this bad influence since two years when we moved to the village. Bad habits are hard to break. But now we have hope.' He smiled graciously. 'Now I shall go and we see you about nine o'clock. No need for me to follow you.'

'Come with me to meet Carl, Mansour. I will leave him with you.' They got up, with Mansour saying many effusive thank yous, and went to find Carl.

'I do like happy endings' sighed Lea. 'Speaking of which, what are we going to do about the boat-hire company? I know Karim is involved – so can we pump him for information without arousing suspicion? And – just what do we ask? Are you trafficking people? Straight to the point? I am joking, of course.'

'We would never have guessed.' I replied.

'As it happens,' Alvaro piped up, 'if we get this evening over with and see where it is leading, it might just be the thing to do. I don't think Karim is involved but – you never know. It isn't a crime to be slimy though he has been better lately. He has been occupied with his dog. You heard about what happened to it in the mine?'

'Yes. Awful. Poor guy. Poor dog. I can't abide cruelty to animals. Or people. Or injustice. Or hate. Or – '

'Think we've got the picture, Lea. And I do agree for the record. In the meantime, I also agree with Alvaro. Wait and see. We need to consult with Louisa before we go off at any tangent. Depending on what happens after tonight, maybe another trip by boat to the kids will flush some other things out. I think taking Francis and another man – or two – could be advisable next time round. They can't murder people by the dozen – whoever and however many are in the tunnel.'

'There's the Gore-Marsdens and that Arab. Coming this way. Wonder if we can pump them too?' We were all still at the table and Uncle rejoined us. Louisa, Esme and Francis appeared. It was a gathering of the clans. They came and sat at the next table so I leaned across and whispered to ask Louisa if she could invite the G-Ms over. Quick briefing of things and an arranged smile as Alexander and Rosalind Gore-Marsden responded to her wave. What on earth could I – we – ask?

'Alexander, I'm told you have a very interesting job and you are actually working while you are here.' They were settling at a table so we could all talk. The Arab looked agreeable.

'Yes, to both. I'm a marine loss adjuster. I get sent all over the world to assess insurance claims made by ships. This time, by pure chance, it was here – so I get paid to be on a working holiday. My colleague was sent over too as this lot on the ship are a bit – how can I put this? Unsavoury. If I say the ship doesn't move till I'm satisfied, it doesn't move. But this makes for enemies, as sitting in a harbour costs money and loses money. I got the feeling I might get pushed over into a cargo-hold area so I asked for back up and James here came to my aid.'

'James – strange name for an Arab!' Lea blurted. 'We saw you in flowing robes. I'm curious. Do tell.' James beamed with amusement.

'Can we ask why?' enquired Louie.

'Er – not really. It's becoming a police matter. I have had cause to go to el capitan here.' All our collective eyes met.

'Then you have met my son?'

'I was in Dubai on a job and I work in those clothes as it's a lot cooler. My preference. I happened to arrive in them. No mystery. I'm as English as Alex. You did have a wobble at the start didn't you, Alex. Had to take Rosalind along for backup. Bit hairy.'

'Yes. I had to go to the ship one evening and wasn't at all keen, so Rosalind came with me and stayed in the car inside the port. The ships are in the commercial harbour which can be pretty deserted at night. They have to think twice before doing anything wrong if they have two people to deal with. One of us could be said to have fallen into a hold – but two? And one not even working. It's a bit of a hot potato, this ship.'

Total confusion from Alex. 'Your son? I remember you saying he was a policeman but I didn't take much notice to be honest. I assumed he was a policeman in England. So – your son is a policeman here?'

'Yes, Alex. El Capitan Spelier-Bielby. A Brit. Born in Spain though.'

'Good heavens. I – we – didn't know. No one gave me his name. Just called him 'el capitan'. What a small world!' The three of them were genuinely nonplussed.

'Well, I can tell you a bit then. I had to hire a boat to inspect some damage on the seaward side above the water line and amongst all the ropes and chains and damage I saw – James and I saw – something sparkling, so we picked it up. Small so you wouldn't normally notice it. Then we saw three more, and something that was bigger and didn't sparkle. Turns out they are all diamonds. One uncut. So we took them to your son, Louisa. We are all waiting for the next move. No one knows we found them. Must have fallen overboard somehow but I'm blessed if I know how, even with a collision involved. You don't stand by a rail with a bag of diamonds in your hand waiting to crash into another ship. Which they must have seen. That's the other thing. Where they were out at sea how could they possibly collide with all the equipment they have these days? They must have been very preoccupied. Bit of a mystery.'

'Absolutely fascinating. You do have an interesting job. Oh, any more please?' Lea looked dreamy. Esme was wide-eyed, Francis beaming. Uncle was rooted to his chair, hoping for more. We all were. We weren't disappointed.

'There is something, but I really can't elaborate. Because I'm not sure yet. I have a funny feeling about the holds. I did some measuring – for the damaged bits – and found some discrepancies in the internal and external sizes. Meaning gaps – for something. Couldn't see any ways into the gaps but maybe panels can be removed. That's what James and I need to investigate next. But we need to tread very carefully in case they can think of how to make two people disappear plausibly. That's as far as we have got.'

He looked at us all and something registered that we were holding something back from him. We all sat there in silence but it must have been obvious our brains were working hard.

'Am I missing something here? You all have a funny look on your faces.'

Continued silence. We didn't know how to proceed.

'Come on. I've told you some things a bit on the secret side – so what gives? Are you going to report me now for blabbing state secrets?'

'Far from it.' Louisa broke the silence. 'We too have some things to tell you. Now that we know you are the good guys.'

'The good guys? What do you mean? I was never a bad guy.'

'No. But we didn't know that till now. For which we all apologise. Don't we?' We all nodded solemnly, and murmured in agreement.

He looked astonished. 'What were you thinking of accusing me of?' said in a less friendly tone.

'We didn't accuse you of anything. But when I tell you what we have been investigating, I hope you will understand why we had to include you, along with others, in the possibility that you were somehow involved – maybe without knowing. Please, before you blow your top, hear me out. Then you can say what you want.' I hoped this would mollify them somewhat.

'A while ago, Babs and Lea came across some disturbing incidents that have escalated into something serious that at some point soon, I will have to make my son aware of. Your 'capitan'. The people you see here around this table – plus one more who isn't currently here – have been investigating people-trafficking.' Here all three moved to protest but Louisa held up a hand. 'Without permission or knowledge of my son. Totally unofficial till we had some proof to hand over. We are nearly there. We had speculated about you and Rosalind simply because you were in various places and we didn't know why. You just happened to turn up. In no particular order – being in the boat near the tunnel that goes down to the sea, us seeing you at night going on to the ship, always late for – well anything, hardly being around, turning up with the person we now know is James, and James looking like an Arab. It was only speculation, but when you don't have all facts to hand, things can add up to more than they should because of other outside factors.'

Alex and Rosalind sat thinking. Eventually Alex spoke. 'I don't know what to say. It's horrifying. All of it. How did you know we went to the ship late at night though?'

Oops, I thought. We did follow them.

'Lea and I wanted to explore one evening,' I replied, 'and we went to the Harbour Deportivo, then on to see the commercial harbour to see how things work for real. Holiday Spain is nice but I like to know how locals function. Even the gas tanks interested us. You really just happened to come along. There was no one thing that as a standalone, would have been incriminating. Same for the other people we have wondered about. We can only apologise, as Louisa said.'

Alex let out a long breath. 'As it happens,' he said, 'James and I were speculating about the missing space in the ship's holds. It did occur to us people smuggling was a possibility but we were going to make sure before we passed this on to your son, Louisa. The ship's crew know nothing of our diamond find and we want to keep a low profile – I mean as much as we can as marine loss adjusters. I was wondering if I could persuade the crew to all take a night off – but I doubt it. Too suspicious. I think we will have to brazen it out – one of us on deck and the other tapping for hollow places. Might be small as in drug concealment. Not people.'

'May I make a suggestion?' We all looked at Francis. 'Several of us go with you. Can you say we're working with you? Or else we can stay very pointedly on shore after conspicuously dropping you off? Any good?'

'Oh, yes, we'll all come with you!' Esme was excited. Alex was amused at the enthusiasm.

'That would be marvellous. Can I think about it – the form of it? Get back to you? The ship's not going anywhere as it hasn't been signed off by me. Also, they will probably want to appoint an assessor to argue their case for money. Bit late, mind you. Should be done at the start. Unless they are so guilty they want to scram. Thinking about it, personally I think they want to scram as fast as possible. They hadn't bargained on having an accident, not only because of delay, but to bring investigation upon them. Most unwanted. The captain is one of the owners, so has a lot of say in what goes on.'

'We have some things to do tonight so take your time. Tell Louisa. Here is my card anyway.' Uncle handed over his private phone number. 'Do you think the boat hire company has any dealings in any of this? We think a lot of to-ing and fro-ing goes on from the sea tunnel. As well as the balloons.'

'Wow. I see. Big operation. I had no idea about the balloons but the boat hire – it crossed our minds, didn't it, James? Transport is all important. Boats fit in with ships. We don't have any concrete proof of how things – diamonds or people – are moved around. Like you, speculation. Fast is all I can say. Get things out of view.'

'At least I came on the scene too late to be suspected,' James chipped in.

'Actually no. Don't take this the wrong way but as you were dressed as an Arab and they do like the odd boy – we thought you might be an important client coming over to choose.'

'Oh, I see. I suppose I asked for that. I caught the sun in Dubai.' He looked sheepish.

We all felt we had got further than expected and had a sense of elation. We talked more then began to split up to re-group for the evening ahead but at the last minute, Alex cornered Louisa and Francis. I heard him ask if they were free to accompany him and James to the ship that night.

He'd talked it over with James.

I sidled over and butted in. 'Great. The more the merrier. Safety in numbers. How about Esme? Anyone else do you think? How about Mr Campbell Casson-Parker or Mr Farnworth-Seager?' I surprised myself remembering their names. It apparently surprised Lea and Louisa too.

Lea had joined us all ears flapping.

'I'll ask everyone,' said Louisa. 'Give them a basic idea of what's going on. We can take two cars as well as Alex's. We have big cars. Mine lives here and it's a massive 4-wheeler. I like to go up a lot of mountain tracks. I'll let you know, Alex. We have each other's phone numbers already, so I'll ring or text later.'

We all drifted apart again, even more satisfied with the rapidly gathering progress. □

CHAPTER SEVENTEEN
Things Get Strong.

As evening approached, we all got ready to do battle.

I wondered how many such battles we would have before handing over to the authorities. It was all nerve racking but at the same time exciting. Francis and Louisa didn't seem to have any nerves, which I envied. Lea said she did but didn't show them. Another annoying trait.

Was I the only one to feel like a jelly? Tonight didn't involve me much but my mind was racing ahead to the next phase and how much danger we could be in. My problem was worrying about what might happen. At uni I would worry myself into a frenzy about exams to the point where I could hardly bear to turn up. Lea sailed through, telling me she enjoyed the challenge. What would she do if she failed, I asked? Be an artist anyway. Take the exams again. Shrug of shoulders. Life would take care of it. Maybe she would get a job caring for animals – her passion.

She annoyed me so much even back then. I often wondered how we had come to be best friends.

She told me once – and it has stuck in my mind ever since – that it is because we are so opposite.

We complement each other's weaknesses and strengths. We feed off each other, one supplying one thing and the other, another, to support whatever we are doing. Symbiotic. It has occurred to me on occasions that I might just annoy her. Rare occasions mind you!

We were lounging in Reception when Hans arrived, all spruced up. Not that he particularly needed to. He was always smart, even when he had been working fitting a jacuzzi for a client. We didn't bother with drinks. Clear heads needed. Gradually everyone drifted in, including all the Double Barrellers. Seems we were all going out at the same time, but in different directions.

'Isn't this a bit late to inspect a ship?' I asked Alex.

'I like to catch them off guard. Besides, there's plenty of light aboard.' He looked around at all the people. His comrades, friends, holiday companions, all come to support him and James. 'I am grateful to you all. I never expected this. What can I say? Drinks are on me later!' A collective 'hurray' came.

'Doubles all round!' Francis smiled. 'Shall we get off? Let's get in groups for the cars and follow Alex. We know where the harbour is but if we get separated we need to meet you at the gate to get us in. How are you going to justify so many of us all going in?'

'I can do what I want but if necessary I'll say you're a corporation interested in investing in a similar ship and want to do price comparisons based on size and condition. Bullshit usually works. I don't think I can get you on board but if you wander around looking as though you are really interested you might be allowed aboard – not that it matters. Your presence is enough.'

'Vámanos!' Francis shooed everyone out.

That left Uncle, Hans, Alvaro, Lea and I. Alvaro was following along to the club a bit later, so we set off to collect Elijah. He was ready and waiting for us, and came scampering out as soon as he heard the car. Mansour followed and just waved.

I was driving this time so Lea motioned Elijah to join her in the back with Hans. Elijah was shy with the others, all his bravado gone when not backed up by his friends, so the sweets Lea had brought along helped. He munched happily and looked to her for reassurance. She got her dictionary out and chattered away in Spanglish with Elijah responding with hesitant English which, while slow, was pretty much correct. It would stand him in good stead for work in the future if he got away from all the bad influences.

It didn't take long to get to the club and I drew up right outside the front door. Uncle and Hans got out slowly talking to us so we were on view – we hoped – for a while. It did the trick and a doorman came out to look at us. We didn't recognize him but someone shouted from inside and he came forward to greet Uncle and Hans. Lea pushed Elijah over, so he spread out in the back seat and stared at the doorman who stared back with immense curiosity. She had told Elijah not to smile and try to look sullen. He did a marvellous job.

Uncle and Hans went in and I roared off, scattering some gravel. I smiled and talked animatedly to Lea in the back seat. She responded with handwaving gestures and laughter. The doorman watched closely, then closed the door on Uncle and Hans. My peripheral vision is second to none.

Elijah asked if that was all he had to do.

'Nearly. We need to pick up my uncle and my friend again, then that's it. Now would you like a tapa?'

'Yes, please.' He smiled shyly. Gone was the brazen attitude he had had when surrounded by his friends.

I headed for the bar Lea and I had been in the night before. We made our second spectacular entrance. We were dressed up to go clubbing again but with a child in tow. As Lea opened the door several of the occupants recognized us and a chorus of greetings went up. Smiles all round.

We went to the tapas bar and told Elijah to pick what he wanted. He asked for orange squash to go with the food. Lea ordered wines for us and we sat down at a convenient table to wait for our food and drink. Greetings kept coming our way so Lea set off on another tour of the room while I sat with Elijah. Fortunately the mountain of food arrived so I didn't have to make small talk – not my forte with children.

Elijah's eyes were wide with surprise and glee at the amount of food in front of him. He managed to explain that this was his first such treat. His excitement was catching, as he squirmed around in his chair tasting first one, then another tapa. Everyone looked and smiled while Lea explained he was a friend's kid out for a treat while his parents were out. I thought we would have to have takeaways but Elijah steadily munched his way through the lot.

I ordered two more wines, making mine a small one, and talk criss-crossed the whole bar, laced with good-natured humour. Time flew. I realized nearly an hour had passed so I shouted to Lea that we should go soon. She extricated herself from her admirers, promising – hand on heart – that we'd see them all again before we went home.

We got back to the club and parked outside the door. I gave a quick blast on the horn. We noticed Alvaro's car parked up. The doorman opened up and saw us. We beamed then he went back in. A few minutes later Uncle and Hans came out, dispensing tips.

When they were in the car Hans said, 'Oof. That was strong!' He shook his head.

Uncle half-turned so Lea could hear but he was guarded in what he said in front of Elijah.

'We've made our point. Alvaro was – as far as I could see or hear from a distance – doing a great job of dropping us in it. We got a few glances. I left a card with my old phone number on. I brought my old phone as a spare. You never know. I'll tell you later but – success, I think! Shall we get Elijah home now? Did you have a good time?' He smiled broadly at Elijah who smiled back engagingly.

'I had a good time. Thank you. Lots of food. I never have this before.' ☐

CHAPTER EIGHTEEN
Amateur Sleuths

By 9.30 am breakfast had come and gone. We continued to sit in the dining room ahead of the day's meetings.

I felt like death warmed up. Hadn't we done enough the night before? Surely we didn't need to plan anything else? Why couldn't I have had my usual morning lie-in? I wasn't exactly grumpy – but I wasn't not grumpy either!

Lea was fizzing as usual. Been up since 7.30 am. She'd seen to her animals, followed that with a swim and had, I noticed, picked a rag-tag bunch of wilting flowers.

'What are you doing with those things?' I commented gruffly.

'Rescuing them. What else? They'll be beautiful when they get into water.'

Uncle looked smart, ready for the meeting at the boat offices. Hans had joined us for coffee and, seeing my mood, had the utmost pleasure in baiting me. His increasing amusement riled me and I responded waspish, which brought even more provocation in the form of Uncle telling me I always had been surly and cantankerous in the morning. 'And she hides it so well!' grinned Lea. She and Hans fell about laughing, and I responded in full Queen Victoria mode only to be told by Uncle that I was being pompous.

I hated mornings, full stop. It was 11 am before I was ready to join the world again.

Alex of the G-Ms and James were elated at how many of the Double Barrellers had turned out. He went round the tables where they were sat, filling in the details of our plan. He had informed the authorities in the commercial harbour that he was bringing some more people on board the ship he was assessing, as demanded by his company.

The start was for all to meet in Reception at 2 pm. Cars were to follow Alex and park just outside the perimeter of the fence near to his car on the inside. The ship was moored near the fence.

By the time we had shared cars, there would only be four of them in the area, and they would all be outside. We hoped this would avoid a row with the security guards. Alex would explain to them that fellow experts were accompanying him on board the ship to give a second opinion. This would be backed up by some official-looking paperwork, courtesy of Louie. Some of this paperwork was in fact genuine, from Alex's insurance company, in technical convoluted English and loose Spanish translation. Captain and crew spoke English, of course, but it was biased towards shipping matters. Louisa was already looking the part of the absolutely no-nonsense authoritarian boss, newly hauled in. She had some ID she flashed around which made me curious, but not enough to move from my chair or ask what it was. The more we learned about her, the less we knew. A deep person. Or at least a woman with a past.

Should eyebrows and questions be raised, we would say that most of the women in the cars were merely accompanying their husbands before they all went off to a social event connected with work.

I listened and observed through a fog.

'Babs!' A sharp call to attention.

'What?' I snapped, frowning.

'Your uncle told me to tell you we should be off in the next half hour. Go and get ready. Smart casual. Hans and I will wait here. Go on! I have our instructions. And take the flowers I've picked. There's a vase so put them in it. Please!'

'Instructions for what?' I took the flowers and thought I must have missed something. My stomach did a flip. Trouble? Danger? I regretted having the cereal and fruit. I felt slightly nauseous all of a sudden. I must have looked awful.

'Instructions about what we should do in the office, and what we're going to say to back Charles up! Nothing to worry about at all. Now, get going. I'll drive – so you can carry on snoozing!' I got going, slightly appeased by Lea's words. Somewhat cheered and having come wide awake with my initial fright I arrived back at the table to join Lea and Hans for another coffee. Normally I had tea but with such an early start it had to be coffee.

Uncle pitched up. 'Has Lea explained what I want from you all?'

'I'll bring the car round. See you in a mo. Not had a chance yet. You carry on, Charles.' Uncle smiled indulgently at Lea. Hans followed her wiggling bottom out through the door. So did Uncle and the rest of the people in the room.

The thought of so many eyes made me cringe. I knew she would be enjoying every second of the attention. I liked to be dressed up, glamorous and melting into the background. Chalk and cheese again.

Uncle turned back to me and saw I was watching him. He drew me to one side. 'Ahem!' He obviously felt guilty. 'Now, Barbara – this morning's meeting. I will be doing most of the talking so you can relax. What I do want is for you both to take my lead and maybe expand on something I say, but nothing too explicit. So it's a bit like when we went to the brothel, only this time with words. Thinking on your feet. You are good at that. Improvising! I am going to suggest some business tie-up so maybe quote some figures. I know you were researching the profits, losses and spending of La Roca before you came out. It will become obvious as we go along, I hope. If not I'll just ask you. Hans is my silent partner for this purpose. So, Hans, take your cues from me too.'

'Queues? I have to wait outside for you in a queue?'

'Hm? Er no. Cue – I mean listen to me and if I ask a question or for an opinion from you, answer me.'

'I understand. You explained me before.'

I heard Lea toot the horn so we all went to the car.

Half an hour brought us easily to the boat hire company 'Blue Sea Boat Company', which had ample parking space in the sports harbour in San Cartana.

Lea and I went on to a different part of the harbour when we picked up our boat through Karim. It had had its own specific moorings. Immediately next door was a large, expensive ships chandlers which was in turn next to an upmarket café with solid tables, matching chairs and colourful umbrellas. Obviously the members of the boating fraternity round here were all well-heeled.

I cast a glance around all the moorings, which were occupied by boats of all shapes and sizes – and, dare I say it, some pretty dilapidated ones. The small dry dock further along in a specially cleared area behind extra fencing had a dirty, practical-looking specimen propped up. This was being worked on, and another was waiting for attention nearby. Busy, busy.

Clothes shops were scattered in between delis, food takeaways of all kinds, souvenir shops, a pharmacy and, last but not least, a sales office with photos of sparkling brand-new boats to make anyone drool and forget their sea sickness problems. Second-hand sales were referred to as being inside, so you had to pass all the new boat advertising first. Sales and marketing!

Uncle pushed open the office door of the boat hire and came face to face with two desks occupied by smart young ladies and a tallish, older man with thinning hair carrying too much weight and leaning on a high-standing metal set of drawers, one of several dotted around. He looked up immediately, latching on to Uncle's eyes.

A smile broke out, Uncle returning it. 'Senor Madden, I assume.' He came forward to meet and greet. 'We spoke on the phone. I am Carlos Atimos.' Had he been wrong in his assumption it could have been awkward, but he wasn't. We were spot on time and his keenness to meet was evident.

'Please call me Charles. Let me introduce you to my niece, Barbara, and her best friend, Lea.' We all smiled now and shook hands.

'Please hold all my calls now.' Carlos spoke to the women and, with a waving arm movement, indicated to us we should follow him.

'Please!' he said. We followed.

Inside his office it was spacious, light and airy. A large desk, more filing cabinets – some lockable I noted as they had keys hanging in the locks – and more than enough comfy chairs for all of us, arranged neatly, ready for us to occupy. Carlos went behind his desk and we pulled up the chairs.

'Would you like something to drink?'

'Water for me, please!' Lea beamed.

'Me too,' I followed.

'Full set,' from Uncle.

'Full set – ?'

'Sorry, I mean water for me too. Full set – means all of us.' Apologetic smile.

'Ah, I see. I am always learning.' Carlos flicked a switch on an intercom and asked one of the girls to bring water. 'Now Mr Madden – Charles. You had some interesting ideas on the phone so can you start, please, and give me more details?'

Uncle got straight to the point – well, one of them. Business-like. 'I want to expand business at La Roca Club. It will take different forms and your boat hire is one form that interests me. Also, your boat sales. Probably more so.'

Sharp look from me. The third thing he hadn't enlightened me about. Now was not the time to mention it. Make mental note.

'I am a new broom.' Uncle saw a puzzled look flit across Carlos's face. 'Sorry, I mean, as I am the new owner, I have many ideas for discussion. I am going to be aggressively advertising – that is advertising a lot – both for my coach tours, which would provide a suitable clientele for boat hire, and with the more upmarket individuals, who would fit possible boat sales. In a nutshell - I mean that is the basic idea.

Many details, both financial and legal, would follow if you are interested.' He drew breath.

'Si. Yes I am interested of course. Talking costs nothing. So, first the boat hire. What ideas do you have for this?'

'There are brochures for this in reception at La Roca as a courtesy for guests but I want something more positive. If they book through us, they get a discount with you but we share commission – exactly how much we can discuss later. Something performance related, if you understand, Carlos? La Roca will be pushing your product, but the big project is boat sales. I will organize sales drives from the UK for clients interested in buying a boat over an agreed amount, for which I would give incentives. For example, free accommodation if they buy or free boat hire for the duration. Ladies, do you have any further ideas?'

Cue for Lea and me. Wish Uncle had warned me he wanted actual ideas.

Thinking on my feet, trying to earn my position in the company, I ventured, 'I think it should be mutual. By this I mean, if we are pushing the boat sales, then Carlos should be pushing La Roca. If he gets a possible client – and we should both consult on aggressive advertising – then we offer the accommodation. It is the same end, but with mutual promotional campaigns we can double the impact. This could take us into TV advertising at prime times, both in Spain and the UK. Obviously, the internet too. Professional blogging. A Facebook page for all clients to follow, both established and new. Make up daily events or stories at the resort, boat yard, sales office, boat hire. Anecdotes for everyone to enjoy and follow. Personalities of all kinds creating massive followings. In fact, create a special department dedicated to this. It can be run from either La Roca or here, if you have the space. Perhaps make it an independent company shared by you both. The two Charleses. Carlos and his English partner, Charles, and vice versa.' Both Carlos and Uncle looked thoughtful.

'Certainly food for thought!' Charles looked at Carlos.
'Si!'

Lea jumped in enthusiastically: 'Why not add themed holidays – to both La Roca and the boat hire company. Carlos, I see some of your boats are aimed at clients who want to hire them for days, even weeks, at a time. When in port they could join in Club-based activities. An example – painting, photography, yoga which is popping up all over these days, with healthy nutritional food. In fact, Charles, I've noticed a large tract of land someway down towards the village which I know belongs to La Roca so perhaps your chef – Gordon isn't it? – could work with gardeners to produce your own microbiotic plants and organic products. You could have a restaurant called 'Gordon Bleu'. Perhaps Prem might be interested in joining in, as she is next door to the field near my horse and donkey.'

And when did she find out the chef's name was Gordon? I felt another twinge of jealousy. Was she serious? Or would Uncle take her seriously?

'How would the horse and donkey fit in? Would you produce your own meat too? Perhaps this is a little far from boats.' Carlos looked a tad confused but not wishing to upset anyone, smiled enquiringly. He was dying to talk and talk and talk, but kept quiet in our company. I could see his brain working, his eyes darting around, assessing matters.

'Oh no. I only meant that it's another string to my bow. They are my pets – well almost.' She looked wistful. 'But with all this mutual stuff going on, you could try it and see.' A trifle less than a professional statement, but what has been said can't be taken back.

I brought it back round to business. 'Lea is more on the artistic side of things. She would be marvellous liaising with the promotional and advertising side of events. She has a degree in art and the tourism and leisure industry.' I stretched it a bit. 'She is also an advocate of healthy living in all its forms, including compassionate animal farming. If there is anything you don't understand, Carlos, do say. We are grateful you speak such good English but maybe we haven't always made our ideas clear. It is considerate of you to indulge us.'

'English is the business language so it is my pleasure. I don't get every individual word but I understand the general concepts. See, I have some good words too.' He seemed gracious but underneath I sensed a man who was smug, self-satisfied and liked the sound of his own voice. A certain TV presenter Lea and I mutually hated would be pleased to meet Carlos. Twins even down to the wobbly chin. 'I certainly need some healthy living.' He patted his bulging stomach fondly and his jowly face wobbled a bit. Somehow I got the feeling Lea's microbiotic plants would send him scuttling to the nearest menú del dia restaurant for the full three courses, plus wine.

Uncle took over again. 'My very able assistants here have been giving all this a great deal of thought, Carlos. It is a big subject. It needs developing and a lot of hammering out. Oh – hammering out –?'

'Thank you I understand. We can do some hammering now? I am agreed in principle.'

We all smiled and Uncle started the financial hammering while Lea and I added promises of doing more research on costs, especially the TV advertising.

An hour flew by and had I not known why we were really there, I would have said there were some good business ideas being discussed. Uncle wrapped it up by saying he was hungry, whereupon Carlos invited us to lunch. Uncle countered that with an invitation to La Roca. Some arm-twisting resulted in Carlos saying he would join us in the main restaurant in half an hour. As we wandered out, we took stock of the harbour again. It was extensive, the boats and yachts seeming to gleam and shimmer in their white-painted coats in the sun.

We set off back, Uncle phoning ahead for a secluded table to be set up for us – but one which others could lurk around and eavesdrop. He had asked Carl, the manager, to meet him.

'I wanted to firmly establish my authority with Carlos. Not that I think he doubts me but the more I can play the adventurous millionaire, the more he will want to please me.

As you heard, I'm willing to shoulder more of the set-up costs until it is all up and running. So, if he can please me in small ways without cost to himself, I am banking on him bending over backwards about the boys. I must say I am genuinely impressed with your ideas, girls, and at such short notice. Sorry about that. It just came to me as we talked. I had every confidence you would be up to the task, Barbara. Well done, that girl.'

He patted me on the shoulder from the back seat.

Lea shot me look that said, 'I told you your uncle was proud of you.' I did feel good.

'It was fine for off the peg. Had we been able to plan it or research, it would have been better.'

'I think it was so good, I'm thinking of implementing some of the things we discussed. If Carlos does get put away for people smuggling I am going to approach his successor with a deal. So, Barbara, please research TV advertising costs and so on. And as for your idea, Lea, I think it worthy of further thought I'll talk it over with Gordon. Have you met him then?'

'Yes. Just in passing. I noticed one day some chicken dishes didn't have legs on so I asked for him, and he came out and we got talking so promised me legs in the future. They have been there ever since. He waves to me all the time and smiles a lot. Such a nice person.' She sighed.

Oh please – not another victim of her unwitting charm!

'In that case, Lea, we'll speak with him together and I would like you and Barbara – no, in fact all three of you – to approach Prem with the organic ideas. We must have a meal there. Another for you and a first for me.'

'Absolutely. I'll drink to that. Fabulous food.'

'Me too,' I said. 'All food is fabulous to you, Lea. If we are going to take some ideas seriously, I think Prem and La Roca should have some mutual backscratching ideas similar to the boat company, Blue – Blue – what was it?'

'Yes!' She grinned.

'Good. That was helpful, Lea,' I said waspishly. No response. I shook my head and carried on. 'Blue Sea Boat

Company. Anyway, Uncle, you neglected to tell me something again. Carlos has the boat sales company as well as the hire company. If I am to come up with ideas, I really need to know these things.' I was emphasizing.

'Ah! Quite right. Remiss of me.' He was suitably chastened. 'Not done on purpose but you weren't around and then I forgot. I'm still getting used to having you in the business. You must cut me some slack for being a single man, used to being sole person in charge. I'm adjusting. It's going well, I believe anyway. I am so proud of you doing things that wouldn't normally be in the job description, but you always seem to get stuck in and go with the flow, even out of your comfort zone. What do you think, Barbara? Are you happy in general?'

'Couldn't be better, Uncle Charles. It is exciting, if nerve-wracking. The people we're meeting are amazing. And Lea has nerves of steel for everyone. On a par with Louisa. Compliments where they're due.'

'I get scared. I just don't show it. But I do like adventure!' She smiled gleefully.

There was a funny look on her face but I ignored my suspicions. 'So what was that all about earlier with the Spanish – example? What was wrong with example?'

'Popped into my head.'

She didn't further it so Uncle filled what was becoming a gap. He never wasted opportunities to push a point.

'I asked Carl to see if he could get a tape recorder of some kind to record conversation with Carlos. Lots of Carls, Carloses, Charleses around. Think I might re-name him 'Duke'. See if he minds.'

'My watch records things,' Lea piped up. 'Got it given years ago by an admirer who had promised me a slap-up dinner but couldn't deliver. So, he got this for me. I think he said he found it on the back of a wagon. Or it had fallen off and he couldn't catch up with the driver.' She had one of her innocent looks on her face. Was she kidding me or was she for real?

'I'd better not ask! Hmmm. When you say years ago – do you mean when you were about twelve?'

She looked at me as though I was being awkward.

'The watch – is it on you?'

'Yes!' She waved her wrist around, still driving perfectly with one hand as she manoeuvred the final corner before La Roca. The watch was a large affair and rather flashy. More jewellery than watch. Bling. Of course it would be.

An awful thought occurred to me. 'How many things have you recorded between us?' I was ready to be angry and it sounded in my voice because Lea answered instantly with a deep frown forming and hand back on the steering wheel.

'Never ever! I wouldn't do that. Not up for discussion.'

She was rarely waspish so I took the hint and apologized. 'Sorry. I didn't really think you would but it came as a surprise. That's all. Honestly.' She was mollified.

'Can I borrow it, Lea?' Uncle asked. 'Does it work under a cuff? It's not my style, is it? so I can't show it and at some point I want you both to leave me with Carlos to get him to talk about meeting young boys.'

'Could it be considered entrapment?' I enquired.

'Possibly. Probably. Maybe. But I think it best to have something tangible, rather than nothing. So I'll run it past Louisa. If she says no, then I'll reconsider.'

Uncle duly rang Louie's number only to get the answerphone. He left a message informing her that if she didn't ring back soon it would be too late – he would go ahead and face any consequences later.

We pulled into our shaded parking area and got out. Lea handed Uncle the watch, showing him how to operate it to record, and then fixed it on his tanned wrist, neatly tucking it under his shirt cuff. He had held his wrist out in pleasure while Lea smiled a little smile to herself.

'There, let's test it.' Uncle and Lea spoke then Uncle re-wound it. Perfect. He re-set it ready for Carlos.

As we were walking to the formal dining room, Carl intercepted us. He had a bulky-looking piece of apparatus in his hand. 'Charles – is this any good? It records well. I use it for dictation for letters. I have your table ready near the service area so I can hide this. I will be serving you to keep an eye on things.'

'Good idea, Carl. I have one Lea gave me, but two are better than one, just in case. Also, if you lurk unobtrusively, maybe you can eavesdrop bits and pieces and be a witness. After the meal, when the girls have left the table. I know you weren't too happy when we discussed certain issues. Perhaps non-committal is the best way to describe it. I will be asking Carlos some awkward sexual questions so be prepared to be embarrassed – it is necessary. You know of our investigation into the child trafficking and sex trade, and now we are preparing to hand over to the police. Louisa Spelier-Bielby, is staying here, is part of Interpol and her son is el capitan in this region. I hope this satisfies you? Louisa's information is to be kept secret, whatever your views.'

'I understand Charles. I'll do my best. The sentiments can't be faulted.'

'By the way – ahem! I was saying to the girls that there seem to be a lot of Charleses one way or another, what with you, me and then Carlos. So – would you mind – if only on a temporary basis – unless you didn't like it – '

The look on Carl's face was a study. Going from an initial 'whatever you want' look to 'what on earth is coming' to 'I think I should be worried.' His eyes got bigger.

Uncle struggled on. 'Er, the name 'Wellington'. It lends itself to something great. And be clear, it's only because there are too many Charleses around – at the moment – would you mind, for awhile at least, being called Duke? As in 'Duke of Wellington'?'

Carl's expression changed to amusement and relief. His shoulders relaxed. 'I see. I wondered what was coming. Umm, yes, fine by me. I can live with being famous. Should everyone call me Duke? I can send a memo around.' You could see the 'Phew!' on his face.

'Excellent idea and thank to so much for indulging your eccentric boss. Much appreciated. Now can we get the tape recorder set up. Carlos will be here soon. We'll go to the table anyway.'

We all got settled at the table while Duke set everything up. Menus were on the table so we were studying them when Carlos joined us. All very natural. Duke was introduced and told to take good care of Carlos any time he should come to the restaurant. Uncle was showing who was in charge in a pleasant way.

Carlos was impressed with the whole set-up and listened to Duke rattle off some specials. We ordered, plumping for at least two courses. Lea would never say no, and Carlos seemed happy, exposing plump pudgy wrists when he reached over to offer and pour water for us all. Uncle had ordered wine but Lea and I declined. Clear heads needed, and space for drinking in the evening.

We all chatted amiably without pauses as we were expanding on the earlier discussions. The wine flowed, for Carlos at least. Uncle only sipped and surreptitiously kept filling Carlos's glass. Finally we took our cue to go.

'Ladies, I know you would like to relax and swim and get ready for the evening, so do feel free. We have made good progress this afternoon so indulge yourselves. Don't forget the fun' – Uncle emphasized the word – 'we're hoping to organize. If you make any progress it would be good.'

I picked up on that and nodded at Lea to back me up. 'Your wish is our command. Both to relax and investigate more fun options. Lea has some young contenders for approval. A secret source she won't tell me about.' I pouted.

Lea went round the back of Uncle's chair bending down and putting her arms around his neck, her face next to his. She had what I can only describe as a cross between a sultry and delicious look, on her face. Since when did she take up acting, I mused?

She stage-whispered, 'Oh I think you will be pleased with my findings – but I think you can do better for all of us. The organization – is – difficult.' She nuzzled her nose against Uncle's face, put a brief butterfly kiss on his cheek and her elegant fingers with the long nails – totally au naturel –

slipped back around his neck as she withdrew. What a performance.

Sizzling sex. Her hair had grown even more since she had cut it on our previous trip and it had partly covered Uncle's head so he caught it in his hand as she withdrew and then let his hand linger on her hers. Then she was gone.

Walking towards reception. I followed, so glad the attention wasn't on me. Uncle and Carlos's eyes followed. One more exit magnificently staged.

'I didn't know you had attended acting school.'

'Who said I was acting?' Her expression was inscrutable, unfathomable. She was almost daring me to further it. So I didn't – darn it. I so wanted to.

We went to our room to change into swim gear and headed for the pool. I was glad to see Lea had ditched the tight shorts, even for the pool. It certainly had taken balls to wear them in the first place.

We settled on our favourite sun loungers and Lea typically fell asleep – but with a big smile on her face.

I remained professional.

CHAPTER NINETEEN
Forward March

Uncle joined us by the pool, sitting on another lounger, under an umbrella. He was beaming and had taken off his formal jacket and tie, sporting a short-sleeved shirt with Lea's watch in all its glory. He took off the watch and put it in his trouser pocket.

'I think I'll put a lightweight blazer on for any more meetings. I've been too hot today. By the way, I'd like to keep the watch, Lea. It may have more work to do. Louisa will be able to download what we have so far.'

'Sure. Be my guest.' We sat up, attentive.

Lea was awake, contemplating a swim in her more modest one-piece costume. I'd been reading, dressed in my ordinary shorts and top.

Earlier, walking past Reception, she had fallen over again. 'You look about as elegant as a giraffe in those ridiculous high heels!' I jibed. 'Why wear them?'

She stared at me indignantly. Because they'd matched her swimming outfit, and she didn't have the short, tight shorts anymore. Dig.

A wit had quipped, 'I can cut the heels down for you, love. Bring them over here.' He waved a sharp-looking steak knife at us as we passed by. Lea with pursed lips, steadfastly ignored the man while desperately trying to rub her ankle and walk all at the same time.

Now the enormous heels had been rakishly tossed aside.

Alvaro flitted around at work but keeping up with events. He had been put on the rota then taken off again. Twice. The gay barman, Miguel Martin, had asked Duke for some leave for personal reasons and then not turned up for work when expected back. He was now on the missing list. Too soon to phone his parents but the time was fast approaching when they should be contacted. He wasn't answering his mobile.

Alvaro hovered. Any event of importance he had missed he would be informed of later and Uncle had specified he should have time off to help us, as of this evening. Staffing was not a problem as La Roca was now the biggest employer in the area, with many people wanting to work there.

Mansour and his wife Shakira would be filling some gaps shortly, his wife flitting between housekeeping, bars and restaurants – she was currently filling the gap in the bar. She was multi-talented and glad to have all the work she could get. It would settle down for her in time. Mansour was starting on the decorating in some of the garish bedrooms. As they had only one battered car between them, a golf buggy was on loan for the foreseeable future.

All this had been Uncle's doing and Duke was beginning to learn what a kind, thoughtful and forward-thinking employer he was. He inspired loyalty by the bucketload.

'That went very well, and we have it all recorded,' Uncle began. 'Two recordings. I must say, girls, you're surpassing yourselves today in ideas, taking up my cues and – Lea, what can I say! I almost thought you fancied me. Carlos certainly thought that.'

Lea didn't even blush. She was annoyingly smug. 'I do what is necessary for the circumstances at the time – but I have to say, Charles, it was easy with you.' She looked at him directly and winked, then settled back on the lounger. 'I may not be the best sharpest tool in the drawer but I have my uses.'

'Sharpest tool in the box, actually! Right, let's go over what's happened.' He became businesslike. 'It wasn't difficult to get Carlos opening up as he was curious anyway. Downright nosy, in fact. Also, a bit drunk. Actually, a lot drunk! I think the success of the meetings today had him in a good mood – and then the personal invitation from me to the hotel, together with lunch, had gone to his head. He is someone who likes to be thought someone, if you know what I mean. There was one amusing moment when he said he'd heard the 'scuttle tit tattle bottom'! I assume he was referring to some gossip he'd heard – shows our schemings have worked. I nearly insulted him by laughing, but resisted the temptation. I managed to sort out what he'd meant between the English and American versions. Close call. Anyway, I digress.'

'Better than a few days ago, when Hans called that annoying guy in the bar one evening 'a total turd' with his computer knowledge. I think he was right the first time. 'Nerd' had nothing to do with it.' Lea proffered this bit of information apropos of nothing. Then followed it with 'Remember when we all saw those glamorous women by the pool bar and Hans looked at a cat passing by? The lawn sprinklers were on and he said it could be a wet pussy soon?'

'Oh, happy days. Now can we get on, Uncle?' I sighed. Lea's little asides could be very distracting.

'Yes, quite. Where was I? I phoned Louisa and she's on her way back. She'll take the recordings for Edward. She said it was time to hand over to the professionals but that we should delay a day or two in order collect a bit more evidence. And that we should leave it to her.'

We digested this.

Uncle continued: 'Supposedly the three of us have a potential meeting for some fun time, unspecified as yet. Carlos is to contact me – on my private phone. I don't know if he found it distasteful, as he was too busy trying to be solicitous. I hinted strongly about what we wanted without specifying and he more or less said it was up to us to do as we wished – he would 'organize and supply the goods' as he put it.'

A pause had us waiting for more.

'He did say he had been unable to get hold of some of his contacts for a while and didn't know why. He referred to a maricón who went by boat to some special places. He needed to get in touch with these, or this, persons. I also pushed having a free, fun balloon trip and he didn't seem fazed. He said he could organize that too – so we might assume the balloon company is connected in some way. Do we know who owns or runs that? I can ask Duke. Or Helen will know.'

'I think we should push forward with our next boat trip to the cave and see what the children are up to,' I said. 'We could warn Louisa to – sort of – warn Edward but make sure we set off before he can stop us. Agree to phone to update him – leave someone in the boat for phoning or getting help or coming to help. We did discuss women only for this so it'll seem less threatening when we moor up.'

'First, Alex's trip to the ship – then decide how to proceed.' Lea was thinking sensibly. 'First things first, if you don't me saying, Uncle Charles? We all need back up for each of these events so don't want half our team on another mission. Some of us should stay here in case they need help or just contact – and some may want or be able to come on the trip to the cave – maybe tomorrow? They can't be much longer. We've all been out for ages now. We should swap stories before regrouping.'

Alvaro offered back up for whenever he could.

'That's good advice.' I gave a small laugh as a memory came to me. 'I remember you told me that on your first day at school, you told your parents you didn't need to go back as you had learned all you needed to know. Clever ploy but it didn't work for me, did it Uncle?'

He smiled with memories of the au pair he had hired for me. She had got me kitted out with all my clothes, doing the feminine side of things. Lea and I had been parent-deprived, she more seriously when hers were killed in an accident. And I was parent-deprived because like many couples my mother and father didn't get on, so parted, leaving me with Uncle and no regrets – on any side.

Remembering her loss, Lea looked sad.

'Um. Life has been a bit like skating on ice. It just flows under you and there is nothing you can do, then every once in a while someone pours oil on the ice and it seems everything is OK.'

Uncle and I looked at each other, confused.

'Is this a good thing? Do you mean oil on troubled waters?'

'No, I mean what I said. Life goes on, you get through things and flow on, like a smooth run on ice, but with some bits that make you slip and fall – then you get an oily patch where you feel like you are able to fly, soar into the sky and be happy.'

Uncle and I were considering how to respond when our compatriots came into view – Louisa, Alex, James and Francis first. Then others started drifting in, not properly involved but heading for the bar to quench their thirst. Rosalind came to join Alex to hear how it had all gone.

We all shifted around. Duke arrived, invited by Uncle to keep him in the loop. All this went on under the manager's nose – we had all agreed it was only fair to keep him informed. We asked nothing from him except basic co-operation. He said 'Hello' all round, stumbling only on Lea's name:

'I hope you like the pool, Lee. We are proud of it though I believe you have some ideas for improvement, Charles?'

Lea was as quick as an athlete on the starting block. 'Lovely pool. By the way, my name is Lea, as in 'azalea'. Le-ah. After all you wouldn't call an azalea bush, Azalee, would you?' She threw a dazzling smile and patted her sun lounger for him to sit beside her. Somewhat bemused – weren't we all – he did as she bid.

The pool improvements were forgotten as Karim's dog suddenly shot across the terrace to some greenery and lifted its leg against the plants, rolling its eyes in sheer relief. Karim galloped after it, seeing us and apologizing profusely as he went. His favour from Uncle had been to bring his dog to work. As he was doing so many hours at the moment, the poor dog had been left alone too much. Evidently staying in the office had been too much for it. We began to laugh. The puddle was becoming a lake but draining down into soil around the bushes in the borders. Thank goodness for pool plants. Karim was going red and spluttering with embarrassment.

'Karim – no problem. Can't be helped. Next time, make sure you take the poor dog out more. We don't mind really. Do we? Any of us? Lea, a job for you I think?' Uncle smiled kindly.

Everyone nodded agreement, still laughing. The dog kept going.

'Oh yes. Love to. We'll work something out. I'll see you later. What did you say it was called, Karim?'

'Willow. And thank you! He escaped from the office. I didn't realize he had drunk so much water but it was hot in there, even with the window opcn' He almost rung his hands in obsequious Uriah Heap style in gratitude. The waterfall from Willow gradually became a trickle and the leg was coming down.

Lea supplied some more gems to ponder on: 'I know so many dogs called Willow. Must be the fashionable dog name at the moment. Still – it's got to be better than Eucalyptus. Mind you, I think Benakee is a popular name for Spanish dogs.'

No one was quite following this but Hans had strolled quietly up in between work sessions and was now leaning against a pillar. His shoulders began to shake in mirth. 'I think you mean you have heard 'ven a qui'. Pronounced as you said it. A 'V' is a 'B' sound here. It means 'Come here'. Someone is calling for their dog.' The mirth gave way to an outright belly laugh.

After the Willow episode and Lea's pronouncements we all gave way to laughter – perhaps we needed to because of the serious matters we were dealing with. A literal relief. Karim collected his dog but Uncle told him to take a break and walk it which he did, gratefully.

I thought I should get us all back to business. 'Now – who wants to go first? Uncle or Louisa?'

'I will.' Louisa spoke authoritatively. 'Most of you know to some degree what I do – did, rather. I'm owed several favours, and my unofficial enquiries have interested several – shall I say 'parties' ¬ in the nefarious activities of some rather dodgy individuals and groups around here. Alex – your ship and its captain for one. Carlos's boat company, the Blue Sea Boat Company for another, and, thanks to you, Babs and Lea, now we can tie in the balloon company and at least one brothel. Small threads coming together.'

'The enquiries are in their infancy but are being accelerated now,' she went on. 'We are all on the radar at various levels. My son has his part to play. It is also amazing how different agencies co-operate worldwide: Interpol, Europol, MI6, CIA, DGES in France, BND in Germany, CSIS in Canada, MOSSAD, to name a few. Many others exist. FSD in Russia. China and Australia have their agencies. Spying, terrorism, smuggling, trafficking of various kinds, are a worldwide problem. We have been told to back off for our own safety as I told Charles on the phone – shame I haven't managed to catch up with you, isn't it?' She grinned. 'I think we need to move fast to get in first – or before we really have to back off.'

'What happened on the ship then? Do we need to go back?' I asked.

'No. I've told Edward about that, and Alex has told his insurance company. For now, we wait so they can be tied in with the rest. The captain was desperate to be signed off today and get going without repairs. Lucky I was there, waving formidable-looking papers around. It got very heated, but he couldn't argue in the end and the port authorities were informed his ship couldn't leave. It wouldn't be worth him risking defying us all. We found big discrepancies in the hold's measured sizes, and indeed other smaller places we sneaked into, with hollow sounds as you tapped around.'

'Do you know what the definition of a ship is – as opposed to boat?' asked Lea looking towards Alex. Bless her, she loves to distract people.

'Size mainly. Leaving out sailing ships, a ship is a large motorised vessel intended for ocean going and deep-water transport. A boat is everything else. Ships have to carry boats, and boats have to be small enough to go on a ship. Of course, there are exceptions, like in the USA on the Great Lakes where a boat could pass for a ship. Some fishing craft can be classed as ships by size but are still boats. And then we have containers.'

Lea was spell bound and was hoping for more, but it didn't come. She was a sponge for information. I wondered if she had followed all this and was trying to clarify things in her mind.

'Are we waiting for the penny to drop, Lea? Or is it a whole euro in your case?' I said rather meanly.

'I thought that was really interesting. Thank you, Alex. As for you, Babs – ' She let it drift. 'I think we should go to the caves tomorrow morning with an enormous picnic and about six of us girls. The boys can hover half a mile away – nautical mile of course – in another boat. I also think we should use Prem's place more for our confabs. Or at least start from there with a coffee. and leave some basic info and phone numbers – just in caseou know. Perhaps we could all play spoof there for rounds of drinks in an evening, just for fun?'

'I agree.' From Uncle.

' Er – spoof? Why? No, I'll ask later. First Louisa, do you know who's in charge of the balloon company and who's in charge of the Town Hall – or should Babs phone Helen to ask?'

'I can tell you.' Hans piped up. 'I met the Town Hall kefe – um boss - when he came to my finca to buy a spa bath. Huge amount of money. I asked myself, from where did this money come? And it was going into a new house he was building. This is a man who works to live exceptionally well and lives to party big time. I tried to fry him while he was playing with my puppets.'

Lea got her own back for the Benakee name. Howls of laughter. Smirks all round.

'Grill him. And I guess 'puppies'.' She was smug.

'Grill? Yes, I said me puppets. It was from a hornet's nest. All from the same family as Karim's dog and Sam at the quayside restaurant down from La Roca.'

We all cogitated on this while trying not to offend with more hysterical laughter.

'I can't guess that one. Oh, maybe I can. From the same litter.' Lea was pleased with herself – again.

'There is no litter in my finca.'

'From the same litter means from the same mother. Puppies all from the same mother. Litter has two meanings.' Hans's penny began to drop. 'Please explain me 'spoof'? I think this rattles my bell from before. Ah, but first you need names and I have phone numbers too.'

He produced these. 'Jefe, boss name – Santiago Lopez.'

Uncle went off to phone Senor Lopez and see where it got him.

He was back in no time, explaining that the jungle telegraph seemed to be working overtime. He had been put through to Lopez immediately, and Lopez had almost fallen over himself to accommodate Uncle. Said he was impressed with what he had heard so far, as a businessman, and would be honoured to help in any way.

My pet project about turning the mines into bars and shops had been mentioned. Lopez hadn't said no but had drawn his breath in, in builder fashion, then let it out with a loud 'Phew!' at the idea of the massive expense and ensuing complications.

Anyway, they were going to meet up now. As Santiago had put it, he had 'only boredom in siesta time' so he was coming here.

Uncle carried on: 'Seems spreading money around really talks. Duke will hover as before on that convenient table in the corner with the second tape recorder, so will you do the same, Alvaro, please? Maybe you can clean the shelves behind the table to look occupied and, Hans, if you have the time, will you sit with me in the restaurant and I will introduce you as my Spanish contact and silent partner. He may talk to you more as a local and he may have heard of our trip to the brothel so it all ties up. If not, it doesn't matter.'

'Of course. No problema. Now please, 'spoof'?' He was nothing if not dogged.

'It's a guessing game with a coin. I could have sworn we spoke if it before, and it does ring your bell or am I dreaming? Time is flying and events are fast and furious so I couldn't swear to it.'

'Lot of swearing going on, Babs! And it's rattle my cage and ring a bell.'

'Funny, Lea. Not. Are you going now, Uncle?' Said quickly before Hans got in his request for clarification.

'Yes, let's get set up.'

The three of them moved off, leaving the rest of us to organize for the next day's boat trip. First, hire a boat again, plus a second one: Lea's department. Arrange huge picnic: my department. Find out who was willing to come along for the boat ride – as it were: Louisa's department.

Volunteer hands shot up immediately. Women's boat: Esme of course, Lea, and I, Louisa,

Rosalind ¬ we silently hoped she wouldn't be too stuck up – and out of nowhere, Theophila Francis Brown-Lowe. We all cheered.

Now, the men: Francis the Air Commodore of course, Hans, Alvaro and Uncle. It seemed only fair to include Alex and James in their absence.

We chatted on, making basic plans, discussing all manner of stuff until over an hour later Uncle rejoined us with Hans and Alvaro, now off duty for the foreseeable future. Their ploy had worked. It was interesting to note – vital even – that some mine tunnels had been let out for storage. Initial excitement but it wasn't helpful. Santiago had been told that one of the tunnels had been rented out to a farmer but, on investigation, he had discovered that no rent had even been paid. He had let the matter go on the basis that it was not worth bothering about. Another tunnel was supposedly rented out to a company. Santiago had the company's name.

Uncle was of the opinion that Santiago was probably unaware of any of the sexploits, and that he was just so greedy for money that bribery was a way of life for him. So, if there was no bribe, no plans would be passed.

Uncle had hinted at sex favours but had drawn a blank. When he moved onto the topic of child porn, human trafficking and smuggling in the world today – and even here, near la Roca – Santiago had appeared genuinely horrified. Brothels were one thing where all were consenting adults. Abuse was another matter. Uncle pointed out that not all brothel workers were consenting, and that a lot of women had been trafficked. This is where it had got a bit dangerous, with Santiago wanting to know what his sources were. Uncle gave the impression that he'd been doing some reading on his journey from the UK. The subject was dropped.

We got back to business swiftly. I offered to investigate the name of the company supposedly hiring the tunnel for storage, and see if it led to something.

Lea had the boats organized, with Francis and Alvaro tasked with running the one for the men. I had gone to the kitchen to see my chef Gordon about the picnic. Uncle had also left it to me to initialize an exploratory chat about a new restaurant with him, the Gordon Bleu, that we had talked about. Exciting and fruitful talk. I was being taken seriously and seen to have authority. My feet were several feet off the ground.

Only the thought of possible trouble tomorrow marred the evening ahead but now it was time to relax, so we all went our separate ways to change clothes, eat, drink and be merry. Uncle, Lea and I, Hans and Alvaro all headed for the Piano Bar after tapas in Las Aqueas, to catch up with Helen and David and update them on events. Louisa had copies of the recordings and Lea had her watch back.

We arranged to meet at Prem's next morning for a final briefing over coffee. Prem was delighted. I hoped she would see it as a useful opportunity to discuss business opportunities. Uncle had after all left that side of things to me.

Prosecco and G & Ts beckoned. The guys were already by the piano talking to David, who was on a break, and Helen was also there, listening intently, leaning on the gleaming piano and getting a mild admonishment from David for leaving finger marks on it.

We joined them, ordered drinks from Shakira, Mansour's wife, who was overjoyed to see us. As she brought the drinks over, we chatted, equally happy to see her.

It did seem that our plans were falling into place.

Could we hope for a 'smooth run', as Lea would say? We certainly were skating on ice! □

CHAPTER TWENTY
Full Throttle

'The world is full of tubbles and pitals.'

We were all musing over coffee at Prems. As it was going on for 11 am, I was awake and in this world. The lounge area was so comfy and elegant that it would have been good to stay socializing all morning. The words got my attention and I looked over to Lea's little group.

'What does that mean and what brought it on?'

'Prem's vegetarian meals. A few of us were perusing the menu.'

Was she back on her big words kick? I mused.

'I've noticed how people say 'vegetable' and 'hospital', especially TV presenters. Most say 'vegetubble', or even 'vegtubble', instead of 'vegetabl', or 'vegtabl'. Then we have '-pitals'. 'Hospital' or 'Hospital'. How do you say them?' She looked directly at me.

Somehow my speech dried up. 'OK, how do any of you pronounce them?' Silence.

'I'll go first. 'Vegetabl' and 'Hospital.' She looked around for volunteers.

Everyone started muttering the words until they got louder and clearer. There were indeed a lot of 'tubbles 'and 'pitals'. Then giggles. Uncle came off best. Hans, as he was Spanish, gave us ' - opital'. I had to work at it but then I was saved by the bell: a stout, flamboyant woman came in. Prem obviously knew her well and they chatted over the bar. I vaguely recognized her from La Roca.

In listening to the 'tubbles' Lea had moved around and was next to me. She whispered: 'Wonder if Charles will mind that she's stolen the bedroom curtains?'

'She hasn't. The curtains are tasteful.'

'Miaow. And so early for you. Anyway, she's probably from Benidorm. You know, full of the type of Brits that embarrass you and only eat full English breakfasts. Their idea of fresh fish and chips is straight from a deep fat fryer – not the fresh catch of the day from the harbour – or burgers and chips with baked beans, washed down with large mug of tea. Britain with sun. The Blackpool or Las Vegas of Spain or Skeggy.' She hardly paused for breath.

'Wow. It sounds awful. And how do you know this? You are on form. Double miaow, Miss Snobby. And what's wrong with Skegness? It's a lovely seaside resort. I have to say that Blackpool is fun too. We went to a hen party there.'

'My point exactly.' Pause. 'You know I'm only kidding. Salt of the earth, these people. 'I watch lots of TV programmes about Brits in Spain or wherever. Fascinates me. I'm pretty sure I'd like to live abroad. After all, I'm already trying to learn Spanish, aren't I? I don't want to be like one of those expats Helen's always grumbling about – nothing to do but bitch on about things and far too lazy to try out the language.'

'Where are the 'cucumber sandwiches and china teacup with pinky stuck out' brigade?'

'La Roca of course. Even the coach tours fit in well. Symbiotic.'

Louisa overheard: 'I suppose you could say Benidorm's fun. It's also full of idiots – idiots from all over the place. Drink mainly to blame. You should go and see for yourselves before you go home. Make sure you catch the magic act – it's run by a couple. They go round all the bars. They start off naked, producing flowers, scarves and much more from amazing places – risqué in the extreme. Then they slowly put all their clothes back on. And they're dancing all the time.'

Our eyes widened. 'Adult bars only?'

'Not at all. Your average bar. It's up to you whether you take your children in. The act's well advertised so people can't say they weren't warned.'

I asked if Louisa knew why Karim had given his dog such an English name but Lea supplied the answer. He'd been shown some photos of England and had asked the name of the beautiful tree he'd seen on one of them. It was a willow so, as he had only just got his beautiful puppy, he named it after the tree.

'First I've heard of it!' I observed tartly.

'Well, you should get off your high horse and start communicating with people!' she replied cheerfully.

This banter kept us occupied till it was time to go.

Uncle had filled Prem in on basics and left contact numbers, including that of Louisa's son as a last resort. We had no reason to think it necessary – we were just erring on the side of caution.

We all parked up at the sports harbour and Lea went to find the young Adonis from our previous boat trip. He was the one who had made this booking. To our surprise, Karim appeared with Willow at his heel. It was his day off, he informed us, and he was needed here in reception as the Adonis – whatever his name was – had something else to see to. Likewise Carlos, so he was holding the fort. Karim looked happy, clearly in his element with the boats. His obsequious manner had all but disappeared. He tried to get us to take on a large boat with a qualified skipper but we insisted we were happy with a small boat that we could deal with ourselves. Karim gave in graciously.

We boarded our respective boats and set off at a lick. It was incredibly calm so we got the full blast of the sun and were glad of the breeze created. Francis took the first turn at the wheel of the boys' boat and Lea at the girls' – ours. Louisa was near the front – or fore – so Lea took the opportunity to pump her for more information on the world's intelligence agencies.

I was prompted to say that if we were Romans her name would be 'Lea-us Annoyus'.

In response she threw her binoculars over to me – at me – to keep me occupied. 'Be a lookout!' she snapped.

Louisa obliged. She spoke earnestly and I was all ears. Spying, terrorism, smuggling, trafficking, forgery, cybercrime – all need eliminating, she said. High-tech equipment on land and in the air, and state secrets of all kinds – these need protecting. An international criminal register was being compiled which would make things so much easier the world around. Mutual co-operation was expected or hoped for in operations to dismantle criminal networks of all kinds. Specialized officers underwent vigorous training in participating countries.

The KGB had ceased to exist in 1991 – had been superseded by the FSK and now the FSB. We should note this was not the only agency. Somehow, the name KGB conjured up images of more exotic, dangerous and times: men compromised by glamorous women – or men by men. Ah, the good old days. Now most of that was in the open. There was a more laissez-faire morality.

And then there was ISIS, a violent and destructive ideology, both to humans and cultural heritage, vicious in a different way.

'Of course,' Louisa added, 'on a more mundane level, the world doesn't work without money. Even spy agencies need HR and accounts departments. After all, spooks need salaries to pay the mortgage.'

She gave us an interesting insight into modern submarines capable of conducting a war from beneath the sea. Your town could be devastated and you wouldn't know where the strike came from. You'd look up into the sky on vain. That reminded me of the weekend Lea and I had once spent in the Lake District. We'd sidetracked to Barrow where submarine technology had thirty years of updating technology ahead of it.

Our lesson continued. Europol and Interpol have a lot to do with criminal gangs and individuals. Law enforcement, customs officers and even naval and military officers are not immune to bribery and have been known to be tempted to turn a blind eye for a handsome fee. Migrant smuggling is a billion-dollar industry, mostly in cash, so undercover operations are necessary.

The UK has the National Crime Agency to deal with illegal activity in drugs, firearms and human trafficking. Indeed, with any form of immigration crime. And it works with other agencies, foreign and home-based, such as Border Force, Royal Navy, European and USA units from source to every level worldwide.

One local popular smuggling route is from Gibraltar into Spain. Also, the Spanish Civil Guard keep an eye on the smuggling of people and drugs from Ceuta, an enclave in the disputed Spanish territory on the North African continent. We pricked our ears up on hearing this.

Shame we are not in the EU anymore as the EMSC European Migrant Smuggling Centre helps EU member states! Louisa told of a case where the Spanish Policia Nacional recently dismantled a migrant smuggling group based in Algeria with the support of Europol who supplied intelligence analysis, identifying members of the gang and providing mobile office deployment during the 'action day', when houses, computers and paperwork were, searched, seized and processed.

Europol co-ordinates joint working between EU police forces, and supports EU countries against terrorism, cybercrime, and serious organized crime of all kinds. But again Brexit has interfered and excluded the UK. Further negotiations were being made. Lea and I sighed.

The Global Criminal Police Organisation – inter-governmental – helps police in 194 countries via a specially secure communications system network. Interpol is concerned with all of this, but on a more global scale, with co-operation among and between police organization in many different countries. It is based in France and staffed by police and civilians. The UK remains a full member of Interpol in its own right.

Whew. What a learning curve. Public knowledge but not many people look into such things. Just as well it was in a nutshell or we could have had to keep going till Morocco to get the detailed picture.

I glanced through the binoculars and could see the mine entrance and landing coming into view. A second boat was moored next to the first one we saw. I called for us to slow down. Both boats cut the speed, slowly nosing up to each other, with various hands grabbing the sides, holding them together so we could talk.

'I think here is where we part company. It's not too deep – ' Louisa was peering over at the depth gauge beside Lea – 'so Alvaro can drop anchor. You're nearest. We girls will proceed slowly to the cave – with caution. Wish us luck.'

Mutterings of 'Good luck! Be careful! Keep in touch! Is your phone working? Have you got the torch?' went on. 'Yes, yes, yes! Thank you! See you!' We didn't wave in case we were being watched. We wanted to give the impression of just having met up by accident and of being simply friendly with fellow sailors.

As Lea approached, the area appeared quiet. We drew alongside the boat we knew and threw our painter over the top of the one already there. It looked neglected somehow, as though the boat hadn't moved in a while with no one looking after it.

Louisa and Lea jumped ashore and I followed. Esme, Rosalind and Theophila were to stay in the boat as back up. Rosalind was capable of handling a boat if push came to shove. They handed out all the many picnic baskets.

With a huge effort we heaved them further up the rocks. Shouted, 'Hello!'

Silence.

We tried twice more then started up towards the mine entrance.

We were nearly there when in a sudden rush the children came out. They stood and stared – an ugly, wild, confused look on their faces.

'We brought a picnic – food – for all of us.' Lea beamed and indicated the hampers. 'We saw your boat and thought we would share everything with you. We've far too much and it's so nice here. Hope you don't mind?' She was friendliness personified.

No one moved. No one smiled. My heart was racing, flipping over and over.

'Come on. Everyone!' Louisa smiled too. 'We're all from the big hotel too and Lea here told us about this great place so we just had to come and see. It's lunchtime so you must be hungry.'

She moved back down a bit to the hampers and made to open them. This got a reaction. The oldest boy we had spoken with before spoke to the other children and they all became animated and went straight for the food. They seemed more raggedy than on our first visit. Thinner, dirtier, something desperate in their manner. Or was my imagination running riot.

Politeness and manners, which had barely existed before, were now non-existent. It was a full attack on the food. Not a word was said to us. Louisa handed the packages out. They were snatched in an instant or else the food was just taken directly from the hampers. It was lucky that there was so much to occupy them. This left the entrance to the mine clear.

Lea was nearest, nearly in the opening, so she slid in. I followed. We saw only the first part as we had to adjust our eyes to the darkness.

We stood blinking. It was empty but there was a strange, very unpleasant smell. A stench, not a smell. A mixture of unwashed bodies, urine, defecation, and –what else ? I couldn't place it. Something rotten. We moved further in. No people, but we knew we were not alone. A shadow, a flash of someone? A small noise? My flesh crawled and the hairs on my neck stood up. Debris was everywhere. Discarded tins. Paper plates with plastic knives and forks. Takeaway containers. Large water bottles, many of them full. We were nearly at the back of the cavern and other passages off became visible.

We stumbled over chunks of rock. Lea nearly fell over on one and when she looked up I followed her gaze back to the entrance. It had darkened, with the children all stood watching us, some with food still in their hands. Louisa behind saying nothing. They hadn't noticed her behind them.

'I hope you don't mind us having a look round? So clever of you to make this a home or play area. Must be fun.' Lea tried the innocent card.

'No fun.' The eldest boy, Yusef, who had been the leader on our previous trip here said unsmiling, 'Why you really come? You want us like the others come here, to take us away, and bring us back after we work for you? In the sex club.' He spat. Hate in his face.

We all stared at each other. This was so sudden. An unexpected turn of events that we should really have expected. It's what we had been working towards but maybe not quite like this. We suddenly felt like the victims not the saviours.

Lea broke the silence. 'No, no! All right – this is why we've really come. We're going to rescue you. I mean it. Can we explain? We have more people outside and another boat waiting for us – all of us. To take you to safety.'

'No safety for us.' The boy sneered. 'We should not be here – and now we have a dead person. You will blame us.'

My mind and body froze when I heard that. A dead body. Who? It took me a moment to realize he was slowly bending down and the other children were following suit. They were all picking up stones.

I drew my breath in horror.

Suddenly Louisa shouted from the entrance.

The noise seemed to spur them into action. They started throwing the stones at us, picking up more so quickly it was unbelievable. The blows were stinging, then as, the volume increased, painful and soon bordering on excruciating.

We tried to get back toward the entrance but as two men appeared from one of the passages, the stoning stopped as quickly as it started with a shout from the boy. Here were Carlos, the boat company owner, and Jose, the brothel manager. Terrified and dishevelled, the children ran towards the back wall. Carlos put his hands to the top of the wall and pushed. It sprang open and they fled through. I suddenly remembered that this was the door we had found earlier.

With our assailants' attention diverted, we headed towards the entrance Louisa was part way down, waving to our boat, but she had her phone in her hand. She came back up.

I saw our boys' boat up anchor and set off at speed. The children had scattered in confusion, some through the door, some down a side tunnel, some caught back in the main cavern. They stood, hesitating. Lea had a knife in her hand and Louisa a gun.

I found myself holding a sharp rock. It all happened so fast it was almost a blur. A sound came from down the side tunnel. A cross between a moan and a strangled shout. Lea and I fled down it. A door in the side of the tunnel was shut, with a key on the outside.

We opened it. There was a rudimentary bed in it and a body on it. The space was partly lit by a dim lamp hooked up to a nail. There was a generator going somewhere, the source of the humming we had heard in the first days of exploration.

The body moved trying to sit up. Filthy, emaciated but alive. Empty water bottles were strewn around. Louisa stood outside the door to make sure we weren't attacked again. The gun had worked its magic when she let a shot off which echoed all round, nearly deafening us.

Esme, Rosalind and Theophila appeared, indicating that they would wait in the main cavern for the men and keep an eye on the children who were left standing beside their leader, Yusef. Esme had produced an evil-looking instrument which she let hang by her side.

Lea grabbed a full bottle of water and approached the bed. She put a hand behind the man's head and offered the water. He took only a sip, struggling to put his legs on the ground. I moved forward to give Lea a hand.

'Who are you?' I asked. 'Can you talk?'

'Gerhardt – I work at La Roca.' His voice was a whisper. The missing under-manager.

'How did you end up here? We've been looking for you.'

'I came for a day out. Went exploring the mines and went down one tunnel. I met a man coming out with a small boy. Bad timing for me.' He stopped to rest. 'Another man came. Between them they got me in here.' Another rest.' The kid fled, I think – but they got him. I saw him again. I knew what was going on. They didn't know what to do with me. Kill me at some point, I suppose.' He sank back on the bed, exhausted.

'I overheard talking,' he managed to continue. 'There were some other people nosing around – They said it was 'big proble'. Then it was something like 'Spiders would work. A warning. Slash tyres. Insects – balcony.' I didn't understand. I hoped someone would find me. Who are you?'

We didn't answer. After such an effort his voice was drifting. We heard more voices and the men appeared, milling around. We felt safe now and my trembling hands began to steady. Lea moved out of the room. She came back some minutes later. She was white but steady. Precise even.

'You need to come and look at this!' She addressed Louisa but the men moved towards her. She went further down the passage to another door. Gasps. OMGs followed. I felt I must go too. In a room with no light but light from the passage the source of the stench was found. Miguel Martinez, the gay barman was lying in a heap, badly bruised and cut. He had been stoned. Nearly our fate. Slowly I noticed a large gash down his middle. We were all staring frozen. Not just the body but the state of it. Part of it missing.

'Is anyone thinking what I'm thinking?' Louisa said quietly.

'The children didn't have anything to eat – did they – after they killed Miguel. There was no one bringing food for them. Their contact with the outside world stopped,' Lea speculated.

'So, I suppose that's why Carlos and Jose came looking today, to see what was happening – and got the fright of their lives.' My contribution.

'Speaking of which – shouldn't we follow them through that door in the wall? We can follow the marks we made when we first came in from the other side.' Alvaro moved to set off with Uncle, James and Francis not far behind. Louisa closed the door on Miguel and we went back to the main cavern. The children still stood in silence.

'There are police coming now.' This was for all of us. 'I called Edward.' Louisa was serious and the gun stayed pointed – just in case.

'Who are you?' the boy asked. 'And what happen to us now? If you find the others.'

'One question at a time. I told you who we were and where we were from – and that we wanted to help you. It is true. We still do in spite of – in spite of –' It was hard for her to finish. 'We'll help you, we'll speak for you. Won't we, Louisa?' Lea spoke firmly.

Louisa did not demur. After what seemed a long silence she asked hesitantly, 'Did you – did you – actually eat any of the dead man?'

'No. We were hungry but we couldn't do it. The – things, bits – are on the floor in that room. You will find them. We wanted to escape but the boat wouldn't start. We didn't know how to open the secret door. We were so hungry.' He hung his head for the first time.

'We all came here with hope. Work in fields, anything. No matter. No parents in our countries so we wanted to get better life. We all from different places came here. Long way.'

Silence then he started again. 'Ship, not nice. Had to hide in small spaces sometimes but then we went in big air balloon. We think this is fun and we have now hope of life to come. Happy here in cave. First steps. Then we never leave – only to go with some men into sex club and we are told we will go as slaves to other places. So one day we – we, killed that man who brought us food. So we could escape.' He ground to a halt. 'What will happen now?'

'I can't say for sure but first, we'll see the police. Then you'll be taken somewhere safe to have food, clean up, and speak with kind people who will know how to help you. How old are you?' Louisa asked.

'I am the oldest. Twelve. So I was in charge. This is bad for me.' Child that he was he looked very scared. It was hard not to have sympathy.

Finally, Alvaro, Uncle, James and Francis came back with Carlos and Jose scuffling along awkwardly in tow, having to be more or less dragged every inch of the way.

Where was Hans? ☐

CHAPTER TWENTY ONE
All Stations Go.

Where had he got to? He had been there in all the melee. Then he wasn't. Now he was nowhere.

My mind flashed through events to see if I could remember when he went missing. We had seen all the men except Alex go through the secret door – and then come back with Carlos and Jose. No sign of any of the children who ran out. The men were all breathing heavily and gleaming with sweat. This was so not what we had expected and events had certainly ramped up to chaos level.

Carlos and Jose looked awful – bloodied, bruised, dirty, roughed-up, frightened, cowed. All the fight had gone out of them. When they had fled, I got a fleeting impression that something had already scared them, that they that had already encountered violence and that it had been nothing whatever to do with us. From the children? I thought I remembered the name of their leader.

I asked Yusef, 'What did you do when the two men came in?'

He barely looked at me. 'Nothing. Not know what to do. The men were very angry. Asked many questions where other man was. Spanish man. We said we wanted to leave here then they started to look round and found the body. Not nice. They went into the room with the German to see if he was alive so we shut them in and locked door.'

'But they got out!'

'Lock, door, no good. Rusty. Broken but was OK when they put the German in. Then he was beaten up many times and no food, only water. We were in rooms the same so we got out ¬ and big surprise for the Spanish man when he came for one of us to work.' Head bowed, he looked up without raising his head. 'Today we heard you. Didn't know what to do. Came for food. Very hungry. But you came in here – more problem.'

Uncle and Alvaro had taken the belts off their shorts and bound the hands of Carlos and Jose behind them. Not that they were going to struggle – but we weren't taking any chances. They were sat on the floor among all the dirt and dust. Carlos was very overweight and the flight, fight and capture had taken its toll.

'Looks like you had a big tussle between you all,' I said.

'We did. Surprised myself. Bits of rock lying around came in handy, and we've got some sore knuckles. Never thought to bring a weapon. They weren't going to give up easily. Far too much at stake – their lives and freedom. Worth more than money. Alvaro's young and fit, though, and can handle himself. James too. Well done, both of you!'

Alvaro smiled looking rather pleased with himself.

James was calm and self-possessed. 'I saw Hans running after another man. They were going up the road that comes down into this mine. A tall, blond young guy. Not seen him before.' He added as an afterthought: 'I didn't see Hans go. He had to pass us. I thought he came out with us but – ? Maybe he went in another tunnel?'

He glanced at Uncle. 'A hot air balloon was coming down into the base here. At least I think it was. It was hovering – some people peering over the sides.'

We all started up – what should we do?

'Let's go and see. Half stay here and half go out. I bet that man Hans was chasing is Adonis,' Lea volunteered. 'Remember, both Carlos and Adonis had gone, Karim told us.'

We split up. Lea and Louisa made instantly to go out, with the Dunkirk spirit I was beginning to expect of them, followed by Uncle, Alvaro, Francis, Alex and James. Once more unto the breach!

I had no desire to join them , so stayed with Esme, Rosalind and Theophila. I wanted to find out more from Yusef and the men. I couldn't reconcile the impression I had of the kids in front of me on this side of the secret door with the idea of them killing someone on the other. Something we had heard but would never have thought possible had happened almost in front of us. An image of the dead Miguel was vivid in my imagination. I felt like a grotesque curtain twitcher.

I would never see these mines in the same commercial light again. They were places of misery and depravity. It seemed obscene that I had ever had the idea of preserving them as some kind of world heritage site with shops, bars and cafes. I shuddered.

Carlos moved around, catching my attention. I decided to make some overture – see how he and Jose reacted – and Jose. 'I assume you own the balloon company too?' I said. 'Everything indicates you've got several sources of income – illegal income. Very clever of you to tie everything up. Boats, balloons, brothel – all for smuggling – people, drugs, diamonds. Anything in fact.'

Carlos gave me a sharp look when I mentioned diamonds. He studied me for a moment. 'How do you – all of you – fit in?' His voice had no trace of vehemence, denial or indignation. It just carried a sort of whispered acceptance, with a hint of anger at having been caught out,

'I don't think you are in a position to be asking questions. Besides you know who we are. My Uncle owns La Roca. My friend and I came to look into the disappearance of the under-manager, the German you have in that small room.' I nodded in the direction of Gerhardt. 'I think we should go and see how he is and let him know what's happening.'

I moved to do this, and Rosalind followed. Esme, Alex and Theophila were keeping a stern eye on everyone.

Esme looked particularly threatening as she wielded her instrument – a long thin piece of strong, pliable metal with springs and a handle on it. I imagined it would knock you out cold if force was applied. I asked what it was.

'Drain clearer. Found it lying around outside in the hotel grounds and it seemed a good idea to bring it. I had no idea if anyone else had anything – let alone a gun.'

A drain clearer! It struck me as funny. I started to laugh but it wasn't the time for levity so I stifled it. Somehow I found it hard to not giggle under my breath. Was I hysterical?

Actually I wasn't. I was cool as a cucumber, my nerves were steady as the proverbial rock. I was surprised by myself.

Gerhardt was sitting up on the edge of the rudimentary bed, tended to by Rosalind and looking dazed and bewildered.

Back in the main cavern we all heard more noise, coming from two directions this time – the tunnel and from outside. It can only be described as an eruption followed by a cataclysm of people. Edward and many officers seemed to explode into the area with some un-uniformed men. Also Hans, the Adonis, the missing children and the men – our men.

A lot to take in. Swirling bodies of authority, stunned victims or perpetrators - view them as you will - it was a moment of mayhem. □

CHAPTER TWENTY TWO
Snippets

The cavern had never seen so many people. The smell was increasing by the minute, with sweaty bodies that had been making herculean physical efforts in a dangerous and unexpected situation.

Adrenalin was positively pumping through the air. Carlos's stomach was wobbling like the jelly it was as he was pushed against a wall. Spanish phrases were hurling hither and thither: 'Murder ... driven to it ... illegal immigrants ... no families ... system failure ... what next!'

Edward made his presence felt, ordering people around, although the un-uniformed men – and one woman, a blow for equality, I hoped – seemed to have their own agenda.

Louisa was pointing out the 'goodies' from the 'baddies'. It was a relief to be accepted as a goodie.

The children had been herded into a room down the passage with the door left open and one officer keeping watch. Edward with others went to view the dead body and looked in on Gerhardt. Rosalind had come into the cavern to see what was happening. She was now clinging to Alex – who, it seemed, wished he was free to mingle. He was a bit of a hero too and wanted his moment of adventure to last, I imagine.

Edward was phoning. How did he manage to get a signal? Near the cavern entrance? He took an opportunity to glare at his mother. Louisa glared back, hands on hips, legs slightly apart in an 'I know better and don't mess with me' stance. Mexican stand-off.

Snippets were flying around. My head began to ache. I was trying to follow the Spanish babble. Low-grade weapons. People-trafficking. Diamonds. Blood diamonds. Ship in harbour. Was the ship referred to the one Alex had been dealing with? If so, it was indeed a miracle he had not been killed and no wonder the captain and his crew had been desperate to leave after the accident. I made out the phrase 'IVA fraud', which I took to be something called 'carousel VAT fraud', remembering something I'd once watched on TV: imported goods are exported, going round time and time again, the VAT being claimed on the same goods each time.

'… must buy a ship – or large boat at least to hire out. I'll have a word with Karim. I saw how happy he was this morning in the Blue Sea Boat Company offices. Depending what the legal and financial situation is now, Carlos will be no longer involved. I think Karim may be the best candidate to take it over … '

'… Bodega Bar – barrels …' Oh surely that lovely young couple weren't involved in anything? My mind was whirling.

'… Santiago Lopez – the Town Hall. Not just bribery – diamonds again, passport forgery, drivers' licences …'

Hans's voice floated over: 'When we can go, I would like to invite us all to my finca for dinner.'

'I will cook. I want to cook a meal with savoire faire for everyone,' Lea was definitely back on the long words.

'Three things!' I stage-whispered across the gap. 'Can opener, microwave and gravy with everything is your mark. And I assure you the savoire faire they sell round here doesn't taste nice. You can feed everyone from the mini fridge in our room. Full of fruit, pate, rolls, butter – should I go on? You think your midnight snacks have gone unnoticed when I'm asleep.' She frowned.

'I suppose you think that's funny, Babs – and I most certainly don't have gravy with scrambled eggs. What an odd idea you have of gravy with everything. Oh, by the way – did I tell you? I want to study, or get into, some kind of pathology.

Seeing Miguel's body was horrifying but fascinating. Mesmerising.'

'You're definitely odd. From food to dead bodies. Besides. how many murders or dead bodies do you think we'll come across in our lives?' I shook my head.

'You know I flit, Babs – but so far in the last few months, including going round Europe by coach, we've seen four more dead bodies than most people – who aren't involved in either medicine, rescue, war, spying etc. So too many.'

I stood corrected.

Lea changed tack again: 'Maybe the children were being seditious, inciting each other to rebel against the appalling authority they had had meted out to them here. Or – and I don't believe it – insouciance. Someone give me a jelly baby.'

'You don't like jelly babies. Did you get that bit about the Spanish going to help the children – and do you understand 'insouciance'?'

'True, but I love biting their heads off. Or a chicken will do – I can rip its head off. And I got the gist of it, yes, and lastly, I think they are very concerned indeed. Maybe the children became atavistic under the circumstances – reverting to some ancient, instinct of survival, even if evil. Or else maybe they took punitive measures.'

'I think either study law or psychology to get them off the hook. You can use mountains of big words then.'

'Yes. All right!'

Just talking about jelly babies and chicken seemed to have a calming effect on Lea. Not that she would have harmed a feather on the chicken's head, except to eat it. She had been huffing and puffing like an old steam engine, which reminded me of an old car she used to have. It was all she could afford at the time and not a lot had changed – so far.

I was taking in the scene around us bit by bit, but at the same time all at once. It was a circus of gigantic proportions.

Edward came to our area looking stern and impressive. And sexy. He gave Lea a fleeting amused look, a flicker in his eyes that was there and gone. Would he be too young to interest her? Would she be too air-headed for him? I looked over to Alvaro and thought I would stick to what I might be able to have with him. Would that be just holiday fun or something more serious?

Oh, dear Gareth – his image flashed in front of me. What was I to make of it all!

'I am very happy for you all that you can discuss dinner arrangements, and gravy with eggs, and dissecting bodies under these awful circumstances. It shows great resilience.' Sarcasm was dripping from his precisely-spoken words with his perfect, upper-class English accent – the accent we had thought funny for a Spaniard when we first met him. I found it such an anomaly when you considered the very Spanish job that he did.

'However, I must remind you all that there has been a murder committed,' he went on stony-faced. 'Two in fact, whether related or not, and the first time I met some of you, it was over the first murder. As you mentioned, Miss Dunbar.' Side glance to her.

'I think this time I do require statements but for tonight I will release you into the custody of my mother. We will re-group tomorrow. Won't we, Mother?' She nodded. We smiled agreement. 'Perhaps I could ask you to desist from any further activity from now on? You seem to have solved most, if not all, criminal activity in the area. Even if you did potentially destroy months of undercover work. As it happens, you drew attention to yourselves which was, I suppose, useful. In fact, I can even risk saying that you all did what you did do very well. Much against my wishes. I can only reiterate, leave something for the police to do! If we can't manage without your help, we'll get back to you.'

He paused for breath. Was there the remote suggestion of a stern twinkle in his eye?

We were chastened but elated at the same time.

'If anything had happened to you, I would have had to take the blame. So – again please stop now. Resist temptation. Desist. Loose ends don't concern you at all. You have been involved with hardened and vicious criminals who will stop at nothing to continue their work. The murder here is another matter. The fact it was done by children is a shameful testament to the fact we were too late to protect them.'

I began to realize how naive we'd been. Naïve! Naïve! Naïve! Stupid – brave – bold. We'd meddled unforgivably. But what alternative had we had? We'd had to follow it through. There had been things to prove to Uncle. My head ached even more.

People came back from further down the tunnels with plastic bags full of – I got a glimpse – blue and red small books and plastic cards – passports and what? I could only guess that they were credit cards or driving licences.

I was aware of Louisa: 'The only reason I didn't mention weapons was because if – let's say you have a knife – if you aren't prepared to use it, it can be taken off you and used against you. It's different for me as a professional. Retired or otherwise. Mind you, not all work is dangerous. There is an HR and wages department. Even the field operators need to book time off and get paid. Not all of them lead James Bond lives. They have mortgages too.' Louisa had that funny 'Am I being serious' look on her face. Annoying but intriguing. One day I would get the courage to ask. She had Esme and Lea rapt – though I suspected Esme had always known more than she let on.

'And gun-running,' she went on. 'There are a lot of reliable workhorse guns left over from the Civil War, and gun-running. Mr Kalashnikov has a lot to answer for. You can borrow them by trading in favours even in this day and age.'

'I do actually know how to use one,' Lea surprised us all. 'I was in a gun club once!'

'You never told me.' I was miffed.

'I don't have to tell you everything.' Defensive. 'Besides, I didn't think you would approve. And anyway, you were off studying in Barcelona.'

I wondered if Lea would have been prepared to use her knife. I would have to ask her later. Our own private interrogations of everyone would be very interesting if not quite in order. Who did what to whom – and how far would

Uncle, Hans et al have been prepared to go? A fascinating prospect.

Uncle cut in: 'I think it would be easier if we all go out for dinner – but thank you, Hans. Some of us will come tomorrow – I promise – but tonight I am treating all of us to a meal out. I think the restaurant at the bottom of the hill from La Roca with the old dry harbour would do nicely.'

Hans gave in to Uncle gracefully and as he said, he would have needed a lot of potato 'purray'.

Our chatter continued unabated. Balloon ballast, cocaine, smuggling, boats. The weather. I was amazed the weather-obsessed Brits could talk about weather under the circumstances. How can you talk every day about nothing but sun? Maybe I was wrong and it was the Spanish talking idly while waiting for more arrivals of the official kind.

More snippets. Human mules. Did we realize that Yusef had said some children never came back and he thought they had been thrown down some air vents? There would have to be body searches. How terrified they all must have been. Mental cruelty.

Just then Gerhardt emerged, supported by a couple of people while he waited for an ambulance. Rubbing his head, he slid down on to a convenient rock.

More people began to arrive. The ambulance for Gerhardt, another for the body, with forensics in tow. People to take the children away. Where to? I wondered. I would have to follow it up. They began to emerge from the room they had been in with mixed looks of abject sorrow, fear, resignation, relief. An impossible situation had come to an end. Adults from a civilized country would handle it now.

Yusef passed by close to me and Lea, and gave us a full stare, stopping briefly. We waited for a comment that didn't come. It was impossible to know what was in his mind and his face gave nothing away.

Lea filled the silence, her words firm and serious. 'We did what we had to, Yusef, to help you in the long term – if you understand long term? I mean you were all in a bad place and had to be rescued. None of us meant to harm you. Ever. I promise I will follow up what happens to you – all of you.'

Yusef nodded before he was pushed forward. He kept looking back at us, as he was led down the main tunnel out through the secret door that had proved too awkward for the children to use for escape.

Lea foraged in the ever-present bag where she had hidden the knife, and came up with two cards with her phone number. She rushed forward and gave one to Yusef and another to the adult leading him. Yusef clutched the card tightly and made to go to her, with his grubby hand extended. She took it, then transferred her hands to his shoulders for a few seconds, looking him directly in the eyes.

'I'll be in touch, I promise. They'll let me know how you are.' Her optimism and positivity were infectious, and he gave her a small smile.

It seemed an eternity before we could get back in the boats. Many questions came, and names and contact details were taken – just in case Louisa lost us overnight! La Roca had its own moorings beyond the sun loungers down the hill. Enough for these boats anyway so we headed back, the sun still shining. We had the boats for twenty-hours so no hurry to return them to Karim.

Showers, change of clothes and out early. Uncle invited Hans and Alvaro to his suite to shower and, as they were all much of the same size and stature, to borrow some clothes. We all congregated in Reception. Uncle had ordered taxis for the journey both ways so we could all relax after the ordeal.

We arrived en masse in the Harbour Restaurant, causing a bit of a stir. Hans and Alvaro were mutually admiring the quality of the outfits they had on loan. Uncle was nothing if not fashionable. Uncle joined them with Lea doing her rat-up-a-drainpipe impression – she was there in a flash – basking in the company of two eligible men. She left Alvaro to me so I went over to start a mutual admiration society with him.

I had made a special effort to dress in a sophisticated, elegant but understated manner with only one piece of jewellery. Darn it – so had Lea, for once forgoing the bling.

With her height and willowy figure she had pipped me to the post again in the fashion stakes but with something she had found in her second-hand shops – or maybe market. I decided not to care, as I had Alvaro's full attention.

Just then Karim appeared with beer in hand and his dog, Willow. He was enjoying some time off. Willow and Sam, the restaurant dog, were playing happily if boisterously. It got a little out of hand, and shouts from an inner room sent them into rear-sniffing mode.

Lea put on a funny voice: 'I'll try the end that doesn't snap or fight back.'

Wilful disobedience was diverted. Finally they settled down.

The owner of the voice from inner room came out to see who had arrived.

Uncle headed towards Karim with Lea on his heels, cooing over the dogs. There was much fussing while we all milled around. Uncle started a conversation with Karim but had to give up. A short woman made a dramatic entrance after Karim – she was introduced as his mother, Lea's 'scary old bat'. She was all fuss and bluster, and her glass of wine spilled over in her enthusiasm to see who was talking to her son. Her golden boy.

Uncle told Karim briefly that he had business plans he wanted to discuss about the boat company. Karim deliberately ignored his mother, saying he would be extremely interested and please to excuse his mother as she was 'an over enthusiastic but well-meaning person'. He looked down and smiled at her indulgently. 'Aren't you, Mama?' She went quiet and smiled, shyly. We were starting to like Karim and Willow.

'You know, Dalmatians mature at twelve and die at thirteen.'

'Fascinating, Lea, but these aren't Dalmatians. Just exuberant dogs. Like Hans's.'

A voice diverted us. 'Welcome. I remember you from a while ago.' This was directed towards me, Lea and Alvaro. 'Please excuse the dogs. How many are there of you? Oh, hola, Hans! Good to see you. Too long since you were here. You have brought friends?'

'My very good friends. Twelve of us.' He beamed.

The English owner rallied, giving her name as Saranne Morales for those of us who didn't know, and started placing tables so we could all sit near each other. Her Spanish husband, Sebastian, started setting up, greeting us all individually – a great bit of PR. We were made to feel special so I understood why this place had such a good reputation.

We settled into chairs, and drinks started flowing – complimentary wine to start with, then what we ordered individually on the bill. We could start to unwind ¬ discuss, assess and, dare I use the word, dissect the day.

'So! Tell us what happened when you went to see about the hot-air balloon?' I sat back to listen to the tales of heroism.

Alex started to fill us in on more details. He'd managed to land a right hook on someone. Louisa had waved her gun around to great effect. Lea had cut a balloon rope with her knife. Not sure why. I wondered if I had I been cowardly in staying behind? I tussled with my conscience and was rewarded with an unexpected comment from Uncle.

'You did well, Barbara, staying to talk with Yusef and Carlos. You get the best out of people. You were the brains while we were the brawn.' I was satisfied I had played my part and began to enjoy the numerous tales of gung-ho adventure, interspersed with speculation on what I had heard. The VAT or IVA fraud for one.

'Well – as I said, Alvaro and Alex were great. James and Lea – what can I say, magnificent! Louisa, a real pro. The balloon was starting to land when the people in it must have decided something wasn't right so they were tipping out sandbags as fast as they could to get going quickly. It was all a bit fast. I was aware police were arriving but still a way off. I got a glimpse of Hans up the road closing in on – what do you call him – the Adonis? The ballooners started to go up again but we managed to throw the bags back, plus rocks, and jumped in ourselves. We had some hand-to-hand fighting. Close call. Very. Then the police were there helping, though

I'm not sure they knew what was going on – just needed to retain every person around. Turns out some of the bags that were thrown out were full of cocaine. Shot themselves in the foot – but not literally.'

Uncle stopped talking so someone else could do some explaining.

Lea continued for him. 'Fortunately for us, the type of balloon used – if you remember, Babs, the different types were explained to us – is the pure gas balloon, best for long distances. It uses ballast. There are three types of balloon and some would have got away but for our luck in managing to throw stuff back in to this gas one to weigh it down. You know, even if they had been run legitimately with ten to sixteen passengers at roughly £125 per person it would still be a good business.' A glimpse into Lea's practical side.

'I think the balloons and boats have been used for many different activities. A picture is beginning to emerge. I can tell you from the grapevine that accusations and confessions have been flying around – people are trying wangle lesser sentences. At least xenophobia is alive and well – various nationalities ratting on each other! That's just from this afternoon. They all know they are in super deep trouble. There are a few loose ends to tie up – the Town Hall boss, Santiago Lopez, and some others are still at liberty. Africa is only across the water. Thankfully religion and terrorism hasn't reared its ugly head.' Louisa imparted this information in her usual enigmatic way.

'So they weren't exactly fanatics, bombing pubs and subjugating women. They were just greedy bastards!'

'Er – I think that about covers it, Lea.' Louie smiled – had to. As did we all.

Then the Spanish owner, Sebastian, came for our orders, but our enthusiasm had got the better of us and we'd put our menus to one side. Sam and Willow the dogs were playing again, Karim keeping an eye on them while he had a quiet drink. His mother had gone. Obviously alcohol was not against any religion they may have had. He always appeared to be at work so didn't seem to have time for social activities.

Any spare time was devoted to his dog, Willow. He seemed happy to be able to relax this early Spanish evening.

Uncle called him over and pulled a chair out for him. He seemed embarrassed to join our company but was intent on Uncle. His expression went through serious, amazed, rapt, interested, surprised, grateful. All genuine, as far as I could tell, so I assumed he was totally off the suspect list. Finally, he shook Uncle's hand and moved off back to the bar area. I decided I liked him. I got the impression we all did.

We had all ordered food during this, and Uncle had said he was having whatever Lea had. Food started to arrive with more wine flowing. We tucked in .

Uncle announced amid mouthfuls, 'I've brought Karim up to speed about some of the goings on and, in a nutshell, have offered him the job of sorting out the boat company. He will remain at La Roca till Gerhardt is back, then go full time with the boats – after sorting legalities out.'

Uncle had made some quick phone calls while we were all getting showers and changing, updating Duke on events and finding out about the Blue Sea Boat Company which he would invest in.

I was both stunned at the speed with which Uncle worked, and full of admiration. I had a lot to learn. I felt overwhelmed all of a sudden. It made me uneasy, worried, excited, hopeful, determined. I stuck my chin out. Bring it on, I thought. Bring it on.

I overheard Hans telling people about his encounter with the Adonis. He had caught up with him and tackled him so they landed in a heap on the ground. It was all hands, legs, feet flailing, fists trying to find places to land a punch. They were pretty equally matched and determined but then the Guardia had arrived and pulled the Adonis off him, recognizing Hans as a local they knew. The rest, as they say, is history.

Hans extended the dinner invitation again, with me, Lea, Uncle, Louisa, Esme, Alvaro and Francis accepting. Lea, Uncle and I would stay the night on various beds he would organize. We felt absolutely delighted to have such an informal get-together, quite childishly happy. Alex would have come but Rosalind vetoed it – much to his annoyance, though he covered it well as he arranged to have a drink with James instead, which in turn annoyed Rosalind. Nails in coffins were positively flying. Lea noticed too. She observed without comment.

'I does all my washing tomorrow before yous are coming. If Lea helps us, me, with cooking I will get gravy for everything. You like gravy, yes?'

'With many things, but not all.' Lea quipped.

The banter went on until we had eaten all we could. We decided to call it a day, missing out the late bar, but arranged to meet at Prem's for pre-prandial drinks, Hans included. Tiredness was catching up with all of us and we were emotionally as well as physically drained. Taxis came and took us to our beds. □

CHAPTER TWENTY THREE
Twists and Turns

A morning meeting at Prem's was becoming a fixture and what a nice one to have. Home from home. We made a happy band: Lea and I, Uncle, Alvaro, Louisa, Francis and Esme. The stalwarts.

We updated everyone on everything. We had spoken with Edward again, full statements being given. There were some people who still needed rounding up, such as Santiago Lopez, the Town Hall boss. The Adonis had implicated him in the passport and driving licence forgeries but not in any dealings with human trafficking or child sex slavery.

Santiago seemed to have some modicum of humanity compared with the others. It was his vanity we had found hard to take – flexing his muscles while speaking, as though his appearance was irresistible to all. It had taken Lea all her time not to burst out laughing, and he had obviously mistaken my smirking smile for admiration.

We speculated on whether he had been picked up yet, was being watched, made an escape or maybe didn't even know what had happened to his colleagues. News can travel fast in such an area, but not necessarily. If his colleagues were all languishing in police cells, maybe he could only wonder why he had no contact.

Mansour and his wife had heard of the dramatic developments so they came specifically to speak to Uncle in the morning. He had told them the whole story. Their reaction was astonishment followed by serious concern, bordering on anger, for what might have happened to their son, Elijah. Luckily Lea and I were able to give our sincere assurances that Elijah had never been in any danger. Lea did superbly in convincing them that his part had been of paramount importance, that they should be proud of him and that they should tell him what a little hero he had been.

Uncle sealed the feel-good factor by saying it was time they moved into La Roca to save the travelling from their house in the golf buggy that was still on loan as transport. He had a couple of units being used as storage at the moment but each had been self-contained staff accommodation at some point. Their job for the day was to relocate the stored items, clean up and paint the units and move in as soon as possible. Enough staff were around to be able to cope today, when no coach parties were expected.

Extra furniture for Mansour and his family was available in the form of hotel furniture that had been superseded by more upmarket items in the hotel. Wardrobes, tables, chairs, sofas – I had seen them stuffed in a garage near the golf reception and thought what a waste when I had found them. It was on a list to mention to Uncle. Find a use or get rid. The Mansours were elated, and any traces of anger were dissipated. I was learning how diplomacy was a big part of what Uncle had to deal with on all levels. My learning curve was going up steeply.

Suddenly I heard: 'Shar – er', show – er, sho– wer'. I looked over to see Lea holding court. She's at it again, I thought. Pronunciation – or big words.

'What are you on about now?'

'I keep hearing people either saying they are going for a 'shar' or 'show – er' meaning 'shower'. It annoys me. I wondered how anyone else said it. How do you say it?'

Once more my voice dried up made my mouth very small like the wide-mouthed frog once did and mumbled very quickly 'shower'.

Everyone had stopped to listen, making me even more self-conscious, but it gave us all a laugh and everyone started saying 'shower'. We got some strange looks from other customers but after our nerve-racking previous day we didn't care.

To add to the hilarity, Francis pointed out to Esme some of the funny books titles that Prem had in her bookcase in the restaurant. Lea and I had seen them before.

'Look at these, Esme. 'It's a Dog's Life' by W U F Barker. 'Climate Change' by I C E Berge.'

'Oh, how clever! Then 'Time' by A Clocke. 'Beasts' by OF Burden. She went on to read more titles. Finally 'Fishing' by AN Angla. Thank goodness for that.

Hans said we should make a move to his place so we paid up, got up and left, telling Prem we would be back another day. I still had to discuss business with her. We piled into our cars following Hans, who went with Uncle and Lea. Alvaro was with me in the hire car. The rest went with Louisa.

We waited for Hans to open his large metal gates, always padlocked when he left or before he went to bed. The eight-foot-high fence was a big deterrent to intruders too. He left the gates open for us and we were greeted by Bessie and Guapa, coming in from the campo. The dogs inspected us from top to toe. After much cooing and fussing from us, they decided we passed muster. It was easy to see Sam and Willow came from the same litter. The dogs sat under a palm tree near the double-fronted showroom doors which were the entrance to Hans's, observing us.

Hans came out with two dog harnesses, heading for Lea.

'Please you to put these on the dogs. I forgot them earlier and if they go out again I like people to see they are owned.' He called the dogs, who stood up, and showed them the harnesses with Lea.

He left her to it. More cooing – by the bucket load.

I stayed to watch while Hans invited the others in for drinks. I saw him offering beer and wine.

The sun was fading now so the temperature was pleasant. The cold lager beer at Prem's had quenched our thirst but now it was wine time. I went to get us a couple of glasses as

Lea didn't seem to be having much luck with fastening the harnesses. I handed her one which she put on a low wall.

'Oh, look!' she said. 'A bu – afly', pointing to an exotic-looking specimen.

'You're on another crusade – and it's getting annoying. Spit it out!'

She stood back watching Bessie and Guapa who stayed, still waiting – for what?

'I like accents – they can be interesting. But I hate bad grammar and lazy speech.'

'So, who's upset you now?'

'Oh, just a crowd of people booking into the La Roca. They couldn't string a sentence together without effing and blinding, or clipping their words. Not the sort of people I imagine Charles wants.' I considered this but decided to ignore it – for now. Travel is for everyone but La Roca by its very nature expected certain standards. To be considered and discussed with Uncle.

'Go on. Try again.' Each dog had a harness on but not fastened. Lea bent to Bessie and went to buckle up. I started laughing. I got the 'we are not amused' look while she carried on struggling.

I pointed, but the laughing took over and I sat on the low wall.

'What!'

'I can see it from here because I'm not on top of it.'

'On top of what, Babs?' Exasperation setting in. She had turned her attention to Guapa with no luck either.

'They're puffing themselves up. Each time you go to fasten them, I can see them breathe in and blow their stomachs out. They obviously don't want the harnesses on.' My laughing rumbled on and on. The others came out to see what was happening.

Hans joined us, saw what was happening and, chuckling, gave each dog a slap before fastening the harnesses quickly.

'Makes them breathe out but you have to be quick. Lo siento. Sorry. I forgot to say it to you. Now, Lea, can you help us please? I have cleared my desk and table, put best cloth on, some knives and forks. Can you put around then do gravy?'

I went in too, sending Lea to do the kitchen duties. Individual lights were low and dotted around, casting dancing shadows as a welcome, gentle wind blew through the open doors. Good smells came wafting out from the kitchen area. The others drifted back in. We organized chairs and sat around in the showroom, which was where we were going to eat.

Louisa asked for a coffee to go with dinner as she was a designated driver for Uncle who had decided to go back to La Roca after all. Alvaro had his own transport. Esme joined Louisa in asking for a coffee, strong and black and could they have it now, please?

I shuddered. Coffee for me had to be milky. Café con leche, here, or latte, back in England. Lea had perfected getting her iced café con leches in quick style, in any bar now. Once learned it seemed to prove popular and was offered to others. We had even noticed it on a menu as a special. I was a little jealous of her success and thought again of how I must try harder to turn off the jealousy tap.

Lea brought out the coffees, announcing dinner was nearly ready and that we were to sit down round the table and desk. Some artificial flowers appeared in a vase that Lea found lurking in the showroom. It gave a certain flair to the occasion. Louisa and Esme took deep swigs of coffee – and all but spat it out.

'Ugh! What's this? Tastes like gravy!' They made faces and Lea was frozen where she stood. Then she rushed back to the kitchen and came out with the large gravy boat. She sniffed.

'Oh! I'm so sorry. The gravy is coffee. And vice versa. I wasn't concentrating on the jars. They are next to each other.' She looked devastated.

'So much for the portion of savoir faire!' I couldn't resist it. 'Coffee and gravy substitutes instead.' Hans came out to see what all the fuss was about. His shoulders shook with merriment. I thought I would twist the knife while it was in.

'Do you know the difference between an elephant and a post box?'

' Erm – '

'Well, I'm not sending you to post a letter then.'

'There's nothing like a good old joke – and that was nothing like a good old joke.' Smirk.

'I will turn dinner down and go to get more gravy and coffee. There wasn't much of either. Please to talk with yourselves and help to drinks.' He went 'immediamente', shoulders still shaking with mirth over the little spat we'd had.

Once we were settled with wine, the talk turned to a variety of topics.

Lea told us that buffalo numbers in America had gone down to only about 7,500 from millions, but that they were on the road to recovery, with a good breeding programme in hand.

Francis was very knowledgeable and had us all listening intently to all sorts. Apparently, each country had a national criminal record bureau but all of them were being cross-referenced worldwide. An international register in the making as we spoke.

Alvaro volunteered that Spain was the most mountainous country in Europe after Switzerland and cycling practically the national sport. We discussed this, which led on to other things in the business area. Catering for cyclists, I thought, with special accommodation in the village – maybe combine it with boat trips. This brought ums and ahs. Odd combination. Conversation is a strange and interesting thing.

Then there was a mini shriek from Lea. She was pointing at the garraspatas. Little black dots were running around the ground. A sort of tick that happens in summer which can't be helped. Better than an invasion of cockroaches.

Lea said she would close the 'puertos doble' to stop the breeze now it was almost dark.

I pointed out she couldn't close the port but maybe she would have more success with the 'puertas' or doors. She sighed.

'Well, I hope Hans can provide some loo paper on his return because I had to drip dry.' She said it in a 'so there' voice.

'Too much information,' I responded.

'Only trying, Babs. I have to try.'

'Quite right too! Never mind!' Uncle chimed in, smiling hugely.

The finca was well illuminated, but just then I caught a glimpse of more lights moving far across the road in what I knew to be a field. A few became a dozen and then more – and more. We all went out to look, Alvaro standing close – very – to me. Suddenly the field was lit up like a football stadium, leaving us in comparative darkness.

'How curious!'

'You sound suspicious, Uncle. Because of current events?' I had a nagging thought that I knew what they were. Not good. Or – ?

'It's my job to be suspicious. You are my family – and friends.' That warm fuzzy feeling came over me.

Just then a car zoomed in, a possible customer for Hans as his gates were open, inviting people in. A gasp went round as Santiago Lopez stepped out of a high-end Mercedes. He seemed neither friendly, nor unfriendly. Non-committal in fact. We didn't say or do anything because we didn't know what to say or do.

He came towards us.

'Good evening. I saw the cars so I thought I would find Mr Madden. The hotel told me he was out this evening – here. Sorry to trouble you, but I am hearing some strange things and I wanted to see what is happening. We have business to discuss but there are bad rumours.' He waited.

Some of the lights started to come our way, moving slowly but purposefully. Santiago had seemed confused. Now his attitude seemed more unpleasant.

Uncle finally spoke: 'What can I do for you? Are you expecting something in particular? You can speak in front of my friends. No problem. There is nothing they don't know. No secrets.'

'I am thinking we have maybe some business but now I am hearing – you are involved in children sex which is not good. I am businessman only. Property. I try phoning some business people of mine but I don't get reply. You know something?'

'Property, eh? How about passports? Diamonds?' Uncle queried.

'I know nothing of these. If you want passports you find them. What is diamonds to do with anything, with you? I import and export them?' His voice took on a note of forced indignation. 'I know only property we discuss. Nothing more. We have deal for property. You want?'

'No. I don't. I don't believe you about passports – and I have nothing to do with children and sex. We are all,' Uncle waved his hand indicating us all, 'part of an investigation into that and much more. The police – Guardia – are now involved. I bet the Border Forces will be interested too.'

The lights from across the road were getting ever nearer. Steady, unrelenting progress.

'Police? Why? 'Santiago now had an edgy look, nervous, uncertain. He was concentrating on Uncle. He took a few steps back towards his car. I wondered what we should do next? Try to detain him? Louisa was quietly moving behind him between him and his car. Alvaro was following her.

'There is nowhere for you to go. You can't just up and leave – unless you have cash, a passport and transport organized as we speak.'

We all edged closer to Santiago. He turned suddenly towards his car, alarm setting in. Louisa had her foot in the door.

'Get your foot out of my door!' Santiago snapped.

'Get your door off my foot.' She suddenly grabbed his hand from the door and put a finger in the middle of his palm which elicited a howl of pain, following immediately with a crippling knee in the groin, doubling him up, then finally shoved him so he fell on the ground, writhing. Alvaro was on him in a flash, sitting on top of him, pinning him down. Lea took the keys out of the car.

The lights were crossing the road and heading directly for us. Esme headed for the big gates to close them and I rushed to help. Uncle went inside to find something to tie Santiago up but had to resort to his trouser belt again.

Santiago's hands were duly tied. I stopped in my tracks near the gates. The lights had become four people carrying plastic containers. They smiled ingratiatingly, almost bowing, reminding me of Karim at his worst. The dogs came back in panting, rushing around and sniffing all over.

Santiago who recoiled. Louisa spoke in Spanish to him. The dogs were guard dogs and would bite if he didn't stay still. He did stay still, although clearly the pain he was in made it difficult.

Hans swept in at that moment taking in the strange scene. He came to an abrupt halt. The container carriers stopped in their tracks, half in, half out of the gate, not sure of their reception now they saw a body on the ground and dogs moving around.

'Hans – all under control. No problema,' Uncle told him.

'That is the Town Hall boss, jefe.' He pronounced it as though he had catarrh in his throat. A Scottish sort of sound, like the 'ch' in loch. His eyes were wide with surprise.

Louisa had phoned Edward, she told us. Hans turned his immediate attention to the half-in, half-out people, waving them in. They stood for a moment with mouths open then came forward slowly. Hans pointed them in the direction of what turned out to be an outside tap where they started to fill the plastic containers. I suddenly remembered Hans had mentioned them before.

'They come for water when they are working in the fields. They take the crops all the night and gone by morning. Put the food in the big trucks.' We looked over to see enormous trucks entering the field and more flood lights going up so the area was now lit up as if it was daytime. We could see the activity now. What Hans had told us a while back was exactly as he had described. Fascinating distraction.

Santiago was put in his car and locked in. He didn't go in quietly, and angry protests continued from inside. Louisa kept the keys.

'Where did you learn to do that – hurt his hand?' Francis was impressed. As were we all. Louisa could never be called Little Miss Mousy.

'I was a tomboy as it happens. I learned that in the school playground from watching the boys fight. It's a pressure point. A very painful one if done correctly. I had the nerve to try it. No one ever bullied me and I was good at head-butting. But I suggest you practise that, because if you get angles and force wrong, it hurts you as much as the victim. Yes, practise it,' she smiled conspiratorially, 'or you may get a smack in the face back as well as a sore head.'

'Nothing to do with work training then?' Francis followed up. No chance of such confidences, I thought to myself.

'What work training?' she smiled enigmatically. A small object fell from a pocket and she snapped it up.

'What's that?' I was quick on the uptake.

'You'd never believe me?'

'Try us.'

'A motorized garotte.' We all stared – then she burst out laughing. Was it or wasn't it? We stayed silent. The less we commented, the more she took us into her confidence – or wound us up.

The Guardia arrived in short time, lights flashing but no noise. The water carriers melted away back to the fields across the road, keen to avoid any confrontation. I wondered idly if they were illegal, or just naturally averse to authority. They looked poor though. Some were young and fit and, maybe much as the UK employs foreign fruit pickers, they just wanted extra seasonal work. Not my business, so I gave my attention to the scene in front of me.

Santiago was ordered out of his car and stood up against it, dusty and dishevelled, looking a bit like sand after the tide has gone down – brown, knobbly and indented. The protests quietened down but didn't entirely subside.

By this time, Edward had arrived and wasn't pulling any punches. Santiago had been well and truly dropped in it: IVA fraud, smuggling diamonds for this purpose, bribery and corruption now investigated and confirmed by various companies. The relevant departments would be dealing with him but in the meantime he was being driven in his own car to the local police station.

Edward turned his attention to us. We all simultaneously had an 'Oh dear, we're for it now' look. If we stared hard at the ground, would he disappear?

'Well!' Silence followed by a big breath slowly let out while he studied us. 'Once again, you have been busy solving and catching our criminals. We are indebted.' We shuffled, waiting for the axe to fall. None came.

'My mother told me Santiago came here of his own volition. Nothing to do with any of you. No enticement on your part. So – I mean it when I say well done! You all have courage. Maybe too much of the adventurous spirit. But– citizen's arrests happen. The public do get involved at times. I will leave it at that and once again especially now you have rounded up and apprehended the last suspect there is truly – and I repeat, truly – nothing else for you to do. Santiago has some small-time people working for him but that is of no importance in the grand scheme of things. I dare to suggest yet again, we can handle that without your help. However, as I said, if we can't, we'll get back to you.' The last wasn't said with sarcasm this time, but with amusement.

We heaved a sigh of relief and began to talk – all at once, which amused him even more.

'Would you like some coffee? I promise not to give you gravy. I have found out the difference now.' Lea directed her words to Edward who was suitably bemused.

'Yes, that would be nice. Um, no gravy. I was about to go off duty when Mother rang.'

Lea started dazzling – or was it sparkling? 'Shall we all go inside and I'll fix any drinks that anyone wants. Is that OK, Hans?' she added as an afterthought.

He agreed, smiling.' De aquerdo!'

We got drinks and settled down in chairs, heaving sighs of genuine relief that it was all truly over. We speculated if everything would seem very flat from now on. Edward was extremely interested in Louisa's answer which was non-committal. She had already had adventure in her life already, she said. What exactly? we wondered silently. But as everything had turned out well, she declared herself happy that others, especially Francis, had had their own slice of adventure. Enigmatic to the end.

'We should meet up regularly for murder weekends!'

Lea got some napkins thrown at her amid hoots of good-natured derision.

I slyly observed Edward, Uncle and Hans. They all looked at Lea with a mixture of fondness, affection and desire.

Alvaro was next to me and put a hand on my knee to get my attention. I tingled.

'Will you miss the adventure, Babs? I think I will.'

'I know I will miss all of you. The sunshine. The hotel, planning the future of it. But we're here for a while yet and if we are to carry out plans for improvement, then trips over here will be necessary. I will look forward to that. I hope we'll keep in touch? You've been marvellous, Alvaro. Uncle will want to see where this goes now. I know he is keen to reward loyal work above and beyond the call of duty. And you have certainly been loyal – way beyond!'

'It is a pleasure and with you around it was easy. And Lea of course – but mainly you. I hope that isn't out of turn for me to say? If so, I apologize.'

'No apology needed.' I smiled warmly and patted his hand on my knee, letting it stay there. We did a classic stare into each other's eyes. Gooey stuff. I was melting.

Gareth annoyingly flitted into my mental vision – and straight out again. Damn!

The background conversations percolated into our trance. People were moving around, Edward talking to Louisa, Uncle with Francis and Esme. For once Lea seemed alone.

I made a move lingeringly away from Alvaro. 'What gives, Lea?'

'I was thinking – '

'Steady on!'

'There you go – that's what I mean. People take you seriously. Me – well, they like me because I look nice. They see me as an entertaining air-head and wonder what sex would be like with me. People fancy me, but they don't respect me or love me, the way they do you. I'm just a sex object.'

She was utterly dejected so I had to stifle my urge to giggle. It was a serious declaration but the way she described herself as a sex symbol made me want to laugh out loud. I put my serious face on.

'Lea, my dearest, best friend in the whole wide world. I love you to bits. So that's one person. I hope you think that's important. It is to me.'

'Oh, of course, Babs. Very important to me. I just meant – oh, I don't know! Everyone else. No one thinks I'm intelligent or worth listening to. That's why I look up the long words. I'm only good for sex.'

'Stop right there!' I said earnestly. 'It was you who went into the mountains and basically started this whole adventure. You did all that research and we listened to you seriously. That's why we are here now, at the end of the adventure, and with criminals in custody. This was your project!'

I went on: 'You're a fabulous artist – remember all the commissions you've got? You've been a hero, rescuing a drowning person, shown courage when I was like a jelly in going into the mines, and confronted the children with a coolness and humanity that can only have helped. You've even been prepared to use a knife! I could never have contemplated that!'

She considered all this, so I continued: 'Uncle and Hans are besotted with you and always listen to you. They are so fond of you they could wrap you up and take you away to a deserted island for life and be happy. They love you as you. The icing on the cake is they do fancy you too because you are physically and mentally gorgeous. You can have the pick of the world. You make friends wherever we go – and I don't. You're the star.' □

CHAPTER TWENTY FOUR
Fandango Finale

Hans had put us in a room near him with a normal bed and a king-size, blow-up bed that was full bed height. We had left the door open during the night as this room didn't have any lights in it. The showroom was illuminated dimly all night, which gave a glow into the bedroom in case we wanted the loo.

Now I could see the sun was shining. It was still a little dull so when I cast around for Lea, I didn't think anything of it. I got out of my bed and headed to the 'throne room' as Hans called it. I gave a soft 'morning' to Lea as I passed the end of her bed.

Returning, I sat on my bed adjusting to the dimness after finding blinding sun in the rest of the living area. I cast around for a body shape in Lea's bed but saw nothing. Must have got up already, I thought. Always an early riser.

I got dressed, which didn't consist of much as we had stayed partly dressed last night, keeping an overnight bag to the minimum. I went into the showroom where Hans was putting furniture back into place ready to open up a bit later. We had all had fun clearing up the previous night, washing up and drying things together like the best girl guides and scouts. A far cry from the luxury of La Roca.

'Good morning. Did us sleep well?'

'Yes, us slept perfectly, thank you! Very comfy bed. Has Lea gone for a walk?'

'Not seen her and the doors are still locked.'

'That's odd. She's not in bed.' We both frowned and I went back to the bedroom with Hans following. We had no reason to worry now events were over but – could some bizarre twist have played out?

I stood at the threshold of the bedroom door and called. A soft moan came from the bed. My heart leapt. Was she injured? Had we somehow had an intruder? I rushed forward – to find her in a massive hollow in the bed. It had deflated and with her weight had sunk down to the floor in the middle. She blinked, focusing. Then started to try and get up, sliding back down into the hollow.

She tried again and failed. 'The bed's not co-operating!'

I began to laugh, with Hans coming over to look.

'Oh, my goodness! So sorry!' His shoulders stared to shake too as Lea struggled but kept sliding down the slippery plastic sides, bed linen getting tangled up round her as she got crosser and crosser.

'Fine! Don't help. This is what happened during the night. It went down gradually and by this morning I was stuck in here. I'm a bit short on sleep now because I kept trying to get out without waking either of you.'

We didn't move. Just stared.

'Well! Don't just stand there! Give me a hand!' She extended an arm, waiting for a pull-out. We both went to grab her and pull, so she came out, flying headlong towards the door with momentum. She only narrowly missed hitting the door posts by putting her hands up to take the force. Gales of laughter now set her in full grump mode.

'This is not we expect from a sex symbol, Lea!' I fell into more quivering laughter. I was being glowered at but I didn't care.

'Tea or gravy anyone?' Hans joined in the baiting.

'Tea, please!' she almost snapped, dignity severely dented.

Hans sloped off to get morning drinks so I followed. Best to remove ourselves from the situation, I thought.

I heard her raised voice. 'Honestly, I think you two are a few puppies short of a litter. Or a few lions short of a pride. Or a few –' She slammed the bathroom door.

Everything comes back to animals, went through my mind.

We took the drinks out into the showroom which was flooded with sunlight, and settled down, the dogs coming to greet us from their corner.

Lea joined us in a few minutes grabbing her tea and drinking it one go. 'Can I make myself another? I was trying to get a drink of water through the night but – '

'Of course. I'll go. Same again, guapas?'

'Si. Muy bien. Gracias.' Lea smiled, recovering her good temper.

As Hans came back with fresh drinks, a car appeared at the gates and a woman got out, peering through the gates.

'Haven't we seen her before? She's orange-coloured with electric socket hair?'

Lea was busy fussing Bessie and Guapa, who had shed their harnesses for the night. Time for the morning battle to get them back on.

'She likes you too, Lea!'

'Hans, I really do think you should take the sign down that says 'Beware Dangerous Dogs'. Or only put it out at night. It would put me off if I were a customer.'

'Oh – si! You said me before, Barbara – but too early for her so the sign can stay.' Hans groaned and watched the dangerous dogs lick the electric orange woman through the gate. 'I have to be in extra good mood. So much time wasting for small sale. I don't open for another hour.'

We sat and ruminated, relaxed, occasionally glancing towards the woman who seemed to be getting more impatient. We took bets to see if she would give up and go away or start rattling the gates. Such small pleasures. We continued to chat and watch the woman. I volunteered to sweep up the garaspatas if Lea put the harnesses on the dogs to which came the reply that I couldn't harm any of them. What? The dogs?

No – the garaspatas. I would do it quickly when she wasn't looking.

'Well – I must be doing things soon but please to stay here as long as you like.'

Lea moved to put the harnesses on, I went to find a dustpan and brush and Hans went to let the orange woman in, the dogs leaving for the campo with harnesses in place as soon as he opened the gates.

Hans had told us he had had the dogs from 'two young puppets' and had to feed them every few hours through the night. His then girlfriend refused to share the bedroom with animals, going back to her home to sleep. It was Hans's salesgirl who helped with the 'puppets' during the day, gaining brownie points and Hans's bed in due course. I idly wondered if the dog harnesses would lead to similar for Lea.

As the dogs grew, Hans told us, they had had to get used to customers coming and going, but not without incident. 'In first place, a woman came to my other shop and I told her to stay in the coché – car – but she heard me not and got out. The dogs jumped in and took her handbag. Shook it round with all things falling out and one dog running around with bag on his head. I didn't make me my sale! I have much amusement but this woman not.' Hans smiled broadly at the memory.

'So – you have slept with some dogs in your time.' Lea quipped. I groaned. Hans stayed smiling probably unaware of the inference.

Lea and I had business do at La Roca and ideas to discuss with Uncle, but we decided to call in on Gerhardt in the hospital on our way back. He was under observation for a few more days. I thought the whole episode might be too traumatic for him to want to talk about it, but what he had to say certainly helped to complete the picture. More to tell Uncle.

We arranged to meet Hans at Prem's about eight o'clock with the 'crowd' who we would round up through the day. I decided it was high time I paid for dinner to thank everyone for their input.

They had put lives on the line, knowingly or not. Dinner wasn't much but it would at least be a nice gesture. Lea volunteered to contribute but I told her she was a starving, if talented artist and she should wait for some of the Double Barrellers to pay her for commissions. She didn't argue.

'Do you know, Babs, I once made some people look good in my portrait of them It was an early commission and I was desperate for money – and they were downright ugly. Like the Spanish Bourbons. Ugly bunch with fried egg eyes, nasty stringy hair, 1960s pancake faces – you know, that awful cover-all make-up you see in old magazines, trying to mute their weak features. But Goya made the Bourbons look good. I suppose he had to – so I am in good company as I had to as well, because I needed the money too. Or maybe he would have lost his head as well as his income ...' She trailed off.

I concurred that it was necessary for both Goya and Lea!

After phoning around with invitations for this evening at Prem's we caught up with Uncle by the shore down from the pool. For once was relaxing to be on a sun lounger under a palm tree. We had changed into swimming gear and cover-ups. No high heels for Lea.

'I'm testing my product.' He reached for an exotic-looking drink.

'The hotel or the drink?'

'Hotel. Now, Barbara, let's hear your ideas, updates, recommendations – whatever you've got in mind. Do you girls want one of these – fruit drink with half a forest in it?'

'Please!' I accepted for both of us since Lea was smiling.

Uncle waved a beach waiter over. 'Well, that's one thing. Wage bills. How much do you spend – or Duke spends? I notice that some waiters don't double up with other duties – like the pool bar.'

We settled on our own sun loungers and updated him on Gerhardt's progress before getting back to business. Gerhardt had told us that, whilst he was tied up, he had overheard Miguel arguing violently with his partner. Seems Miguel had taken the partner to the mine to show him what was going on and to try to convince him about how much money they could make together. The partner was horrified and a row had broken out.

Edward now had forensic evidence about the murder, and after Gerhardt had told him what he had overheard, Miguel was arrested as the murder suspect. No one doubted that he was guilty.

'Staff – they do move around, but sometimes they get stuck in one place depending on who is off for whatever reason. It was good Alvaro could have time off to help us. I think it's useful to have a small safety margin in staff numbers to maintain smooth service. But I take your point. Now we can concentrate on business, we can study how efficiently and economically things run. After all, I've inherited things being run this way. Duke is very amenable to new ideas. Has some himself. We should all get together. '

'Yes, indeed. You're still very hands on. Depending how much you expand or what new projects you take on, I wonder how long that'll last?'

'Well, Barbara – that's one of the reasons you're involved. I don't want to be so big I lose sight of my personal interest in things. I wouldn't be interested in buying something simply as a business takeover. I want to be able to put my personal mark on any ventures. Speaking of which, I think that buying a large boat – through Karim and the Blue Sea Boat Company ¬ would be an advantage for La Roca. We had a long talk this morning and he will be taking over running it, after I have bought it – and a boat.'

'Fait accompli! Do you really need my input?' I'd been feeling left out.

'Yes, Barbara. I most certainly do. As you are still learning I can't, with all due respect, put business deals on hold. What I should do – and I hold my hands up to this – is discuss ideas first. I know I've apologized before and you have my abject apology on this and I won't do it again. If it seems I am about to, remind me. You are full of progressive ideas and I'm looking forward to exploring them with you. I think the bar or café in the mine idea is a non-starter though. At least for now.'

'I don't think it would ever be suitable now after all the horrible goings on there,' I agreed. 'It would be morbid. Ghoulish even. Come and see where murder took place! And human misery by the bucket load! No! Not for a long time.' I had to admit defeat.

'Well, we've come full circle, haven't we?' Uncle sighed. 'You told me both Hans and Helen spoke of the corruption that was rife around here even though many didn't come across it. It was ironic that it was Gerhardt's disappearance that set you off on the trail that led to the discovery of smuggling of all kinds, murder and finally back to the corruption. Which will be at an end now.'

He continued: 'I think this whole area can breathe a huge sigh of relief. I spoke with Louisa and Edward this morning and he's picked up a couple more of Santiago's colleagues. He is singing like a canary to get a deal of some kind. He's petrified apparently and his family in shock. Never knew that side of him. Just thought he worked hard. One minute the world is run of the mill and next, turned upside down.'

'What about the ship and crew?' Lea asked.

'Oh, yes. Arrested too. Ship impounded. Thanks to Alex first getting involved then the rest of us.'

Sneaking admiration from Edward though he's always reserved in his praise.'

'If you buy a boat, Charles, do you realize it needs to come out of the water every two to five years for a major overhaul?' Lea peered at Uncle closely, waiting for a reaction. His look invited further comment.

'So, depending how many boats or ships are booked into the dry dock it can be out of service for a long time, losing you – and costing you – money. Wouldn't two boats of middle size be better? Then you're never without one and they can each cruise different areas. Also depending on costs and what is around second-hand, it may be best to build from scratch. Brand new is always good. You've got teething troubles but what about the problem of keeping an old girl going?' She seemed satisfied with her information. 'Just saying – and if you need new-build funding, you could sell timeshare on it. It has been done.' She scrutinized us again.

We were silent. I think a mild shock at her knowledge and her suggestion had tied our tongues.

'And you know this how? And why?' I finally said.

'I take it you don't like the idea?' She was crestfallen. 'Like I said, Babs, no one takes me seriously. I will have to stay a sex toy after all.'

Argh. Here we go again, I thought, and after all I'd said!

Uncle and I both chimed in simultaneously Brilliant idea. Just taking it in. Honestly, well worth more research. Perhaps you could do more, then we all get together. What got you onto this subject?

She perked up. 'I did it as a project at uni – from the design side of things really. We had to take a technical subject and make it arty. I got so interested I followed it all the way through. Even got a shipping company interested, but the idea fell down when funds couldn't be raised. No one would take a chance on selling the timeshare upfront either. They said if I got it going, they would re-evaluate it. Of course, I never took it any further.'

'I am impressed, Lea. Truly. It's something to be worked on. Can I leave it with you? I'll keep you on the payroll, of course.' Uncle was beaming.

Lea glowed and basked in the praise all at once. It seemed our paths were destined to keep crossing and I was very happy about it. A team was forming and maybe Lea wouldn't need to starve anymore.

'Don't ever change, Lea. You are lovely as you are, believe me!' Uncle winked and, as he was getting up, planted a kiss on top of her head then ruffled her unruly, fast-growing hair. She went all coy again and Uncle went off – to do whatever he had to do.

'Well, my smart friend! You've impressed my uncle and me, so quit while you're ahead. I think we should now concentrate on a swim, sunbathing and slowly get ready for tonight. Absolutely everyone is coming so Prem has closed the restaurant for us. All the Double Barrellers, Helen and

David, Alvaro, Hans Alex, Rosalind, James ¬ and us, of course. Have I missed anyone? She's arranging some dance music, did I tell you? Should I invite Duke and Edward?'

'Why not? Everyone's played a part, if only a 'bit' part. Tell Louisa to ask Edward and I'll find Duke on our way back to the room. All the DBs can come. The Bailey-Pullens – anyone.'

We plunged in to calm, balmy, blue sea for a good splash around before going to get ready.

Taxis all round this evening and we had our best swanky, bling gear on. We had told everyone to push the boat out, men included. We suddenly remembered we should return the boats to the Blue Sea Boat Company but it was too late now so we found Karim and apologized. Tomorrow would do, he beamed. No extra charge.

Arriving at Prem's we found Lea's farmer indulging in a drink. As soon as he saw Lea he sped over – as much as overweight bloodhounds can – to greet her effusively. His old, wrinkly, hangdog face was alight with pleasure.

'See, Lea,. I told you everyone loves you. Invite him to stay.'

She did and they got chatting in Spanglish. People were turning up in dribs and drabs but in half an hour everyone was ensconced in chairs or propping up the bar.

Lea was holding court: 'Did you know – Puffins mate for life and their babies are called 'pufflets'? Isn't that cute? And Platypus babies are 'puggles'.'

Then later, from Hans: 'Oh I am such an eager platypus sometimes.'

I heard someone say, 'Goodness, you went from two hundred pounds to eighty? That's amazing.'

'I mean money. I'd be about dead if I only weighed eighty pounds.'

'Oh – I see.' That was more like my Lea.

Francis and Louisa were deep in discussion over a mole they found back in the UK that was moving. When they went to rescue it and pick it up they were horrified to find a load of maggots falling out. It was moving because of the maggots writhing around.

I wished I hadn't heard that ahead of dinner!

Helen and David's contributions included: 'For evil to succeed it only takes good men to do nothing. Like a lot round here. It takes an outsider to see it all and do something.' I gathered it referred to us and not for the first time I idly wondered where that quote came from.

'... they get smaller. I'm not a good cook. Omelette. Omlette. Omlet. They're all oxymorons to me.'

'Not quite, Lea. Oxymorons are self-contradicting statements – I don't think omelettes of any size are contradictory!'

I didn't get any further before she put a hand up, pronouncing firmly, 'Another time. Thank you, anyway, Babs.'

Alex had slipped away from Rosalind, mixing happily. I overheard her say with a deepening frown: '...stay on a caravan site? Bit common but I suppose they can be nice. The booze, snooze Brits! And, no! I don't like standing at the bar with a load of bickering old expats.'

Oof, as Hans would say.

'... Yes, it was the gay barman, Miguel, who put all the spiders on our balcony,' Lea was answering Duke. 'The children went into the tunnels like the Viet Cong or Khmer Rouge.'

'I do think Edward is quintessentially English, in spite of being Spanish. Is that an oxymoron?'

Just then he appeared, leaving the question unanswered. As Lea was leaning against a wall at the time, he stood next to her. Very close, engaging her in conversation.

She smiled a lot but I could see her imperceptibly widening the gap between them until with a flourish she ducked away with a final comment: 'I agree. He is very anal. That's the criminal mind for you.'

Edward looked surprised but couldn't comment as she headed immediately towards Uncle and Hans who were deep in discussion.

I joined them to unashamedly plug my new pet project. A microbrewery.

'Uncle have you noticed the trend in Brits starting microbreweries because expats are fed up with lager beer?'

'No. But I'm sure you're going to enlighten me. I assume this is your new project in the absence of utilizing the tunnels?'

'Indeed. I've been looking into it and I think in one of your empty buildings at La Roca it would fit in perfectly. You have a captive clientele and with aggressive marketing it could supply interested Brit bars far and wide!'

'I'm open to it, Barbara. Let's talk with Duke – and Carl when he's back. They'll have a lot to take on board for the future.'

'May I suggest we relax and leave business for later?' Lea smiled sweetly, batting long eye lashes. I noticed she had had them done in the hotel beauty salon. How did I miss that and not find time for myself. 'Now, Babs asked me – challenged me – to find something good about people who are not. So – whilst they were all beyond the pale and that's putting it mildly – Attila the Hun, after murdering his own brother to gain power, did have a smidgeon of humanity when he agree to rescue Honoria, a Roman woman from a marriage she didn't want. He was to marry her but unfortunately, he was killed before he could.'

She had that satisfied look. 'Then, we have Ivan the Terrible. About the only thing he did was orientate Russian foreign police towards Europe. And my final offering is Vlad the Impaler. What a hugely nasty, horrible, vicious, sadistic unforgiving person he was. But he defended Europe against the Ottoman Muslims. The Pope was grateful.'

I graciously accepted the 'offerings'. She was certainly into her research: long words, languages, animals and rescue missions. Did I feel a little dull? No! My microbrewery awaited and – and – such fun!

Edward's amusement with Lea's offerings knew no bounds. He was smiling hugely. His contribution to the conversation was more sobering. 'We've found drugs sewn into carpet edges, curtain hems, shower curtain rails, real jewels worn as clothes accessories on shoes, belts, you name it – it's been tried and sometimes got away with.'

We were all ears. 'It's not possible to keep an eye on everything and everyone without ten times more the manpower, though modern search equipment helps. We wouldn't have thought of hot air balloons before. Just goes to show. There is poly criminality on a frightening scale. Criminals actually advertise portfolios of what they can offer so we need computer experts to dig it all out from deep within.'

Edward's audience included a rapt but tense Lea. I speculated on that. Uncle and Hans had moved over to listen, with Lea visibly relaxing.

James added some of his experiences: 'Sea smuggling is rife. The routes are so varied, and they're worldwide. Like Greece at the southeast, then the central Med, entry via Italy or southwest Spain, then the long haul, Red Sea via Yemen, Gulf of Aden and much more. Our work for the insurance company had led to finding other things which we don't really want to get involved in, but sometimes we have to. If it's bold, it's hard to turn a blind eye, though our own safety is paramount.'

'Can we do a quickie?' Eyes widening in the company. 'I mean a photo of us all of course.' Sweet smile from Lea.

Several photos later we sat down to dinner, the farmer joining us. What a happy man, with tales to tell of these odd expats. He coughed an old man's cough and got general sympathy.

'Un tos,' said Hans. 'Cough.'

'So – you could say he was a toser.' Lea pronounced it tosser. Smirks all round. 'And, do you know, I found a dogging site twenty miles from here. You need to keep an eye on that, Edward! Lewd behaviour or something. Leave murder to the amateurs.' She was in a wicked mood.

Poor Edward didn't know how to take it but Uncle and Hans loved it. I speculated that Edward thought maybe Lea was a bit of a handful. It took the more mature man to handle her.

Prem and her team finally cleared away and started making space for dancing.

The music began. All kinds. What Uncle called rain dancing, rumba, waltz, fandango, some flamenco where we all made fools of ourselves, and plain smooching which Alvaro and I took advantage of and which Lea avoided. She was happy talking with Uncle, Hans and Edward who all eyed her up as the intelligent sex symbol she was. She obviously felt safe with Hans and Uncle, so she could be wicked and flirt with Edward who by now was a tad wary. Could bridges be mended or did she even want to?

My observations were put on hold when my phone rang all of a sudden and I got a shock as I saw the incoming number. Gareth. OMG. What a jolt. Bad timing. I decided not to answer but listened as he left a message. He was thinking of coming over for a short holiday and maybe Colin too. What to do. What to do. Panic. Guilt. Did I or didn't I want that? I still had time to enjoy Alvaro. I waved Lea over for a quiet conflab.

'Gareth phoned and wants to come over for a holiday – with Colin.'

'Colin!' She almost shrieked.

Uncle looked our way. 'What's happening with Colin these days? Nice boy.'

'No! Do something, Babs. Gareth is up to you – but Colin. No way! I'll see him for a cup of tea when we get back. Maybe. It's not disloyal. My life has simply moved on. That's all!'

She looked at me almost guiltily. Perhaps she expected a rebuke. It never came. I was feeling much the same as she did, I think.

I saw Uncle take a call too. He talked for a while then sidled over to us.

'That was Karim. One of the boats we discussed that I will probably invest in has some trouble with the crew and the person who hired it. Apparently this person hiring the whole boat was remarketing it for holidays. A real go-getter. She'd put aside all the best and biggest cabins for a company she thought wanted the cabins for what on the booking form said 'labradors'. Other people refused to book when they thought the boat would be full of dogs so she added a premium to cover the loss. She'd been informed by the company that made the booking that they wanted all comforts possible for 'labradors'.'

He looked a tad harassed. His first venture into oceanic travel had already given him a headache.

'So – she's neurologically challenged – or at least diverse?' Innocent stare from Lea. Wide-eyed glare from two pairs of eyes.

Uncle went on. 'But then she found that the company had booked for 'labradors' which, translated into English is 'labourers'. It had wanted to thank these 'labourers' for the exceptional effort they'd put into a project.'

'That's like the Spanish woman on the TV programme who kept saying 'the sheeps were all at sea'. We thought she meant the sheep were being transported for slaughter but she meant 'ships'. Now I speak Spanish, I know an 'i' sounds like an 'e.' Smirk.

'Don't push your luck, Lea.' I retorted.

Uncle ploughed on: 'Now she's stuck with the company booking, and the company wants the good deal she negotiated with them but without the doggie comforts for which she was charging extra. Some very bad feeling has ensued. And all the extra dog facilities and treats have been bought. She had even created a temporary dog toilet.'

'Wow. Impressive! But did she – the nameless one – have permission?' This from Lea.

'No. Another factor for you to sort, plus profit margins etc. Too many people wanting a share of the proceeds. Needs a soothing diplomatic touch with some good negotiating skills put to use. I wondered if you and Lea would like to go there tomorrow to start sorting things out? Then the boat can get going.'

My brain worked frantically. Now Lea and I had the perfect excuse for delaying Gareth and Colin's arrival.

I said brightly, 'Of course. Look forward to the challenge. But is tomorrow negotiable? We have a few things to sort out with Hans and Alvaro. Not to mention some potential business projects, such as Prem's restaurant ideas. Just long enough to set up proposals and get them worked on. My thinking anyway, Uncle.'

A short silence ensued while he considered this. 'Good idea. Let's say the end of the week then and Karim can relay this to the captain and this woman.'

As an afterthought he added, 'Then you might as well join the boat yourselves – test it out as tourists! See how it all goes before I make my final decision on buying. It's already chartered to Karim's – our – company, which is why the profit margins are of paramount importance. Buy the thing, I say, and get on with it but – this a good opportunity to get to grips with the financial side of things, Barbara. And Lea, you have some experience here with the project you did on timeshare.'

Lea and I looked at each other, smiling. Oh, happy days! Gareth and Colin could wait – for now.

'I must have missed the name of where you want us to go, Charles, and the woman in question,' Lea enquired innocently.

The music got louder and the fandango started up. Uncle waved his arms about, saying something we couldn't hear.

It didn't matter.

We were about to sail off into the proverbial sunset.

The End

Printed in Great Britain
by Amazon